Prophecy of the Flame

Book I: Love's Dawning

By Lynn Hardy

Illustrated by: Yivgeni Matoussov
© 2006

All rights reserved. This book is protected under the copyright laws of theUnited States of America. No part of thispublication may be reproduced,stored in retrieval system, or transmitted in any form or by any means - electronic, mechanical, photocopy, recording, or any other - except forbrief quotations in printed reviews, without the prior written permission of the author.

Text and Illustration © 2007
Resilient Publishing

Chapter One

Bonnggggg....Bonngggg.....

The second alarm, tolling in the distance, leads to profound silence: I hear the whispered breathes of four men accompanying me. As shock turns into comprehension, Darren unsheathes the tinfoil sword from its cardboard scabbard. Stretching out long legs, he takes the stairs three at a time, loping downward. The mousy-haired professional pauses long enough to shout over his shoulder, "Two gongs... attack at the front door!"

The fanning stairway broadens. Ten-foot oak doors loom before us, barring the entrance. Huffing, our band of out-of-shape would-be heroes heaves a collective sigh of relief: The entryway is secure.

Scanning the foyer we find only a reception table and the game master who will record our progress. "Not even enough time to get know each other and a blasted bells sounds!" George grouses, his eyes darting daggers at the game master.

I grind my teeth as my hand snakes out to twitch his shirt, "You're coming out of character in game-time. Do you want to loose points for something like that?" George's lips twist into a disdainful sneer.

"Awesome dude, we beat the invaders," Chad's warm smile encourages me to shrug off George's attitude, "Should we wait or, like, go out to meet them?" Comprehension dawns: those blonde streaks Jamison sports are from hanging out at the beach with a long board.

We ease past the table with Chad, Darren and Allen to one side and George on other. I bring up the rear, hanging back. Cursing under my breath, I whisper, "I can't believe they outlawed offensive magic in this game. What good is being a mage without battle spells?"

A metallic squeal pierces the stillness as the front doors ease open. Bronze hockey-masks hide the enemy's identities but their brown garments mark our foes as gremlins. The enemy slides single file through the cracked entryway before splitting into two groups. They charge our motley group of stunned heroes shrieking like deranged cats.

Allen shoves his way past Chad knocking the bleached-blond to his knees as he slashes at the closest invader. Over eager to make his first score, Allen misses the intruder by a good six inches. Before he recovers from his vigorous swing, a gremlin scores a hit on his sword-arm. Taking the weapon in his left hand, he swings ineffectively before diving for protection under the hearty oak desk in the center of the foyer. George joins him under the table after receiving a disabling blow to his sword arm as well.

Swarmed by a group of gremlins, Darren and Chad turn back to back. The duo manages to keep the enemy at bay, scoring some hits as they shield each other's position.

Jabbing at a pair of attackers with my staff, I focus on the gremlins determined to take my weapon. A firm tap on my elbow lets me know I have been ambushed from behind by a third attacker. Instinctively, I drop my magician's rod, knowing I cannot wield the staff one-handed. Using the table as a prop I kick like a mule, planting both feet in the chest of the invader, taking him down and out for the count. *Six months at kick-boxing class are paying off...*

Seeing a mage without a stave, the other gremlins

rush to score their first kill. Taking flight like a startled gazelle, I mount the table. I pivot like a gymnast kicking at the leader's head. Knowing George and Allen are pinned under my position, I make my way around the table, striking out with a booted heel at each bronze mask. The drab antagonists take a step back.

The game master scribbles furiously on his notepad while the gremlins huddle momentarily. Breaking apart with loud fiendish gibbering they dash up the stairs. I smile, long legs pounding the floor as I race after them with the other defenders in tow. *If only Tony could have seen that! I wish he had followed us here instead of going back for seconds at the breakfast buffet...*

Darren, uncharacteristically enthusiastic, interrupts my silent musing, "Now that was fun! I got two. What did you get?"

"Two, maybe three. I think one might have been fatal..." *Boonnnngg.* The gong drowns out the rest of Chad's recount.

"One alarm for the dining hall..." Darren roars. "They're attacking the breakfast gathering!" Shrieks and peels of laughter echo as we dash into the entryway at the top of the fan-shaped stairway.

Tony looks up from what is left of a breakfast that has lost its appeal. Eggs, sausage, toast, and chocolate milk - what could be finer? But not all mixed together! A quick leap keeps the engineer from wearing the mess as a gremlin strikes the jumbled tray. The quintet of white tops decorated with distinctive blue sashes race across to the dining room. Tony follows at a jog, anxious to see his wife in action.

Making two turns, following the screams and shouts, we enter the left wing of the domestic quarters. I lope down the hallway, head swiveling from side to side. All five players skid to a halt. This corridor is a dead-end, with no gremlins in sight.

"Shit!" I pace like a caged animal. "Shit, shit... SHIT!! We've taken a wrong turn! Let's backtrack. If they are still here then they can't be far..."

Bong. Bong. Bong.

"End of Round One," shaking his head, Darren interprets the gaming signal, "Time to see how we scored." We do an about face, heading back to the foyer at a more sedate pace.

"You have been here before?" Allen's inquiry draws the attention of the entire group.

"Yeah, I'm a real veteran..." Darren grunts.

"How long do they give us to heal our party?" The needs of the patients are never far from Chad's thoughts, even in a game of fantasy. "We could use the time to work out a game plan for the next round."

"They claim each campaign will be original," the gangly engineer shrugs.

"I bet the King is pissed. We made a real mess of breakfast. What will that take off our score?" George, an accountant, mentally tallies up the scores as he and Allen discuss their wounds and possible hits.

I glance over my shoulder at Tony. Sharing a smile with my husband, I try to portray a little of the optimism that comes so naturally to him, "Surely they didn't expect us to kill all of 'em. I got one - wounded a couple of others."

"Well I got at least that many," George harrumphs, reaching for the scorecard lying on the reception table. Reading the results of the first round of Live Action Gaming, the number cruncher is fractionally disgruntled, "72 out of 100 points! That friggin' game master has his head up his ass!"

"With three out of five of us injured? We're lucky they only docked us fifteen points for each hit," a wide slash of white stretches across Allen's ebony face, "Good thing two of our characters claim to be ambidextrous. " With a scarecrow body and balding head, his levity takes some of the punch out of the score that is purely average.

Glancing up, seeing Tony head my way. I hiss with frustration, "If they had only let me use some of my spells, any of them, I would've had them contained in the foyer! Those Gremlins would've been no match for a force-field or even a wide-ranged stun spell."

A thundering clamor fills the air around us. Startled, I lock eyes with the engineer whose ring graces my left hand. Hair on the back of my neck prickles, goose bumps surge across my body as a white flash consumes the world around me.

Color seeps back into my vision, inky blotches fading from the world around me. Amid the cloudy haze in my mind a slow but startling realization of my surroundings penetrates my thoughts.

Have my eyes recovered from the lightning strike? The room is darker. The tingling that set every hair on end hasn't entirely left. My nerves are on a caffeine high: awake, alive, and sensitive beyond belief. Bewildered, I glance at the long pole grasped firmly in my right hand.

A staff? I left mine leaning on the table...

My eyes flutter and my brain bogs down like a sports car in a mud pit. Through the fog in my brain I take in the walls around me. *A real torch? The thing gives off more smoke than light.*

Faint predawn-beams slanting from narrow windows are the only other source of illumination. We are in a round chamber formed out of dark rock, not the granite wallpaper covering the hotel walls. *What part of the Renaissance Resort is this... the dungeon?*

Baffled, I turn to the man standing next to me, "Allen? Your clothes...?" My mouth

hangs slack as my brain catches up. A deep knowing settles into my soul, warring with logic and reason. *That can't be Allen...*

I just met Allen when we were placed on the same team for Mischief, Mayhem, and Murder: a role-playing game at the one and only Renaissance Hotel and Gaming World, but I am positive this is not the same man. Yet something inside me insists that it is. *This is nuts!*

Allen is in his early to mid-thirties, five foot ten,

black, balding, skinny and altogether an unremarkable guy. Like me, he was dressed in blue jeans and a white shirt with a blue sash around his waist. *No way this is the same guy.* But deep inside I *know* Allen is standing next to me although this guy is a twenty-something year old who could easily win the Mr. America contest: over six-feet tall, smooth midnight skin over broad handsome features, full sensuous lips, raven braids halfway down his back and weightlifting shoulders. He's wearing what will be a big hit at the Renaissance festival: authentic breastplate over chain mail, complete with a set of gauntlets.

"Who else would it be…." the question trails off, as his mind registers the sound issuing forth. Allen's voice has a distinct nasal ring, which is far different from the satin smooth and honey sweet tone this man used.

A shouting match ensues when the three other strangers standing with us in the center of this bizarre room recover their voices, all at the same time. A very, very short, black bearded man - That's *Darren?* - bellows to be heard over Allen, only to be paralyzed by the deep rumbling of his own words.

"What the…" begins the seven foot, wire-thin man with pale alabaster skin. The soft soprano tone of the man my brain insists is George silences the question.

"Will every one chill for a minute!" Chad steps into the middle of the group trying to bring reason to a totally unreasonable situation.

Now that voice I know! But the sandy-haired, short and stocky medical student is not standing before us. This man is much taller than the Chad of old, built like a quarterback, dirty blond hair darkened to a chestnut color, but still undeniably Chad. There is no mistaking the similarities in the face. It is as if an artist moved the best qualities - the kind, compassionate eyes, the straight nose - to a more suitable frame, just touching-up where needed.

Something so familiar yet still so unexplainable achieves the quiet Chad demands. No one dares intrude on the stillness as the unmistakable squeal of a rusty-hinged door echoes into the chamber like a scene from a bad horror flick.

   Carrying a metal pot with a wick burning in front of a shiny metal plate, a medieval guard steps through the dark doorway. *My God, a stairway around the room... without a guardrail! Talk about a lawsuit waiting to happen!* I give a harrumph at my internal musings: even situations this bizarre fail to steal my sense of humor.

   A robed man and a He-Man looking character enter behind the quintessential soldier holding the antiquated lantern. Light glints off gleaming hilts. *Are those swords made of metal?*

   I shake my head trying to dislodge the illusion. *Surely, if this were a dream I would not be thinking in the archaic clichés Tony teases me about? Everything, including my speech, would be more gothic.*

I strain to catch what the new arrivals are saying, "Merithin, nemdinn sund i minna enn korter getur petta ekki bidid?" my brow furrows with irritation as I realize the futility of eavesdropping.

Out of pure frustration I follow my gut instinct, sarcastically muttering words that blaze into being inside my head, "Oh my gosh! How can it be? Their speech is foreign to me. What I don't have, and I really need, is to know these words instantly."

Lifting my hand in the direction of robed figure coming down the stairs, I finish the rhyme with a sigh emanating from the depths of my soul, "I am in a hurry and assume it's fine, so copy the info from that mind to mine."

Fierce tingling cascading from my head to my toes causes my jaw to hang slack. My eyes widen further when blue light arcs from my hand to the robed figure, retuning back to me before I blink an eye.

"Your Highness, I assure you, the War Council will be very interested. I think I have summoned what will be the answer to the demons plaguing our kingdom," The robed elder pleads with He-Man, "When I meditated on the need to conquer our foes and performed a scrying, I was shown these five warriors in the dream-state. I have never accomplished a seeking across the planes so quickly as when I sought and found these soldiers. I know I was destined to use my Summoning for this purpose."

"Merithin, what can five men do against the legions of demons besieging us? I have studied war all my life. I do not see how these five men, or even five hundred men, will be of that much assistance!" the princely hulk sulks.

Thoughts fly quicker than superman running from a kryptonite hailstorm... *I can understand them! How? Was it that awful rhyme and that blue light? What else could it have been? Hold on a minute... I'm in a robe and carrying a staff, surrounded by an armed entourage...*

Glancing to my right, I see our hosts have made it

halfway down the stairs. *I'm running out of time!*

"Humph." My brow crinkles as a thought occurs, *If I'm a mage with magical powers... how 'bout another spell? Hell, it's worth a shot.*

"Well here I am and really confused,
It's unfair, I feel totally abused.
I'm calling a 'time-out' as anyone would,
Using my magic, as you know I should.
Time will speed up, but only for me.
Until I count deliberately, one-two-and-three."

Intuitively I give another push from within. My thoughts center on the movie about the guys whose molecules sped up so fast time around him seemed to stand still. An orgasmic tingling sensation turns my palms numb as a blue flash tinges the world around me.

"I did it! Oh—my—God...I really did it!" I shriek, as the silence of room, void of even the melody of the flickering flame causes my voice to echo. "Now that I have a little time let's sort things out," I mumble to no one in particular.

Taking a closer look my companions, the solution hits me like a freight-truck. I step over to the reed-slender giant to confirm my suspicions. I move the white locks revealing pointed ears. When I take my hand away, the ivory strands stick straight out instead of falling back into place. It *is* George. *Ok this is just too weird... Let's see if I can wake up the others.*

"Like the guy with the watch in the movie I've seen,
I have gotta have help from the rest of the team.
So with a quick touch unfreeze them I will,
That way they can help me, the blanks to fill."

Oh great, now I'm sounding like Yoda. I hope it worked. This time my hands feel as if they are light as a cloud when an azure glow surrounds them, sinking into the skin. With a shake of my head I place my staff on the ground and begin one more rhyme:

"To grab the spotlight when they awake,
A mirror from this staff I now make."

A bolt of blue arcs from my hand, encompassing the rod. I hardly notice the pins and needles as the wood splits down the middle contorting and stretching. It rises from the ground, a gaping hole framed by oak. Blue fog congeals in the gap. In a matter of seconds a six foot by six foot mirror stands in place of the staff.

Walking over to the group, I stride toward Chad first. *At least I can reason with him.* My fingers graze the hand he rests on his sword hilt. "Have we hit the Twilight Zone or what?"

"Rebecca?" the questions tumble out of his mouth like water from a broken dam, "You are so short… And where'd you get the shiny robe? How'd you change so fast?"

When the flow of confusion ebbs, he glances around the room, choking on whatever he was about to say. The frozen world renders him speechless.

"I'm not short, you're tall," as I pull him over to the mirror, Chad gapes like a newly caught bass, "Listen for a minute, that is all I ask…"

"If you can explain any of this, I'm all ears," the armored man's eyes rove the reflection of his enhanced physique.

"You remember our gaming characters? Do our companions seem familiar? Did you hear the thunder and see that weird light?" As I pause for a breath, he gives a cautious nod. "The guys on the stairs, I heard them talking. The robed one is a mage and I think the other is royalty. The mage said something about summoning us from another plane, as in… dimension. Call me crazy, but I *don't* think we're on Earth any more." Filling my lungs, I prepare more evidence.

Before I can utter a syllable I feel confusion ebbing from the man next to me, as palpable as a shout of denial. Chad thrust his hands out before him, "Whoa, what do you mean you heard them? You can understand what they said? Whatever language they speak, it doesn't sound like anything I have ever heard. I have traveled Europe and parts of Asia, know Latin and some French, the intonation is similar but I can't understand a word."

My lips twist wryly, "I will wake the others from the time-spell if you will keep them quiet long enough for me to explain what I've pieced together. I would rather go through this just once."

A knowing smile brightens Chad's handsome features as we maneuver the mirror into place. I move from each one of the familiar strangers to the next, tapping each in turn. My new ally trails behind pointing out the mirror, making sure they notice their unrecognizable reflection.

"You guys want to know what the hell in going on here?" Chad's voice rings out as I wake George last, "Rebecca is one step ahead of us."

Taking a deep breath, I clear my throat, drawing their attention from the mirror, "I have cast a spell to give us a few minutes to figure things out. Where we are I don't know, but let me tell you what I do know. We have been summoned to this world by that mage," I tilt my head toward the stairs, "across a trans-dimensional barrier. This kingdom is under attack. The mage's meditation and scrying told him we are the answer to a war they can't win on their own. So he brought us here."

"And how, oh wise one, do you know all this?" pipes-up the same old pessimistic George in a voice pitched a few octaves higher.

"Take a look around, it should be obvious," a sigh escapes while I attempt to reign in my impatience. Stepping in front of the mirror, I draw their attention to the object once more.

"My gaming character was an ArchMage. Chad was the MasterHealer. Allen certainly lives up to 'Charles the Prince Charming.' George, have you noticed your ears? The Druid Elf lives. And Darren, wasn't your crusader a Dwarf. Is this what you all envisioned your gaming characters to be?" Slowly, four very stunned men nod.

The rest of the puzzle falls into place. "Somehow the mage must have scryed and found us role-playing. When he pulled us from our dimension, the spell reconfigured us to fit this world according to the mind-set and powers of our adventure characters!" Sensing disbelief overwhelm the minds of some of my companions, I stumble in mid-thought.

"Like whoa man... Bump that! I couldn't even score a hit on those damn gremlins with a *fake* sword. Man, there is absolutely no friggin' way I am a swordsman. You cannot gain instant knowledge, much less skills!" Allen's cheery demeanor evaporates under the blazing glare of chaos that sorcery and magic invokes. "Boo, there gotta be a logical explanation for all this... this is just a dream. That's it...just a very realistic fantasy."

I recall Allen stating he was a program engineer. Science majors are so grounded in the world of facts that explaining this world of magic to him is going to be a royal pain in the butt.

"How do you think I figured out what they said? I used a spell to learn their language in less time then it has taken me to explain it to you." I feel Allen's pig-headed logical stubbornness as tangibly as a shouted refusal. I grind my teeth muttering, "Helvitis asni (stupid fool)..." *Do they think I can hold this spell forever? We don't have time to be for this bullshit.*

"Fine, you think this might be a dream. That is understandable; after all, this is pretty surreal. Just don't start acting like this is not real life. If you charge up those stairs, trying to slice your way free of this dream, someone is bound to get in a lucky shot. Or maybe that mage has a lightning bolt with your name on it," I jab Allen's broad chest. "Will you feel the pain as cold steel pierces warm flesh or will you wake up? Is there chance, no matter how unlikely, that dead will be dead?" I pin him with my best motherly gaze, then turn to include the rest of the gang. "Until we have absolute proof, we had better start acting like this is our reality."

I spin on my heel, pointing to our approaching host. "They brought us here to be some sort of heroes in a war we know nothing about. Until we find out exactly what's going on, we had better get our act together and play the part of the people they expect us to be!"

From somewhere deep within, words well up and spill forth. "We were ready for a weekend of live action role-playing. Now, we might be playing for our lives. We can't afford to take the chance that this is not our new reality. If we wake up then one of us is going to get a good laugh. Until then, better safe than dead." As heads nod I get down to business, "First off, we need to know everyone's character strengths."

"Who died and made you the first woman President?" George manages to sound insulted, arrogant, and snide all at once, "We may be stuck in the Middle Ages, but we can still operate like a democracy. The first thing we should do is elect a leader, someone to speak for us as a group. Let's introduce ourselves and the characters we created, their strengths and their weaknesses. Then we will vote on who we think should represent us. I will go first."

"I received a promotion to Assistant Manager of our accounting department; that means I've got great people skills. I am also at least ten years older than all of you: more world experience. Keep that in mind. From now on I am Allinon. As a druid I have an affinity with nature. The magic I possess deals with living things as well as enhancing the properties of herbs. Right now I can tell by the crisp feel of the air that winter is almost at an end. I'm a MasterArcher," drawing his slender, delicate looking weapon for emphasis he continues, "and a MasterSwordsman. I have never handled a sword before, but this feels completely natural." Sheathing the long blade he makes a lame attempt at humor, "If the world has gone mad it has taken me with it."

Chad steps up before Allinon can elaborate further, "Jamison the MasterHealer. I am also a MasterSwordsman and Master of the Martial Arts. This being my first gaming character I hadn't decided on anything else."

"I'm Charles," says the raven swordsman, "I am a Paladin with high charisma points. Like the typical paladin, my aura acts as a defensive barrier, slowing down attacks and reducing the damage I take in a fight. Also I am practically impossible to poison. Unlike the typical paladin, I can't work even the most basic healing spell. Due to my character's lack of….ummm ….piousness," his leer leaves no doubt that promiscuity held a large part in the penalization, "the gods have taken that ability from me. Life's not all bad though, I have worked at weapon skills instead. I've mastered all known weapons and some my gaming group invented."

Darren speaks next, "Jerik the Dwarf. No magic 'cept what I use as MasterSmith. Dwarves are incredibly resistant to sorcery and poison. That axe-" he points to the weapon strapped to his back, "-is my weapon of mastery. My character has one unique ability: besides being able to enchant weapons, I have got a slight telepathic skill. Telepaths are almost unheard of in dwarves, but our Dungeon Master allowed an exception because of a history I wrote. The short version: Jerik comes from a colony of Dwarves who have developed this trait. It can only be used with other telepaths."

Why does the Dwarf seem so right for Darren? The engineer has undergone the most dramatic change. Jerik has morphed from a six-foot tall brunette to a four-and-a-half-foot tall, black-bearded, axe-swinging dwarf, I have no problem associating the new Jerik with the old Darren I met this morning.

A deep breath focuses my mind, the world becomes clear as a crystalline lake, "Call me Reba. Not only am I an ArchMage, but I have also mastered the dagger and the staff as well as all known martial arts. I can communicate telepathically."

"Jerik, can you hear me?" I send a tendril of thought to the dwarf. His bushy brows rise in shock. "That might come in handy if we ever split up. I have only the most basic healing skill, but I have above average empathy points and extremely high intuition points." I take a moment to meet the eyes of each member of our party.

"Having said this let me tell you why I should be our leader. I feel like these people are good people and we should help them. I also have a strong feeling I should act as our leader." Allinon rolls his eyes and I pin him with a glare, "Beyond that there are several reasons to elect me as our representative. When you role-play, who is your most powerful player? The mage. Who was the first one to figure out our current situation? I was. Who is the only one who can understand their language? Yes, me again," I put all my cards on the table, revealing a royal flush, "Most importantly, who is your best chance of getting home?"

"Really?" I perceive a challenge as Allinon jerks his chin, "And how do we know you can work magic here, or that any of us can for that matter? All I've heard is a couple of unintelligible words and you sputtering a lot of unsubstantiated claims!"

God! Of all the idiotic, lame, childish... and I can't even blast him, we might need him later! Growling I stalk over to the mirror muttering,

"Ab-bra-ca-da-bra and al-la-ka-zam,
Turn back to a staff for this irritating man."

The mirror begins its metamorphosis, shrinking back to its original shape. Even with my back turned, their simultaneous intake of breath cannot be missed. I time the retrieval of the stave with the completion of the spell.

"Hot Momma, you got my vote," Charles murmurs melodiously.

"Looks like the position is yours, Reba," Jamison's smile stretches from ear to ear.

I knew I liked that man the moment we met. Feeling a time crunch, I begin to chant,

"The language of the land I have gained,
Shall be passed along to the rest of my gang.
If heroes of this world you are destined to be,
I must pass to you what is inside of me."

Even with the ambiguous words, the meaning is clear. The enchantment is so strong goose bumps surge to life. Tickling energy races from my outstretched arm to surround the four men who have accepted my leadership.

With my position secure I forge ahead, "I'm not sure how long I can hold the slow-time spell. Let's get an act together that will impress the hell out of these guys."

We work furiously, hammering the details. Satisfied with the plan, I give some final instructions, "If you will form a half circle behind me, I will release the spell." As the men move into position, I intone, "One, two, and three..."

Chapter Two

"They look impressive, Merithin, but still, they are only five men," looking in our direction He-man adds, "How long ago did you summon them?"

"Not even a candle-mark has passed, My Lord," the robed elder studies our group as he musses, "I thought the transfer would have been much harder on them."

Followed by an armed entourage, I pace to the end of the staircase, then bowing from the waist, wait for our host. Their complex language feels as natural as my own when I declare, "Your Highness, may I have the honor of introducing the Crusaders of the Light?" Since I shine like a beacon in this robe, the nomenclature seems appropriate.

"You have leave to continue," The hulking blonde gives a slight dip of his chin.

"Allinon the Druid Elf, Charles the Paladin, Jamison the MasterHealer, and Jerik the Dwarven MasterSmith." Each sketches an elegant bow as I call their name, "I am ArchMage Reba, the leader of the men before you."

"Having summoned us from a vast distance, I know your need is great. I sense a growing force of malevolence outside the walls of this place, and goodness within. For this reason, we freely pledge our services to aid your kingdom." I bring my hand to my side. Relief washes through me as several knees join my right one on the chamber's hard marble floor.

"I am not King nor Crown Prince that I may accept this as formal pledge to the Kingdom of Cuthburan." I am unable to read any emotion from the Prince, his stoic face also refuses to divulge what lay beneath the spoken words, "I will, however, accept your offer as a request to join the forces, which I, Prince Szames of Cuthburan, command. Before we proceed, may I see the face of the one who has pledged himself?" he continues to explain as if teaching a young student, "For this oath to be binding I must know from whom it comes."

Looking up into the eyes of the man to whom I have just dedicated our small force, I set my staff on the ground beside me. Reaching with both hands I remove the forgotten hood: the material is translucent to my vision. Slanting through the narrow window, the warmth of the sun strikes the top of my head, providing a halo as I rise. *I could not have choreographed that better if I was making a movie!*

"The Prophecy..." mumbles the guard turning a ghostly shade.

"The One..." gasps someone further up the stairs.

Even if the mutterings are a bit over the top, the shock is justified, what with me being a woman and all. But the fleeting look of hope from Prince baffles me.

Feeling the direct route is best, I plunge ahead, "Prince Sha-mes," I struggle not to pronounce the American name James. "May I inquire, Your Highness, how stands the condition of your army?"

Prince Szames clears his throat, "The Kings army stood 5,000 strong until last night. We lost 300 men and another 200 were wounded in the first and only battle so far," surprisingly, Prince Szames gives more than the requested intel, "My brother, the Crown Prince Alexandros, took a mortal wound in the skirmish."

Jamison steps up beside me, his concern for the injured overwhelming his sense of protocol. "You have wounded? How many healers are in your army? I am a Master of Healing with a large resource of magic available."

"You are a Sorcerer-Healer?" Prince Szames' words tumble out in his excitement, "If you are a physician who wields magic then you have come at Cuthburan's desperate hour. All efforts to cure Prince Alexandros of the jarovegi wound have been ineffectual. Perhaps it is magic that is needed. Come with me."

His entourage flattens themselves against the wall as tall-blond-and-hunky does an about face, charging up the stairway with Jamison at his heels. Long strides bring me to the physician's side as he attains the landing at the top of the circular staircase. As we charge into the hall with the rest of the group following behind, my comrade elbows me, whispering in English, "Du-ude, you should see your hair! It's awesome man."

"My hair? We are rushing to cure the Heir to the Throne when we don't even know if you can use the magic in this place and you want to take time to discuss my hair?" *Men! And they call us vain!* "Jamison, what if your magic doesn't work - then what? Not exactly the great first impression we had hoped to make!"

"But did you see the look on their faces? It has to be your hair, I have never seen anything like it," Jamison persists as we turn into yet another hallway.

"Maybe you are onto got something. We are in a world of magic and scrying. These people are facing what seems be a hoard of demons. Some prophet in the past must have caught a glimpse of this future. Our coming could have been foretold. Maybe my hair color is being used as a way to distinguish the true allies they need to win the war. What is it, purple?" I give a shake of my head, dismissing it as frivolous. "No, don't answer that... forget I even asked. We need to concentrate on healing, not hair! Do you use herbs? Can you use my power to augment yours if we establish a link? Have you even tried activating healer's sight?" *That should give him something to think about other than the aesthetics of my mane.*

"Let's see," Jamison pauses. The hair on the back of my neck prickles, "that's got it. Switching to healer's sight is just a matter of concentrating to stabilize my vision." His smile broadens, "Whoa! Your hair isn't the only colorful thing. Your aura is so bright it's almost painful to look at..." as I sigh, he hurries on, "Being new at gaming I constructed my character according to what made sense. No herbs are required, only the knowledge of what needs to be done. Using plants will probably mean using less raw energy. As for joining powers... why not give it a try."

The prince is leading us in what is more like a slow run rather than a stately walk. I am in awe of the muscles I have seemed to gain in the transport here. We have come twice as far as we chased those gremlins and I'm not even breathing hard! Two stairways and several turns lay behind us, enough that I will never be able to find my way back unless someone hands me a map, even then it might be kind of iffy.

I've got a feeling I'm going to need mage-sight. Even though I can see my spells, I don't want to walk into a magical booby trap... Hmmm, this should work for general healing as well:

"When it is magical work that I am doing,
Saying 'sight' reveals the power I'm using.
When I am through and done for the day,
'Sight' again leaves me ready to play"

"Wow, *dude*, that was, like, way cool. Limericks, is that how you access your magic? A blue field of some sort surrounded you then was, like, sucked in through your eyes!" in his excitement Jamison lapses into surfer speech.

We make yet another turn, this time into a much wider hallway. I motion for Allinon to join us. "Can your Druid skills help the prince?"

"Hmmm…" his brow furrows as he thinks, "Well,

most of my healing requires herbs. My power plays upon - in fact depends upon - nature. If there is an infection I might be able to break it down, but without the right plants, my assistance will be minimal," as usual Allinon can be counted on for the "glass is half-empty" point of view.

The doorways grow further and further apart, the doors themselves doubling in size. *These suckers have to be at least ten feet high...* Prince Szames comes to an abrupt halt before the next entrance, a set of double doors. Looking up into his clear blue eyes, I concentrate on my empathy trying to get a look behind the royal façade.

"Princess Szeanne Rose is with Prince Alexandros," his tone echoes with sadness I cannot sense, "If you cannot cure him, it will not reflect badly upon you or your skill. Our physicians have pronounced this wound as fatal."

If a Royal Prince looses his composure, how bad off is his brother? I rack my brain, trying to think of something, anything, to ease his anguish. "Let us take a look at what we are facing," I qualify our abilities, "Jamison, Allinon, and myself all possess a certain amount of healing magic. There is a chance we can help where your physicians could not. The less disturbance to Prince Alexandros the better. The three of us will be able to determine what we can do for him."

The door slides silently open as Prince Szames holds the colossal giant motioning for me to proceed. "ArchMage Reba, MasterHealer Jamison, and Druid Allinon: if you will follow me, the rest may wait in the Reception Chamber." The others are forced to file in behind Szames and the sorcerer.

A massive bureau sits a few feet from the wall, dead center between two doorways leading from either side of the room. Rows of books line the shelves behind the escritoire. A fireplace big enough for Jerik to stand in occupies each of the sidewalls. Besides several uncomfortable looking chairs, the room is empty, giving the study a look of intimidating spaciousness. *Reception*

Chamber? It looks like Donald Trump's library!

The prince once again holds the door as I walk through it and to the right. His exemplary manners afford me the opportunity to get a look at his brother's injuries without having to worry about schooling my expression. Single minded in my effort to spare relatives what will assuredly be my own bad reaction, I cross the huge room stretching out my legs for long, efficient strides.

I have never seen someone close to death, or even someone badly wounded, but as I look down at the figure in the bed I know now I have seen both. Black hair, wet with continual perspiration, is slicked back from the Prince's brow. The ashen visage of the twenty-something year old looks more like a wax sculpture than a living man. Even though Alexandros is covered to the neck by a sheet I know our patient holds onto life by the slightest of threads.

Jamison takes a steadying breath as he pulls back the sheet, easing off the blood-soaked bandages covering the prince's shoulder. Braced for the worst, I am nonetheless struck by the extent of the injuries. Serrated flesh is parted, as if repelled by its deplorable condition. Ghastly white bone shines through ruby tissue, swollen and splayed.

Within seconds I recover my composure. I am no doctor, but this wound doesn't strike me as a mortal one. *Gruesome and highly infected, yes, but fatal… how? Maybe it's something else.* I whisper, "Sight." My vision ripples for a second before it clears.

An inky writhing mass is leached onto the patient's aura, spreading out from the wound like an ameba. "Holy…" my stomach churns as revulsion cause it to flip-flop. Rocking back on my heels I grit my teeth and stand my ground. "Jamison, Allinon, do you see that… thing? Is that some kind of poison?"

"Needless to say I have never seen anything like this, at least what is shown by healing sight. But I will state the obvious if only to give my brain a few minutes to try and figure this out." Jamison sighs chewing on his lower lip, "The redness indicates the area of bacterial contamination. Reba, my best guess is the inky blob is some kind of magical infestation, not a poison. I can cure his wounds, those will be a synch: at least with healing ability they should be. But he has lost a lot of blood and he is dehydrated too. Compound that with the black massed 'Aura Virus' draining his spirit and you have a mess way too complicated for me to handle." Jamison closes his eyes for a few seconds.

With a sense of renewed conviction the healer continues, "Reba, we might have a chance if you can remove the AV, for lack of better terminology. Severe dehydration and blood loss... well that's something even a modern hospital might not be able to cure. I don't know how much of a chance we stand of saving him, but we have to try. You got any ideas, Allinon?"

"The aura is made up of our essence, spiritual DNA if you will. Genetically we pass DNA on to our children. For a reason that is beyond me, I know auras work the same way. Our siblings have a little of the substance contained in our aura around them in their auras. Even though each person's pattern is unique, what it's made of is similar to the auras of our family members or grandparents. Perhaps, I can try to reenergize his energy field ...." Allinon expels a breath, shaking his head. "This is all theory of course."

"I can handle the AV. I think I may have a solution to the rest of the problem." I sketch out my idea and the others nod as they get the picture I'm painting.

A slow smile replaces the grimace the Elf has worn since our arrival. "You know, if his family supplies DNA, the potion could act as a link. I will be able to pull directly from their auras, like a blood transfusion only it will be a spiritual transfusion instead," Allinon's self-gratifying tone lacks warmth or compassion.

"Ex-cell-ent! Faced with an impossible task, all we have to do is get creative with the forces at work, and *voila*," Jamison snaps his fingers, his jovial nature fully restored, "a life is saved. You know this world of magic might not be so bad."

The chestnut haired healer turns sheepishly to me, "But, Reba, I'll let you explain to the Prince what we need to get this job done."

The healer's support is all the encouragement I require. Looking around I spot Prince Szames standing by the door, engaged in a quiet discussion with the sorcerer and someone who has to be the sister he mentioned earlier.

The woman stands at least six inches shorter than me; her head only comes to Prince Szames' chest. She is petite and he is massive, but the family resemblance is there none-the-less. They have the same flaxen hair, a true blond not sandy or dirty. Every single strand is the same exact hay color. The eyes are also carbon copies of the same sapphire blue. Coming around the end of the bed I make a mental supply list.

"Your Highness, I believe we may be able to help Prince Alexandros, but I am going to need a few things. Time is of the essence." I pause. As I discern hope rise in a sharp pinnacle in his companions I begin the request. "We need a large tub, big enough to hold your brother. I need it filled at least halfway with one of every kind of food: meat, poultry, fish if you have it, vegetables, flour, sugar, even a pinch of each type of spice your cooks use. Put all of it into the tub and bring it to the reception chamber. Also we need warm water, enough to fill it halfway. This we must have immediately," With a brief dip of his chin, Prince Szames dashes to the door yelling for someone named Herald. *So I manipulated them, life is more important...* I shrug off guilt.

I turn to the Princess, hoping, though we haven't yet been introduced, that she will trust me enough to help with the rest of the plan. "Is Prince Alexandros married?" Her eyes flutter as my new line of questioning takes her by surprise. "What I mean is, does he have any children? The rest of what I need is just the cooperation of his family, especially any offspring he has fathered,"

I perceive tension rising in the princess. Knowing her support is crucial, I urge, "It is necessary for any blood relation to be present at the healing, our success depends upon it."

Merithin and the Princess exchange glances. As the sorcerer gives a slight nod the Princess addresses me, "Prince Alexandros's mother died in childbirth. Prince Szames and I are his only siblings. Prince Alexandros has sired a bastard, Andertz, unacknowledged by King Arturo." Although she seems calm enough, I sense her objection to her father's attitude. "Is it absolutely necessary for both King Arturo and Andertz to be involved?"

I take a moment to form Aura Theory into Iron Age words and concepts. Prince Szames joins us as I begin, "Whatever attacked your brother has left part of itself behind. It is nesting in Prince Alexandros's aura, his spirit, draining that which defines him, that which makes your brother unique. This Aura Virus is also hindering your brother's ability to heal."

The sorcerer nods, but I receive blank looks from the nobility. I smother a sigh, "Most of what we are, as people, comes from our parents and is passed on to our children. We will draw on the part of each of you that is also present in your brother. By transferring a little of that substance to Prince Alexandros we will stabilize his aura, his inner being, and keep it from slipping away. The body will naturally rebuild itself. Jamison will speed this recovery, but your brother has lost so much of his inner-self, I fear he may not wake without aid to his aura as well. Having no mother to be here, it is not only necessary, but vital, that both Prince Alexandros's father and his son, as well as Prince Szames and yourself, take part in this healing." *Will the love of a son outweigh family pride?*

"I will fetch King Arturo. Princess Szeanne Rose, I trust you will obtain permission from Andrayia to allow her son's attendance." Prince Szames turns to me, "I will explain to King Arturo the necessity of Andertz's participation. Anything proven necessary to aid in the recovery of his first-born I am sure my father will assent to. I thank you for your patience in explaining the importance of this matter. I shall leave you to your preparations." With an inclination of his head and a smile he shares with his sister, Prince Szames dashes from the room. The princess likewise, gives me a nod before departing.

Doing my best to suppress a grin, I turn to Merithin, "Why do I get the feeling the King stands alone on the issue of his grandson?"

The aged sorcerer returns my smile. I continue as Jamison and Allinon join us. "I have one last request. I need a quiet place to prepare for my part in the healing."

"Yes, of course, if you will follow me." Merithin gestures for us to precede him. The robed mage leads us back to the Reception Chamber where Charles and Jerik are waiting. Merithin crosses the room heading for the doorway on the opposite side. Entering a new level of luxury, my jaw hits the floor. *Thank God for the manners of the upper class. With them holding the door they don't see me gaping like a bumpkin!*

An immense table dominates the room. The wooden plateau will seat a dozen or more, comfortably. What is most impressive, though, is not the size but the quality of the work.

Intricately carved foliage glowing like pale amber leaves clinging to summers warmth creates a scalloped edge around the tawny wooden expanse. A marvelously knotted tree-trunk serves as its base, darker than the sides and top, an altogether different hue, both blending and contrasting with the golden crown of flora. Even the outer supports are carved with great precision mimicking the leafstalk they represent. The entire table gives the appearance of a living oak petrified, preserved perpetually in autumn.

The chairs depict animals, the antlers of an elk-like beast forming the back support of the closest seat. The settees must have taken a master craftsman a lifetime to complete.

Placed in the center of the masterpiece is a pair of candelabrum appropriate to the woodsy scene. Cast in an enigmatic metal looking like a mixture of brass and pewter, five birds varying in shape and size nestle together forming the base for half a dozen candles.

Tapestries, so intricately woven you would swear they are paintings, grace each of the four walls. The tableaus illustrate different hunting techniques. In one, a hunter stands his ground against a massive bear holding nothing but a spear, his wounded companion leans against a tree in the background. *This is not a dining room it's a work of art!*

I school my composure turning to Merithin, resigning myself to the fact that this grandfatherly gentleman is the one who yanked us out of our world, "This will do. Would you care to join us for our council?" My magesight, still active, shows the senior's dull aura, some brown and burgundy are present, as well as traces of yellow, but blue is by far the dominant color in his aura. *Blue must be the affiliation for magic.* Oddly, it contains not even a trace of green. A loud growl emanating from Jerik's stomach gets a chuckle from everyone before Merithin has a chance to respond.

"First let me see about sending for some refreshments, but yes, it will be an honor to join you." The sorcerer goes in search of what, for us, will be lunch.

Charles gives a low whistle of appreciation, "This crib is tight!" he cruises over to the tapestry on the far wall, "If we save this prince, along with the kingdom, ya think we might get a little sum-summ'm for it?"

"So this place is real enough when it comes to money! Well, I'm hoping part of any reward includes a trip home." Now I have their attention. "I have the feeling we are going to more than earn it."

"If we are going to save the prince we had better get organized. I think it best we don't mention to anyone, just yet, that this will be our first time trying anything like this. Let's stick to the role of experienced crusaders." Within minutes I have outlined a plan of action.

"Are you always this organized or is this some new ability?" Allinon sucks-up managing to sound somewhat genuine. However, I still feel animosity lurking in the background. "I'm beginning to think we picked the right leader."

I shrug off the insincere lip service, "We have a long way to go before we get home." I pause, rethinking what I am about to say as the door opens and Merithin rejoins us. "Merithin, Jamison and Allinon are going to explain to the others what we are going to do for Prince Alexandros. I'll use the far side of the table for my preparations."

"Certainly. We shall take this end, Milady," Merithin motions to the portion closest to the door. Following me to the opposite end, the gentleman manipulates the chair at the foot of the table with elegant nonchalance. He then joins the others the head of the table.

Pulling a slim dagger from the sheath belted around the top of my boot, I cradle it in my hands, resting them on the table. A limerick flashes to mind. Deep in thought I mutter:

"Razor sharp you are, so what can be gained,
By causing those you cut a stinging pain.
Your edge will remain true no matter its use,
You will never break, whatever the abuse.
No pain shall you cause no matter the cut.
It is the price you shall pay, never to rust."

An aqua light emanates from my hands, feeling a shadow weight upon them. The radiance envelops the dagger, sinking into the blade. The weapon has a faint teal glow as I place it on the table.

I endeavor to focus on the larger problem. Thoughts skitter through my mind, like mice avoiding a cat. *Removing a substance... isolating an infection, banishing, rebuking, exorcizing...* I struggle to pin down a solution to the AV. *It needs to address magic. It's gotta to be comprehensive of the situation. What I really need is a pen and some paper to help get me organized ...*

"To keep my spells from being a bust,
A pen and paper are a definite must."

The space above the table wavers like a desert mirage. Instantly the legal pad and fine point 'Bic' pen I have pictured in my mind materializes. A smile glides across my lips: This world is going to be one hell of a ride!

With the new implements I jot down the parameters needed to evict the amoeba. Three pages later I finish a limerick I am reasonably sure will get rid of the AV. I sit, silently going over the rhyme to commit it to memory. The door opens as I decide once again to weave a spell.

"There are many words, some must rhyme,
A perfect memory will grace my mind."

A soft wave of dizziness swamps my brain. When the world stops spinning I am able to recall the constructed enchantment as if reading it from the paper before me. My task complete, I join the others.

A squire places a serving tray containing a large bowl of fruit, two loaves of bread and several different types of cheese on the table. A second squire follows with plates, napkins, a pitcher and several goblets.

Taking my cue from Merithin I use the softer cheese as a spread on a dark slice from the loaf. Famished, I work my way through several pieces of fruit as well as three large hunks of bread and a considerable amount of cheese. *How'd I manage to eat so much? It can't be more than two or three hours since I had breakfast with Tony.*

As if reading my thoughts, Merithin supplies an answer to my musings, "I apologize for the oversight. I should have had something waiting upon your arrival."

"Your timing was perfect. The food is delicious, thank you," I mumble popping the last bite of bread into my mouth.

Nonchalantly Merithin remarks, "Though your participation in the trans-location was minimal, the summoning spell is taxing to all participants. Frankly, I'm shocked to see you up so soon after your arrival. Your auras seem unaffected by the passage across the planes."

"Traveling across the dimensions is not practiced in our land." I ease into the topic, "I have a few question about the processes used to bring us here. May I inquire?"

"Knowledge is unrestricted in this kingdom. We, as a culture, pride ourselves on science and research. Feel free to inquire about anything that is a curiosity." Merithin is most congenial, "Arcane principles vary from world to world and dimension to dimension, so if you have questions concerning the mystical forces, please ask either my apprentice or myself. Nemir assisted me in the summoning. He is indisposed, but will be available on the morrow." The powerful elder smiles warmly.

"Have you summoned many people from different worlds?" I ask.

"Each of us is able to perform a summoning once in our lifetime, no matter the amount of power we control. It is our First Law of Magic," the elder seems to evade a direct reply.

I continue to probe, "Are there others here with the ability to do this type of magic?"

"Only one out of every hundred sorcerers has the power and discipline to achieve Master status which is required for trans-dimensional summoning. I know of four other sorcerers, who are Masters of the Art; two are no longer with us. I have trained over twenty apprentices of various talents but have never had the honor of guiding a sorcerer to the MasterLevel." The aged magicians thoughts wonder, "Although there was one with the potential, but he didn't have the discipline…"

While giving us important answers, Merithin has the

demeanor of a wise grandfather sharing the legacy of the knowledge collected over many years. A transformation takes place, taking years off the wrinkles as he continues with childish anticipation, "Jamison, you mentioned something about demonstrating this healing magic?"

I grin at the sorcerer's exuberance, "Jamison, use this enchanted dagger," I hand the ensorcelled blade to my companion, "Allinon perhaps the three of us should demonstrate the link we will use in healing Prince Alexandros, if one of you guys will volunteer to be a patient."

Jerik's gravely voice is like the rumble of thunder in the silent room, "I'll do it. Never been healed before."

His brow bunches up into a scowl as Jamison wields the knife. When blade makes contact, the Dwarf relaxes. "Strange, all that blood yet I feel nothing."

I take Jamison's left hand and Allinon takes mine as the healer places his right hand on Jerik's forearm. Closing my eyes helps me focus on slow, even breathing. My shoulders jump when I feel a tugging sensation: like a high-powered fan is sitting right beside me, only it doesn't pull air away from me: it is pulling something from within. I make a conscious effort not to resist the insistent drag sucking energy from the very fiber of my soul.

Certain now of the power I control, or my lack thereof, I open my eyes eager to get a look at a genuine healing. A green light surrounds Jerik's palm. The illumination intensifies as the wound narrows and the bleeding slows. The skin melts and blends. In a matter of minutes no sign of the incision remains. *Incredible! And Jamison thought my powers were cool!*

"Good as new," Jerik wiggles his fingers, "Other than tingling, didn't feel a thing."

"That was amazing, truly amazing. And this healing works as well for larger wounds? Can you mend bones? Is this procedure taxing for the patient as well as you?" Merithin seems twenty years younger in his enthusiasm for exploring a new magic.

"Excuse me, Sir Merithin, the requested tub and supplies have arrived," although he is addressing the sorcerer, the Page's eyes dart in my direction. He can't be more than twelve and he is working!

"Thank you, lad. We will be along directly," turning to us, he sighs, "It seems my questions will need to wait for another time. The skill you've demonstrated gives hope that Prince Alexandros is not yet lost. Thank you for the demonstration."

The Reception Chamber is devoid of most of the human occupants. A large wooden tub occupies the center of the room and, as requested, it is half-filled with a variety of foods. On the far side of the room, seated in a chair next to the princess, a woman holds a small boy on her lap.

Walking in that direction, my attention is absorbed by the princess and Andrayia, for that is surely the identity of the young woman accompanying her. They pair of females have the same exact color of hair. *Oh great! Please don't tell me we've been transported to the World of Golden Locks! I gotta remember to lay off the blonde jokes.*

Although their mane has the same hue, these two women will never be mistaken for sisters. Judging from their seated position, Andrayia is even shorter than the princess, and that is the smallest of the differences. Where the princess is petite, Andrayia is voluptuous, in features as well as figure.

Rotund almond eyes evaluate us as Jamison and I cross the room. The women rise as I near them. My prediction proves accurate: Andrayia is a good two inches shorter than the princess. The top of her head doesn't even reach my shoulder.

Andrayia sets her son beside her and curtsies with a bowed head as the princess makes the introductions, "Reba the ArchMage, I present Andrayia and her son Andertz."

Pretending I am used to people bowing in my presence, I incline my head as Prince Szames did.

Princess Szeanne Rose continues, "Milady ArchMage Reba, may I be of further assistance? I have knowledge of the bodily arts: I have studied medicine for many years."

"Your Highness, that is a most welcome offer. Jamison, maybe you two can discover which herbs will aid in the healing process?" Finding a secluded corner, the pair immediately put their heads together.

I address Andrayia, "I thank you for your timely arrival. I assume this means you're willing to allow Andertz to participate in the healing of Prince Alexandros?" *Why do I perceive hostility? Could it just be tension?*

"No harm will come to him?" When I nod she continues, "Then my permission is given."

Definitely hostility, but why? What have I done?

"You are a pretty Lady," squeaks a small voice from beside her.

Squatting down so we are eye to eye, I address the smallest member of our impromptu healing group. "Thank you, young man. You are Andertz, right?"

His head dips as he retains a tight grip on his mother's skirt. "My name is Reba. How are you today?" This boy is going to be a real lady-killer. Emerald eyes combined with jet-black hair and a porcelain complexion.

"Good, but Poppa is sick. Are you going to help Poppa get better?" The love I feel from this child brings a lump to my throat.

"Yes, but I need your help. Would you like to help me work some magic, so your poppa will get better?" His eyes widen but once again he nods.

Hearing the door open, I glance to my right. Prince Szames ushers in a distinguished, gray-bearded gentleman whose elaborate robes speak of great importance. After rising from a bow with the rest of those assembled, I turn back to Andertz, "You will have to be very brave."

"I am a big boy, and very brave too. I want to help Poppa get better," demands the youngster as he lets go of his safety net, putting his hands on his hips. This child can't be more than four, five at most. *A truly brave boy, indeed.*

Pulling the enchanted dagger from its sheath I show it to the child, "This is a special knife. We will need to poke your finger so it will bleed, but I promise it won't hurt, not even a little." Andertz immediately sticks out his tiny hand.

Andrayia nods her consent. I take the offered appendage in hand, leading Andertz over to the tub filled with foodstuff. *It won't hurt him… it won't hurt… it won't…* Willing my eyes not to close, I use the tip of the dagger to prick the diminutive index finger.

Blood from his fingertip wells then drips into the tub. While the precious drops we require are deposited, I ramble, trying to distract him from what I find to be a disturbing sight. "The blood will help Allinon use what is in you. I will also need a lock of your hair." I carefully take three stands of hair out of the ponytail he wears. His adorable eyes cringe as I yank out the roots.

Allinon hands me one of the napkins from our lunch, signaling we have enough fluid. I pass him my blade so he can start on the others.

I press the cloth to the wound. "That wasn't so bad, was it?"

"My hair hurts, but the finger was fine, just like you said," Andertz beams at me. *I was right, with a smile like that, a lady-killer indeed.*

I grin as I make my next request, "You know, I bet a boy your age really knows how to spit." His smile broadens as he gives a nod. "Well, now what I need you to do is spit real big, right into that tub. Can you do that for me?" With a profusion of enthusiastic Laning, Andertz leans over the side of the tub to donate his last piece of DNA.

His brows drawn in puzzlement as he turns back to me. "Is this magic?"

With an aura like that you might get to work magic of

your own some day. "Not yet, this is just the preparation. See the tall gentleman over there with white hair? His name is Allinon. In a few minutes he will work some magic on all this stuff so it can be used to help your poppa. Then we will all get into a circle around him and hold hands."

Glancing around, I notice an audience has gathered now that everyone has finished making their own DNA deposits. *Will a child's explanation be adequate for all of them?*

"This is where more magic comes in, where I will need your help. What you will do is to sit in your mom's lap, holding hands with the people next to you. You will close your eyes and try to relax, maybe even pretend you are napping. You are going to feel kind of funny: like a strong wind is blowing past you, only it will be coming from inside of you. It's very important to stay relaxed and don't fight against the feeling coming from your insides. That is just going to be Allinon and Jamison using the magic inside of you to help your poppa get better. Do you think you can do all that?"

"Sounds easy. I relax, with no fighting. But if I close my eyes I will miss the magic." Andertz lips form a diminutive pout.

"It is very, very, important that you stay relaxed. If you see the magic you might get excited. If you get excited and forget about relaxing you could cause all the magic to stop. If this happens, your dad may get much sicker. That is why you need to close your eyes, all right?" I am satisfied this remarkable child fully comprehends his role in the healing process as his face turns serious and he nods again.

"I tell you what. You can watch Allinon work some magic right now." This brings back the smile I am quickly falling in love with.

Standing up, I look to the adults, "Allinon will use Druid magic to make a potion out of the tub's contents. We will then need to wait until the bath is filled halfway with water before the healing can take place. That leaves a few minutes in which I can address any concerns."

Turning from the royal participants, I address my comrades, "Jerik, would you and Charles arrange the chairs? We need seven encircling the tub. Merithin, can you retrieve the pitcher we used at lunch? I would have you fill it with the potion Allinon is making, before it's diluted. You will need to pour this over the wound as the healing is performed," having given the final instructions, I lead the others to the corner where I met Andrayia and Andertz.

Once there, I turn to face the royalty of the Kingdom of Cuthburan as Prince Szames makes the formal introductions, "Arturo, Sovereign King of Cuthburan and Princess Szeanne Rose I present to you, Reba the ArchMage, leader of the Crusaders of the Light." I curtsey, eyes downcast. Looking back to the ruler of this kingdom, I note the family resemblance.

King Arturo's salt and pepper hair was undoubtedly once black like Alex's and Andertz's. His eyes are the same sapphire blue as Szames and Szeanne Rose. The King's voice holds the same inflection and mannerism as Prince Szames and the younger son has also inherited his father's strong, straight nose and square jaw.

"Your Majesty, I am honored. Do you have any questions regarding the healing process upon which we embark?" I try to sound dignified.

"My son has explained the reasons behind our necessary participation. We have never before participated in anything magical. What may we expect from our roles in this endeavor?" though his voice remains calm as he uses the royal plural, I perceive a building tension as he talks about his involvement in the supernatural.

"Your Eminence, you might experience a small amount of fatigue, but nothing permanent, I assure you." The feeling is still present. If the tension transmutes into resistance the link could be jeopardized!

"Jamison is a MasterHealer with 'the Gift.' The Gift

is what we call the ability of someone who can use his life force to harness the power in our auras. In Jamison's case it is somatic essence he uses. From the hue of her aura, Princess Szeanne Rose also has an affinity for this type of magic. You, Prince Szames, possess an affinity for corporeal magic such as Merithin and I command." This is not helping… if anything he's more agitated. Let's try a different angle.

"Your son lies close to death, therefore I cannot guarantee our success, but time is of the essence. We can perform the healing without your participation, but our chance of succeeding will be greatly reduced. Unless you are willing to give yourself whole-heartedly into my care with absolutely no reservations, your participation may be more hazardous than your exclusion."

Trying not to single out my new Monarch, who will undoubtedly resent my eavesdropping on his feelings about magic, I include the others with a glance in their direction, "You must ask yourselves, all of you: are you willing to trust the intentions, motivations, and capabilities of a mage you have just met. I realize I ask much, but Prince Alexandros' life hangs in the balance. There is no time to earn your trust, therefore I have no choice but to ask that you to give it blindly for the sake of your son and your brother."

"You ask much. We three represent the ruling sovereignty of this kingdom. We declare this not to justify our lack of participation, but so you, ArchMage Reba, know the measure of trust we place in your hands. We will shy from nothing, no matter the risk, that will spare the life of Crowned Prince Alexandros," as King Arturo embraces our healing as the savior of his beloved son, I discern the tension siphoning away into nothingness.

Bowing my head, I show acceptance of his gift, "Never in my life have I betrayed a trust given to me. If it is within our power, your son will be spared. His chances are good with so much support to draw upon."

Glancing behind me I see the tub is now half-full

with a silver liquid. The potion is diluted with the water necessary to restore Prince Alexandros's bodily fluids. Knowing it's best to strike before apprehensions can resurface, I rush on to the final stage.

"Your Majesty, if you will take a seat at one end, Prince Szames you will be on his left at Prince Alexandros' knees. I will sit next to you. Princess Szeanne Rose, you will be seated on my other side, with a cushion to pillow Prince Alexandros' head. Jamison you will sit between Princess Szeanne Rose and Andertz. King Arturo, since Allinon will restore the stolen life force to Prince Alexandros, he will sit between you and Andertz for you both possess the strongest spiritual ties to him."

I was either victorious in answering all their questions or I have successfully impressed upon them the urgency of this operation. The mentioned participants go immediately to their respective places. *Only one thing left undone...*

"Your Highness," I reach out, touching the arm of Prince Szames before he can assume his place, "Would you assist Jamison in bringing your brother? We need to place him in the tub." If Charles is Mr. America, Szames is Mr. Universe. *Why am I so sure I'm not dreaming when the entire royal family looks this good?*

Prince Szames manner stiffens fractionally. "I am honored you place this responsibility with me. Will we commence immediately?"

Taking his hesitation for a quandary, I explain, "You seem the least disturbed by what is about to take place; therefore I am hoping you won't require as much time to relax. Even with the water heated it will be a drain on your brother. We will begin as soon as possible." *Then again he could just seem relaxed. I can't read him like the others.* Turning my thoughts back to the healing, I approach Prince Alexandros' mistress and her son.

"Andrayia, if you and Andertz will take the seat to the right of Allinon?" I squat to better address the smallest member of the healing circle. "Andertz, are you ready to help us work an enchantment?" As he nods I take his hand, "Prince Szames will bring your poppa and put him in the water. Your father's shoulder is going to look really bad, but don't be scared; that is what we are here to fix, ok?" He feels excited, yet calm. If only everyone had the faith of a child!

I sit, holding the hands of a prince and a princess as I close my eyes, taking a deep breath to center myself. The tingling sensation accompanying me since my arrival finds a focus.

Resembling vibrations from an electrical device, I don't need to touch the carrier. I discern the trembling: the stronger the vibrations the larger the source of magic. It is just a matter of pulling the outside magic to the large white mass that is my center of power. As I entwine and fold a small piece of the foreign magic into my personal reservoir, it forms a bond.

The tricky part is letting go of part of my essence at the same time so I can share energy. *I have no idea how I know what to do. I just know that I know, that I know what I know...*

After examining the links to make sure they will hold, giving it a few more minutes to establish a current, I watch the flow of the outgoing energies. *Looks stable.* I open my eyes. In the short time it's taken us to prepare for the healing, the prince's aura has noticeably decreased. The writhing inky mass of the AV, the aura virus, is growing. *No time to waste!*

"We seven are joined in agreement,
Alex won't be martyred by your treatment.
It's of magic you're made, and it's magic I wield,
Be gone from his body, against us you have no shield."

Aqua light shoots out from my long slender hands, heavy with power. Magic surrounds the AV. The blob rolls and boils like someone has set a match under it. In a matter of seconds the AV dissipates like fog under an autumn sun.

In a blink of an eye a green haze settles over the wounds and brown mist rises from the sliver liquid enveloping the lower half of the prince's body. As the mossy cloud intensifies the mangled flesh melts, beginning to close. The coppery fog thickens as shimmering liquid evaporates. The grotesque wounds standing out on his alabaster skin like scarlet paint are reduced to the pale pink of a carnation as his skin darkens to beige.

Second by second the hued patterns of the Prince's aura become apparent. Besides a small amount of blue corporeal magic and a strong fuchsia streak, his aura has no affinity for magic, just like his father's. Whatever talent the purple streak represents, he was the only one of his siblings to inherit it.

As the energy we invoked disperses I look up from the sentinel I am keeping into the eyes of young boy. The child doesn't look scared, horrified, or even slightly disturbed by the sight he has just witnessed, against my instructions I might add. He looks fascinated, in awe, and he is wearing a smile so wide you would think it was Christmas. In the face of such enthusiasm my lips curve and my eyes light up.

Turning my attention back to the patient, before my lips part to ask Jamison if our healing has been successful, Alexandros, the Crown Prince of Cuthburan, opens his eyes.

Butterflies take flight in my stomach as he gazes at me with the most gorgeous green eyes I have ever seen, framed by long, thick lashes. Prince Alexandros gives me a week smile. In a voice rough from disuse he inquires, "Have I died and gone to Heaven? Are you an angel sent to take me to the Afterlife?" Having exhausted what little strength we restored to him, Alexandros drifts into sleep.

Blushing like a teen who just received her first kiss, I sit back in my chair as Jamison and Prince Szames lift Prince Alexandros from the tub. Mind whirling, perfunctorily as a sleepwalker I trail the men, waiting hesitantly at the door to the bedchamber.

Laying his brother gently back on the pillowed surface of the bed, Prince Szames whispers, "Barely conscious and you have already out-maneuvered me on the battlefield of her heart. No, Brother, I will not fight you for her love, no matter how my heart beats stronger and my blood races when she nears. No, I am not a fool. I will not wage a war I cannot win. Does not *The Prophecy* foretell her to be your bride?"

Though enhanced hearing brings the words clearly to my ears, the sounds are meaningless to my befuddled senses.

Chapter Three

Jamison delivers his professional diagnosis: Prince Alexandros will make a full recovery. The others rejoice while I scramble to gather my scattered wits. *Come on Rebecca, get it together. It's not like you've never received a compliment before. You are married, remember! How can you let a gorgeous set of eyes and a come-on line affect you like this?*

Hands trembling, it takes a conscience effort to still them-and calm my racing heart. *Now I know there is something else that needs to be done. Oh, yeah, thank God I've got that improved memory.*

Recovering my senses, I notice Prince Alexandros has been delivered back to his bed. Only the royal family and Merithin remain. The trio is engrossed in an animated discussion.

The rest of the visitors from Earth are clumped together in a corner like a heard of frightened sheep. A few long strides bring me to them. "Jamison, didn't the prince mention something about over two hundred wounded? You don't have the strength to heal them all, but I was thinking: how long will it take to teach the basic technique to a group of physicians already trained in the mundane herbal methods?"

"With the Gift and some knowledge of how the body works, it wouldn't take long. Once I show them how to access magic, I could demonstrate on a couple of the patients with them following along. Most would be able to pick up enough of what's needed to stabilize the majority of the patients." Jamison's brow furrows, "but they have never heard of using magic for healing. Surely if someone had the Gift they would have figured out how to use it by now."

Words come fast and quick in my excitement, "I studied your link with Princess Szeanne Rose. There is a barrier set around her inner reservoir of power. Something is restraining her magic, yet it still let you access it. I'm betting with the right spell I can bring down the obstruction so the princess can detect and use her own Gift."

Jamison gets a second wind of enthusiasm. "Well what are we standing around here for? Lives may be lost with each minute wasted! Allinon, do you feel up to breaking down another batch of food for a healing potion?"

"I can do better than that," Allinon smirks, "Reba wasn't the only one paying close attention to our first healing session. I watched the way you handled that AV. It's similar to how I broke down the food. If there are any more people suffering from that malignancy, my druid skills will exorcise it."

Jamison turns to me with a broad smile, "Reba, how fast can we get another tub, this time have it filled all the way to the top."

Having heard all I need, I stride to where the prince, princess, and Merithin stand: The king must have left for the council meeting. My patience is lacking. I fail to wait for royal acknowledgment, "Pardon me, Prince Szames?" I barely retain manners enough to hold my tongue until he turns to look in my direction. "You mention having other wounded?" A look of surprise steals across his face. The rebel in me delights in breaking the royal façade of total confidence, even if it is just for a minute.

"Yes, of course. The wounded are being kept in the new barracks where the healers can better tend to them. Milady ArchMage Reba, should I have another tub of food assembled?" Prince Szames words rush in his haste to assist.

A pang of regret wounds my heart because remorse colors the princes reply. "Another tub is exactly what I have in mind," hastily, I fill him in on the rest of our needs.

I phrase my final request with care. "Your physicians are the other things I wish to discuss. With your permission, I may be able to help your people access their Gift so they will be able to heal as Jamison does. Princess, as I have alluded to, I believe you have a somatic affinity. If you wish, I can open up the channels to release the Gift you have within you. Since you have knowledge of herbal healing and how the human body works Jamison will be able to teach you the basics of wielding your magic so you may assist in tending to the wounded." My speech is halted as I see the open-mouthed surprise of Princess Szeanne Rose. Her lack of composure is not at all humorous, for she does not even attempting to regain it.

Oh please! Don't tell me it's against protocol for her to be seen with soldiers, even for healing! "I apologize, Your Highness, if I have transgressed some rule of propriety," turning back to Prince Szames I continue, "Some of your physicians might also have the healing Gift, Jamison will be able to train all who possess even the slightest affinity for bodily magic."

"Milady ArchMage Reba, I will have the physicians assembled in the foyer of the barracks at once. If you will give me a moment to dispatch my page for the needed supplies, we will be on our way," with a quick bow Szames excuses himself.

"ArchMage Reba, are you saying there may be those who possess the incredible power Sir Jamison wielded in the healing of my brother?" Princess Szeanne Rose stammers into the brief silence, her voice a mere whisper, "That I may possess such ability?"

As I nod affirmatively she continues, "Men have died, many more lie sorely wounded and may die before the day ends. If the power lies within me to save another's life, as you have spared Alexandros', I feel it would be a great wrong not to use it."

I take this opportunity to re-examine the woman standing before me. She is gowned in a fine-woven material with a satin sheen to it. The garment is tight fitting from the neck to the waist. Not as broad as the southern-bell dress I wore to the senior prom, but there is some fullness to the floor length skirts. The attire is a somber brown, providing a perfect contrast to her peaches and cream complexion. Her golden locks are pulled back into a tight braid.

The whole ensemble speaks of the seriousness with which she regarded the duty she undertook while caring for Prince Alexandros. I feel the compassion and the truth of the words she has spoken, as if an echo surrounds her.

"Your Highness, I cannot guarantee the success of the spell that will let you access the healing Gift within you, for I am unfamiliar with the laws of magic governing your world. But I can promise you this: If my attempt is unsuccessful it will not be harmful. You already have a basic knowledge of the human physique, if your Gift is activated, then you will be able to heal as Jamison has. It requires focus and concentration to use the Gift, along with knowledge of the problem. With time and practice, if your skill increases to equal Jamison's, the difference in power will not be great enough to matter. Do you wish me to release your Gift?" She utters a single, affirmative syllable in response. I continue. "You must relax as you did when we healed your brother. Listen to the rhyme and rhythm of my words. Clear your mind of everything except your desire to heal others."

"The magic is within you, I feel its power,
We need its force in this desperate hour.

Respond to her will after my touch,
Unless it will cause you harm or such."

Feeling pins and needles as if my arms have gone to sleep, I graze the woman's forehead releasing the mystical force within her as Prince Szames approaches.

"We can add one more healer to our list of assets?" The prince's smile is tight and approving, "With scores of wounded men your help will be appreciated."

Jamison joins the group, handing my knife back to me. "Your Highness," he nods to Prince Szames before instructing his new student, "Princess Szeanne Rose, if you will pick an object. Reba's knife will be excellent." After a pause, "Now focus on the knife, only the knife. Keeping the blade in view, try to focus on the space behind it. When you see the blue-green light surrounding the blade give a push from the power you sense within. This will activate healing-sight."

"Oh!" Princess Szeanne Rose gasps, closing her eyes, "I must have pushed too hard." She quickly schools her composure, "ArchMage Reba, you are surrounded by the most brilliant rainbow of colors. The blues are so bright they seem to dance! That is the 'aura' you mentioned earlier? Jamison, you are completely green, such beautiful shades, too."

I chuckle as Jamison's cheeks bloom like a flower in the spring sunshine, "Your Highness, somehow, I don't think you will have any problem picking up the basics." I hand my knife to Jamison. "The numbing aspect of this blade will be helpful in your work. Prince Szames, if you will lead the way, I look forward to seeing if any others possess a dormant Gift."

"As do I," Prince Szames agrees, "ArchMage Reba, if you will follow me."

I suppress a chuckle as Jamison rushes to hold the door for the princess and myself, hoping the others are picking up on the subtle mannerisms of this culture. Or could it be that Jamison has another interest? *Whatever the reason, I'm not complaining.*

Why do I feel like we are rushing headlong into danger. What am I missing? Turning to Jamison as we start down the hallway, I explore a new train of thought, "Jamison, do you know the Hippocratic Oath?"

"I was due to take it in six months. I have been going over it for weeks now." Jamison catches my mood so quick it seems like we have known each for years rather than hours, "You're onto something."

Still organizing my thoughts, minutes pass before I respond, "You know the old saying, 'with great power comes great responsibility?' Let me tell you, I am feeling that weight. We are about to create a whole new type of magic, the likes of which this world has never seen: neither has ours for that matter. Are we releasing something into this unsuspecting paradise that is more destructive than the enemy we are facing? The doctors of our world must pledge the Hippocratic Oath before they can wield their skills. With the power we are giving them, shouldn't we have something more than a simple oath?" *With all the talents we possess surely there is some safeguard we can impose.*

"Jeez… it never dawned on me that someone would use healing maliciously," Jamison pauses as we turn yet another corner in the meandering trail of halls through which Szames is leading us. Looking up, I realize I have no clue where we are. *I should have asked for a better sense of direction for my character!*

Mulling over Jamison's words, the answer to our dilemma pops out at me. "Jamison, that's it!" I bark, "Can you come up with a version of the oath for these people?"

"Sure, no problemo. Would something like this do? 'I swear, by the god I hold sacred, that I will serve my king and kingdom in their best interest. I shall refuse my services to none in need, nor will I use my powers in harmful ways… etcetera, etcetera…" He gives me a mock glare as I grin, "Now give it up. What's churning inside that head of yours."

Hastily I fill my comrade in on the details and the role he will play.

"It's perfect!" he crows, "Now we can use any available power without worrying about a loose cannon running around. Since Allinon will handle the AV, I assume after the initiation you will start to work on a magical defense for the castle?" Jamison shakes his head with a wry twist of his lips, "If they lost ten percent of their men in one battle I'd say their defenses are in need of an upgrade." *Does he have to be so confidant that I will have a solution to everything?*

Our fast pace brings us to the servants' quarters. In the narrow hallway the doors are crowded close together and the lantern contraptions are so sparsely placed that dark pools litter the corridor. Unable to see in the dim lighting, Jamison stumbles over a rough patch on the wooden floors while I step nimble over the uneven boards. It must be the Mage thing - aren't all magic users supposed to be able to see in the dark almost as well as daylight?

A few minutes later we approach the end of the hallway. Sunlight shines through cracks around the door, the brightness emphasizing the gloom in this section of the castle. A small figure waits by the exit holding several garments. Szames and Merithin turn so we can huddle into a group as much as the constrictive foyer will allow.

"ArchMage Reba, here are cloaks. The walk to the barracks is not long but spring has not yet taken a firm hold on the land. The weather is still quite bitter, especially this early in the day," Prince Szames offers before he continues out the door.

A blast of chill wind sweeps inside. "Wheeew.... this mail feels like a block of ice strapped to my chest." Charles reaches for a cloak. *Thank God he spoke in English!*

"We are seasoned warriors remember? Think tough-macho–football-player. Would a little cold bother them?" I reprimand him in our native tongue. I pull up the cowl on my robe, "I'm beginning to appreciate choosing a Mage for my gaming character. This robe is enchanted to maintain a constant temperature in a field surrounding my body." *Field surrounding, protecting...hmmm.*

Turning to Charles I give his arm an impulsive hug. "Charles, I could kiss you! You are a genius." *That mail really is cold!*

"Who me? What'd I do? But, hey...if it is affection you want, a charming knight like me would never pass up a kiss from a hottie, even if she is a witch!" Charles silky voice teases me with a Cheshire cat grin and a rise of his handsome eyebrows.

Now that sounds like the Allen I know! "Better watch it, Princeling, or this witch will turn you into a toad and have some fun seeing if there are any fair maids willing to kiss your warty hide!" I chuckle, aiming a mock swing in his direction.

The air is brusque and the day outside is bright. *I love the smell of wood stoves... what a beautiful day.* Looking ahead, I analyze the state of the king's army by the quarters they keep.

Six large wooden structures stand in three parallel columns with two buildings in every row. Each construction is a precise rectangle, making them appear modern. The only thing giving away the medieval work of the quarters is the lack of glass in the windows, and the fact that each immense three-story structure has eight large chimneys from which a continual stream of smoke pours. As we draw near I can make out the individual logs framing the outside walls. They are so straight they look like manufactured siding. Squinting against the wind I notice the smooth finish, like sanded wood.

With living quarters this advanced surely they have made similar progress elsewhere. What kind of army can cause such damage to an advanced medieval culture? Having decided I need a little more information, I lengthen my stride.

"Excuse me, Your Highness. Is now a good time to find out some basics about your...er...our strategic situation?" I ask, wishing I had paid more attention to protocol at the renaissance festival.

"I will be happy to answer any questions you have, though our knowledge of the Demons is limited." His smile seems genuine.

"How many men make up the besieging army? Are they more advanced in--"

"Men? Hump! If we were facing mere men our situation would not be this dire," with a crinkle in is brow, Prince Szames continues, "Milady, you believe we to be facing an ordinary army? An army such as we house in these barracks?" He gestures to the buildings. "An army made up of human flesh and bone?"

The arrogance! Is it because I'm a woman or is it just a princely superiority complex and his male ego that makes him think I am so simple-witted I need to be hand fed? Well, two can play at that game. I keep a tight reign on my Irish temper, modifying my bitter tone to something more reasonable. "Often, when people are faced with an enemy whose tactics and weaponry are foreign to all they know: whose appearance is startlingly different from what they are used to, they believe their foes are demonic monsters. In reality, they are just men who have evolved different customs, beliefs, and traditions, forming an unusual, even bizarre, culture. But they aren't demons, just immensely different. If you have a sketch of the invaders I will try to dispel this notion of demons. The revelation should restore the morale of your army."

The six barracks are behind us as we pass between two elongated single story buildings. The aroma emanating from the structures identifies them as the mess hall. Another large single story structure, "v" shaped with a square portion common to both wings faces us. The exterior looks exactly the same as the other buildings, yet intuition tells me this is the new addition.

The Prince takes no offence at my obtuse reply, "ArchMage Reba, I am afraid we have somewhat of a miscommunication. When I use the term 'Demon' it is with no metaphorical reference. We believe a sorcerer has opened a portal to another dimension and has somehow stabilized it. As you have stated this other world has developed far differently from ours. Of those who attacked, some had wings and flew, some were more than ten times our size, and some burrowed underground. All have claws and fangs which shredded our armor like a hot knife through a wax seal and none have been sighted except at night."

Oh my dear God, actual demons! Like from hell, demons! What have we gotten ourselves into! Swallowing hard to cover my loss of composure I ask a question I am sure he has already contemplated, "You mean there is a mage, excuse me, a sorcerer who is foolish enough to make a portal connection with a dimension that is demonic in nature?"

Prince Szames sighs as he reaches for the door, "Milady ArchMage Reba, that seems to be the case."

Chapter Four

Entering behind Princess Szeanne Rose, I am able to conduct a full examination of the physicians as they bow in the presence of royalty. It is a mixed group: most of the fifteen or so men are older than me, except for a couple of youths gathered in one corner. Other than the requested tub of food, a large sturdy-looking table and several chairs lining one side of the plain timber walls, the room is as striped of essentials as is a nudist colony.

"Your Highness, Princess Szeanne Rose," a gray-bearded gentleman at the front of the crowd bows, ridged with formality. He continues as the princess gives a slight inclination of her head. "What an unexpected pleasure."

"Your Highness, Prince Szames." He bows again as Prince Szames enters. His eyes goggle, as first Jerik then Allinon file in behind the raven-skinned Charles. The four-and-a-half foot Jerik's can't be mistaken for a child with his broad shoulders, and long arms, not to mention the six-inch braided beard. His shortness highlights Allinon's seven-foot stature which towers over Prince Szames, who seems tall for men on this world. "Can it be true? By your presence here I assume the rumors must be true. Has Prince Alexandros been healed of his grievous wounds?"

"Yes, my brother will make a full recovery. ArchMage Reba, leader of the Crusaders of the Light, I present to you MasterPhysician Tupper," Prince Szames performs the formal introduction, "Tupper, are any wounded in imminent danger of passing?"

"Only one. Captain Youngmen received a blow from the same jarovegi that wounded your brother. Nothing we've tried seems to aid his recovery. I doubt he will survive more than a few hours," as the physician answers, I feel despair threaten to engulf the professional before he pushes the emotion aside.

"ArchMage Reba, are you and your men up to another healing?" waiting only a moment for my affirmative nod he continues, "Tupper, this is MasterHealer Jamison who wields sorcery in healing. Bring the patient to him." The front door opens as Szames finishes his instructions, and the physicians spring into action.

"Your Highness. I brought as many as could be gathered quickly," the squire manages a small bow, even loaded down with wineskins.

"You did fine, Robert. Set them by the tub," I take down my cowl as Szames turns to address me. Ignoring the gasps and whispers I long for a mirror as he asks, "Will these be sufficient for your needs?"

"Yes, quite. Thank you. If you don't mind I will perform a simple enchantment to make them more suitable for holding the potion Allinon is creating?" Seeing Merithin's interest I include him in my offer. "You are welcome to observe."

The crowd of men part as I follow Squire Herald to the tub where Allinon is breaking down the raw material for a new batch of healing potion.

Picking up one of the wineskins I turn it over in my hands. Covered in some kind of animal hide with a wooden cork it looks like it will hold water, if just barely. *As important as the potion is going to be, I'd feel a lot better if these were Rubbermaid.* Inspired I mumble:

"Containers, your construction is lacking.
Now you'll be clear plastic; never cracking.
With a hourglass shape, easier to grip,

A screw-off cap whose threads won't strip."

"What a beautiful glass bottle. Such delicate lines. Is it watertight? How does it open?" With inquisitiveness a cat would envy, questions tumble forth from Merithin only seconds after the transformation is complete.

"Water will not escape even if the container turns upside down. The cap twists off, like this," taking off the stopper I toss the bottle to Merithin who doesn't react quite fast enough. I wait, my stomach clenched in expectation as the sorcerer juggles the canteen from one hand to the next. Prince Szames rescues the fumbling object with a skillful catch, putting an end to my hope of a dramatic demonstration of durability.

"It is much lighter than expected," turning it over in his massive hands he taps the side of the bottle, "This does not sound like glass. Is it some type of material prevalent in your world? Or is purely magical in construction? Is it similar to glass in anything but looks?" A fraction of a smile turns the edge of his lips as, without preamble, Prince Szames tosses the canteen in my direction.

I take a step back so it is clear I intend to let the canteen fall to the ground. As it bounces with a loud hollow clack I get the satisfaction of witnessing stunned amazement from both Prince and sorcerer. Reaching down to grab the canteen after the second bounce I explain the properties of synthetic polymers.

"This material is called plastic and it is rather common on my world. It doesn't occur spontaneously in nature but is made somewhat like glass. Other than the method of manufacturing and its translucency, plastic doesn't share many other properties with glass. This container's biggest weakness is heat. It will hold boiling liquid just fine, but you cannot heat something to boiling by placing this over a fire: its melting point is much lower than glass."

Handing the canteen to Merithin for a close inspection, I continue, "As you can see, a solid drop will not break or even harm it. The more common material in my world will eventually become brittle with time. I used a preservative incantation so this will remain forever as it is now." Glancing around I notice the patient - Youngmen wasn't it?- is being brought in.

Two men carry the patient on a stretcher and, as instructed, place him on the table in the center of the room. I get a glimpse of Youngmen's injuries as Jamison removes the bandage wound around his upper leg. *Ugh! What a mess!* A cavernous gash has shredded the flesh of his outer thigh from the hip to the knee. *That must be a part of the hipbone. Good thing it was his outer thigh and not the groin area, if the femur artery was hit he wouldn't have survived the blood loss.* Glad to have something to take my mind off the gore, I turn my attention back to Szames and Merithin.

"You call this 'pla-stick'; does the name hold any magical significance?" Merithin hands the canteen back to me, continuing as I indicate the lack of magical reference, "I would love to take a closer look at a world where such marvels are manmade and require no enchantments."

I share a tight smile with Merithin, glancing at the bathtub which now holds a shimmering liquid. I don't have time to transform each bag into a canteen. *Maybe I can use a duplication spell. Only one way to find out...*

"With magic you were made from a common substance, All you touch will have your properties in abundance."

Tossing the canteen onto the pile of wineskins with the completion of the limerick, I smile as light surrounds the entire stack. In a matter of seconds a clattering fills the room as fifteen canteens settle to the ground. Wiping sweat from his brow with the back of his hand, Allinon bends to pick up a translucent container resting near his foot.

"Plastic. And with a screw-on cap," he heaves a sigh, "Reba, I appreciate your help. This stuff is not easy to make." The elf stoops, filling the canteen with iridescent liquid.

My cheeks color at the sincerity of the compliment, "With our combined talents there is nothing we can't accomplish. It looks like they are ready for us - do you want to handle the AV?"

Allinon attempts a grin, but only manages to looks like as if he's suffering from constipation, "Sounds great." The slender giant hands the newly filled bottle to Merithin, "This should be poured over the wound as Jamison performs the healing."

"Gladly," Merithin bends from the waist, delighted to get a better view of the procedure.

The MasterHealer stands midway down Youngman's torso with Princess Szeanne Rose beside him. There is a space to Jamison's right, directly in front of the leg wound, obviously intended for Merithin. *Better him than me. In this world blood doesn't make me swoon, but I would rather not have a ringside seat.* There is a space to the left of Princess Szeanne Rose, presumably for Allinon.

Without a clear view of the actual healing, I discern what is transpiring. The breakdown of the AV proceeds without a hitch. *I'm glad Allinon can handle the virus; I am not sure my stomach is ready for a full day of visiting wounded men.*

"Youngman's aura is still weak. If he survives the night, with time, he will make a full recovery," Jamison lets out an audible sigh, "Princess, were you able to follow the procedure?"

"Yes, using 'The Sight' I could see you connect my energy to yours. I then witnessed the combined forces surrounding the wound, penetrating the injury. Now that I have witnessed the process, I believe I will be able to access my Gift. But I am still unsure how to make it respond and do what I wish." As if her response is a cue, the silent room erupts.

"Enough!" Prince Szames does not raise his voice, much, but the tone of absolute authority gets immediate results.

"Tupper, please see that your men make Captain Youngmen comfortable and the table is put back into place," men jump to carry out Prince Szames' commands.

"ArchMage Reba believes several of you may possess the 'Gift' of healing Jamison has demonstrated. It lies inside you, camouflaged like a deer in the brush, waiting for the right touch to set it free. In fact, the ArchMage has already released the Gift within Princess Szeanne Rose. She was able to join with Jamison and follow the entire process. Are there any among you who do not wish to have the Gift awoken if you possess it?" complete silence greets his question. "ArchMage Reba, I believe you and your men have made a favorable demonstration of the importance of the Healing Gift. Are there any here who possess it?"

"Yes, Prince Szames, most of the men have the Gift to some degree. Whether or not I can activate the Gift is another matter. Before I attempt an Awakening, I ask that you allow Jamison to lead these men in an oath," I turn, tilting my chin to meet the eyes of Prince Szames. *Please… please don't fight me on this…* "In my world our healers make a covenant pledging to use their knowledge and skills to the betterment of mankind. Considering the depth of what we are about to do, I feel a similar oath-taking is in order."

With a twinkle in his eyes Prince Szames begins, "Our physicians also have an oath they take when they begin their training. I agree the gravity of this situation demands another vow be made with the bestowing of the newly discovered Gift. ArchMage Reba, if you have something commonly used in your world I feel it will be a perfect counterpart to the Awakening of the Gifts you uncover."

With a brief nod of acknowledgement, I step forward. "Tupper, if you will have your physicians line up in three rows; I must perform an incantation for each individual.

"You must be completely relaxed. Open yourself to magic if you wish the Awakening to be successful. Jamison will lead you in the 'Healers Oath'," I whisper out the side of my mount to him in English, "Have them repeat the words in their minds."

Jamison gives a fraction of an inclination to his head before he begins, "Raise your right hand and repeat after me: 'I swear, by the god I hold sacred, that I will from this day forth, serve my King and Kingdom in their best interest…'"

I close my eyes, taking a deep breath. Concentrating on my empathetic ability, I stretch out my senses, soaking in all the emotion in the room as the chant continues. "I shall refuse my services to none in need, nor will I use my powers to harm human or beast…"

Excitement, joy, enthusiasm... nothing more than expected. *Wait a minute, what's this?* Disgruntled fear, seeps into my awareness. I direct my focus to the left corner of the room, concentrating on that area. "I shall keep in confidence anything disclosed to me by my patients, or obtained though the use of my Gift…"

Almost there, just a moment more. *H a t e…* "*I'll show them, I know what is best. My Gift will be superior, then they will be sorry, all of them.*" A rogue physician's thoughts come through as if the man is whispering in my ear.

Jamison concludes, "Unless it directly endangers the life of others, or the sovereignty of the Kingdom of Cuthburan."

I open my eyes. I have no problem finding the individual transmitting such heart-rending cruelty. Droopy eyes, thinning mousy brown hair and a thick middle house the destructive emotions I have eavesdropped on. I whisper "sight" as the last few words of the Healers Oath are repeated.

I miss the rest of Jamison's instructions as I approach the MasterPhysician to begin my part of the ceremony. After being submerged in the foul animosity of the mysterious dissenter Tupper's emotions wash over me like a refreshing spring shower. *Such hope, compassion and joy, no wonder he is a MasterPhysician.*

"Magic is within you, I feel its power,
We need its force in this desperate hour.

It'll respond to you after my touch,
Unless it will cause you harm or such."

    As tingling fingers graze his forehead, I give a push releasing the power of my Gift. With sight still active I see a blue radiance surround the center of his power before energy swells past the broken barrier
    I give an affirmative nod to his questioning look. His chocolate eyes sparkle with unshed moisture as I move on to the next physician. Although Tupper's aura is not the strongest among those here, I will lay odds that he gets more done with his power. I bet he's incapable of putting less than one 110% into each and every patient.
    I pass by only two who possess not even a trace of the Gift. One such is an elderly gentleman. I meet his eyes and shake my head "no." When tears gather in the pair of matched ovals, he blinks to regain them in. Sensing kindness and compassion ebbing off the senior in gentle waves, my eyelids flutter to keeping my own emotions from overflowing.
    My eyes widen with surprise as the physician reaches out with one gnarled hand, grasping my fingers. "It's alright child. Andskoti has bestowed many blessings upon me, one more or one less makes my life no less joyous."
    A give a determined bob of my head before I hurry on before the sorrow glistening in my eyes overwhelms my composure.
    After working my way down the row, I stand before the source of all the negative vibes. The plain, middle-aged, man with mud-brown eyes isn't any taller than I am.

A smug sucker, but he certainly doesn't look dangerous or deranged. Could I have been wrong? I open my senses once more, and find anger bound so tightly inside I am surprised his hands aren't trembling. A memory flashes through the healer:

    Though the white hair is now red, I eyes of the kind elder remain the same. His voice takes on a hard edge, "You know better than this, or you should by now. A dose of this size could harm an adult or even kill a child. I'm afraid I cannot pass you to the next level. Perhaps next year…"

    The vision wavers as a red haze clouds all thoughts. Malice so strong it borders on murderous intent, rises up with indignation.
    Yeah, that's him.

"Magic is within you, I feel its power.
We need its force in this desperate hour.

It will respond to you after my touch.
Unless it will cause you harm or such."

    Uttering the words, I never reach for the power lying with my being. I touch his forehead. Meeting his eyes I murmur, "I'm sorry, your Gift is beyond even my reach."
    The wolf in sheep's clothing casts his eyes to the floor, giving a show of acceptance. I feel palpable disappointment, crushing frustration, and hatred laced with overwhelming resentment in his soul. *Who knew such a meek exterior could house the destructive nature of an atom bomb.*
    Completing the last row with greater speed, I stride back to Prince Szames and Tupper to give my official findings, "Out of seventeen there were only two who possess no affinity for healing magic. There was also one

whose Gift was beyond even my reach: the brown-haired, middle aged gentleman on the left end of the second row."

"That would be Malegur." Tupper supplies the name.

"There seems to be a common strength, at least among those gathered here. Tupper, you are at that average level. There are one or two who are above average. Jamison and Princess Szeanne Rose seem to be on a level all their own," I share what I have gathered with magesight.

The outer door bangs opens as a gust of wind hurls the door into the wall. Herald, the page, enters carrying a large tray of food. The other squire, Robert, and several servants follow loaded down with more trays of food, several pitchers, and a few dozen wooden plates and cups. They make their way to the table in the back as Jamison and Allinon join us.

"ArchMage Reba, Merithin has informed me that one of the main requirements for a speedy recovery from any magical working is plenty of food and drink. I hope you and your men have found our cuisine palatable," Szames queries.

"Thank you, Your Highness. That is very considerate of you. I think I speak for the entire group when I say that, although your food is somewhat different from our common fare, we find it very palatable."

First the cloaks and now the food. Are all here on this world so thoughtful or is it just princely manners? Turning to the others gathered off to the left, I continue, "Jerik, Charles, would you like to sample more of their unique repast?"

"Are we eating again so soon? Well, I think my stomach might be able to hold a little something," Jerik replies in his deep bass voice.

Prince Szames extends his hand motioning for me to lead. I make my way over to the table with Princess Szeanne Rose, Merithin, and the rest of the group falling in behind. With four trays of food, it is more like a buffet than a meal. There are several types of meat cut into thick slices, most look like a dark roast of some sort and several legs of a fowl. Deciding that bird is the safer choice I select one of the latter, along with one of every type of fruit and vegetable. *That snack couldn't have been more than an hour ago.* Noticing the tart apples we sampled earlier, my stomach rumbles.

I add a couple of wedges of cheese and a slice of bread. They have even got that tasty cheese spread we had earlier: it tastes like a cross between sweet-butter and parmesan cheese. I pour myself a cup of water and, seeing no silverware except a pile of knives, I help myself to one of those and a napkin before moving off to one side.

Will it offend anyone if I take a chair before the royals? A loud rumbling emanates from my midriff. *I can't eat standing here. Besides, I feel like a fool holding this heaping plate.*

As I set the cup on the ground beside me, Prince Szames approaches carrying a fully loaded plate. "MiLady ArchMage Reba, may I join you?" A curve of his lips suggests approval of my position.

"Please do," I motion to the chair beside me, "actually, I was hoping to get a chance to speak with you. Would it be inappropriate to discuss business over a meal."

"Are all women on your world this direct or are you unique?" as embarrassment tinges my cheeks, he qualifies the statement, "I ask not out of offence. It is not typical behavior in our society, for either men or women."

"I'm afraid you've lucked out…" I grin as my slang gets a puzzled look from the prince, "I am considered somewhat blunt, even on my world. Please tell me, is my directness inappropriate?"

Szames answers my question with true royal grace, "Inappropriate? Perhaps. But I believe our current situation warrants a change in what we consider appropriate. I, myself, find it refreshing." I get a fleeting impression of attraction - or is it admiration? - before my empathy is once again blank.

"I'm relieved you are flexible on the issue, I have no patience for pleasantries when an important matter is at hand. Which brings me to the issue I mentioned earlier: I believe I have a way to secure the castle and city from the demons. It will require a great deal of magical energy, more than I possess." *I wish I could get more than a stray feeling from him...* "If you can be speared from your duties I could use your assistance."

Seeing a brief look of puzzlement, I expound. "Even though you don't seem to be able to access it, your aura still holds a tremendous amount of magical energy. Since we have worked together in the healing of Prince Alexandros, you will be an easy source from which to draw. Between the two of us I should be able to surround the castle in a spell that will keep the enemy at bay for a week, maybe even two." *I perceive such awe or fear from everyone else it may take more energy to draw magic out of them than I can spare.*

While I wait for his reply I try to eat with all the manners of my upper-middle-class upbringing, considering a knife is my only utensil. The food is so tasty, after a few bites, my appetite comes alive and I have to restrain myself from shoveling in food with both hands. The fowl taste like the expected chicken, of course. The vegetables are scrumptious, especially those looking like a long-limbed cauliflower. It tastes like a cross between broccoli and cauliflower, two vegetables I adore.

"Prince Szames, ArchMage Reba, may I join you?" Merithin, getting a slight nod from Prince Szames, takes the chair on the other side of me.

"You intend to encompass the entire city in a spell? I would think it will require more energy than we have between us two if you intend it to have enough strength to keep out the number of demons who are bound to attack once they see magic acting as a defense." The prince raises a skeptical eyebrow.

You look like a brawny football player, but please, don't to all pig-headed-jock-like on me. "The enchantment is a variation of one commonly used to contain attackers. I don't think I can explain the principles of the spell in your tongue. The only obstacle I see standing in my way is time. If the energy we have is going to be sufficient we will need to make a complete circuit around the entire city, preferably as close to the surrounding wall as we can get. Will we be able to accomplish this before dark?" *Come on, use your head: a few hours ago you didn't know magic could heal someone.*

"We will be able to walk around the city on the battlement, but if we are to complete a circle before nightfall we must begin soon. It will take the better part of a day and mid-morning is upon us," doubt still colors Prince Szames' voice.

I push, just a little, "If you are unavailable to accompany us, may I take a look at your men to choose those who have an aura suitable for the task at hand?"

Szames smiles, "One of the benefits of my position is administration. There is very little I cannot delegate if necessary. It will be an honor to assist you in forming the spell which will protect our city."

Turning to his squire, Szames continues, "Herald, please tell ArmsMaster Stezen to meet me in the stables in a half-mark," he switches his attention back to me, "ArchMage Reba, how many of your men will accompany us?"

"Allinon and Jamison are needed here, but both Jerik and Charles will act as escort." When he makes up his mind, he doesn't waste time.

"Merithin, will you also be joining us?" As Merithin nods Prince Szames turns back to Herald who has finished the food on his plate like a starving wolf. He stands ready to receive the rest of his instructions. "See that the StableMaster has six horses readied." Herald gives a brief dip from the waist before he hastens on his way. A fleeting look of surprise steeling across his face as he looks at my empty plate betrays a little of what he feels. "If you are ready, ArchMage Reba."

Placing the cup on the platter I rise from my chair, "Yes, Prince Szames, I am, but if we have a moment I wish speak with my men."

With his nod, I attempt to give a formal dismissal, "Jamison, I must leave the wounded to you if the walls are going to be secured from the demons by nightfall," At the word "demons" Jamison's eyebrows lift, "I leave these gentlemen in your capable hands. Between Allinon and yourself, their education in the art of healing will go swiftly."

Jamison replies with all the decorum his jovial nature will allow, "The fact that most are trained in herbal healing will help smooth the process, I'm sure. We can pair up the three with no ability to use healing magic with youths who have little training. By the end of the day we will all be exhausted, but with any luck, none will be left in critical condition."

Spotting the others in a corner near the buffet table, I make a beeline to the warriors. "Jerik, Charles, if you're ready, we need to leave for the battlement encircling the city. I intend to have the entire populace surrounded by a force-field by nightfall. The majority of my magical resources will be tied up in the spell-casting for the duration of the excursion. Your protection will be invaluable." I remark, hoping their fighting abilities have been incorporated into their new forms like my mage abilities have.

"Finally, a chance at some action. How soon do we leave?" Charles is boyishly enthusiastic, practically flexing his new muscles.

Prince Szames, Merithin, and Squire Robert are waiting by the door. "Immediately," I command, spinning on my heel striding for the entryway.

Chapter Five

Exiting the building, Merithin and the prince lead with the squire trailing a respectful two feet behind to the prince's left. Tramping back through the barracks, we continuing on a path parallel to the keep. To my right is the wall surrounding the castle, but I am too far away to make out any detail or even guess at the height.

Charles and Jerik have taken up a position to either side of me. I address both in a volume I am sure won't carry to the others. Just to be sure I use our native tongue, "I had a talk with the prince about what we're facing." *How do I tell them we are up against demons? Actual toot-and-claw, fanged-and-flying demons?*

"Well, out with it. Can't be all bad…" Jerik grumbles as the silence stretches out.

"I guess you really need to know. When they say we are facing 'demons' they literally mean demons. It's not a figure of speech." My nostrils flare and my brows draw down as I work up the nerve to add, "They have claws and fangs, they fly, and they only attack at night."

"Dawg, that's off da chain - real-life demons." Charles crows. "We get to slice and dice some real monsters!"

He's got way too much testosterone…this is not the time for bravado! "They are not beasts out of some fairytale. This is your worst nightmare. Some are huge monsters while others poison you with a mere scratch, and most of their claws cut through armor as if it is homespun wool. We've got to overhaul this kingdom's weapons, armor, and equipment - not to mention fighting techniques - if we are going to stand a chance of surviving the first battle." Charles' coal black eyes grow in diameter while I describe our foes. I give a "humph" of satisfaction.

Jerik's response is as direct as the hammer he will wield. "With the help of the smithy, I will reinforce their weapons with a Dwarven enchantment. It will increase the strength and sharpness of any edge. With over 5000 men, it will take me a week at least. How long will that force-field of yours last?"

Mouth agape, I find myself unable to respond. I am overcome by the grandeur of the sight before me. A beautiful woman in flowing robes is a centerpiece of the fountain we are passing. She stands in a marble garden of blossoming flowers. Past the figurine, blue-gray marble creates fanned steps to frame the main entrance of Castle Eldrich. We advance down the gravel path opposite where we have come, exiting the foreground to the palace. The beauty of the sculpture makes me re-examine the situation, trying for a little more optimism.

"If there's any kind of intelligence coordinating these demons, the defense won't last much more than a week, but you should get at least seven days." The monumental size of the task in front of us is daunting: useless armor, an army with record-low morale, and just one other sorcerer with his apprentice for magical support. I hope this is one hell of a prophecy everyone keeps mumbling about. Lord knows we need the help!

The unmistakable fragrance of horse brings me out of my musings. Closer now, I identify the large building as the stables. The barn is complete with a door to the hayloft above a double-gated entrance.

A grizzled old man and two boys are leading several mounts from the shadowed entrance, tying them to the hitching post out front. The prince angles us toward the soldiers waiting beside the doorway. The uniformed men bow, straightening as we come to a halt before them.

"ArchMage Reba, Jerik the Dwarven MasterSmith, and Charles the Paladin: this is Lieutenant Craig and ArmsMaster Stezen," As Szames makes the formal introductions, both men bow in my direction. The older gentleman joins us while the boys continue bringing out saddled mounts.

"Your Highness," the StableMaster bows, "Your horses will be ready directly."

"Thank you, Mik. Stezen, ride with us to Westgate," the prince's tone makes it more of an order than a question, "ArchMage Reba, do you require time in which to prepare for the spell casting?"

"This particular enchantment is a variation of one I'm already familiar with. The ride to the outer-battlement should be sufficient for making the necessary adjustments," pausing, I cock my head to one side, "Lieutenant Craig has an aura with a large reservoir of corporeal energy. If he has no objections to magical workings I would like for him to accompany us around the city, in case I have misjudged the energy required for this spell."

Intuition tells me it is approval I see in Prince Szames' eyes as he pronounces, "Lieutenant Craig, how are you disposed toward magic?"

"Your Highness, I've not formed an opinion one way or t'other," Craig states with a more relaxed style of Cuthburish sounding something like a country drawl, "but any request coming from a beauty such as this I won't be refuse'n."

Prince Szames' voice has a hint of a scowl as he commands, "Find a horse. We leave for Westgate," he gestures toward a mare who looks so old she is probably only days away from the glue factory, "ArchMage Reba, if you will allow me the honor of assisting you?"

"Thank you, Your Highness, if you will hold my staff, I believe I can ascend on my own." Just because I'm a woman he saddles me with a nag?

Having both hands available I take a closer look at my robe. An overlapping flap hides a row of buttons.

Undoing the robe to the waist gives me a little more freedom of movement.

My lips compress into a thin line of determined. *If I prove I'm no greenhorn so maybe next time I can get a horse that doesn't look like it will die on us before we finish the job.* A controlled jump allows me to plant my left foot in the stirrup. With acrobatic agility, I straighten my knee, throwing the other leg over the saddle which is missing the western horn.

My new and improved muscles are good for more than walking. I could have vaulted into place. My coordination has increased tenfold. The reins in one hand and my staff in the other, I watch the others mount. Jerik stands rock solid. Fists on hips, he glares at the stirrup hanging just below his chin.

Edging my mount up close to his, I frown with the concentration it takes to put a stranglehold on the bubbling laughter threatening to spew forth, "Having difficulty?"

"Whatever gave you that idea?" he grumps, "You know, I've ridden a few times. I claim no great skill in horsemanship, but this time it is different. Just looking at this animal turns my stomach."

Continuing, his voice drops to menacing whisper, "Dwarves aren't known for their love of ponies, much less full size horses. Where long distances are concerned I could outdo even a pack-mule. Is it necessary that I humiliate myself by riding this animal?"

A chuckle escapes me, "I'm afraid so. We need to complete a circuit of the city by dark and every minute counts. Hold still, I will spell you into the saddle."

"While you're at it, you might as well shorten those stirrups," Jerik grouses.

"Dwarven you are and your legs show the lack,
For placing you with grace upon a horse's back.
With magic I'll aid you, help you out,
Even shorten stirrups, without a doubt."

Watching the results of my spell, the chains binding my self-control shatter. Raucous laughter escapes in a flood, as Jerik's eyes pop open when azure mist surrounds him, lifting him into the air. The stirrups, having shrunk, are now child-size.

"Ha, ha, very funny." Jerik grumbles, "We will see whose legs are lacking halfway around the city."

"I'm sorry," Schooling my expression, I try to reign in my laughter, "but you should have seen your face!" Chuckling, I add, "I didn't know you had such big eyes under those bushy brows."

I see that by now the prince has concluded his discussion with Squire Herald. The rest of the group is waiting on us. I straighten in the saddle, gesturing my readiness. Prince Szames takes the lead with ArmsMaster Stezen beside him. Lieutenant Craig joins Merithin, who is stationed behind the prince. Jerik and Charles take up positions to my right and left as we head toward the barracks at a fast trot. In a matter of minutes we are in sight of the main gateway to Castle Eldrich.

The wall surrounding the castle is cut from stone identical to main-keep, a blue-gray marble. Like redwoods squared and trussed together, the gates are colossal. Hinged metal beams run the entire length of each gate acting as support. Pairs of soldiers stationed to either side of the entrance come to attention as we travel through. *That wall is made of solid blocks!*

Leaving the castle grounds, we hang a right. The street is cobblestone and broad. Two and three-story mansions line the avenue. A few of the estates are constructed from the same stone as the castle, but most are wood structures like the barracks. Each dwelling that doesn't have a massive wall surrounding it has a stone-lined walkway trailing through a manicured courtyard. In the quiet street only a score of people are out, rushing about like a herd of whitetail evading a pack of hyenas.

Traversing the disquieted metropolis, the tension I sense from the people hurrying from this place to that, or hiding behind locked doors begins to try my patience. It is like angry bees swarming around me: I keep waiting for a sting.

Surprisingly enough, the horse's gate isn't as bad as expected, although she does have a packhorse mentality. Sticking her nose in the tail of Craig's mount, she needs no encouragement from me to follow his lead. *One advantage of being stuck with a nag: it affords me an excellent opportunity to develop the force-field spell into something capable of protecting an entire city.*

Placing my trust in the docile mare, I put the staff between my leg and the stirrup then block out the world around me. With the ease of a photographic memory, I go over the spell I developed for the role-playing game. Absorbed in overhauling the mantra, I'm startled when I open my eyes and have no idea where we are. *Lost again it seems...* Our group is traveling down a cobbled street with no sign of the castle.

The streets are broad. The houses remind me of condominiums. They are stacked like sardines in a can. The only things differentiating one from the other are signs and an occasional picture window. The advertisements are unexpectedly artistic: standing out brightly against unbleached wood. One shop has several gowns displayed in the window, and a wooden plaque showing a large spool of crimson thread. Squinting, I see chicken scratches I assume are words, printed neatly under the picture.

The outer wall looms before us. It takes minutes to reach the three-storied structure. The fortification is made up of cobalt marble, which seems to be the foundation of the city. The guard station is an extension of the wall itself, constructed from the same stone as the rest of the castle and its fortifications. Twenty feet square, the sentry post continues up the side of the wall, ending above the battlement where it serves as a sheltering overhang.

A guardsman dashes into the building as we approach. Another soldier takes the prince's horse after greeting Szames by crossing his right arm over his waist touching the hilt of his sword with his fist, snapping heels together with a curt bow at the waist. After words are exchanged, the prince motions for us to accompany him. ArmsMaster Stezen bows from his saddle, also touching his fist to his saber, before heading back to the castle. Hastily we move to follow the hunky blond prince into the building.

The solitary source of illumination is from a pair of narrow windows placed at either side of the entrance. Though the day outside is bright, the light fails to reach the corners of the dim interior. A stairway follows the opposite wall, continuing up through the wooden ceiling. Other than a stained, rough looking table, a couple of chairs, and a few piles of straw nestled around the edge, the room is vacant.

"This leads to the battlement. ArchMage Reba, are you are ready?" Prince Szames inquires as soon as all are gathered in the small room.

I give an affirmative nod, starting toward the stairs. I take them two at a time. My breath comes in quick bursts by the time I halt in front of the entrance to the battlement, but I am not yet winded. Starting as Prince Szames reaches past me to open the door, I squint allowing my eyes to adjust to the dazzling morning sky. Easing my way to the edge of a crenel where the wall dips below my chest, I take my first look at the country I have sworn to protect.

Winter's harsh embrace grips the undulating hills in an unforgiving embrace. Whispering "sight," I scan the open vista. If they are out there, they are hidden beyond even magical sight.

"Charles, would you please take point?" The ebony warrior quickly complies with my request.

"If you're ready, Your Highness. It will be just like when we worked on your brother. Just relax…" I take down my hood. Turning to the prince I extend my left hand.

Prince Szames hesitates. My heightened mage senses pick up a prolonged inhalation. Assuming he is having second thoughts about working with magic I expound, "A physical connection makes borrowing energy easier. Once I finish the incantation we will walk. We need to make a full circle of the city before I can complete the spell." Seconds after our hands meet I get a glimpse into the emotions at which I have, until now, mostly guessed. The fleeting sensation of sensual arousal disappears like lotion on scaly skin. I dismiss the insight as irrelevant, concentrating on the task at hand.

Prince Szames gives a nod indicating his readiness to proceed. I close my eyes. Securing the connection, I combine our powers. With the world sealed away along with my vision, I begin the most powerful spell ever contemplated:

"As I walk the path of this magnificent wall,
Following in my wake I leave a magic hall.
Power flows through this corridor unseen,
Awaiting my instruction, my idea is so keen.

On my command power will spread,
Forming a dome far over our heads.
Far underground magic will go,
Spreading thin but impregnably so.

A force-field you will form, surrounding this city,
Keeping it secure from any malevolent entity.
If to this kingdom you pose a dire threat,
Touch this field and vaporized you will get.

Their energy you'll capture for your power,
You will guard us well through our darkest hour."

An orgasmic sigh escapes through my clenched teeth as I fight to remain erect. My body feels as light as a feather, as if I could walk on air right off the side of the battlement.

Magic spills around my feet. The flow steadies. I ease

my eyes open. Prince Szames gives an inquiring gaze. I nod and we begin to stroll along the wall following behind Charles, leaving a trail of magic behind us, just like Hänsel and Gretel leaving a trail of hope. *I pray this endeavor turns out better than their breadcrumbs.*

The magic continues to stream behind just as I pictured in my mind. I focus my concentration on the pathway the magic is taking intent on stabilizing the flow. *There, now I should have a little more freedom of thought.*

Looking to my right quite a bit of the countryside is visible. Stark as it is, the beauty touches my soul. Before me is the most striking winter-scape I have ever seen: so many shades of brown. *Is it the scenery, magesight, or just the world we are on?*

Smiling I turned to Prince Szames. "If all your land is this fair then your kingdom is rich beyond words."

With an unconscious smile, Prince Szames' voice is a mere whisper, "This is but a pale shadow in comparison to the sight of her crowned in full glory. Castle Eldrich is known for its beauty throughout the world, but spring is the season for which she is famous. The knolls shimmer with colors so vibrant you would think the hills have gowned themselves with gemstones."

"Why, Prince Szames, I didn't know the soul of a poet could inhabit the body of a warrior. Or do all the men in this kingdom possess a natural affinity for words that let them speak with tongues of silver?" *A little flirting often loosens the tongue better than wine.*

Pouty lips curve downward. His brow furrows showing the honesty of his puzzlement, "I am afraid you have mistaken me, perhaps for my brother? I have never been one to manipulate words for a flattering effect. I speak of what my heart sees in an honest fashion, I know of no other way. Perhaps the company I keep has inspired my heart to communicate more intimately with my mind."

"Then your heart sees beauty where others might not, and you speak of it in a fashion that makes me long to share your sight." *Touché and en'garde: the battle begins.* "If it is my company that inspires you to speak with such passion then we must keep company more often. A heart filled with such as yours is wasted if it is not shared." Prince Szames cheeks brighten with my compliment. I discern a surge of arousal from the warrior, but it disappears as I try to pinpoint it.

Please don't tell me I've made this movie star of a man blush with a little compliment. Surely, being the Greek god he is, he must get constant attention. Hmmm, maybe I should take it easy with the flattery until I learn a little more about this place: women might flirt to let a guy know they are ready to hit the sack. Denying a princely proposition may cause more trouble than the information is worth.

The smile he sports is dopier than ever. "It will be my pleasure to accompany you whenever you are in need of an escort. As I have said before, rank does have some privilege. It will be an honored to guide through this world."

Yes, I will definitely have to watch the flirting. "Your Highness, I thank you for your offer and will keep it in mind. I have a feeling I will be in need of a guide. Your world differs from mine in more ways than I can count." My lips curve to reassure him while I provide a way out, "but I don't wish to monopolize your time: add more demands to your schedule of duties."

"Please, call me Szames, as my friends do when the situation does not demand otherwise. Milady ArchMage Reba, I would like to count you among my friends," his deep voice holds warmth and thoughtfulness I dare not take at face value, since I can't sense what he is feeling.

"Then I insist you call me Reba," my thin lips nearly disappear as my smile broadens.

"Reba, you tell me your world is greatly different from mine? In my youth, when I had a greater amount of time to call my own, I loved to study history and science." Szames eyes light up, "Other lands across the dimensional planes were not suitable material for a prince, so my father always held, but I must admit they fascinate me far more than any topic this world holds. Perhaps we could exchange information about our worlds. I will provide you with a guide through mine, while you provide me the forbidden knowledge I long to study."

"Szames, you have yourself a deal. An exchange of information it is." *Oooh, careful now. Is he more than a dumb jock: an over-muscled football player? Could he have brains behind all that brawn? I shake my head in denial of the bothersome thoughts. No way! I've just been out-maneuvered on the field of flirtation: he's a playboy philanderer, not a genius in disguise.*

In the distance two guards stare at the horizon. Hearing Merithin and Charles approach they turn and salute, as the others have done, ending with heads up and eyes straight. As Charles passes they glance in our direction. When the wind brings a startled whisper to my ear I wish once again I had taken a look in that mirror with my hood down. It seems my looks make a profound impression even from a distance. The sentries snap to attention again as they recognize my escort.

The silence expands as we stroll along hand in hand. I have not been for a walk holding any man's hand but Tony's for so long. *I'd forgotten how small, how delicate a big guy makes you feel.*

Tony's five-foot eleven and not too big. Lord knows, being five-eight I don't feel petite often. Szames' hand is so huge… *Yep, now I remember this feeling from high school. It used to intimidate me, feeling so small. But now I don't feel intimidated at all, even though the man outranks me as well as towers over me. It must be the tremendous store of magical power: now size doesn't matter…* A chuckle escapes me at the unintended pun.

"It sounds like that much fun, this exchange of information? Reba, you are an unusual woman," Szames interrupts my wandering mind.

"I'll take that as a compliment… I think," I hesitate

to correct his misconception.

"I assure you I mean it with complete admiration," Szames returns my smile.

Any male model would kill for a smile like that, goofy as it is. *What am I thinking! I don't have time for this.* Turning my thoughts within, I check the progressive flow of magic. Everything looks good.

Spotting the stairway overhang I realize we are approaching the southern guard station. *I should have no problem with the energy supply. I'm not even feeling the drain yet.* I tilt my chin to peer at the clear blue sky. The sun is past the mid-point.

Unsure of when we began the journey around the battlement I ask for second opinion. "Szames, will we be able to make a complete round of the battlement by nightfall?"

"It will be close. Will your spell be affected if our speed increases?" he inquires.

I monitor the power stream as we speed up. *Everything is still peachy-keen.*

Off to my right a new vista steals my breath. A cerulean ribbon sparkles as a river winding its way through the hills. A crystalline curve and a patch of sand denotes a bend in the waterway. Further north, just below the horizon, lays a dark smudge. *A forest perhaps? I get the strangest feeling we are being watched.* Determined to ask Szames about that later, I reinforce my effort to stay focus.

"How many - " My question stumbles to a halt. I find no word for "hours" in versatile language of Cuthburish, "How long until dark?"

"It will be several marks before dusk, much less full dark. Will there be enough energy between the two of us? " Szames supplies the requested information, taking into consideration my future needs.

"As things stand, there should be plenty of energy, but I would prefer to keep the Lieutenant around, though, just in case we hit a snag," with business taken care of

I can't resist broaching a new topic, "Since we were speaking of differences in our worlds I won't feel like a complete dimwit asking this: What precisely is a 'mark?' I understand it refers to an increment, the amount of time it takes for a candle to burn a certain distance, but I am unsure of what amount of time it represents, even in the vaguest sense."

"Hmm, an interesting question. I had not realized the term might be unfamiliar to you. How to account for a mark?" pausing, Szames gives a comical half-smile and shake of his head, "I never realized explaining something so simple could prove to be such a difficult task. Maybe the best reference is the bells. Have you heard the tolling?"

I nod. I heard bells when we first arrived.

"The bells are spelled to toll eight times a day. Once at midnight, once at dawn, once at midday, once at sunset, and once in-between each of these, dividing those times in half. A little more than two marks separate the bells during the day and about three marks separate the bells in the evening at this time of year. There are roughly twenty marks in a day."

"Interesting…" *A wristwatch is so much easier.*

"If not with a mark, by what do you measure the day on your world?" Szames interrupts my musings.

"My world divides the day into twenty-four equal parts: hours. The hour in which the sun sets and rises changes with the season, but the hours in a day are always numbered the same. In the winter the sun rises later than during the summer. So if your mark equals one of my hours then we would have four more hours in our day… but more likely marks and hours differ. Without a clock, which we use to measure an hour, we will never know." I respond, determined to "magic-up" a digital one later.

"It would be fascinating to compare the flow of a day on two worlds. These 'ow-ers' of yours are measured on a 'cla-k?' Is that a type of candle? If you know the dimensions perhaps I could have one made?" Szames' interest seems genuine.

"A clock" I begin, stressing the "ah" part of the word, "is a very complex machine. I am not sure how it works but I will tell you what I know: it is composed of many small wheels of varying sizes rotating at constant speeds. These wheels move a lever held stationary at one end. The other end of the lever moves at a consistent pace around a circle inscribed with numbers representing the hours of a day. The movable end of the lever points at the hour it is," chuckling, I finish what feels like timepiece lecture, "Now aren't you sorry you asked?"

Who would've thought describing a clock would be such a task! We will have to watch what we say. One wrong word and we could inspire the invention of gunpowder, a grenade, or something worse!

Looking toward Szames to see if he took my words in the jovial manner I intended, I hear a deep chortle. My eyes never meet his, however, for they refuse to look anyplace but the city below. Tiny houses are lined up on a perfect grid with streets so straight they look as they were laid out on a drawing board. The buildings are shabby, some more so than others, but not as bad as I assumed they should be in this horse and carriage society. The streets, though, are what strike me as the most odd.

"Reba. I have no doubt our time together will be fascinating. If a clock is any indication, our worlds are quite dissimilar indeed. I look forward to learning more about the differences as well as their similarities." The surge of attraction I feel tells me volumes, before it blinks out of existence.

My eyes light merrily, as I return his smile. *At least I'm used to dealing with unsolicited attraction from men I can't read. Perhaps this exchange will be in my favor even with the handicap of blinded empathy.*

A breeze ruffles my hair as I walk holding the hand of a gorgeous prince admiring the picturesque beauty of the town below. *Is this all a dream? A town of this era shouldn't be this clean. Hell, I've been to cities whose streets weren't half this organized!*

There is a smell of wood smoke in the brisk air. It's all so real - more than real. It's like all my life I have been dreaming and now I'm awake for the first time. This world is so vivid and alive. Up ahead we are closing in on Eastgate. *We are almost halfway done?* I haven't heard the mid-afternoon bells yet, so we must be making pretty good time.

As we draw near, I spot someone standing under the outcropping. After a few minutes I make out a table and several stools positioned under the overhang. My brows knit in perplexity as I look to Szames.

He gives a shrug of his massive shoulders. "I hoped to make it to this point with time available so we may take a short break. I thought a snack would be needed."

"How thoughtful, thank you. The spell should be fine as long as we don't move from this path." *If I keep eating every few hours I will be as big as a house before I leave.*

Five stools surround the table. A cloth covers the contents. We slow to a stop as Squire Herald bows to Szames. "Your Highness, your arrival is most timely. I believe the bread is still warm." He gestures to the covered portion of the table.

Chapter Six

"Merithin, Charles, Jerik. Would you care to join us?" Szames inquires.

"Your Highness, you must know little about dwarves. There is seldom a time any of my race will pass up a chance for a meal," Jerik's booming voice rumbles as he comes around the table, taking possession of a stool.

Herald removes the cloth covering bread, cheese, and assorted fruits. Szames gestures to the remaining seats, "Reba, do we need to stay linked for this rest-break?"

"Let's separate slowly. I will monitor the link to make sure it remains stable." I pause, turning my concentration inward as our hands part.

"The spell's holding. The less distance we put between us the less energy it will require to keep it intact, so if you wouldn't mind…" I indicated the two seats placed side by side. Szames reaches to pull the right out for me.

The food is placed upon another cloth covering a roughhewn table. It is a simple fair laid out before us. A single knife rests next to the bread lying beside a wooden tub of butter-cheese and a more solid block of cheddar. A wooden bowl holds fruit somewhat like the apples we tried earlier except they are a little more pear-shaped, larger on the bottom than the top. *Now this is what I expected a medieval world to be like.*

"Milady, would you care for some bread?" Herald slices into the loaf.

"Yes, thank you." *Boy, they take "ladies first" to heart.*

Charles's silky voice eases into the silence, "Merithin has been telling me about the attack. He says the walls weren't broken in the assault; that most of the demons just climbed straight up them, the ones that didn't fly, that is. What I don't understand is how they managed to get close to the city with all the sentries?" Prince Charming elaborates upon his rhetorical question. "Since you doubled the night watch with four men stationed at every guard-station and at every midpoint, by the time they were at the walls you should have been able make pincushions out of them."

Charles bites into the fruit he slices into quarters, talking around the mouthful. "With four men at each post, you weren't betrayed from within. That leaves two options: an aerial attack taking out the sentries, or magic." He tilts his head, waiting patiently.

"You reasoned such, with a limited amount of information?" When Charles nods, Szames continues, "Merithin, it seems you have summoned us a powerful sorceress and a military strategist. He has deduced what we needed you to point out."

The prince continues, "The corporeal plain had been significantly disturbed in the area south of the attack. All reports of demon assaults have come from the southern duchies, and the skirmish was lead on the southern wall. It stands to reason that a powerful sorcerer disguised their approach. Since none of the enemies we destroyed were human, the only possible conclusions are either a demon with the ability to work magic," Szames' voice takes on a menacing growl, "or the sorcerer who performed the summoning is still working with the enemy."

"Reba, the way I understand it: the closer you are to something the less power it takes to perform the spell?" As I nod Charles continues, "I'll wager it was a sorcerer and he is still out there."

The harrumph Szames gives has definite approval in

it. "I have the same feeling."

"It is illogical to waste a sorcerer powerful enough to disguise an invading force on a mission never intended for success. The fact that the demons were spotted a couple of hundred feet out indicates the sorcerer didn't come very close to the castle, else he would have continued the spell until the sentries had been slain," he pauses for emphasis, "No, I don't think you were lucky enough to take out a magic wielding demon. Our mysterious sorcerer is still out there, watching, waiting for another opportunity to probe for a weakness. This was just a test to see how armor and swords will match up against claws and fangs. Unfortunately, Prince Szames, it isn't a test you scored very high in," Charles concludes with a grimace.

"A very perceptive analysis, Charles. Not many of my officers would have done as well. Have you led many troops or has your knowledge of strategies been gained through book learning?" Szames asks.

"I have studied history and great wars. There is very little practical experience to be had on this type of battlefield. My only battles have been small skirmishes where strategy wasn't a deciding factor," Charles shrugs modestly.

"Lieutenant Craig, please assume point position with Charles. I believe he will be most interested in whatever details you may recall from the night of the attack," Szames commands, "If we are going to make Westgate by nightfall we had better get moving."

"Merithin, if you would like to join Prince Szames and myself," I ask as Herald and Craig move the table out of the way. "I'm interested in your assessment of the strength of the enemy mage."

"I would be delighted, ArchMage Reba," Merithin bows.

The sorcerer wastes no time. He launches into his findings as we continue the circuit of the city. "By the time I arrived the demons had been destroyed. I didn't get to see the monsters in action. There were no reports of magic used in the attack except that which brought them unseen to our gates. A quick scrying helped me locate the residual power, which kept the demons from our sight. Fifty men accompanied me as I followed the trail of magic southward. Unfortunately, I was unable to find the sorcerer who wove it. The spell was not a powerful one but there was enough residue to make out a partial pattern. The energy signature it depicted seemed familiar. Until you asked about the summoning process I failed to identify the magic insignia. Thinking about Master Level disciples helped jog my memory, though."

"Merithin are you saying you know who has unleashed these demons upon us?" Szames demands.

"I am afraid so. The information I have concerning this sorcerer is about twenty years outdated but I believe the signature belongs to an old apprentice of mine, Gaakobah of Dunmore. The only absolute fact I know is that he had the capacity to become my equal."

Szames interrupts again, "Your first apprentice? You trained our enemy? Merithin, we must have every detail you can recall of this sorcerer."

"Yes, well, he may have been my apprentice, but he did not complete his training under me. I have no idea from whom he would have received further instruction, but I'll tell you what I know."

Merithin takes a deep breath before continuing, "As I said, he was my first apprentice many years ago, the son of a dear friend. Gaakobah was a quick learner and appeared to be the perfect student: very helpful, attentive even. After spending a couple years schooling him in the ways of magic, I began to realize Gaaki was not as stable as he outwardly appeared. Inexperienced, I was unsure how to handle my discovery. Having known Gaaki since he was a lad, instead of dismissing him I convinced myself it wasn't as serious as it seemed, that deep down he had a good heart."

"But no matter how I tried to reason out his odd behavior, I still felt uneasy about his mood swings. As the months went by I lingered over Journeymen skills and basic spells he mastered. I scrutinized his behavior hoping to find my suspicions were misplaced. They were not. When his progress was stymied as we continued to review the same spells, Gaaki became morose. His spell working became unpredictable. Instead of focusing on the internal issues as I hoped he would, Gaaki's depression grew."

"Now it's not well known, but all apprentices are allowed to experiment on their own once a level of competency has been achieved. Although I had not granted permission for him to work unaccompanied, I noted some time back the lad's experimentation in his free time. When his behavior became erratic, I grew curious about what sort of work he was doing," I glance over at Merithin as he pauses. I feel sadness, regret, and fear washing through him.

"Searching for a reasonable explanation so I could continue his education, I sent for Gaaki's father, hoping he could help shed some light on this perplexing problem. The afternoon Gaaki went into town to escort his father to the cottage was the perfect opportunity for investigation. The memory of what I found still haunts me...." though I sense no magic, Merithin's tale comes alive before us, as if we are transported through time.

The youthful MasterSorcerer glances around the room: nothing seems amiss. Peering intently at the foot of the bed, he examines what seems to be the remnant of a light spell.

Pride washes over the plain features, when Merithin realizes he recognizes the concealment spell and a dispersal-spell are interwoven. 'Concealment' is an advanced spell Gaaki has picked up on his own! Even more astounding, he figured out how to combine it with another enchantment!

"Pushed aside you will be, let me see inside of thee." The Master chants.

Blue light, streaming from his fingertips, surrounds a square object. The stronger magic penetrates the weaker spell moving it aside. A sturdy chest is revealed. Corporeal magic emanates from the chest with a deep pulsing throb.

"Box who is revealed to me, locked you will no longer be."

As the mantra ends a loud click fills the dim room. Revulsion puckers the sorcerer's lips as he removes the lid. Merithin's pride curdles into disgust.

Two half-starved animals occupy the storage place. One of the pets is a black cat, not much older than a kitten just weaned from its mother. The other is an ordinary kitchen rat. Both creatures have enlarged craniums despite their malnourishment, which can only be the result of the intense application of the 'increase-intelligence' spell Gaaki has mastered.

"But there must be more," Merithin murmurs, as he tries to separate the weaves of magic into a sensible pattern.

Suddenly the design and purpose of this monstrosity becomes clear. Horrified, the sorcerer takes an involuntary step back.

A magical barrier divides the large box in half. The enchantment is, once again, two spells interwoven: the "look away" and the "aggressive instinct spell." The "look away" portion imprisons each animal in its half of the cage, for now.

The half-starved animals will perish from malnutrition or become desperate enough to break the barrier, encouraged by the "aggressive instinct" enchantment. Once past the concealing enchantment the enraged beast will slaughter the other victim, gorging itself on the remains of its fellow prisoner. Until then, both animals are experiencing horrendous mental anguish from the constant barrage of conflicting emotions.

The rat dashes toward a small hunk of cheese placed close to the shield. As Merithin looks on the true purpose of the atrocity is revealed.

"No!" The shouted plea escapes the MasterSorcerer unchecked, as loathing for the one who has lived with him for the last few years takes firm root.

Two piles of tattered rags, saturated in Gaaki's aura, lay in respective corners of the container. The cloth holds a third enchantment, aptly named "Dispel Magic." The pain inflicted by the magical barrier is not only used to increase the violent tendencies of the animals, it is also forcing them to remain on their nests for relief. Gaaki's aura becomes their sanctuary.

The youth's passionate, almost fanatical, interest in Merithin's familiar, SwiftWing, now makes sense. His apprentice is trying to force a one-way bonding!

Usually, when a familiar is taken each gives a part of themselves to the other for the Bonding. This exchange is what makes communication with a beast possible, but it also leaves the sorcerer vulnerable. No familiar lives as long as his sorcerer and when the familiar passes on, a piece of the master dies with the companion. It is like the death of a best friend and a brother all at once.

What Gaaki is attempting is an abomination: he is forcing a one-way bond. This will create an animal that will respond and do his bidding as a mindless slave to a master.

"Magic called by another... Disperse," Merithin recites one of the first enchantments a magic user learns. All the magic in the vicinity of the chest dissolves under the barrage of azure light coming from the sorcerer's outstretched hand. Sitting on the end of the bed he reaches to free the rat.

Mouth agape, long fanged teeth lunge at his fingers. Merithin yanks back his hand. Dodging injury by a hair's breadth, a furry mass springs up onto the sorcerer's lap. Startled by the playfulness, the kitten's purr reassures the sorcerer that no permanent damage has been done to at least one of the victims.

Merithin gives an involuntary shiver at the vivid emotions the memory evokes. "Gaaki hid his inner self well. His outer portrayal of kindness, helpfulness, and the jovial nature covered his inner cruelty, ruthless ambition, and mental instability."

As we pass the Northgate the forest is closer, within plain sight. Engrossed in Merithin's tale, I note in passing that some of the houses are little more than shacks. The few two-story buildings occupying this area are in such bad shape I am amazed they are still standing. Odor permeates the walkway. The rank smell emanates from a long single-story building equipped with eight smokestacks. *A tannery?*

"After finding some leftover chicken and feeding the kitten a small amount I meditated on finding a way to tell my friend, Goran, that his son is a dangerous man. With his father's permission, I would bring an end to Gaaki's use of magic, maybe even erase the last two years of apprenticeship from his memory.

When Goran arrived I invited him into my study, while Gaaki saw to the horse and wagon. Amazingly enough, although Goran was disappointed by my findings, he wasn't surprised. He often suspected more lay under his son's cool exterior, but was never able to 'catch his hand in the hens nest,' so to speak. After dinner we debated long into the night about whether or not to take Gaaki's memory along with blocking his Gift, for memory removal is chancy at best and could result in permanent damage."

"We finally decided to see how Gaaki took the news of his dismissal and let that be the deciding factor. Perhaps if he could own up to his behavior it would be a turning point in his life. How he handled criticism of his inner-self would be the telling sign of what he was truly made."

Looking up, I am shocked to see the Westgate in view

again. The sun is on the horizon, painting the western sky brilliant shades of pink, purple and mauve. It looks like we'll make the Westgate by sunset, but only by half an hour or so. "How bad off was he? I expect he was pretty defensive when you confronted him."

"We never got the chance. The next day we awoke to find Gaaki gone. Goran left a few days later promising to send word if he turned up in Dunmore. I figured the lad overheard part of our discussion and fled rather than face punishment," Merithin shrugs.

"Since I was on good terms with both of the Master Level Sorcerers I let him go. I sent messages to the others of my guild with a description of Gaaki. When he failed to resurface, SwiftWing and I scouted the surrounding area. We spent the next several years investigating all reports of rogue sorcerers. When we found no sign of Gaaki, I assumed he must have fallen prey to bandits or some other peril of a solitary existence. I dismissed him so completely from my mind I did not register the pattern of the energy signature until I was explaining to Reba the scarcity of Master Level apprentices," Merithin concludes his explanation with a resigned sigh.

"So you know little about Gaaki's training. But we have learned that he is a quick study and as powerful as you, given the right training. It is knowledge than we had to two days ago," Szames summarizes.

I turn to Merithin, but the bizarre view off to my right causes me to loose my train of thought, "Merithin, what do you make of that?" Everything is covered with a red haze.

"What? I don't see anything. Are you using sight?" Merithin queries.

"Yes." It never occurred to me to disengage it.

"Vision," Merithin mutters in Old English with a heavy accent on the "s" making it sound more like a "sh." Then in Cuthburish he adds, "It is a shield. It has the same energy pattern as the magic used in the attack. Let us see what's behind it…"

"Magic called by another, I command you: Disperse."

A deep azure light shoots out from his hand, encircling the haze. The crimson fog reacts like oil flooded by water, recoiling into round goblets. Merithin's magic surrounds the scarlet beads penetrating them. In a flash of light both energies disappear. *Merithin spoke in English - Old English. It must be the language of magic! But he didn't rhyme and it still worked.*

In the distance trumpets bleat out the alarm as Merithin collapses to his knees. His aura is so faint I can't detect a single color variation. The drain from the spell was too great.

A loud shriek arises from what Merithin has revealed. *What the Hell are those?*

"Demons!" Szames swears under his breath, "It is a quarter-mark till dark?"

Sunlight must not be fatal, just painful. The beasts have leathery skin and long beaks with oblong-shaped heads, like a pterodactyl, but their craniums are large so their heads are more of a pear-shape. Two limbs support the top of the wings ending in clawed hand-like extensions with four fingers. The wings are almost transparent and they have thick legs like a bat. A cross between a pterodactyl and a wyvern, the four creatures soar toward the battlement. Grasped in the winged demons' hind talons is an enormous humanoid. Each wyvern clutches a hair covered appendage, carrying the ogre closer with each beat of their wings.

"Craig, guard Merithin, get him to Northgate," Szames's bellow is a shallow whisper to my ear as a flash, similar to the one that brought us here, tinges my vision.

The sky, bright seconds ago, is now the deep violet of a newly fallen night. I choke as acrid smoke fills my nostrils. Turning to the city, my jaw hangs slack. The pristine town is ablaze. Demons dive-bomb like sparrow hawks, taking a human in each run, dropping them down upon the troops filling the streets. Other monstrosities swarm over the walls like ants attacking a picnic table.

Again, light causes me to blink long and hard. This time I soar over a farming community. Everywhere homes are ablaze. A certainty settles in me, this is occurring everywhere on this world.

A third flash blinds my vision once more. I force my eyes open, afraid of what I might see. The brightness of the day makes me squint, but I can make out Charles' figure in front of us.

Deep inside a knowing forms. High intuition points have given me a premonition. I have seen what our future holds, if we continue on our present course. I turn to my escort, "Ready to make a run for it?" Szames nods and we match strides sprinting for Westgate.

Our dash for safety comes to a skidding halt as wyverns swoop toward the battlement. A demon-bird emits a loud screech, and the pair of fliers holding the legs of the ogre releases him. Within seconds, the winged demons holding the arms of the beast free the towering humanoid. The monstrous foe drops the remaining ten feet to land solidly on the path before us. The giant humanoid lands midway between Westgate and Charles, who is in point position. *Intelligent beasts.*

Mesmerized, I watch as the dark prince draws his long-sword. The shining blade looks like a rapier as he parries the spiked club the ten-foot ogre wields.

"Clank…" the grime-covered hide flexes outside a caveman fir-wrap as the monster counterattacks seconds after Charles's deflects the latest blow. Although its forehead has a Neanderthal slope, the technique shows cunning.

A raucous screech breaks the paralysis tying down my limbs. I release Szames to give him full access to his sword, which he transfers from the other hand. Spinning more gracefully than a ballet dancer, the prince squares off with the wyverns plunging toward us.

The prince remains rock-still in a crouched, defensive

stance. As the flyer draws near he leaps, straightening to his full length, slashing out with his sword. His blade slices the creature's hind leg causing it to let out a night-piercing shriek of rage.

Knowing Szames has my left side covered, I turn to the right. A second demon is barreling toward us in a swooping dive. The beast is so close I don't even have enough time to bring up my staff much less cast a spell.

I watch in fascination as a battleaxe appears out of nowhere, lopping the head off of my attacker. Jerik's dashing pace carries him through the inky spay cascading from the decapitated foe as he charges toward the ogre.

One down, three to go. But I'm immobilized. If I move from this spot, the force-field spell will be disrupted and the backlash could incinerate our party along with half the city. *This staff isn't the best weapon against giant flying bats. What I need is a shotgun; or even better - my laser spell!*

"We are under attack, the situation is dire.
What will even the score is a little laser fire.
When I am in need all I must say
Is 'laser' and start blasting away."

I smile in anticipation as blue light envelopes my hands, disappearing under the skin.

"Where'd you go, you ugly SOB," I scan the area for a target. Looking back to Northgate I see one of the creatures hurtling toward Craig, who is standing guard over Merithin's prone body.

Extending my right hand I whisper, "laser."

A bolt of light shoots from my fingertips. The beam catches the wyvern in the side, exactly as I picture. The creature's swoop turns onto a nosedive. *Two down, two to go.*

I check on the progress of the sun. *Better hurry, night is almost here.*

"YAAH-YEE!!" the battle cry echoes in my ears.

Szames rises from a crouch, leaping over four feet straight up. Holding his sword in both hands above him, he slices at the underbelly of the demon plunging toward us. Veering to avoid the blow, the demon only succeeds in crippling itself as the sword catches a wing. A downward spiraling ends in an auditable thud.

"Szames, there's one left, do you see it?" Panic puts a sharp edge in my voice: dusk has arrived and full darkness is setting in. My head swivels, searching.

I glance ahead to check my comrades' progress with the ogre. My mouth falls open as I see Jerik standing in the crenel between two merlons. He has a hold of the edge of the upper parapet with his fingertips. In one fluid motion the dwarf heaves himself over the side. Taking off at a dead run, he jumps across the gap formed by the teeth of the battlement. He's trying to get on the other side of the ogre!

"There it is," Szames points to the Paladins right, "Charles, behind you!"

Parrying the ogre's two-handed swing, the swordsman glances over his shoulder. Seeing the wyvern plummeting for his head, he leaps to one side, warding off the ogre's next strike.

Holding out my hand again I shout, "laser!" The beast goes down but the bolt is seconds too late. The beam nails the wyvern squarely in the back as claws sink into Charles's shoulder.

"AAUGH!" an inhuman roar tears from the paladin's throat as he drops his sword and is hauled bodily to the ground by the demon's dead weight.

The ogre lets out a throaty, almost childish giggle. Smiling, the giant reveals a row of jagged teeth. Raising the spiked club over its sloped forehead, Frankenstein's playmate brings the weapon down for a bone-crushing strike.

The Dark Prince pulls himself free of the flyer's claws rolling to the side, seconds before the club takes a chunk out of the marble battlement. Snatching his sword with his left hand Charles springs to his feet thrusting upwards with the blade. The Neanderthal is faster than his size suggests. He snaps back, standing straight. Charles only etches an oozing scratch across its midriff, failing to disembowel the creature.

I extend my hand to release a laser bolt with the creatures name on it, but again I'm too late. Jerik's battleaxe swipes through the ogre's thick neck, felling the giant like a Redwood.

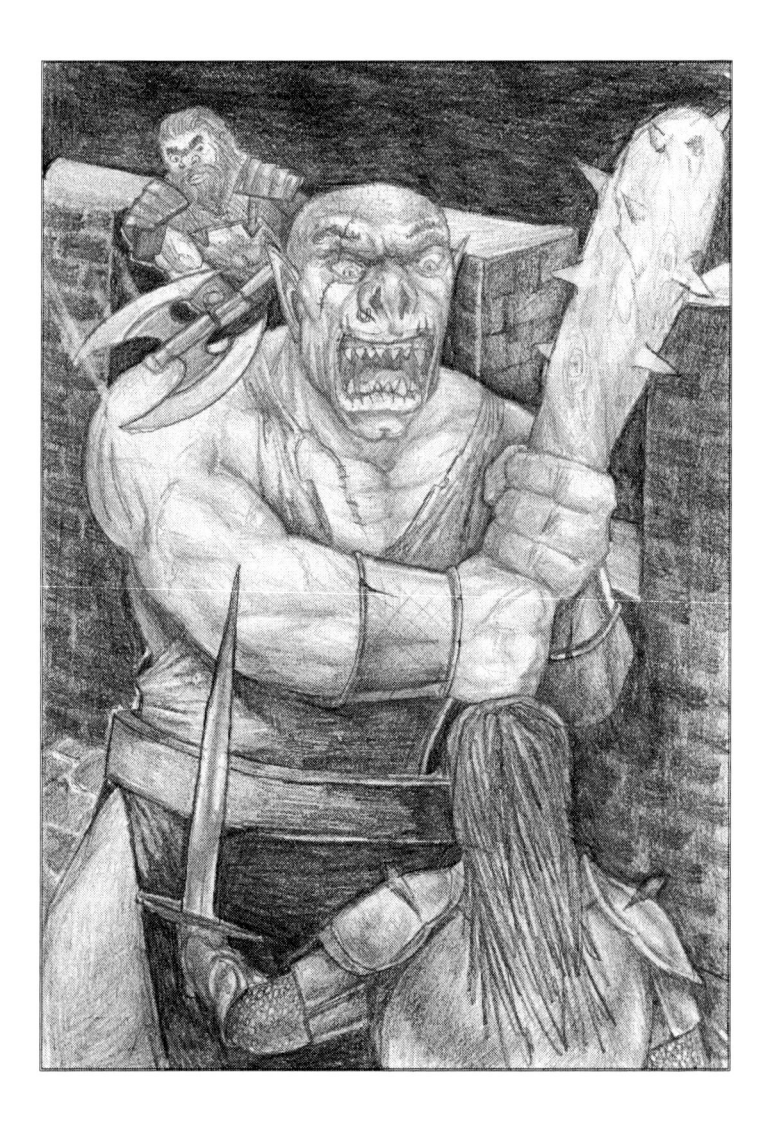

"We must finish this spell, now! I will pull extra energy from you, enough that you will feel drained." I hold out my hand to Szames.

"Take what you need to keep the demons at bay," Szames seizes my hand, "Set the quickest pace you can."

Making a six-minute mile look like a leisurely jog, we reach Westgate in record time. Dark is now upon us. I motion the others to the stairs, handing my staff to Jerik.

"Szames, please, just do what I do," I instruct in the seconds remaining before the sun sinks below the hills. Retaining his right hand I begin by holding my arms out to either side.

"The circle of power I have completed,
And my powers are now much depleted.
I command you to take form and roam,
Over our heads, making a protective dome."

Pulling Szames' hand with me, I raise both arms, clasping my right one with our two joined ones. When I feel the prince's other hand join ours I intone the next line.

"Your form is now good halfway done,
But this last verse is an important one."

Every nerve vibrating with power, barley able to move, I ease my right arm back to our sides, while envisioning blue light spreading in an arc across the city. Fighting a wave of euphoria that threatens the hold I have on the harnessed energy, in measure with the chant I lower our joined arms, bringing my hands together below our waist.

"To protect us from enemies who abound,
You must also travel far under ground."

Giving a firm thrust from within completes the massive undertaking. Disconnected from the ocean of power, the world spins. Gritting my teeth I manage to stay on my feet as the world dims around the edges. Turning to Szames I let out an exhausted sigh, "Well, that should keep us safe for the time being."

"What exactly will the spell do?" Szames sucks in air, as if he has just ran a marathon.

"Any evil presence or anyone who poses a danger to this kingdom will be turned to ash if they come into contact with the barrier. Unless you harbor a traitor among your guards, they should be fine." Minute by minute I feel steadier, and minute by minute I begin to ache. My head, my muscles, even my bones ache.

"That is some spell. I have never heard of an enchantment powerful enough to protect anything as large as a city." He shakes his head as if to clear hazy thoughts. "We had enough energy between the two of us to complete it?"

Entering the guard station I ignore the redundant question. Charles is seated on the bench wearing only his chain mail: even with his 'natural tan' he looks pale, ashy. As Jerik moves aside shredded armor, the warrior's lips thin with a grimace. Remnants of a blood soaked shirt lie underneath. Jerik eases that aside as well, exposing a puncture the size of a half-dollar on Charles' upper back and three parallel gashes on the front of his chest. Five quick strides bring me to Jerik's side.

"Charles, can you move your arm? Is that the only place you're hurt?" I demand.

"I think my shoulder is either broken or dislocated, I'm not sure which..." In agony, Charles lapses into English. "Man it hurts like a mother-fu**er!"

"I don't have much healing power, but I can ease the pain a bit. The wounds should be washed clear by the blood you have already lost. I can stop you from loosing more."

Charles grunts through gritted teeth. "Stop jabbering

woman. Heal the damn thing and make the fu**ing pain go away!!" *Thank God he's using English. What would people think of a soldier treating his leader this way?*

"Charles, healing the wrong thing could cripple this arm. Give me a moment to organize my thoughts," placing my hands above each side of his shoulder I focus inward, ignore the pain stabbing through my head. A peaceful calm envelops me, I feel as if a warm rain is sprinkling down on my hands while I concentrate on my Healing Gift. It takes only seconds to stop the flow of blood. Next I ease as much of the pain as I can.

Through the haze of exhaustion, I register the admiration in Szames's voice, "Here, use my baldric for a sling." He removes his scabbard from the decorative strip of leather holding the sword across his back.

"Ugh, God that feels better, thanks, Reba. Sorry for my… lack of patience--" pain halts the apology as a grunt is forced from him when I place his arm in the makeshift sling hanging over his good shoulder.

"I'm sorry I couldn't do more: that is about the extent of my healing ability. Let's get you to Jamison; he will get you fixed up." *I wonder if he still thinks this is just a dream? At least we know that we won't wake up if Charles is hurt. Let's see - that means if this is a dream it has to be either Allinon, Jamison, Jerik, or me. God, my head hurts! This is way too complex to be thinking about with this skull-splitting headache.*

Chapter Seven

Charles manages to mount his horse without the use of his right arm. Holding the animal's reigns, the guard's star-struck gaze never leaves the Ebony Prince. "Is it true? Did you and the little guy take down an ogre?"

"The ogre never laid a finger on me. It was one of those flying demons that did this." Fierce whispering ensues as the guardsman returns to the loitering soldiers. The reinforcements were too late to be of any help in the skirmish.

Once again Jerik hesitates, his eyes shooting daggers at the equine provided for him. "Reba, I refuse to ride this animal. I can keep any pace you set," his jaw is tight as his hands ball into fists the size of grapefruits. "I will be right beside you the whole way, without riding a blasted mule!"

"Whatever you want, Jerik. I'm too tired to argue. If you can keep up, more power to you." Jerik moves to position himself beside me as I whisper, "You saved my life not more than half an hour ago, it is the least I can do." The stout warrior bobs his head, the wooly beard failing to hide the smug grin.

Szames, having briefed his officers, mounts and assumes the lead. "I will escort you back to the castle. Hestur, the MasterSteward, will have your accommodations ready by the time we finish dining."

I am not surprised when the dwarf maintains a slow

jog matching the pace of our horses to the tee. "Jerik, will you keep an eye on the mare I would like to trance. I gotta recoup some energy." *Or at least get rid of this blasted headache.*

The stoic dwarf bobs his head.

Szames is caught up in his own thoughts I proceed with the meditation. Slowing my breathing until it is even and steady, I turn my thoughts inward and clear my mind. Picturing the traces of energy around us, I picture myself as a living sponge, soaking in the powerful essence with each breath.

It seems only seconds have passed when Jerik touches my knee. My horse halts beside Prince Szames as he pulls up next to the sentry at the gate. The throbbing pain is gone and so are the muscle aches. *I still feel wrung-out, but that I can deal with.* I look up, checking on the force-field, which appears whole.

Suddenly the sky above erupts like a Forth of July rocket exploding over our heads. The colors are dominated by orange and red, but there is a bit of blue mixed in. The cerulean force swirls down into the protective dome. *It's working!* The demons are vaporized and reenergizing the barrier at the same time.

"ArchMage Reba, one of the guards will escort Charles to the infirmary while we continue on to the castle," Szames states.

"I thank you, Prince Szames, but I will sleep better if I see to Charles' well being myself." *Almost courteous to a fault, or is it thoughtfulness?*

"Certainly, this way then," The quizzical look speaks of surprise as well as approval.

Thanks to the horses, we dismount in front of the door to the new infirmary before I have time to regret my decision. As Charles slides off his mount he stumbles. Jerik appears by his side, propping up the warrior before he can protest. *Those short legs are swift.* I hustle through the door Szames holds open.

Idly slicing a piece of fruit, Allinon occupies one

of the chairs pulled up to the table. With his stature, he towers over the young healer seated next to him. Their conversation ceases with our entrance: Allinon's wide-eyed companion bolts out of his chair bowing in my direction. Giving a nod in recognition, I approach the elf.

"Allinon, we were attacked. Charles is wounded. I have stabilized the wound as much as I can. Is Jamison tied up right now?"

"I'll get him," the elf glances at the doorway where Jerik is half-carrying the stumbling Charles into the room. His pace quickens. He sprints into the adjoining room. By the time Jerik and I have Charles seated, Allinon is back with Jamison in tow.

"We have been here less than a day and already you're dancing in the limelight?" Jamison tries to lighten the mood. He looks tired. His aura is nearly transparent, yet still he maintains a great bedside manner. A tired grin of approval spreads across my haggard face.

"Yea, glory, that's what I'm after. How can I be Prince Charmin' if the ladies don't swooning at my feet when tales of my valor are told?" Charles makes a valiant attempt at banter, "Reba dulled some of the pain, but it still hurts like hell. Give it to me straight, snowflake, how bad is it?"

Jamison eases the shirt aside. His face betrays nothing as he examines the wound. "Oh, not too bad. Whatever it was that hit you could have done a lot worse. It's a good thing Reba didn't attempt to do more: with her level of skill this would be tricky work. No offense, Reba."

"None taken," we exchange smiles like best friends though we just met this morning.

The MasterHealer focuses on the job at hand, "Those lacerations on your chest look messy, but I will be able to heal those right now. Your shoulder on the other hand, well, it's going to take some time. The scapula, or shoulder blade, has a hairline fracture on the top edge. Even with the healing it will be a couple of days before you have full use of your sword arm again."

"Two days we have," relief washes through me. I sigh, pulling up a chair across from the patient determined to add to my knowledge of the healing arts.

"You completed the spell? That is welcome news. Within a week all of the men who are going to achieve a full recovery should be there. Unfortunately there will still be almost a score of them that will never be whole," as Charles moans, Jamison turns back to him, "Let's get you taken care of; then I will brief you on the rest."

"In a case like this, you need to heal the internal injuries first and make sure those are stable," Jamison narrates for my benefit, "You will be able to see those injuries if you can achieve a full healer's sight, not just magesight. Bones need to be healed and back in their proper position before you move on to any other tissue damage. The outer muscle tissue will act as a support for the restored skeletal structure."

Jamison continues his narration with his hands hovering over Charles upper back. An emerald light, visible to magesight, emanates from the outstretched fingers, penetrating the mangled flesh until only a thin beam of green is manifest, "Charles, it looks like some of your paladin skills are still intact. Knitting a bone usually requires a bit of energy, even for someone of my skills, but healing you took very little. Your blessing for quick recovery is still active. Now for those cuts."

Allinon has reappeared. While I observe Jamison's healing technique, the elf pours a generous amount of the potion from the plastic canteen, soaking the puncture wound as Jamison activates his Gift. The liquid draws into the wound. The energy absorbs the potion like a sponge in the noonday sun. Jamison is incorporating the fluid in the regeneration process, putting it to use to rebuild the tissue.

"Ahhh, that feels…. better." Charles sighs as Jamison moves on to Charles' front shoulder.

Prince Charming's spirits rise as the pain ebbs. He

elaborates on his encounter, "Yeah, I'd say my Paladin skills are in effect, or my shoulder wouldn't be attached. The shield my aura emits slowed down the attack, softening the blows. As it is, my sword arm went numb with the first strike."

Paladin shield – I have got to remember that. It might come in handy. Gulping air like the wind has been knocked out of him, Jamison completes the healing reducing the wounds on Charles's shoulder to faint pink lines.

"That feels great. Are you sure I need to knock off at sword practice tomorrow?" Charles flexes his arm, testing its strength.

The MasterHealer wipes sweat from his brow, "Even though the pain is gone, bone takes a while to heal. If too much tension is placed on it before it is fully recovered you might pop that bone apart. One more healing session and it should be as good as new after a twenty-four hour integration lag." Jamison gives his final instructions wearily.

"Here, Jamison, take my chair." I jump up to retrieve another one. But once again I am too slow for my escorts: Szames and Jerik are retrieving extra seats for those of us without one. "Would you like to accompany us back to the castle for dinner?"

"All of the patients have been stabilized as much as possible, but I will feel better if I am here incase complications arise. Seventeen men died before we could even get started on the healings. We lost twelve men regardless of the power we poured into them and another fifteen aren't yet out of the danger zone: five of those I don't expect will see the sun rise. As I said earlier, almost fifty will retain some disability, either limited use or loss of a limb. That leaves over three-hundred men who will be ready for battle within the week," Jamison pauses, his eyebrows knitting with his reflection.

"Tupper tells me there are additional students at the Consortium. If any of those possess the Gift we will have most of the men up and around sooner, providing you are up to another awakening, Reba." When I give my immediate assertion he continues, "The more healers we find with even a trace of talent the better. I never dreamed the Gift would prove to be so limiting. As it is I need food and rest before I can perform even another minor miracle," Jamison finishes his report with more pessimism than usual. *Is loosing patients taking a toll on his optimism? I've never seen him like this.* I shake my head in denial: I just met the man this morning. *But he feels down.*

Szames clears his throat, "Jamison, you are truly a MasterHealer. I had not believed more than one hundred of the wounded would survive, much less have a full recovery, and now you say all but fifty will and with only a minimal amount of loss. You have worked a miracle that will be talked about for generations to come. This is truly the time of the Prophecy. Is there anything you need to aid in your work?"

Faint pink flushes Jamison's face as Prince Szames praises his work, but when he speaks his voice is clear steady, no sign of lethargy remains, "Since you mentioned it, there are a few supplies we need. Another two tubs of healing potion, more containers, and some sterile bandages, the latter we could use right away. Due to the limited amount of healing power we weren't able to close all wounds; that will have to be done in stages. Reba, if you could stop by in the morning to convert those?"

"You shall have them. If there is anything else, please do not hesitate to bring it to my attention," Szames acknowledges the Master-Healer's request before signaling for Herald.

"Jamison do you have any meditation techniques to help you recuperate faster or maybe an enchanted pendant?" With Szames is occupied with his squire, I use our native tongue for privacy.

Jamison shrugs, "I hadn't developed my character that in-depth. I have never even role-played. Is this something easy to learn?"

Not wanting to appear rude, I continue our discussion in Cuthburish, now that Szames has once again joined our discussion, "I know an enchantment that will enable you to recover faster. But I need something solid, preferably medal or glass to center it on. Do you have something on you? A pendant, ornament, or even a decorative chain will do."

"I don't think I've got anything like that..." A quick search of his person leaves him empty handed.

"I have a medallion that may work. Please, accept this in appreciation for the work you have accomplished today," The elderly healer, the one I was unable to grant even the slightest Gift to, quickly removes the pendant from around his neck.

"Thank you Laeknaen, I don't know what to say," Jamison's sober reply shows his appreciation.

"No, thank you. If it will enable you to speed the recovery of those in need, then you are the rightful owner of the Physician's Medallion of Excellence."

Jamison hands the emblem to me. The medallion is three times the size of a quarter and much heavier. It is made of the same type of medal as the candleholder in Prince Alex's dining room: neither pewter nor brass, but a mixture of both. The medallion is exquisite in its simplicity. An engraved pair of hands is cupped together as if offering something. Writing is arched above and below the symbol.

"What are the properties of this medal? Does it rust or tarnish?" I try to get a better feel for the object before I cast the spell.

"It is a metal alloy we call perinthess. It is a mixture of brass and corinth. It does not tarnish nor rust, and is more malleable than iron," Prince Szames explains.

"This will be perfect." I hold the medallion in my hands, letting the chain dangle between them. Feeling a pressure on my bladder I glance around. *No time for that now, besides who knows what kind of facilities they have.*

Though exhaustion nags me I know this is something we need tonight, not tomorrow. Centering myself, I reach once more for the magic tingling just beneath my skin.

"The Gift has been used and with its power,
Many lives have been saved in this dark hour.
Yet more work is there still to be done,
The war we wage is still to be won.

If my soul is good, helpful, and kind;
You will aid me in the strength to find.
As I rest with you placed against my skin,
Recharge my reserves, normal speed times ten."

The world spins about me as I give a push at the end of the mantra. I grit my teeth until my jaw aches, determined not to swoon. A teal light surrounds the medallion sinking into the brassy surface. To magesight it now has a soft aqua glow. Not the most poetic of rhymes, but hey, it worked!

I hand the necklace back to Jamison, "You will want to wear this under your shirt. It will help you regain your energy. If the other healers have an accessory suitable to hold an enchantment, I'll take care of those when I stop by to help with the containers."

"Thanks Reba. With this, perhaps all the soldiers will be on their feet in the next few of days," Much to my embarrassment a loud rumbling emanates from my midsection into the silence following Jamison's heartfelt acceptance.

"Milady ArchMage Reba," Szames bounds to his feet, "dinner is being kept for us," he remarks, placing a hand on my chair to maneuver it for me.

Is this also courtesy or have I offended him by taking charge? Lord knows it wouldn't be the first time. I just wish my empathy wasn't blank. "That sounds great. Allinon are you coming with us?" I rise as the prince assists me.

"There is no reason for me to stay. With the AV taken care of, my aid is limited," the Druid's pessimism sounds odd in his soprano accent.

Mounted, the trip to the castle is swift. In the frigid darkness, once again we enter through the more convenient servants' quarters. Entering the warmth causes my overworked muscles to relax and exhaustion slams into me like a semi-truck. My muddled brain refuses to focus on the world around me. I concentrate on raising one foot and then the other, unable to even glance at the direction we are taking.

How'd I get seated? All thoughts focus on the plate and utensils placed before me. I nod yes to Jerik who offers to pour a cup of mulled wine. He also spoons a couple of the large oval vegetables onto my plate. They resemble beats but are lighter, almost pink in color, surrounded by a thick burgundy sauce. My stomach rumbles as the dwarf continues to serve a little of everything on the table, until my plate is heaping. With a knife and fork, I eat quickly, barely remembering to place a napkin on my lap.

Whether due to my ravenous appetite or the food I will never know, but everything tastes wonderful. I eat every scrap on my plate. I help myself to seconds of almost everything, including the beets.

The door behind us sweeps open. Rejuvenated by the meal, all my senses are alive once more. The whisper of the well-oiled, four-inch, solid-wood door sounds like someone standing beside me, *whoosh-ing* into my ear.

An elderly gentleman hastens around the end of the table. I perceive his shock upon seeing me, although his face betrays not a hint of surprise. *Is it because I'm a woman, or what Jamison says is my "colorful mane" that causes everyone to do a double take?*

"ArchMage Reba, this is MasterSteward Hestur, head of the castle's staff," the balding gentleman bows stiffly. The way he bends his wiry frame nearly in two speaks of his strict adherence to protocol as does the crisp gray shirt tucked into creased royal blue trousers. His slate-hued belt mirrors the color of his polished shoes.

"I am honored, Milady ArchMage Reba. I will personally escort you to your rooms," his nasally aristocratic wine is a perfect counterpoint to his antiquated style of clothing. A shirt balloons out of the trousers, which are similar to dress pants with an extended waistband above the belt. They are formfitting through the waist with legs like the slacks I am used to seeing. *Where are the tights and calf-boots?*

"Jerik, Charles, Allinon?" As the others indicate their readiness, I stand and Szames stands with me.

"Prince Szames, I appreciate your help today," *How do I say goodnight to a prince?*

"It was my pleasure. If I may be of use to you in the future, do not hesitate to ask," Szames replies.

"I will keep your offer in mind. There is much that needs to be done," I turn a critical eye on the man I have spent the entire day with, trying to get some kind of feeling.

He is taller than the steward, as he has been of all men I have seen: only Allinon stands taller. His broad shoulders match his stature perfectly. Big men usually don't have legs that fit their torso so well. Add to that his movie star good looks: a chiseled jaw, strong chin, and straight nose, not to mention the blonde hair and blue eyes, and you have standing before you every woman's dream.

His clothes add to his physique. The suede trousers aren't tight, but they don't need to be, they provide mystery. You can tell by the way they are tucked into his boots that they hide well-muscled legs. Chain mail covers him from shoulders to mid-thigh, so that makes his butt status inscrutable as well. No matter what is left to be revealed he is, in all honesty, a drop-dead gorgeous man, and a prince to boot! *Never trust anyone that good looking. I'm glad I have Tony to go home to or I might be tempted enough to get myself into trouble on this stupid world, even though blonds really aren't my type.*

"I am at you service," he concludes with a slight bow.

"I bid you, goodnight," I reply hoping for sophistication not pretentiousness.

With a slight shake of my head I dismiss the empathetic efforts as a lost cause. "MasterSteward Hestur, if you will lead the way? We are ready to see our rooms."

Chapter Eight

"Right this way, Milady ArchMage Reba." Hestur bows again then reaches to hold the door. The MasterSteward leads us into one of the more elegant hallways where five uniformed women are waiting. I feel surprise reverberating like a shockwave through the ladies.

Even though they curtsey without hesitation, their eyes dart from Allinon's great height to Jerik, then toward Charles' unprecedented ebony and back to me. *Boy, what I wouldn't give for a mirror!* Women are taken back by my looks, even compared to a dwarf, an elf and so far the solitary black-skinned man in this city!

"ArchMage Reba, these chambermaids will see to your needs. They will escort your men to their quarters and I will personally show you to yours," his voice rings turgidly.

Turning to "my men" I relate in English, "Though I would prefer not to be separated, it's probably not considered proper for us to share quarters. How 'bout meeting first thing tomorrow morning," as the three nod in accession I continue, in Cuthburish, "I will see you a mark after first light for breakfast, in my chambers."

They mumble their agreement as three of the women from the rear of the group approach. Each of the chambermaids stand before one of the guys, and after a curtsy, they start down the hall to the right.

All five of our escorts are gorgeous, not to mention thin and busty. Two of the women leading my friends have the same mahogany hair Jamison now sports and the other one is a redhead with a mane the color of Lucile Ball's. That leaves a blonde and a raven-haired servant. *Talk about surreal! Almost everyone we've met at the castle could be part-time models. Or have we been running into the lucky few?*

Hestur, with a sniff of approval in the direction the others have gone, turns on his heel moving in the opposite direction. I follow with the two remaining chambermaids trailing a few feet behind.

Ingenious contraptions, resembling kerosene lamps with a metal back-plate, light our way. Even though the walk is short, the energy boost the food gave me is dampened by the time my guide stops before the first double-door entryway we come to. He grasps the doorknobs with both hands pushing in a grandiose gesture. When I get a glimpse at what will be my accommodations for the duration of my stay, it acts like an injection of caffeine into the bloodstream. My head snaps up and eyes pop open.

It isn't my room, but rooms! I enter a carbon copy of the reception chamber to Prince Alexandros': two large fireplaces, a massive desk and bookshelves filled with books. *Come on Rebecca, don't stand here gaping in the doorway like a bumpkin.*

As I enter my new suite, Hestur hurries over to the right, opening the set of doors before proceeding to the opposite side of the room. Glancing into the first area, I govern my expression, noting I also have a private dining room. *What do they think I am royalty? I have never seen rooms this fancy, much less stayed in them.*

My escort waits, with one hand extended toward the next room. I move in that direction without fulfilling my curiosity about the other accommodations. *I wish he'd leave. I need a few minutes to make sense of all of this.*

Without glancing at the room, I turn to the

MasterSteward, "Thank you, Hestur. These rooms will be quite adequate. If you will excuse me, it has been a long day," I declare with what I hope is a firm tone of command.

"Yes, milady. MasterTaylor Edward is waiting, on Queen Szacquelyn's request. A new wardrobe has been ordered, with all possible haste. Shall I command him to return at first light?" he queries in a voice less forceful, but irritating nonetheless.

An elongated sigh escapes me, "No, if it is the Queen's wish to supply proper attire then we had better get started. Please, have him shown to my reception chamber."

With a vengeance, my bladder reprimands me for ignoring it for to long. As Hestur leaves I turn to the blonde, the maid who has always taken the lead position, "Excuse me, I am ArchMage Reba and you are?"

"Crystal, your head chamberlain, milady. This is Bernadette. She will be Jamison's chamberlain." She curtsies keeping her eyes downcast. "Is there way we may aid you?"

"Actually, what I need right now is a place to take care of," I clear my throat, "'a call from nature.'" When all I receive is a blank look I try a more direct question, "I need a place where I can relieve myself. I believe it is called a chamber pot."

Inspiration brightens her blue eyes, "Oh, of course. Right this way."

I follow her to the far end of the room, which is half the size of my house back home. The bedroom has a complete living room and even a small dining set. I hurry on, the pressure on my bladder insisting I examine the room at a later date.

Straight down the wall from the doorway, Crystal stands holding another door open. "Milady, what you require is located through the door on the other side of the bathroom. Will you require my assistance?"

"Thank you, no. I can handle it from here," I enter at a brisk walk.

Noticing a candleholder occupied by a fat candle, lit and burning, I take it with me as I hurry to the far door. The room smells musty and even with a mage's night vision I can tell that it is dark: All the colors are black, white, and shades of gray.

Looking down I shake my head at my first sight of a chamber-pot. A large metal container is positioned in the center of the small room. It has a round bottom narrowing to short neck that flares out, forming a three-inch lip. *It looks like a giant spittoon!*

Are you supposed to sit on it or squat over it? I hate squatting, even in the forest. Frustration consumes me. *I can't see this happening right now.* Longingly, I picture the toilets back home, and begin a rhyme:

"The day has been so long, really tired I am.
This pot won't due, even if they call it 'the can.'
Of magic you will be made and maintained, that's right,
Porcelain, but warmed, so clean, so shiny and so white."

The power coursing through me only serves to highlight fact that the last time I relieved myself was more than twelve hours ago. Azure light envelopes the metal pot, which disappears as the magical force moves toward the back wall. The brightness intensifies, making me squint, before all the illumination is once again snuffed out.

If magic holds true to form, taking more from my mind than from the rhyme, this toilet should work automatically. It will whisk away the used water to the approximate center of the earth when weight is lifted off the seat.

Even before the spots clear from my eyes I am beside the new piece of brightness that's been added to my suite of rooms. I have my robe off and pants down in record time. The leather laces on the black suede pants are tricky, but when you have to go that bad, your mind and fingers seem to make a direct link, working on their own accord. Sinking onto the familiar surface gives me the freedom of thought that comes with modern facilities like these.

Now this is a pretty cool outfit. The suede pants are snug from the waist to hip. They are on the baggy side after that, fitting like the slacks Hestur wears. My calf-boots are also black and my shirt too. The button-up blouse is made of the same soft suede as the pants. The shirt is rather plain. The sleeves are not tight and are cuffed securely at the wrists, leaving room for maneuvering. Unable to resist I unbutton my shirt to investigate my new body, and immediately pull it closed again.

Shivering in the chill air I glance at my robe with longing. *A variation of the duplication spell should work:*

"Despite the chill you keep me comfortable, you do.
The air that surrounds me stays cool and warm, too.
Decorum prevents me from being clothed in your substance.
Now my skin will share these properties in abundance."

The goose bumps, arising from more than just the cold, retreat from my body. "Much better." *Now let's see what the transfer here has done to my body.*

A little thinner, especially around the thighs, but not quite as bony in my college days. Great muscle tone, though: no cellulite dimples anywhere. When my gaze moves upward I sigh in disappointment.

You know, since they were improving my body you would think that they could've increased my boobs just a little. The cloth brassiere, shaped like a sports-bra equipped with lace-ups in the back, looks like it still holds B-cup sized breasts. Athletic maybe, but aesthetic - definitely not.

In a flash, all the childhood taunts of "stick" and "too-tall" come rushing back. *Well, my height doesn't bother me anymore, but at least now I have the power to change the other, easily and painlessly.* With that final thought I begin an enchantment.

"In all this garb a B-cup isn't flattering,
A 'c' plus will help fill in for the padding."

    I smile as light surrounds my chest: the bra, boobs and all begin to expand. In a matter of minutes I have the cleavage I have always wanted.
    I'm already going to be acting more like the men on this world, at least with these killer feminine curves there will be no mistaking my gender.
    Hmmm… I don't want to have to worry about by weight while I'm here. Those twenty pounds will come back fast. I was contemplating a youth spell before I left…

"Since I've been taken to this foreign place,
Trying my best to save the human race.
With this spell so I won't grow old or fat,
Breast will stay firm and my tummy flat.

And let's not forget the most important part,
My mind will always stay focused and sharp.
Magic around me will be in constant use,
To repair the damage from nature's abuse."

    A wave of dizziness causes my stomach to flip-flop. *I think I need a little more time to recover before casting using magic again.* Having succeeded in attaining my dream figure, and somewhat confidant I won't be loosing it, at least not on this world, I reach for the Charmin and begin struggling into the pants which came off with such ease. On my way out to the bedroom I take time to examine the rest of the accommodations a little closer.
    The far end of the next room contains a sunken tub: snow-white marble with hairline traces of cobalt providing a beautiful contrast to the dark blue-gray rock from which the castle is made. The recessed structure is shaped like

two teardrops joined in the middle like Siamese twins and is as big as a twin-sized bed. The walkway around the Roman Bath is either solid stone, the same as the walls, or so well tiled that finding the seams will mean looking closer than I am ready to. Turning around to examine the rest of the thirty-foot room a glimmer catches my eye. *Now let's see what all the fuss is about.*

Across from the tub, a mirror is positioned over a waist high cabinet occupying the entire wall behind the doorway to the bedroom. The reflective surface stretches from the ivory counter top to the ceiling. My reflection glares back at me.

Oh my dear God! What did they do to my hair? I realize I hadn't decided on hair color for my character, but couldn't they have chosen just one!? With the light streaming in from the bedroom and the candle I hold, the colors are faded but distinguishable.

My hair is a dark auburn at the roots. A few inches from the scalp the colors lightens to a more true red color, another four inches and it blends into an orange red or a carrot top. Eventually all the red fades, leaving a couple inches of blonde on the tips. *No wonder everyone is doing double-takes.*

My decorative mane has gone from mostly straight to cascading waves of gentle curls. The hair is pushed forward with a pearl headband, creating volume in the front yet holding the hair out of the way. My tresses flare up a good inch behind pearly arch of the band.

Examining the decorative hairpiece I notice a faint blue light emanating from the pearled base. *An enchantment to hold my hair?* My hood must have an enchantment that nullifies the one in the band or my hair wouldn't fit inside. When hood is down the style allows even someone in the front to have a view of the full range of colors.

A whispered whoosh of a door opening sounds from the next room. I turn to peer into the bedroom. As the light from the candle strikes my hair it flares to life like God's famous bush.

Ohhh, now I get it. With even a small amount of light my hair gives off the impression of a living flame. The prophecy must be about their savior coming with flaming hair. *Boy, when the sun hit my head as I introduced myself to Prince Szames it must have been quite a show! No wonder it nearly gave the guards a heart attack!*

Examining my facial features, I find not much has changed. I still have mostly straight eyebrows. High cheekbones, an average nose with a slight ball on the tip, and unfortunately I still have the same thin lips. *Is it the same?*

Moving closer I find I still look the same, but it is the same as I look with make-up on. *I know my face is bare.* My lips are fuller than my normal thin, almost non-existent mouth. My eyes are a little larger and my eyelashes are long, thick and curved, even more so than when I wear mascara. And best of all, my skin tone is a light beige, with a slight blush only on the cheeks.

Well, this I can handle. I was, what I consider, above average with out make-up. Unfortunately if I wanted to be pretty, or maybe just feel pretty, I had to wear make-up. Now I have that look full time…

"Milady ArchMage Reba, the MasterTaylor has arrived," the chambermaid interrupts my thoughts.

"Thank you, Crystal, I will be there directly," We had better find out about that prophecy, pronto: it seems I have been custom made to fit the bill.

Taking one last glance at the mirror, shaking my head in disbelief at the fortune I have been granted, I head into the other room carrying my robe over my arm. Crystal holds the door for me as I enter my very own reception chamber.

A grizzled man, short and balding, bows as I enter, as do the two ladies flanking him one to each side. Giving a nod I introduce myself.

"I am ArchMage Reba, and you must be MasterTaylor Edward," I sense his shock. Whether it is my colorful looks, my gender, my attire, or a combination of all three,

I can't tell, but only a slight twitch of his lips betrays the intense feelings.

"A pleasure, Milady ArchMage Reba. This is my FirstApprentice Jhelum and my daughter April, my Second," he says politely, "I know the hour is late, so shall we get started? Would you like to see some sketches of the different styles of clothing I can have ready for you on the morrow?"

"That sounds like a prudent course. I appreciate your thoughtfulness concerning the late hour. Perhaps I can help narrow the selection down before we begin," with my hands behind my back, I explain my needs.

"I have much to accomplish in a short time. My clothes, therefore, must allow a certain freedom of movement a dress will hamper. I will undoubtedly be on horseback a great deal. A skirt would not be suited for that endeavor either. However, I know propriety calls for a certain amount of modesty. I am unaware of the exact standards to which your society holds. Perhaps if you have something like pants, but which has enough material to it that it might appear skirt-like and, therefore, feminine?"

"Milady, it's not unheard of for noble women to dress in a fashion that is not too dissimilar from what you are wearing, when out riding for the hunt. However, for everyday attire we will need something that, as you suggest, gives the appearance of a skirt at least. With the detailed description of your needs you have saved us marks of searching. I believe I have just the thing," I perceive excitement building as he smiles at his apprentice, "April do you have the sketch of the - what did we call it - the Fall something or another..."

"Father I know the one. We called it 'Fall Comfort.' It won't take me more than a moment to locate it," responds the brunette Edward introduced as his daughter. With a robust nose and rotund body, she is a full-figured gal. *So not everyone here is a beauty.*

"Excellent." The MasterTaylor pulls out several

feet of string and begins to loosen the tie binding it. He addresses me once more, "Milady, if you would like we can get started on the measurements."

"Of course. Where would you like to begin?" I ask, longing for a bed.

As Edward measures, April searches. Within a few minutes she approaches, a piece of paper thrust out in front of her like a shield. The top of the woman's head fails to reach top of my shoulder, as with all the females I have met on this strange world. *I guess I could be called an Amazon here, and with good reason.*

I feel her nervousness. *If I was half that anxious I would be trembling.* People here are terrified of me. Halting April curtsies, bowing her head before turning to her mentor, "Father, I believe I have it. Is this the one you were thinking of?"

"Yes, that's it," taking the parchment from her Edward holds it out for my examination, "Milady ArchMage Reba, this is an idea we had for a more relaxed look for the nobility. It is a three-piece ensemble intended to allow greater freedom of movement. There is a blouse, which as you see is quite voluminous, yet with the cut it still appears utterly feminine. Both that and the skirt are tucked into a wide belt fastened from behind. See how it reaches halfway up the torso, curving to form a peak in the center?"

Edward beams as he relates the inventive new style, "That will accent the feminine physique. We have several of the belts in various colors. Oh, yes, I almost forgot the most important detail. I believe I can use some of the fabric in the skirt to form a separation so it will wear more like pants, but still appear as you suggested, dress-like," immersed in their passion, his fear is forgotten, "Do you have any color preference?"

"Edward, I will leave that decision in your capable hands. I can see why you are a Master-Taylor. You certainly know your work and I trust you implicitly." I mean to be reassuring; however the compliment causes the man to blush. I perceive baffled desire stir in the man who is old enough to be my father. *Note to self: watch the flattery.*

"In that case, Milady ArchMage Reba, I bid you goodnight," the MasterTaylor sketches a courtly bow. The trio heads toward the door so I turn back to the bedroom.

"Milady, shall I have a bath drawn?" Crystal asks as Edward departs.

"Thank you, but I prefer to bathe in the mornings." A yawn escapes me. "If you will have the water ready by first light I would appreciate it. A candle burning by the bed will be the only other thing I require this evening." I pause, discerning Bernadette's expectation of instruction as well.

"Bernadette, Jamison intends to spend the night with the other healers. I need you to deliver a message to him. If he requires no further assistance you may retire for the evening as well," When her heart pounds like a mouse scurrying from a swooping hawk, I pause, concentrating on my empathy.

"Bernadette, why are you so frightened?" not knowing what else to say, I am too tired to be anything but direct.

"The dar-r-k, milady," Speaking of the evil lurking in the night causes her fear to escalate to a new height, "and the de-emons," she stutters.

"I placed a magical wall between the castle and the countryside. You can't see it, but you can see the demons when they touch it. If an enemy flies into the invisible barrier you will see fire blossom in the sky, taking the life of any demon that comes into contact with my magic. There is no reason to fear. The demons can't get inside the city walls," I smile as I perceive her anxiety ebbing. Quickly, I relay a message for Jamison.

"Your summons is as follows then: if possible, the ArchMage Reba requests your attendance at breakfast with the others of your group," She paraphrases beautifully.

"Yes, that will do," Turning back to the bedroom, I wonder if I am supposed to give a more formal dismissal.

The door opens and closes behind me. *I guess I did well enough. I just wish I knew the proper rules of decorum.* Wanting nothing more than to shut my eyes for a good, long while, I saunter to the pillowed plateau.

I note where the furniture lies, incase I awaken to a dark room: to my right is the fireplace and a table with two chairs. Between the dining set and the bed lie an uncomfortable looking chair, two loveseats, and several tables of varying size. Someone, mindful of my needs, has laid a nightgown on the bed. A thick cotton robe is draped over the closest chair and slippers by the bedside.

After stripping off my clothes, I climb into the pajamas. Even though I prefer to sleep in the buff, I know if an emergency arises I will need the covering.

Crawling into a bed almost twice the size of the king sized pillow-top I usually sleep on, the lethargy I have been ignoring overcomes me. I lean to blow out the candle resting on the nightstand. The fade colors from the room. *I forgot, I can see in the dark: so much for memorizing the furniture pattern.*

Will I awake in my own home? I hope not. I would really like to see a little more of this world before I go, or wake. But just incase I am still here in the morning…

"Now I lay me down to sleep,
I pray the Lord my soul to keep.

If I'm here when I awake,
recharged power I now make.

As I slumber peaceful and deep,
magic into me will now seep."

As the last words are either thought or said, I know not which, I drift into peaceful bliss.

Chapter Nine

"Tony, you aren't going to believe the strange dream I had, it was so real." I mumble, searching for the warm body located not too far from me. Finding only cold emptiness, my eyes pop open. I bolt upward sitting straight up on the massive cushioned plateau. Gazing around the large room at all the muted colors, I shake my head. *Is it all a dream, then? It seemed so real, but now the colors are faded.*

I shake off the haze of sleep when I hear a noise from my right. *The bathroom was over that way.* A door opens in the corner, well past the location of the lavatory. The room shines, coming alive with a kaleidoscope of vibrant hues, as a blonde enters caring a candle on a metal holder.

"Milady, is there something I may bring you?" Inquires the woman wearing a dark blue, floor-length skirt and a gray blouse.

"Ah, Crystal." *So it wasn't a dream after all.* "Some water would be welcome. Do you know how long until sunrise?"

"It is still almost two marks before morning bells, milady," Crystal replies, striding over to a dresser sitting next to the armoire in a corner.

Well I feel rested, even if it is an ungodly hour. Matter of fact I never feel this energetic in the mornings. Throwing back the thick pile of covers burying me to my chin, I move to the side of the bed as Crystal approaches with a glass in one hand and the candle in the other.

"Milady, would you like to start with the correspondence that came in last night?" She queries, handing me the requested water.

"Correspondence? I've been here, what, a day?" Baffled, I shake my head, "Yes, I suppose I should start with those."

Stepping into my slippers, grabbing the robe, I hurry to follow the chambermaid as she marches out of the bedroom. Looking up at my entrance, she pauses in the process of gathering items on a metal tray.

"Thank you, but I will take care of those in here." As a Crystal hesitates in the doorway for a fraction of a second, I perceive confusion. Wondering if my lack of etiquette is already causing problems I dismiss the foreign emotions from my thoughts, determined to learn more on the subject before I do something that is taboo in this culture

I move to the chair behind the desk. The ebonized wooden chair is solid. The pillowed seat makes it almost comfortable. Crystal places the two folded manuscripts before me then exits the room. Looking at the immense expanse of the desk I have no clue where to begin.

Picking up the missive on top I inspect the letter. There is something scrawled on the front and it is heavier than expected. On the back, blue wax has been placed where the folded edges meet. The seal has a castle stamped into it. *I'm going to need some additional skills: reading and writing. Well, I feel much better, rejuvenated as a matter of fact. It's time to get with the program.*

"The Cuthburish language I now know,
Reading and writing are needed so,
Magic will copy from this written note,
The necessary skills from he who wrote."

I concentrate on the effect I want to accomplish.

After a thrilling wave caresses me, I open my eyes to see a blue light move from the letter to my arms. With a thought I can now recall how to affix a seal to any style of correspondence I wish.

Until a few minutes ago all I had was a vague idea how to do that. It also occurs to me that this seal, the one with the castle, belongs to the reigning King of Cuthburan. *A letter from the king?*

Sliding open the center drawer I find a fascinating assortment of items: an inkwell, several quills, a container holding fine grained sand, a rectangular stick of red wax, a thick stack of parchment, a seal, and yes, a long thin letter opener.

I wonder whose signet this is. I take out the metal stamp along with the letter opener. Engraved on the signet is what I first assume are conjoined teardrops, but looking closer I see the individual lines depict a flame.

I suppose that would make this my stamp. Prying open the wax with the slender knife I lay the first letter, the one from King Arturo, flat on the desk in front of me.

> Milady ArchMage Reba,
> The War Council of Cuthburan is meeting on the morrow at mid-morning bells in the Council Chamber. We respectfully request the honor of your attendance.
> King Arturo of Cuthburan

Liking the simple and direct correspondence, I set it aside. Taking the next letter I turn it over to break the seal which resembles a flower. It reads:

> Dear Milady ArchMage Reba,
> In order to convey my sincere appreciation for the services you have rendered, I ask that you join me, in my chambers, for lunch on the earliest day of your convenience.
> Sincerely,
> Princess Szeanne Rose of Cuthburan

"Wow, two invitations in one day! Well, I should be able to do both today." I pronounce to no one in particular, while giving myself a mental reminder to get some additional info on the 'flaming' situation.

Taking out the inkwell, quills, and the box of fine-ground sand I compose replies accepting both offers. Finishing the last one I bring out the stick of wax, which I heat over the open flame. When it starts to melt I press it onto the envelope where the folded page overlaps. Blowing makes it stiffen slightly before I press the flame signet onto the waxy surface. Placing the finished product in the center of the desk I rise to stretch.

Who knew that writing could be such a chore? I never thought it would take so long to scrawl a few lines. I saunter over to the door on my right.

I pause, putting my thoughts in order: I had been mulling over a security spell while writing out the replies. As I turn my focus inward, the words appear in my mind. I pace around the room, reciting the limerick:

"Nosey people will want to see,
What's taking place inside of thee.
Whatever is spoken inside these walls,
Will be heard by none, however they call."

Like a rush from an alpine stream, power flows through my veins. I feel feather-light, almost floating along the edge of the room. After uttering the last word I arrive at the door to the reception chamber having made a complete circle of the room. Whispering "Sight," I watch the enchantment's progress.

Blue radiance resides along the path I have taken. It oozes along the walls, the floor, and the ceiling until the entire room is surrounded by shining barrier. *And there we have it, my very own home security system!*

"Milady, your bath is ready," Crystal utters from behind me.

Is it daybreak already? "Thank you. There are some

correspondences on the desk, will you see that they get delivered this morning?" With one last look at the walls, making sure the privacy field has no gaps, I murmur "sight," and turn on my heel moving to the door.

Crystal follows me into the bathroom. I nearly jump out of my skin when she reaches for the collar of my robe. This is going to take some getting used to. *I'm not a prude, but I am used to getting out of my clothes by myself!*

I pull up the nightgown as the soles of my feet make contact with the tub's first step. The water is lukewarm, so I take off the gown, sinking down until I am up to my neck. Reexamining the shape of the bathtub I see how the contours represent a flame, the marbling adding to the impression.

"I have some additional hot water when you are ready." Crystal indicates the two steaming buckets as she saunters past the door leading to the new toilet.

I drop my temperature shield with a thought, "A little warmer would be nice, thank you." I discern confusion pass through her as she empties the steaming liquid from the closest bucket into the tub.

"Ahh, that feels much better." I lean into one of the curves of the flame's base, trying to relax as Crystal hustles to the cabinet. *Sure, relax while a strange woman hovers in the room and you're in a tub without even so much as bubbles for cover?!* Relaxed or not, I am desperate for information. "Are you familiar with the protocols of the nobility?"

"Familiar? Yes, milady. I'm somewhat familiar with the protocols of the nobility," she answers from right behind me.

Placing a towel on the floor she kneels. I start as her hands gather my hair out of the water, reaching for the clip I forgot to remove.

"Crystal, I am not sure how much you've heard, but the land I come from is much, *much* different from this one. Because of this, some of my ways might seem strange. I have no wish to offend someone with my lack of manners, or to be thought less of because of an error in etiquette. I need your help. I realize this is probably a strange request, but I must know what is proper here," I explain as she manages to undo the clip and begins stroking my hair. *This isn't so bad. I have always loved having my hair done, and with the warm water... this is heavenly!*

"I understand your predicament. I am here to assist you. I will gladly do anything you require of me," Crystal responds and I once again sense her confusion.

Suspicion springs up from somewhere deep inside. Something tells me 'anything' is not just referring to lectures on protocol. *Is it the fact that I am naked while she is combing my hair or my heightened intuition?*

"First I need to clarify a couple of things. We don't have chamberlains, such as you, in my homeland." I use the Cuthburish title, referring to her position as head of my personal quarters. "I apologize if my assumption is incorrect, but the five women assigned to us, you aren't here to just clean up, and fetch things, are you? You would literally do anything you thought would make us happy, including things of a --"...*just be blunt* "-- of a sexual nature," I manage to spit the words out.

"Yes. We are the best at providing services within the entire castle staff. Therefore, it is our privilege to be assigned to you and your men. Not all chambermaids provide all services, but there are a few who have fully dedicated themselves to the care of others. Because of your status only the best have been appointed Chamberlains of your personal care," her unabashed answer is straightforward, "If you aren't inclined toward me, I can arrange for your companionship with someone who will be most discrete."

"No!" As her hands pause in their work I realize I nearly shouted the denial, "I mean no offence, but I am only inclined toward the opposite sex and I have a husband waiting for me back home. I won't be requiring any of your 'special' services." Again I sense confusion rise. "The second thing I need, besides information on protocol, is to know what behavior of mine causing you such bewilderment. Please be frank."

"How could you know of my confusion?" she mumbles. With a shake of her head she reorganizes her thoughts. "Of course - you are a sorcerer. Milady, you have a husband? It never occurred to me."

"Milady, I am unused to the courtesy you have shown me since your arrival. At first I took your kindness to be a proposition, but now you have stated otherwise. For the first time since I have taken a position here I'm unsure of the needs of the person to whom I have been assigned," Crystal explains as she wets a sponge, lathering it with a fragrant soap. As she hands the bubbly mass to me, I struggle to form a reply.

"Oh, I see. Well, the kindness I have displayed is known as 'common courtesy.' Anyone raised with any amount of upbringing on my world extends this to all they interact with. I'm sorry my behavior is confusing to you, but I am afraid it is something I will not change," I pause as she takes the sponge to wash my back. "Do you understand?"

Crystal empties the contents of the second pail, reheating water that has grown tepid. Retrieving a metal ewer, she fills this with liquid from the tub, pouring it over my head to wet my hair she asks, "But you are nobility, and I am a servant. What difference could your behavior toward me possibly make?"

"You are just as much a human being as anyone else. Why should I treat you with contempt?" I perceive the confusion abating as she mumbles assent.

Our conversation pauses while she puts something into my hair, lathering it like shampoo. The floral smell is pleasant, even relaxing since there is no sign of the allergies that plagued me before our magical transport to this world.

I continue, reiterating the original question, "Other

than my treating the castle staff with too much kindness, what are the other rules of etiquette? I will be meeting with the War Council this morning and having lunch with Princess Szeanne Rose this afternoon. I need to know what is proper."

"I have never been trained in proper decorum, but I can tell you what I have observed." Crystal starts the rinsing portion of the salon treatment. "Almost everything is determined by the position one holds within the monarchy. The person of lower ranking is always presented to the upper-classed noble. Even though two may be of the same linage, therefore equally entitled, their favor with the king may be noted with a simple introduction. The higher status nobles will dip their heads when bowed to by someone of lower status if they deem them worthy of recognition. You should always address someone by his or her full title unless you wish it to be known you are on intimate terms with the individual." By the time a creamy conditioner is applied she is finishing her lecture. "Also the lower ranked personage always waits until the other has taken a seat, with ladies assuming their chairs first, this goes for eating as well."

"Would you like me to inquire about other key issues?" She wraps my hair in a towel.

"No, that will be sufficient, thank you." *I'll have to watch the sitting thing...*

"Milady, if you are ready we should start on you hair," Crystal suggests.

Since the water is lukewarm again, I immediately accent to her proposal. I rise, snapping my protective shields back into place as Crystal hands me a thick bath sheet, passing me a robe after I am dry.

While my attendant answers a knock on the door of the reception chamber, I wander back into the bedroom. Seeing a vanity on the other side of the bed I move in that direction. Alone for the first time, I have a chance to take a closer look at what has been delegated as my chambers.

Light streams in around thick curtains covering almost a third of the wall on my left. Noticing a loose tie at the edge I pull back the thick velvet material. *That's better.* Even though I can see in the dark, the light will help me make out more details.

A set of French doors leading to a balcony lies behind the curtain. Glass partitions, so foggy they are opaque, are placed in-between delicate cherry wood. The doors add illumination, but the view is obscured. Turning back toward the bathroom I spy another door next to the lavatory, opposite the vanity. *Ah, Crystal's room.*

Now that I have better light, I find myself even more impressed with the room. Thick cream-colored rugs blanket the hardwood floor. The wood furnishings are the same color, or colors, making a beautiful bedroom set.

Each piece holds to a general theme: flames. Take the bed for instance. The bases of all four posters are a deep mahogany. About a third of the way up, it changes to a more honest cherry-red color and the tops are the same amber color of the leaves on Prince Alex's dining room table. Lines have been carved into the posts, weaving in, out, and around the poles in no discernable pattern. Everywhere I look I see a blazing pattern. *How long these rooms have been waiting for me?*

Crystal returns, carrying a load of hanging clothes. *Are those mine?* Mixed in with a stack of garments are my silver robe and black leather outfit. "Milady, you said you will attend the War Council this morning?" as I dip my head she continues, "If I may make a suggestion?"

"I would appreciate any aid you can give, especially if it is concerning those. I don't have the greatest fashion sense, even on my own world."

"Since the council is made up of men, if you were to wear your original outfit it may remind them that you are more than a mere woman," A hint of mischief tinges her voice.

"That sounds like an inspired idea, I believe I will," as she puts the other clothes in the armoire, laying out my cleaned garments, I ask a question I have been curious about since my arrival. "Tell me something, Crystal, and I again encourage you to be forthright. I know there is a prophecy about my arrival, but what is it, exactly?"

The chamberlain comes around to my side of the bed, gesturing toward the vanity. As I take a seat she gives me much more than the answer I request.

"I believe I will speak plainly with you, Milady. You are… different… than any of the other nobles I've encountered, and with them I wouldn't dare. But I think I have figured out what it is you need from me and I believe this is part of it.

I don't know the official version of the Prophecy of the Flame for I have no proper learning, but everyone knows it, in a general sort of way." Having combed out my hair, she applies ointment from a jar on the vanity as she continues. "When someone is faced with what seems to be an overwhelming task, it is often said: I don't see the Flame so I'd better get to. There is no help coming. Or when a new law is passed that someone disagrees they often say, 'Where is the flamed-haired one? His rule is bound to be better than this. I'm sorry but that is all I know."

Mary, Holy Mother of Jesus! They can't really think that I'm here to take over, can they? I inhale long and hard, trying to catch my breath. "Thank you Christine. That does help clear thing up." I cock my head to one side as a revelation dawns, "You guys weren't expecting a woman, were you."

"I will say, we were quite taken aback by you being a woman," She pauses for a moment. "Many don't believe it yet. They think it's just a rumor: our savior can't be a woman. I was one of those, until I got my first look. It's not just your hair. There is something about you that says you are what we have been waiting for."

"Crystal, I thank you for your candor. I hope you will always be open with me," a wry twist tweaks my lips, "At least that explains why everyone is so shocked."

She sets the pearl hairpiece back into position, pushing it forward to create a loose look in the front. Without warning, the locks behind the combs flare, giving my mane an untamed look. Before I am able to probe for more information, a knock sounds at the reception chamber door. As Crystal goes to answer the summons, I hear bells ring in the distance.

That must be the guys. I hope they've found out more than I have. The ruling class can't be happy to see the revolutionary usurper to the throne. Unless the laymen's interpretation is off by quite a bit I'd say we are standing in a swamp surrounded by quicksand, and the clouds are gathering on the horizon.

Chapter Ten

Hastily I struggle into the cotton underwear I arrived in. I am starting on the bra when Crystal reappears. With her help lacing up the strings in the back, I am into my clothes in just a few minutes. She confirms the arrival of the three gentlemen from last night. Since she doesn't mention Jamison, I am not too worried about being late.

"Milady, shall I serve breakfast directly?" Crystal inquires with a curtsey.

"Within the mark will be sufficient, thank you," as I smile, she walks toward the doorway over past the bathroom. *There must be a backdoor out of her room.*

Entering the Reception Chamber I hear Charles' low whistle, "Man check it out. This room is got some serious bling-bling, just like that prince."

"We sure are getting the short end of this stick," Allinon's soprano grumps with a nasal inflection.

Crystal squeezes past us, rushing to answer a knock at the outer door.

"Sorry I'm late. You guys are a ways from the barracks," Jamison offers.

"No worries, was running behind too," as I head to the dining room Jamison rushes to open the door for me. Crossing into the ensorcelled walls I let out a breath I didn't know I was holding.

"Has your day been that bad already?" The healer slides up beside me.

"If only you knew." Taking a good look at the room's furniture my patience evaporates. "And would you look at this place, just look at it? Flames!! Everywhere I look its blasted flames! I swear it's gonna give me nightmares."

Predictably, the table and all ten chairs have the same coloring theme as the bed. The tapestries on the walls are just as detailed as the ones hanging in Prince Alex's dining room. These, however, show the castle in various stages of construction.

"Ooooh, you poor thing. Stuck in all this splendor while we're living in servants' quarters," Allinon's sullen sarcasm whines as he takes possession of the chair at the head of the table.

"Come on Allinon, our rooms aren't all that bad." Charles's raises an eyebrow adding silkily, "And hey, I sure like our maids…"

I just bet you do! Now, where do I start? There is so much they need to know. "Allinon, if you can assume the identity I've been given, I'll gladly trade rooms. If no one has any objections, why don't we start with a reality check? I don't know about the rest of you but I have discovered some things that are making me question my sanity."

Getting down to business helps ease the tension building since our arrival. "Let's go around the table, telling something about ourselves, our real selves. Make it unique or special. It should help reassure us that this is our new reality."

"I'm not having problems with reality. I'll go first," rumbles Jerik, as Jamison examines Charles' shoulder, "Back home I was an architect, only been out of school less than a year. Been married for three years. We don't have any kids." the dwarf looks quarrelsome as I sense a mental frown. "Our D & D group stayed at the hotel for our senior break, this was my second visit. That's all there is."

"It looks like I'm next in line. At least I know I don't have a hard act to follow," Charles ribs Jerik, "I've got nothing special either: My boy is five and I get to see him every other weekend. There's a girl I have been dating for a little over a year and a job I've had for a year and a half. I have been gaming since high school."

"I've got the two of you beat," Allinon boasts, "I have been gaming for fifteen years, since my senior year in college. Allinon was my first and favorite character. I have two kids, a boy and a girl, and a marriage headed for divorce. We have been separated for two weeks." *A divorce? Big surprise.*

"Allinon, you got me beat too, thank God," retaking his seat, Jamison gets a chuckle from our little band, "Not even a girlfriend, much less a divorce or kids. I was a third year med. student when some guys invited me to a party where everyone had on medieval costumes. I thought it was so cool, we talked about gaming all night. As the party got going the Jamison Whiskey I was pounding loosed me up. By the end of the night I earned the Ren-name "Jamison the Good." The following summer when I met my foster parents in Hawaii for summer vacation I mentioned my new interest. Instead of the usual week stay at the Club Med Golf Resort, I got the Renaissance Hotel trip for Christmas."

Jamison gives the warrior an approving nod before adding, "Charles, that shoulder looks better than I expected. I wish all my patients were Paladins. You should be okay for practice today, but no rough and tumble stuff 'til tomorrow."

"So far you guys are scoring low on the creative scale," I take my turn at shoveling a little camaraderie shit, "But I guess if it were my dream I'd make up something a lot more dramatic. Let me give you guys a reality fact, though. I have never gamed, I went to a Renaissance fair once, played on the computer, and read some books. And you're gonna love this: I'm an identical twin. We used to look more alike before I got this trans-dimensional make-over."

"No way! You? A twin? You gotta be kiddin' me,"

Allinon's snide soprano interrupts my autobiography, bristling with the usual sarcasm.

"Oh really? Ya' think so?" *I've had enough of his crap,* "And if I can prove I'm a twin will you cut out the pessimism for the rest of the day?"

"You're on. And if you can't convince the majority, then you will introduce me as your Teacher in the Arts of Magic from here on out!" the elf proclaims.

"Come on man. There's no call to bust a move like," amazingly, it's Charles, not Jamison, coming to my defense.

"It's okay Charles. Allinon, I'll take your bet, as long as you agree to tone down your attitude for the rest of our stay when you loose," as we reach across the table to shake on it the door opens and Crystal enters followed by three austere servants. They set the table around us while I concentrate on the necessary rhyming lines to suit my needs.

Blocking everything out, I begin the enchantment:

"I recall some pictures that we sisters had taken,
Lani and I: for each other are often mistaken.
To remove the twin mystery
I must have them in front of me."

Despite the awkward wording I feel the power pulled from me as an explosion of blue goes off like a camera flash. Sitting on my plate, as I imagined, is a stack of photos.

"Aahh!" One of the servants hits the floor in a dead faint. Jamison rushes to her, and with a touch of healing magic, she is up in a few seconds.

"Milady ArchMage Reba, I apologize for the interruption," Crystal laments as she escorts the trembling woman from the room. I give what I hope is a reassuring smile.

"Here take a look at these while you eat," I pass the photos across the table to Jerik.

"But we wait until everyone sees them to comment, that way no one is prejudiced by preconceived notions!" Allinon is intent on getting in his two-cents.

"Whatever you want…elf." *Like it'll matter…*

I pass on the eggs but take a thick slice of ham. There is also jam, or maybe its preserves for the bread, and some fruit-filled pastries. Crystal is back before I take my first mouthful.

"Crystal, is she okay?" I sigh.

I perceive puzzlement as she mumbles, "Yes, Milady."

"It might be a good idea to interview all of the servants," I recommend what seems to be a logical solution. "If any have an aversion to magical workings they should be assigned elsewhere."

"Yes, milady. I will see to it," she bobs her head, accepting my suggestion as gospel.

I manage to clear my heaping plate. Nibbling on a pastry, something like a Danish, light and fluffy with apple filling, I wait for the guys to finishing up their meals.

"There's no way these are real." The elf thumbs through the photos. "You just made them up," Allinon's high-pitched snort is almost comical.

"You'll notice the picture of me in white: standing beside me is my twin sister, Lani, with her hair put up. Well, that was one of my wedding photos: hence the white dress. The other pictures ones are my sister, Cheryl, took the year before I met my husband."

Allinon flings the visual biography down the table as the servants clear the table. I arrange the pictures in two lines, putting the 5x7 glossy with both my sister and me between the two columns.

"We chose our own poses and clothes. If you compare the photos of me with of those of her, I think the personality comes through. I have always been more sweet and innocent. She is more aggressive and flirtatious."

"When we were young, one of our friends once said

about us, "You're the kind of girl a man looks to marry and she's the is the kind you look to date." I think these demonstrate the different attitudes, unless that is, you think I'm a split personality." the guys nod their ascension.

I give a sickening-sweet smile to my adversary. "So you got anything you want to say before we vote?"

"Okay, okay, I know when I'm beat, no need to vote. Who knew? A twin sister? It just seemed like a ploy for attention." his sarcasm grates on my nerves, "Besides, Lani and Rebecca, what kind of names are those for twins."

"Our names are RaLain and Rebecca. We went by Berta and Becky when were kids, then we both changed our names. I started going by Rebecca and she by Lani," my pressed lips narrow into a straight line and my tone takes on an icy sheen, "So Allinon - you are gonna lay off the pessimistic sarcasm for a while?"

The Elf shakes his white locks. "My wife complains about the same thing. I guess maybe it's something I need to work on."

"Thank you Allinon, I appreciate your effort," I acknowledge his confession, not buying his act for a minute.

"Now, on to business. Does anyone mind if I lead?" Everyone immediately assents.

With English revealed as the language of magic, I inform them of the possible security breach, as well as the ensorcelled protection of the dining room. Only Jamison is surprised by the strict rules of decorum. As the servants leave the room I conclude, "Finding out about this Prophecy of the Flame must be our top priority. This Prophecy is a foretelling of our coming and, Jamison, you were right; it has to do with my hair. It's so popular even the lower class is familiar with it," with a sigh I pass on my findings, "I dearly hope what has been filtered down to them is, at the very least, inaccurate."

"Word, dat…" Charles mutters, flashing his teeth in a good-natured grin.

"You said it. Unfortunately, the treatment I have received seems to indicate the nobility is under the same impression as the staff. I mean look at these rooms, equal to those of the crown prince, and Prince Szames seated me before himself."

Reflexively, my hand slaps down on the table, "Let me make one thing real clear right now, I have no intention of ruling anyone - absolutely none! Politics and formality are a total pain in the ass."

I pause, sipping the tea while I regain my composure. "We need to find out what this prophecy says word for word. They must be assuming a meaning, like they assumed I would be a man. We've got to find out what other possible meanings there are for this foretelling."

"And how do you suppose we do that? Just ask to see what must be one of their most sacred documents?" I shoot Allinon a dirty look as his pessimism reasserts itself. He gives me a sheepish shrug.

"Since it's a prophecy about me I don't think it will be kosher to inquire about it. That means it's up to you guys. Charles, why don't you see if you can use some of your charisma to dig up some dirt." He rubs is chin absently, then gives a leering wink.

"That brings us to the last piece of business. We've been invited to attend the War Council this morning. I have accepted the offer. I think it's important that any of you who can make it, come with me." I smile at my favorite comrade. "How are your patients?"

"We lost four men last night, and another two aren't out of danger yet. I was planning on heading back there as soon as we are done, unless you want me with you, Reba." He defers to my judgment.

"If the rest of the guys are attending, then they need you worse than me." I sigh shaking my head, "Anybody have something else they want to go over?"

"I got nothing, kripes, all I did was go to bed and sleep… mostly." Charles gets a chuckle from the men.

"Milady, your page is here to escort you to the

Council meeting," Crystal interjects into the silence. *So in other words, if you don't want to be late, you'd better be going.*

"Thank you, Crystal." Jamison moves to pull out my chair. Speaking in Cuthburish I add, "How about making this breakfast meeting a regular practice?" When four male voices reply, I move to follow the blonde.

A young boy dressed in cobalt and silver is waiting in the reception chamber. The youth can't be more than twelve, thirteen at most, but when we appear he stands strait and bows stately.

"I am ArchMage Reba, you must be my new page," I pretend he is an adult, not the child before me.

"Page William, at your service," he responds.

I don't get an overwhelming sense of awe like in the others. "William, we need to get to the Council Chambers, take us by the quickest route you know." I enjoin.

With a bow he marches straight to the outer door, holding it for our party, "Right this way, Milady ArchMage Reba."

We hustle back the same way we came last night. As William assumes the lead, Charles moves up beside me. "I was hoping to get a chance to talk to you. Do we have a few minutes?" I probe, switching back to my native tongue.

"Sure, wassup?" He flashes me a smile.

"Ugh, well, I don't want to offend you. What I have to say, well, it's... kind of on a personal level. " My cheeks begin to burn before I even get started.

"It must be something good to make you color like that," Prince Charming coaxes. "Come on, spit it out...."

"It's about our chambermaids. I had a little heart to heart with mine this morning. It seems we've been assigned some very special servants. They are the kind that will do anything, and I do mean *anything*, you ask. You might not even have to ask, it seems politeness to someone of their station can be taken as a proposition."

Charles's lips stretch so far across his face they

become as thin as mine. I rush to divulge the reason I brought up the topic. "I'm not gonna preach at ya, your life is your own. Just remember, people use pillow talk for espionage."

"Reba, you hooridin' me about slippin' up when I'm hittin' it with the phat chicks?" Charles's eyes twinkle.

"Just giving a friendly reminder, that's all. Live out your fantasies to your hearts content, but make sure you keep your mouth shut except for tales of valor. And if you will pass on the info to the other men, I'd appreciate it."

"Well I appreciate the advice, Little Momma." A moment of solemnity overcomes him. "You know, I wasn't all that much of a smooth talker, back home I mean. Here the words come easy. I guess I should monitor what's coming out."

With a rise in one brow his mood swings back to jovial, "So tell me, how did you find out about all this, I mean you have female servants too?"

"W-well, she-e...," I stutter, cheeks flaming. Furiously, words shoot out of my mouth, "Ah Hell! Because I was nice to her, Crystal thought I was coming on to her. When I told her that I'm straight she offered to get me a discrete man!"

"Boo-yah!" Charles crows. "Tha sistas' are 06'n hoochie mama's."

Nervously I glance around to see if we are drawing attention. "It's not like I don't have enough to worry about without having a maid that bats for both teams!" As Charles lets out another guffaw I throw a punch at him. "Just watch out for ulterior motives –'kay?"

Stifling laughter, red tinges his dusky complexion. "Fo' real, she was willing to, you know, with you? Man oh man, this is wicked. Talk about maximizing your R & R," Charles is unable to get the revelation off his mind. As I pin him with a glare he adds, "Well, don't worry, I plan on taking full advantage of my new looks and charm. I will be getting jiggy wit' it enough for two...

or with two!"

I think he's serious! Ugh... men!

William has taken us back to the same hallway outside the kitchen then through one of the doorways on the right. The passage twists and turns then ends at another door, which the page holds open. I squint, my eyes adjusting to the bright corridor.

"Right this way, ArchMage Reba. The Council Room is the second door on the right." William gestures down the hallway where two guards stand at attention outside an entryway.

Kerosene lamps shine from the walls about every five feet as our soft leather boots click on the polished marble floors. I stop before the indicated door, while Charles announces our party. "ArchMage Reba and the Crusaders of the Light."

A sentry moves to open the door as bells sound. Unsure of what my reception will be, I enter with my head held high, whispering "sight," under my breath.

The Council Chamber is a square room with royal blue banners hanging on the walls. A likeness of Castle Eldrich is sewn on the surface. Not too impressive after seeing the set of rooms I have been assigned. A long table, only slightly bigger than the one we ate breakfast on, takes up most of the space in the room. There is no sign of anything magical, but that fact offers little comfort.

The sound of wood scraping stone greets me. All but two of the eight men in the room bow. I give a nod to the other men, as King Arturo and Prince Szames come to greet me.

"ArchMage Reba, I am pleased you could make it. Let me introduce you to the Council of Cuthburan. ArchMage Reba and the Crusaders of the Light: I present to you Duke Rokroa of Kempmore; Duke Gabion of Everand; Marquis Vinfastur of Rhymon; Count Anzin of Gandrus; Count Baulyard of Mountview; and Baron Eldhress of Brightport." Each bows in turn as King Arturo calls his name.

"A pleasure, gentlemen. There is much to discuss. We have many things to accomplish while we have the luxury of time," with a smile I conclude my greeting by asking a question I already know the answer to. "Your Majesty, may I inquire if anyone has magically sealed this room?"

"We are in the heart of the castle. Your shield already surrounds the city," his brow crinkles in puzzlement as he exudes offence.

"The shield I erected only keeps the physical enemy from the city. Sorcerers have the ability to trance, seeing into places far distant. We are facing a rogue sorcerer of unknown abilities. I suggest we secure this room. I further suggest that no one mention our plans once they leave this room." I bow, remembering I am addressing one of the most powerful men on this planet. "With your permission, Your Majesty, it will take a brief moment for me perform the necessary enchantment to keep all that is said inside these walls."

I feel shock, disbelief and outrage echoing around the room. *Is it because I'm a woman, a subordinate, or have I neglected some protocol Crystal doesn't know? Only Prince Szames is apathetic.*

"Magic of any kind has been forbidden in this room since it was built more than two centuries ago. However, this is the first war that has been fought with sorcery since its construction, therefore we believe the time has come to break with tradition. ArchMage Reba, your logic and reasoning are sound. If you have a spell that will further secure this chamber it will be preformed before the council session begins." King Arturo declares, sounding as if the precaution is his idea.

"As you wish, Your Majesty." I return to the door. Father and son return to their places, to stand in front of their seats with the other men. I quickly reenact the spell I used on my dining room.

After checking to make sure the barrier encases every inch of the room I turn to address the King, "Your Majesty, the room is secure. All conversations held within these walls will be heard by none but those present,"

The King nods his approval, motioning to the empty chair on his right, "Merithin is unable to attend today's council. We would have you sit, here, in his place to advise us in his absence."

"I would be honored, Your Majesty." Charles pulls out the chair. As I take a seat with a trio of bodyguards standing behind me, the War Council reclines as well.

"First order of business, last night we lost two dwellings to the demons. They dropped torches on the city after many of their number fell to the shield ArchMage Reba erected. Other than archers posted along the battlements, any suggestions to deter the demons from firing the city tonight?" King Arturo addresses the council.

"Flaming brands?" Realizing our enemy has circumvented my impregnable defense, anger blazes to life, "Your Majesty, do you mean to tell me: these demons used fire to get through my shield?"

I hesitate long enough to receive his affirming nod before I charge on, "How many lives were lost?"

"A dozen townsmen perished before we could get the blaze under control," Prince Szames supplies when his father's face remains blank.

"Why was I not woken when a flaw in my defense was discovered?" My voice becomes as sharp as the blades I carry.

"It was our judgment that you would be too exhausted to be of any aid with your prior effort to erect the necessary defense," King Arturo asserts.

I discern his indignation at the questioning of his procedure, but my perfect memory hounds me. *I made a toilet, increased my boobs, kept myself from gaining weight, and even more! Twelve lives lost while I dorked around!* I advance full steam ahead regardless of the feeling in the room.

"Your Majesty, I assure you I had more than enough energy to handle a few fires last night. What I didn't personally have I would have borrowed from another. I highly suggest: before judging what magical resources remain at my disposal, inform me of the situation. I will tell you what I am or am not capable of." Pausing to regain my composure I continue, "As for the demon's fire, I will adjust the shield. Archers on the walls are a good idea, as long as they stick to the inner side of the battlement they should be safe."

"If you can change the defense already in place then we leave that issue in your capable hands." King Arturo dismisses my concerns, and the outburst, though we are both still as prickly as a couple of saguaro.

"Next order of business, battle plans." King Arturo turns to his son, "Commander, you and the ArchMage have battled these demons, what do you suggest concerning fighting techniques?"

"I believe pikes will be the best offence. Most of the demons have far superior reach and strength; pikes for the larger ones are the only solution. ArchMage Reba, you and your men handled an ogre last night, what do you suggest?" with a turn of his lips, bordering on smugness, Szames invites my input while his father stifles a sigh.

"I have put much thought into this very matter, Prince Szames. The way I see it, we need considerably more than just pikes," I outline the ideas I have been forming, while silence envelopes the room like a black hole, "… They are superior in both armaments and in strength. I see this plan as the sole solution to our survival." The room erupts.

"We have had a treaty with Kypros for centuries forbidding magical warfare." Count Baulyard expounds.

"It defies honor use a strategy like that on the battlefield." Duke Rokroa shouts to be heard over the Count.

"We should hide, cowering, behind our mother's skirts!" chimes in Marquis Vinfastur.

"You want us to lure them like a fisherman baiting eel? We are warriors, not trawlers!" Baron Eldhress of

Brightport bellows over Edmond's protest.

"Order! Order!!" King Arturo's fist comes down hard on the table as he shouts to be heard over his subordinates. "Gentlemen, this behavior is unacceptable in our courtroom and is doubly so here! Now, if we can continue in a civilized fashion…" The king's tone is sharper than the one I used earlier, "Commander, you are the only of us to engage these monsters in battle. Does what ArchMage Reba suggest have merit?"

"I have battled these demons twice. When they first attacked, we outnumbered them almost thirty-to-one, but it did us no good. We eventually killed all twenty of the monsters, but not before they killed over one hundred of us and wounded four times that many. This means if our enemy strikes with more than one hundred demons, we cannot win, even with every man we have on the field." Rising, he continues as he leans on his knuckles. "As for the Kypros Treaty: we also have a treaty that states they will come to our aid if we are under attack. We have sent requests for aid. Has help come? It has been proven the demons use magic in their attacks, so where honor is concerned, none is lost on meeting an enemy on a level field for battle."

When Szames pauses for breath, every man is as immobile as the marble statue gracing the entrance to Castle Eldrich, "There is one last thing I wish each of you to think on. Your sons and your kin will be in the coming battle, fighting for your lives and the lives of everyone in this city. If what Reba suggests will allow our beloveds to retain their lives, is it not worth the damage it will do to our pride?" With a reassuring nod in my direction he reclaims his seat.

"We now know this is the time of the Prophecy, with this fact in mind, I would like to hear your recommendations concerning ArchMage Reba's suggestion," King Arturo calls for their decisions without giving anyone else a chance to speak, "Vinfastur?"

"I still do not like it, but it seems we have no choice

in this matter," he relinquishes his position with very little grace.

As King Arturo continues around the table, all but Duke Rokroa agree to the measures I suggested. "Taking all of your opinions into consideration, it is our proclamation: The archmage strategies will be implemented. ArchMage Reba, are there supplies you will need for the magical workings you propose?"

"Yes, and it is a long list. All weapons must be gathered and brought to the forge where Jerik will work. I can use weapons or armor you feel is damaged beyond any further use in one of my projects. We will have to assemble portions of the troops in small groups daily: they will need to wear leather armor and all clothing they will don on the day of the battle. In addition I must also have several wagonloads of sand; four hundred wooden posts at least thirty feet in length; yards of material and people who can sew; and food for the additional troops. Also, Prince Szames aided me in the construction of the protective shield, I could use his help in the modifications."

"We do not have the manpower to fill your requests, not when all the troops will be training under your men for battle maneuvers you have suggested," scoffs Duke Rokroa as pessimistic as Allinon has ever been, "Where do you suggest we get all these supplies, oh great ArchMage?"

Refusing to rise to his bait, I ignore they way he phrased his question and respond to the core concerns, "From the townspeople. Right now they have nothing to do but sit around and think about the demons waiting outside. I suggest we send out heralds asking the populace to gather outside the castle to be addressed by their King. Let them know what they can do to help. I think you will find the outcome surprising. When faced by unimaginable terrors, I believe the human race will unite to conquer any enemy."

"An excellent suggestion, ArchMage," King Arturo replies over the grumbling of the nobles, "We have a few revisions. Instead of our making a request of the townspeople, we will present them to you and you will make the request. And the address will wait until tomorrow. Tonight you and your men will sit at the royal table, and we will formally introduce you to the nobility of Cuthburan."

"As you wish, Your Majesty. Since I will be making requests in your name as well as compensation for services rendered, shall I send you a copy of tomorrows address?" My voice is rock-solid though I quake at the though of public speaking. *God give me strength... And presented at dinner... it all begins tonight.*

"No, that is not necessary. You know what is needed. As long as compensations are just, we see no reason to approve each individual action. ArchMage, will tomorrow night be soon enough to begin the assemblage of the troops?" King Arturo is more relaxed now that talk of change has ceased.

Preoccupied with thoughts of the address running through my head I mumble, "Yes, tomorrow will be fine. How many will be in attendance?"

King Arturo looks to Szames, who says, "No more than thirty the first night."

"Have them assembled in the courtyard at sunset tomorrow. And, Your Majesty, I think it will be best if you participate in the ceremony, if you can spare the time." *I can't have him thinking I'm trying to sway the loyalty of his men.*

"ArchMage Reba, if it is your wish, we will see you tomorrow evening," his tone is one of finality on the subject.

"I appreciate the faith you have place in me, Your Majesty. With these new developments I have much to accomplish. I am no tactician; that is Charles's expertise. With your permission I will leave the Paladin, Charles, here in my stead, to work on the rest of the strategy for the up coming battle. I take care of the matters pertaining to magic." *I need to come up with at least ten new enchantments not including battle spells, a speech for people I know nothing about, and a 'just' method of compensation!*

"It is a wise man - or woman - who knows their own strengths as well as their weaknesses. The time of change is upon us and we welcome a fresh point of view for our strategy session. ArchMage Reba, your task in this war is possibly the greatest of all those gathered here. Your presence will be missed, but we understand your task lies elsewhere. A permanent place will be made for you at this table. You may rejoin us when time allows. We dine at evening bells." With his words he dismisses me with regret, but I sense the relief washing over him.

"Thank you, Your Majesty. Your Highness, when you have time, I could use your aid with the modifications to the shield?" *I'll not be caught short of energy again. I will use all I can from others.*

"ArchMage Reba, it will be my pleasure. How much time will be needed to make the adjustments?"

"Prince Szames, if your disposition for magic remains the same and you have no fear of heights, we will need no more than a mark." I smile in anticipation.

A brief twitch of his eyebrow hints that I have captured his attention. "Milady, I will see you at mid-afternoon bells, if that time is suitable?"

"Mid-afternoon bells it is, Your Highness," My lips tilt in a crooked-smile.

Charles once again takes hold of my chair as I rise. All the men at the table rise with me and Allinon follows me to the door, holding it open as I retire from the War Council.

Chapter Eleven

The page stands waiting for me outside the Council Chamber. "William, how long until the afternoon bells?"

"A little more than a mark, milady." He dips his head.

"In that case, please lead the way to the chambers of Princess Szeanne Rose." I instruct the lad, hoping showing up early won't be considered bad manners. Grateful for a few minutes to sort out my thoughts before I have to deal with protocols and insinuations, I follow the youth.

After a much less direct route, William stops before a set of doors that look identical to mine. Struggling to pull myself out of the haze of guilt and self-doubt enveloping me, I focus on the chambermaid who answers a set of large doors as the page declares, "The ArchMage Reba, here to see the Princess Szeanne Rose."

The servant ushers us into a reception chamber, which differs very little from my own, then disappears into a doorway on the right. A door opens and the princess joins us. "ArchMage Reba, I am pleased you could make it. If you will follow me, lunch will be served momentarily," She indicates the doorway she and the maid have used.

I remain silent, unsure how to reply. In a stately procession, I follow her from the reception chamber to commence my first royal luncheon. *Wow, now this is a bedroom.*

Princess Szeanne Rose's private quarters makes mine look stark by comparison. A plush teal rug covers the floor of the room. Creamy velvet curtains off the balcony, the three-inch border of lace giving it a feminine frill. Elegant chiffon surrounds the mattress in soft waves, enhancing the delicacy of the carved bedposts. The cushions are aqua with a brocade floral print and ivory silk ruffling the edges. An enormous vanity overpowers a corner of the room. A wealth of bejeweled holders litters the surface. A three-sided mirror is snuggled between four armoires. So this is what a feminine room is like. *I guess they were expecting a man.*

"Your Highness, I am honored by your invitation. Time did not allow us to get aquatinted yesterday. I am delighted with this opportunity," I begin our conversation as a chambermaid shuts the door, leaving William in the other room.

"It is I who am honored by your coming. The demands on your time are great. I wished, nonetheless, to convey sincere gratitude for your actions yesterday," She motions to the furniture in the center of the room.

Taking a chair, feeling more and more awkward, I dismiss the tribute, "Your Highness, gratitude is unnecessary. I played a small part in the healing of your brother. Anyone with the knowledge and the ability would have done the same."

"I am afraid you misunderstand that to which I refer. Do not mistake me: I am truly grateful for the aid you gave Prince Alexandros, my brother would have been lost without your intervention," Princess Szeanne Rose ignores my denial, "The entire kingdom is in your debt. I, though, am twice indebted. You have aided me in another, more personal situation. Not only did you restore my brother to me, but you also gave me the desire of my heart, one I had come to believed was unattainable."

When my brows crinkle in puzzlement, she takes a deep breath as if such openness exhausts her. With a scrutinizing gaze, as if trying to see into my very soul, she continues, "Since I was a girl I have taken care of every injured creature to cross my path. I persuaded MasterHealer Tupper to tutor me in the healing arts even though it was unheard of for a woman to take up the study. I have tended to all of my brothers cuts, scrapes, and bruises, all the while dreaming of a time when I could convince my father to let me practice my skills at the Healers Consortium."

Hope and excitement tumble inside her, quickly overcome by anger and frustration. Disappointment builds as she speaks. "Last spring, the dream I strived toward for years, was destroyed. When I mentioned my idea to Father in passing, he exploded. It seems His Majesty, while negotiating a treaty with Tuvarnava, has arranged for me to marry Prince Varpalava of Tuvarnava. His Majesty feels it would be inappropriate for the future bride to be dealing with peasants," I feel her mood shift, lifting from darkness into wonderment and awe as a light of comprehension dawns.

"Yesterday you gave me the opportunity for which I have waited a lifetime: even more than I dreamed possible. All the hours of study I believed had come to naught, you gave them value. I was able to use what lay inside me to save the lives of those who fought so bravely to defend my home. Even though it was only for a day. Milady ArchMage Reba, you made it possible for me to live out my dreams," Princess Szeanne Rose concludes with a dip of her head, "For that I am forever in your debt."

Blushing, I feel my cheeks heat as I perceive genuine gratitude. "Your Highness, I don't know what to say, except to remind you of this: I provided the means but you had the courage to grasp your aspirations in both hands, using the opportunity to accomplish a great good." *Should I take this opportunity? Dare I? Ah, what the hell,* "The world from which I come differs from yours. I am unaccustomed to your ways and some of my ways may seem strange or even offensive."

As I extend myself verbally, I expand my empathy to

its limits, "If I could ask but one thing in return it would be to have your aid on social matters," *Shock, curiosity, slight mistrust.*

"If you would be kind enough to guide me in the ways of your world I would be indebted to you," *disbelief, curiosity,* "I know I am different from the women of Cuthburan; I am even considered blunt and direct in my world. All I ask is that you let me know what actions of mine are different from yours and which might be taken with offence." *Sympathy, comprehension and admiration.*

"And, Your Highness, please call me Reba, just Reba. I was born without title or rank," I wait for her reply while servants carrying large trays file in from a door located in the far corner of the room.

"If we are going to be friends then you must call me Rose. I will tell you one thing. None of the women with whom I am acquainted would be so bold as to make the request you have just put forth," Her smile lets me know she is not offended, "I likewise would have never disclosed my aspirations to them. Yes, I believe we are predestined to be friends. And I am going to enjoy having someone around whom I do not have to try to interpret the meaning behind their words, although it may take some getting used to."

As we both chuckle she indicates the table. "I believe our lunch is ready."

Rose continues her lecture as she begins to serve herself, "In a way the fact that you are a novelty will be of great benefit. No one will expect you to adhere to our customs. As for your lacking a title, you should know, with your arrival here you have been bestowed an honorary title, second only to the King."

When she takes a small portion of all the vegetables on the table and a larger portion of each of the meats I follow her example. Delighted to see a fork positioned next to the knife by my plate, I dive in.

"So my behavior will be overlooked, at least at first.

That's a relief." I savor the delicate spices my sensitive pallet reveals. Each bite bursts with exotic flavor. "Tell me, was your father enraged by my granting you access to your Gift?"

"I do not believe he has discovered it… yet. I have never before defied my father's wishes and I am unsure how he will react," She sighs with resignation.

"You can tell him it was my command. My behavior seems to annoy him," I shrug, "I don't think one more thing is going to hurt."

"I appreciate the offer but I will only use that as a last resort. Times are changing. Father must accept the changes in me along with rest of our world," Rose's chin is set and her eyes blaze as she cuts into the slice of red meat on her plate with a viciousness that projects her mood.

"What about the treaty and your future husband. Will your interaction with the commoners create difficulties?" I probe.

The princess chuckles, serving herself a second helping of many of the dishes, "That is the truly ironic element of this entire predicament. I believe Father has merely used the upcoming nuptials as an excuse to deny me what I have studied so long to accomplish. Everything I have read about the Tuvarnavan culture indicates their ladies have much more freedom than we do. I suppose the elevated stature of their women stems from the fact that their deity is a goddess: many of their higher religious positions are held by women. I do not think anything I have done will offend my future husband or his people in the least."

"In that case, after we finish our meal I will be heading over to the infirmary. Jamison could use some help with the rest of the patients. Would you care to join me?"

A mischievous grin spreads across the face of my new friend, "I would love to."

All conversation ceases while we dig into our plates with a renewed sense of purpose. In less than a mark, I am ushered into the reception chamber while Rose changes into something more suitable for work.

I address the bowing page as I enter the room. "William, I don't believe I will need your services for the rest of the day. If you will report to my quarters for some final instructions at the mid-evening bells you may have the rest of the day to yourself."

"Thank you, milady. I will see you at the min-evening bells." His grin makes him look more like the little boy he really is than the professional he has been performing as. He bobs his head with childish enthusiasm before charging out the door.

Rose appears wearing a thick cloak with a fir-lined hood before I have had enough time to begin contemplating the spells I will need in the next few days. We start out the door and down the hall without any further discussion. The princess leads the way.

"I have to admit, I'm fascinated by arranged marriages." I bring to light the question lurking in the back of my head since she mentioned her impending nuptials. "Parents no longer take such measures with children in my homeland. If it isn't inappropriate for me to ask, what does Prince Varpalava look like? Or do you even know?"

"No, it is not inappropriate, although not many of my friends have been brave enough to question me so," Rose smiles warmly. "I have seen a portrait of him. He is average looking with brown hair and eyes. Not ugly, but I would not call him handsome either. He is eight years older than I and stands a few inches taller: I suspect this is part of the reason he is interested in taking me as a bride. With a simple enchantment, his sons will be much taller than his subjects, not to mention improving the countenance of the Tuvarnavan Royals," she replies without vanity.

Even a princess on this world is used as a brood-mare. *I'm glad our society has outgrown that. Or have they? Weren't they advertising supermodel eggs for sale on the*

Internet? I guess the desire is still the same, only the methods have changed.

I try to lighten the despondent mood shift, "Well, there are still a few months before you have to walk down that isle. I bet we can get a lot of mileage out of your newfound freedom in the meantime." The princess smiles, but still feels down.

Once again we travel through the servants' quarters, exiting the castle into an overcast day. My disposition darkens as my nostrils are flooded the cloying smell of char.

Holding open the door for Rose I sigh, struggling against a tide of guilt. I look for Jamison in the crammed foyer as we enter the infirmary. Tupper approaches as I fail to find my companion among the crowd.

"Your Highness, ArchMage," He bows to both of us before asking, "I assume you are here for the awakening?"

"Yes, among other things. If you will send someone for Jamison and arrange the new group of healers as we did before? I would like to be on my way as quickly as possible."

"Of course," The graying gentleman nods, going at once to fulfill my requests.

This time there are fourteen candidates who line up in three rows. The other fully gifted physicians stand against the walls intent on observing. The awakening goes smoothly, with just one candidate who possesses no affinity for healing. As I report this to Tupper and Jamison, the new initiates begin to disperse.

MasterHealer Laeknaen moves toward us, strides long and sure for an elder. The young woman accompanying him would be considered rather plain with straight black hair, ordinary features and a hawkish nose that is too large for the rest of her face, except for her brilliantly striking eyes. These astounding orbs are so dark they appear as black as her hair.

Bowing, Laeknaen makes the introduction,

"ArchMage Reba, I take great pleasure in presenting to you, my granddaughter, Alicia. She has had no formal training in the Healing Arts, and for this reason she could not be presented with the other healers. But she has inherited my love of medicine. Alicia has studied with me since she was a small girl. If a woman could be recognized among our ranks I would personally testify: she is approaching a Master level of training," Alicia blushes at her grandfather's praise.

I look to Tupper, "And will you confirm her knowledge and skills?" I continue as he assents again, "Then I see no reason why I can't perform another awakening, if it is her wish, and if you have no objections Tupper," As I receive his approval I add, "Tomorrow at mid-morning bells King Arturo and I will address the city to inform the populace of many changes. One of these deals with the place of women in times such as these."

When Alicia repeats the Healers Oath, I perceive compassion, sympathy, and an iron core of dedication resounding from within. With great pleasure I begin another Awakening.

"Magic is within you, I feel its power.
We need its force, this desperate hour.

It will respond to you after this touch.
Unless it will cause you harm or such."

With a tap on her forehead I send a tendril of magic into the center of her power. The boundary around the glowing sphere fades and the white mass pushes outward.

"Laeknaen, it looks like your granddaughter has the Gift as well as the knowledge and the desire you have given her," I grin at the girl's abashed look.

As he hugs his granddaughter he beams at me over her shoulder, his eyes filling with tears. I cough, clearing the unexpected obstacle in my throat, "Jamison, how did the medallion work? Were you back to full strength this morning?"

"That medallion was awesome!" His enthusiasm overflows, "It worked like a charm," He chuckles at the unintended pun. "Even though I didn't get a lot of even sleep, I am back to one hundred percent."

"I'm glad to hear it." I smile in return. A sigh escapes when my perfect memory brings my to-do list to the forefront of my mind, "I have about a million things begging for my personal attention. If you've got some other things gathered for me to spell I should get those taken care of and be on my way."

"Do I have some things? You're kidding, right? Have you taken a look?" As he gestures to the table in the back we move in that direction, "As soon as I mentioned you would be back to enchant anything fitting the description you gave me I lost over half my staff. Anyone who didn't have something suitable took off on a shopping spree."

The mentioned table holds a multitude of objects: one end is cluttered with them. There are several types of chains with assorted pendants, rings and even a bracelet all laid out in tidy rows like a table at a swap-meet.

"I should have guessed everyone would jump at a chance for a free enchantment." I sigh. "Jamison, can I barrow that medallion of yours?"

"Sure." he brings out the chain hidden beneath his shirt.

"Sight," I check to see if any of the items already hold a charm. Clasping the chain with the medallion dangling at the end if it, I contemplate the fastest way to enchant all of the items before me. It takes only moments to mentally change the lines of the much used duplication spell:

"Those with a Gift you restore their power,
Lives have been saved in this dark hour.
Yet more work is there still to be done,
Although helpful, you are only one.
Touching another no matter the substance;

They will share your properties in abundance."

Giving a push from within, I lower the chain taping one item after another with the medallion. Cascading waves of energy roves through my body. The power's caress of my inner being rejuvenates my humor. When the last item glows with a turquoise light, I close my eyes, sensing the power draw deep into the material. The objects are enchanted to the core.

"That should do it," I hand the borrowed necklace back to Jamison, "Will you be making it to breakfast in the morning?"

"I don't see why not. We have less than fifty patients left and half of those will be back to the barracks tonight," his eyebrows extend, "Your day is getting better?"

I shake my head, "What can I say, magic helps. Oh by the way, we've been invited to dine at the king's table tonight. We are to be presented to the nobility of Cuthburan," I smirk as Jamison's jaw drops, "Yah, you'd think with a war on they would have more important things to do than waist time with formalities."

My favorite companion shakes his head in agreement. "I suppose following tradition is comforting."

"But we are stuck putting up with the tedium of it all. I'll see you at evening bells for dinner." unable to resist a friendly jab, I add in our native tongue, "I'm sure the Princess will appreciate an escort," When Jamison's cheeks turn crimson I burst out in full-throated laughter. *Ah, it feels good to have something to laugh at.*

"Go ahead, laugh it up. A rip-tide is waiting for you at the next beach," Jamison elbows me, his voice filled with mock foreboding, "So dinner tonight it is," He adds in Cuthburish as Rose approaches.

"If you can't find the way, I'm sure Princess Szeanne Rose will be able to aid you," To my surprise, Rose blushes as she nods her approval. A silly smile plasters itself on my face, "Let me take care of those wineskins then I really have to be going."

"Will you be free for lunch again tomorrow?" Rose probes.

"Will mid-afternoon bells be too late?"

"Mid-afternoon bells it is," Rose flashes a grin of appreciation.

Chapter Twelve

Instead of taking the pathway through the barracks I cut behind the buildings, continuing on around to the side of the castle. Stretching out my legs for long quick strides, I block everything out, zooming in on the needed modifications to the force field. Completing the lines of poetry that will give the desired results, I refocus on the world around me. Glancing over my shoulder, I am surprised to see the military barracks are so far behind. I have nearly marched passed the palace. Off to my left are the practice grounds where rows of soldiers are going through drills with five-foot pikes.

Curious about the exercises, I put up the hood on my robe to conceal my telling locks. *As if this shining silver beacon of a robe isn't a dead giveaway.* Edging closer, I make my way to the far side of the exercise field.

Charles, Allinon, Szames, and ArmsMaster Stezen are engrossed in conversation, huddled-up like football before a kickoff. Allinon looks up, waiving me over to join the discussion.

"ArchMage Reba what a pleasant surprise," Szames' polite recognition is mannerly, but I still fail to sense anything from him, "I am almost through here, if you are ready to proceed with the modifications to the shield."

"As a matter of fact I am, but there's no rush." At lunch I was feeling like an Amazon; now, surrounded by these big guys I feel tiny. *I suppose Stezen must feel the same, the others tower over him by at least six inches!*

The ArmsMaster's broad shoulders and large hands speak of power but those he is with make him seem lacking in height. He is a nondescript man, average-featured with brown eyes and brown hair, some gray at the temples and scattered in the well-manicured beard.

"Stezen, if you will round up the candidates for the new training detail then notify the officers of the new program? If there are questions they will have to wait until after dinner. Further more I expect my orders to be followed to the letter. The consequences will be dire for those who choose to ignore these changes," he phrases his request with courtesy. The tone implies a direct order from someone who wears the mantle of command with ease.

"Your Highness, should I have the papers drawn up for your signature?" Stezen inquires.

"I am afraid there is no time for the usual procedures. You will deliver my orders verbatim, just as I have stated them. Please take note of anyone choosing not to follow them. Have a list on my desk by this evening." Stezen's brow draws down fractionally. I discern an internal upheaval that would register an eight on a Richter scale. But still he nods stoically, "I trust you to take care of any details I have forgotten as well. Please choose an assistant, two if necessary, to complete the tasks you have been assigned," Szames' dismissal declares finality on the subject. Stezen bobs his head again before gesturing for Charles and Allinon to precede him. Szames stares after the trio, unpretentious confidence chiseled into every line in of the princely face.

"Reba, if you are ready?" When I incline my head, he continues, "Shall I send for the horses to be readied?"

"Actually, I thought we would just fly?" I exude nonchalance.

"Why do I get the feeling you may mean that literally?" The arch of one brow hints of his astonishment.

"Of course," My lips curve innocently, as I try not to

laugh while Szames makes a physical effort to close his mouth. "If you're afraid of heights we can ride, but it will be much quicker and more magically economic to fly up to the center of the shield."

"I have no problem with heights, Milady Reba. Your suggestion sounds like an experience that will forever retain a height of a remembrance, which until moments ago, I believed could get no more memorable." Szames bobs his head as if succeeding victory to a challenger, "What must we do?"

"If you will take my hand while I set the spell, it will be just as before," Szames grasps my hand in his while I recall the flying spell I constructed the night before I was taken from my world. I close my eyes concentrating on joining our powers, drawing more from him than I have previously so that my power only acts to guide the flow of his force. Opening my eyes I begin the spell.

"Christopher Reeve starred on the big screen,
Battling with the bad guys who were so mean.
He was able to fly just like a bird and a plane,
He even flew with a woman named Lois Lane.

Like he did with her one night,
Take my hand, share in the flight.
By saying his name fly like him I can,
All I must say is the name 'Superman.'"

A tingling sensation spreads throughout my body. With the completion of the last line a heated rush akin to an orgasmic climax envelopes me from head to toe. A sigh escapes my parted lips as I relish every second of the magic's sensation.

"Szames, are you ready for your first flight?"

"I am," he rejoins.

"You must keep hold of my hand. That is what enables you to fly at my side," I give a final warning, "without the connection you will not stay aloft." Taking a deep breath

I whisper "Superman," in my native tongue.

I concentrate first on the ground, picturing myself easing away from it. Our feet leave the earth and we head straight up. Szames's grip on my hand tightens. *At least my fear of heights seems to have disappeared.*

I reposition my hand, threading our fingers while moving my elbow to the inside of his arm to secure our connection. I perceive a stab of desire from Szames so sudden that it causes me to lose my focus, momentarily pausing our ascent. Before I can pinpoint what exactly is causing the stimulation, the emotion disappears.

Unexpectedly, being this close to another man still makes me feel like a girl at her first dance. Blushing I change my focus to the world around me, using the castle as a direction-finder for our mobility. *It's not like I can let a prince fall to his death because I'm disconcerted by someone invading my physical space.* Even though the rationale makes me feel a little better I still can't help noticing the overwhelming size of his hand. *It is so large and so strong, and his arm - rock hard, solid, and secure.*

Like a meteor blazing to life in the middle of the clear blue surrounding us, I feel a surge of excitement from Szames that I am sure has nothing to do with flying. The sensation evaporates like fog on a sunny morning, as if it is a figment of my imagination.

Besides, just like every other jock, he is all brawn and no brains with an overactive libido, an expanded ego, and all the sensitivity and compassion of a rock. Definitely not anything I would be interested in even if I weren't already married!

The mid-afternoon bells toll in the distance as I hammer a steely determination of purpose into place. I take down my hood to improve the range of vision and whisper "sight." Looking at the shield above me, I get another surge of interest from my companion that is, like the last one, snuffed like a candle in the wind.

At least he's attempting to show some control. Or is

he just covering hidden desires along with the rest of his feelings? Confident in my flight, I increase our speed. Closing in on the thickening of the mage energy indicated in the center of the force-field where the magic merges, I smile in anticipation.

Keeping us in place takes a brief thought, before I turn to my companion, "Are you okay?" Szames gives me a little boy grin and my heart softens a little. "We need to bring our joined hands over our heads to reach the focus spot."

He follows my lead. Since we are standing perpendicular to the ground instead of flying in a more horizontal Superman fashion, our upraised hands make contact with the center of the force field. I focus on the lines of rhyme I explored earlier today. Drawing a capacious amount of energy from my partner I direct it to pool around our hands. Taking a deep breath I begin:

"You worked hard throughout the night,
Keeping out our enemy, stopping the fight.
But our foes are very determined to win,
They used objects to penetrate your skin.

Modifications are a definite must,
Let in nothing that you don't trust.
Only things of nature will come through you,
Sunlight, moonlight, wind, rain, and snow too.

Anything else an enemy will be,
Treated as such from you and me,
Other objects falling from the sky,
Will vaporize, before our eyes."

I grunt with the effort of pulling the final surge of power through the bond, keeping a firm visualization of what I expect from the magic. My back arches and I throw back my head as magic explodes inside me. I use every ounce of my will to keep us aloft while pleasure courses through the fiber of my being. The sapphire energy I have stored over our heads streaks outs across the shield, disappearing at the outer walls. As spots clear from my eyes I see the shield is a darker blue now, more of a true blue instead of the baby blue it was when we begun.

"Well, that should do it," The lazy smile falls from my lips as I recall the reason for this procedure, "But incase I missed anything, please, wake me tonight. As you see, it only takes a moment to adjust the shield."

"I will leave instructions, it shall be so," His tone serious, but the smile still hasn't left his face.

A breeze coming from the east brings with it a disturbing odor. Smoky, yes, but there is something odd about it. Realizing it must be the remnants the fire prompts me to speak, "Szames, do you know where the demons struck last night?"

"Over in the northeast quarter, I believe," he points straight ahead.

"Would you mind if we have a look?"

"Not at all," The massive, mountain of a man, shrugs.

I tilt us so we lie horizontal to the ground. In true Superman form with our hands still outstretched, I take us behind the castle and off to the right. Approaching the wall my nose wrinkles as the char smell intensifies. Szames points farther to the right and I veer in that direction.

This is the slum portion of town I noticed yesterday, the area containing the tannery. Still, the remains of the fire can be smelt over the rankness of the rest of the section. Our vantage point allows a clear view of last night's destruction.

One of the buildings is reduced to a pile of blackened rubble. A few tall support beams are all that remain: a testimony to a building that would have been one of the few two-story structures in this part of town. The other is, or was, a one-story building. A single wall is still mostly intact. I circle around, trying to picture what kind of people had made this building a home.

Noticing figures moving around inside the rubble, I choke out a question, "Were there any survivors?"

"I believe there are two children, a boy of eleven and a girl of nine," Szames musses.

"What will become of them? Do they have relatives to take them in?" *Two kids, now orphans because of my mistake.*

"I am unsure. If no relatives are found they will be made wards of the Church," His answer is as pensive as I feel.

I rotate back toward the castle, "If I knew which rooms are mine I would land us on the balcony," I ramble, still thinking of the kids.

"I believe I can point it out for you," Szames offers as we cross the inner battlement, flying over a tiny forest. *Is it an untamed park?* "It should be the only balcony facing the northeast on this wing of the castle," Szames indicates the entire side of the fortress located between two round towers.

The stones of the castle don't seem to be held together with mortar, there are no obvious seams. The blue-gray stone is a marbled weave. Seeing the palace from this distance I shake my head in disgust. Close up it is not as noticeable, but from a distance you can see they have been placed purposefully. All the veins run vertical and it's laid out to give the impression of flames.

A dejected sigh escapes before I can control the emotions threatening my control of the flight spell. The blue-gray and white blazing pattern is breathtaking, but it implies so very much. As Szames indicated, I possess the sole balcony on the entire wall.

"Reba, is there something you find amiss?" Szames ask anxiously.

"I'm just beginning to wonder how long you have been waiting for my arrival." I scowl. *And how much you expect out of me. And if you will let me go home?*

"Now that is a story which will be long in the telling, if it is done right," Szames evades, as I land us gracefully on the balcony outside my rooms.

His reluctance piques my interest. "It is a story I would love to hear," I flutter my eyes hoping to persuade him into revealing what I am desperate to know, "If you're free for dinner tomorrow maybe you will tell it to me then?"

"Dinner? With you?" His deep voice stumbles as he reaches to open the French doors, holding back the velvet curtain. "Tomorrow?"

Entering the room, the enormous plateau of the bed stands before me. The alarm in this voice causes me to panic, "I apologize if it was inappropriate of me to ask. I just thought…well you know…" with burning cheeks I stammer, "that exchange of information we talked about yesterday. I was thinking it would be a relaxing way to enjoy dinner…" I hasten around the offensive piece of furniture toward the door to the reception chamber.

Szames' long strides bring him to the door before me, despite my haste to be away from the all-too-obvious love nest. Opening the door for me, he begins awkwardly, "No - I mean yes, I would love to join you for dinner. And no it was not inappropriate."

Within minutes he recovers his egocentric secure confidence that he is supreme and everything is right in the universe, "You merely caught me off guard. It is not often that a woman I have just encountered has the boldness to extend such an offer."

"Tomorrow, here at my chambers, it is then." *If he thinks dinner implies more, maybe I will have a better chance at hearing that Prophecy. I'll live with the consequences.* "I was wondering if making another request would be out of line?" My lips curve as if nothing is amiss.

"Of course not. Whatever you wish, if it is within my means, I will supply it." He rejoins with a smile that seems sincere.

"You haven't even heard my request, yet." I coo, keeping up the charade. When he chuckles, I continue, "I don't know your customs, your ways, so please tell me if what I ask is… unacceptable."

My mood turns somber as I present the proposition I began forming on our flight back from the ruins of last night's fire, "I would like to have the surviving children assigned to my personal staff, if they wish, and if there are no surviving relatives. I feel responsible for what occurred. The creation of the shield antagonized the demons into attacking and my oversight allowed the demons to penetrate the defense."

"What you ask is not unacceptable, I will see to it that they are made aware of your offer. But Reba, trust me when I say you are being too hard on yourself. This is war: loss of life is part of any conflict," Szames laments, looking as if he wants to reach out, "even you cannot change that."

Staring into his blue eyes I feel compelled to expostulate my position, "Casualties may be part of battle, but I am going to see to it that we take as few of those losses as possible--that's my job. Last night, in my arrogance, I failed to take the proper precautions and it cost innocent people their lives. I am going to do my best to see to it that that never happen again." I blink, holding back tears.

I temper my emotional request with logical reasoning, "Aiding these children will not only help me to forgive myself for my mistakes, but if they are close by, they will serve to remind me to think things through more thoroughly."

"Your compassion shames me and my kingdom," Szames sighs, "Your work, your magic, has already saved so many lives, we accept the limited losses we take as a blessing. We have forgotten that, a fortnight ago, all would have lived to see the spring." For once I sense something from him: sadness and regret.

"Mine is a fresh perspective. Having no previous expectations it is no wonder my tolerance for death is much lower. But speaking of perspective, I'm curious."

With deftness I didn't know I possess, I maneuver the conversation. "Have you started to change the sleeping schedule of the men to get them used to being awake all night?"

"As a matter of fact we have. Charles suggested it at the War Council. It was decided a gradual change would be best. Tonight the training will continue until the midnight bells and reveille will sound at mid-morning," Szames's mood lifts with the proactive topic.

"Then we'd better plan on mid-evening bells for dinner, if that will suit your schedule." As Szames agrees the door to the bedroom opens.

"Milady ArchMage Reba, will you need dinner served?" Crystal curtseys.

"I will join the royal family for dinner to be presented to the nobles at evening bells." I reply by rote, my mind still worrying over my dinner-date with the prince.

"Milady, if you like I can assist you in preparing for it," she has my full attention as she adds; "We will need to hurry, m'lady, if we are going to keep you from arriving unfashionably late."

"I can escort you if you wish?" Szames offers.

"Yes, I would appreciate that, thank you." I smile over my shoulder, heading toward the door Crystal holds open.

Chapter Thirteen

I undress, thoughts racing inside my head, while Crystal rushes to the armoire. As my brain centers on the proposal I made for the orphans, the world flashes white. Standing before me are two bedraggled children. First the young boy bows then the dark haired girl follows suit in an awkward sort of curtsy. Before I can blink, a brilliant light tinges the world once more.

"Whoa…" I shake my head, attempting to jar some logic into it.

"Milady?" Crystal inquires from my elbow.

"Crystal, at what age does training for chambermaids begin?"

"I came of my own accord at the age of fourteen, but that is considered late to begin training. Most start instruction around the age of ten, milady." She approaches carrying a red and gold outfit.

"Would it be possible for you to take someone under your tutelage? Like an apprentice?" Loosing my patients with small talk, I get right to the point as she nods affirmative to my question, "There are two survivors from the fires night last. One is a young girl. I have requested she be placed on my staff, if she wishes. When she shows up tomorrow, I'd like you to take her under your wing." *Lord knows she is going to need someone to help her adjust!*

"Of course, milady. I will personally take charge of

her training. But if I may ask, why have her assigned here? Did you know her parents?" Confusion overwhelms her as she tries to follow my logic.

"I arrived yesterday and I cast a spell that set off the demons like a hot rock on an anthill. They found a way around the defense I put into place, taking the lives of innocent people, leaving two kids orphaned," Pausing as she helps me into the blouse I decide to probe to see if she still retains any depth of emotion or if her "special services" have hardened her heart beyond reach.

"Overnight this child has been made homeless, motherless and fatherless. Not to mention scared half out of her wits. Right now she needs more than just a roof over her head; she needs someone to help her find a new way in life. I don't think this falls within your job description: I ask it as more of a personal favor."

"You want me to supply her with a big sister?" Crystal summarizes what I have implied, "For me to be a big sister to her?"

I nod, yes, as she fastens a belt around my waist, not daring to speak, afraid it might ruin the way her emotions are trending.

"When I was younger, before I left home, I often wished for a sister" stretching out my senses I discern her response: *duty... curiosity... sympathy... compassion...* "Yes, I will do it. If she comes here I will take her as my sister from that day forward."

"Thank you, Crystal. I owe you one. If you ever need anything, just ask," My shoulders feel as if a condor has just found a new place to nest.

The maid directs me over to the standing mirror, now that I am clothed in evening attire. *I'm not sure I want to see this, two shades of red combined with a gold belt?*

The ensemble comes together better than anticipated. The cuffs and collar of the scarlet blouse are darker than the rest of the shirt, the same shade as the burgundy slacks. Someone has even taken the time to embroider a golden flame on the each of the four tips of the collar, which is accented by the gold belt at the waist.

The outfit gives me a tall, thin, athletic look. The curves of the belt highlight my bust and the cut of the blouse makes my feminine figure apparent. Even though this look can't be called sexy by any stretch of the imagination at least I look a little more like a woman and a little less like a ninja.

"Thank you Crystal. I would've never picked this to wear." I turn away from the mirror. "Well, I don't want to keep the nobles waiting."

"Not quite yet, milady," Crystal replies, hastening from the vanity at a quick pace. Opening a small jar, she touches the contents with her fingertip as she halts before me. She applies the contents to my lips and administers a pick-like comb to my hair, "There, now you're ready."

Turning back to the mirror I am shocked at what a little thing like lip-gloss and a well placed stroke of a comb can accomplish, "Crystal, I don't know what I would do without you," I give a grateful as she ushers me to the door to the reception chamber.

I cross my ankles, dipping at the waist in my first curtsey as the prince comes to his feet. Looking up, my gaze is captured by an adoring pair of sapphire eyes. Blushing, I give a curt not to cover my embarrassment, "Your Highness, if you're ready?"

"Milady," is the only word my escort utters as he manipulates the door for me.

The prince extends his arm in the age-old courtly gesture. The mannerism seems out of place on a man dressed in chain mail with unruly flaxen hair. With my hand on the top of his, he steers us down the hallway. We pass the hall leading to the MasterChief's private kitchen. The walkway is well lit and the rooms are wide-spaced, but not as far apart as the ones around my chambers. None have the double doors gracing my entryway. The walkway ends in a right-hand turn.

The evening bells toll in the distance as we come to a grand staircase. The stairs are at least twenty feet across and two stories high. My hand remains captured by my hunky escort as we walk down the plush rug lining the center. *I feel more out of place than I have since my arrival. Being a battle mage feels more natural than not the royalty they are treating me as. I'm just a common housewife.*

The floor below is tiled in blue-gray and white marble. The exact color of the granite depends on how much dark gray, blue, or white the piece of rock contains. I find it awe-inspiring, even though I discern no pattern to the beautiful mosaic, for no two pieces of tile are the same size or color.

Glimpsing the far wall, my mouth falls open as perception of the design rises from my worry-filled mind. *A forest!* Not the trees themselves, more like the shadows of trees or the spaces in between the trees of a forest.

Looking back to the floor, taking in the entire area, the tiles come alive. The individual pieces are placed together, depicting a flowering meadow. Budding flora of all manor, shapes, and sizes are strewn together, the edges of one overlapping to form the borders of another.

"Szames, it's beautiful. Absolutely beautiful! The craftsman was a genius," My prior discomfort is forgotten, "Tell me, is it the same person who created my chambers?"

"Yes, as a matter of fact it was. The same man created not only this castle, but the entire city as well. His name was Rikard of Kempmore."

We enter the castle's foyer. A set of massive doors, large enough to emit a freight train, lies at each end. The doorway on the right has a hallway to each side. The other entryway opens into the courtyard. The prince leads us toward the farthest hallway.

"His story is a fascinating one. Sir Rikard was a Master Stonemason by twenty. He was then discovered to have the gift of magic. In his third year of training he had a vision from Andskoti. Once a priest sanctified Rik's testimony, King Sheldon did not hesitate. He authorized everything needed to fulfill the prophecy."

"The Masonry Wizard led the workers straight to this hilltop and set them to digging the sewer system. He then took another group of recruits to the Northern Reaches. They were unmapped at that time, so it was considered a risky venture. Unerringly he led them to the largest deposit of marble ever discovered. Rik used his magic to cut each piece of stone himself while the workers began the transportation. He then used his powers to place each piece, reforming the marble into a solid block. Though he spent his entire life devoted to the project, it is said he passed on sill talking of its completion. Finished or not, his work is known as the crowning jewel of Cuthburan. This city and Castle Eldrich are his legacy."

Szames concludes his story as we approach a pair of doormen stationed beside an entryway. As the prince nods, they sweep inside, holding the twelve-foot doors open.

"The ArchMage Reba and Prince Szames of Cuthburan, General of the Forces of Cuthburan," One of the men intones.

The room echo's with the rustle of clothing and shuffling of feet as hundreds of people come to their feet. Szames looks down at me, a question in his eyes. With a dip of my chin I signal my readiness while I work on convincing my knees to stop quaking.

With my head held high I concentrate on placing one foot in front of another and not on top of each other. Ignoring the deep silence followed by a gigantic intake of breath, I try to quiet the thrumming of my nerves, while Szames steers us down the middle of the room then along the front of the head table. When we come around the end of the twenty-foot dinner tableau and sweep back toward the center, I steal a glance past my escort to the crowd of nobles.

Two rows of eight tables are lined up at a ninety-degree angle to the massive table where the royal family sit facing their subjects. Each table is a little larger than the one in my dining room, seating close to sixteen people.

That means that there are more than two hundred and fifty people out there. The realization nearly causes me to stumble. *Calm down, don't think about them. They are just rich and snobby anyway, right? And you can snob with the best of them.*

Szames makes a quick turn, stopping before an empty chair on King Arturo's left. With an encouraging smile, he relinquishes his hold on my arm.

King Arturo's voice booms out capturing the attention of everyone present, "Many of you have heard the rumors of my son's mortal wound and his miraculous recovery. All of you have seen the fire bloom in the sky as the demons besieging our city meet the magic put in place only yesterday. The time has come for you to meet the one who brings such miracles and many more changes in the days to come," the room remains silent as he pauses, masterfully manipulating the moment.

"ArchMage Reba and the Crusaders of the Light, I present to you, the Nobility of Cuthburan," Every man in the room bows and the women curtsey as the king again pauses, this time for shuffling feet to silence.

"Let there no longer remain any doubt: this is the time of the Prophecy. We, the sovereignty of the Kingdom, proclaim it to be so. Embrace what is asked of you, as it is written: change is our salvation in the days to come," King Arturo finishes his speech in a triumphant shout, "Tonight we dine with the Flame-Haired One!" In unison every person in the room pounds a glass on the table twice in salute.

Servants file into the dining room carrying ponderous trays. I turn to my right as a refined voice remarks, "Milady, I am delighted to see my angel has not returned from whence she came. I am in your debt and at your service."

He continues sketching an elegant bow, "Please allow me to introduce myself, I am Prince Alexandros, and you, of course must be the infamously beautiful ArchMage

Reba," taking hold of my chair, he maneuvers it out for me.

Frozen like a deer seeing headlights, I gaze into a pair of piercing emerald eyes surrounded by dark thick lashes, and framed by picturesque black eyebrows.

"Your Highness," is all I manage, around the frog that has taken up residence in my throat. My knees weaken. I barely manage a curtsey before collapsing into the waiting chair.

I was starving on the way here, now my stomach is tied in knots! How am I ever going to manage to eat in front of all of these people, not to mention sitting next to him! Just look at him - he's tall dark and handsome: the man of my dreams. Refined, chiseled features, arched brows, not to mention perfect skin surrounded by elegant ebony hair and a smile that just makes me want to melt.

A servant appears, displaying a tray of mushrooms stuffed with an unidentifiable mixture. I nod yes, convinced I won't be able to eat a bite. *Come on, get a grip. You are married, remember? And those are just people; people you will never see again after you leave this place in a couple of weeks.* Keeping that thought firmly in mind I look out at the nobles once more whispering, "sight."

One out of twenty has magical affinity in their auras and not many have a healing pattern, although most have a trace of green in their coloring. Whispering "sight" once more, with little more self-confidence and a lot more self-control I take another look at the nobles while uniformed servants continue bringing trays with a variety of appetizers.

Noblemen wear thick velvet material of varying colors and styles, everything from the Musketeer's tunic over a white shirt to English coats with puffy shirts and trousers. The ladies' styles are quite conservative: "southern bell" dresses, some are low cut and others have high lacey collars. All are floor length with voluminous skirts.

Hairstyles vary too. Some of the men have short hair, even as short as a buzz, while others have long hair; flowing free or neatly tied into ponytails. The noble wives have long tresses: either piled on top of their heads or pulled back, spilling down their backs. Even with all their differences, one thing is the universal throughout, the hair color varies from red, black, brown, blond, and gray, but each shade is the same precise hue. There are no sandy-brown, auburn, or sun-bleached heads.

With the more scientific train of thought, I find myself famished once again. Looking down at my plate I realize I have indicated wanting several items. *I hope that's not caviar - ugh, fish eggs.*

Placing the napkin on my lap, I glance at the plate next to mine get a clue how to eat the strange assortment of items I have selected. My brow crinkles in concern when I see King Arturo has yet to take a bite.

They aren't all waiting on me? Well, Rose did say my rank was next to the king's, so maybe it is above the Queen's who should, according to protocol, begin this mess.

Grasping the cracker with purple balls on top with two fingers, figuring it is safe to pop the entire thing into my mouth, I begin my first formal dinner. Not as bad as I imagined. Salty and fishy tasting, but not overpowering. *Is it caviar?*

Quiet sounds of the populace eating arise, along with hushed whispers. I finesse my way through the appetizer course making a point to not look at Prince Alexandros, unsure how it will affect my stomach, unwilling to chance upsetting it again.

A brownish vegetable-bean soup is served next, and before I know it waiters appear with the main course. This time an entire plate is place before me. Shaved meat rolled and sprinkled with a white cream sauce occupies the center of the large platter. Orange vegetables, a little lighter than yams but not as dark as carrots, litter the edge. Tiny onions are intermittent between potatoes placed on top of flat round items reminding me of pickle slices.

Panicking at the fancy display before me, unsure where to even begin, I glance to my left. When my mahogany eyes meet with a pair of emerald ones, I see no choice but to engage in conversation or appear rude. "Your Highness, you are looking well. I trust your recovery is coming along swiftly?"

"Yes, quite, and from a wound that should have taken my life," he pauses to slice a piece of meat, and spearing a potato, he proceeds, "Since I first opened my eyes, I have been overwhelmed with news of your marvelous works. I was beginning to think I was to share an entire dinner with the infamous ArchMage without hearing her relate even one tale."

With a smile and a twinkle in his eyes he teases, "If this remarkable meal is any indication, then the stories must be true, for you are not only the most enchanting dinner companion I have ever encountered, but by far the most intriguing."

My cheeks flush but I keep my wits in a stranglehold, determined not to run from this battle. Taking a bite gives me time to phrase a rejoinder, "Tales of my workings? Your Highness, I beg you, believe only half of what you hear. Stories have a way of growing larger with each repeating. If I have been remiss in my social obligations, I apologize. I will gladly set you straight on any of the rumors captivating your curiosity." *I hate gossip, especially when it's about me!*

"Let me see, I have heard a tale of your battling ten demons without taking a scratch? It has been said you are seen soaring over the city like a bird? And of course there is the one about bringing back my soul from edge of the heavens, making me forever a slave to your will?" I nearly choke on the food in my mouth when he adds, with an arch of an eyebrow and a half smile, "Not that the last would be all bad, I am sure."

Taking a sip of wine I answer the easiest one first, "Your Highness, let me set your mind at ease. It was your brother and I who flew over the city to make some adjustments to the shield. And it was a mere five demons that attacked a group of us: Prince Szames, Lieutenant Craig, Merithin, and I along with my two companions, Charles and Jerik. I hardly battled a hoard of demons by myself: And I am sorry to say Charles took a shoulder wound in the skirmish. As for the last..." I take another bite contemplating my repartee. "Many people aided in your recovery, including your family. The part I played was miniscule," I make false thrust to engage his wit, "If I was to bewitch you, I assure you, you would be the first to know."

"Oh but you have, My Lady, you have," Prince Alexandros replies without a trace of humor.

Gazing into his eyes I feel my cheeks heat once more, along with the rest of my body, while butterflies set flight in my stomach for the second time in as many days. *Traitor! Not even separated from Tony two days and already you let a man seduce you. And believe me, if you were alone with him you'd be as good as bedded!*

"Ding, ding, ding." A utensil is applied to the glass on my right, breaking the hypnotic potency of the Prince's eyes. I take my glass in hand, awaiting the pledge with the rest of the guests.

"A toast," King Arturo booms into the immediate silence, "To the ArchMage Reba and the Crusaders of the Light. May they guide us well through this time of darkness."

"To the ArchMage and the Crusaders of the Light," the entire room replies.

I finish the contents of my glass then focus my attention on the plate in front of me, trying to forget the presence on my left. No longer feeling hungry, I taste none of the food as I clear my plate.

Guests begin to leave as I maneuver my way through the desert course. I turn to my host making a calculated retreat, "Your Majesty, thank you for the honor of dining at your table this evening. If courtesy allows, I have much to accomplish before I retire."

"Your presence has honored us all, Milady ArchMage Reba." King Arturo's lips curve, but the gesture doesn't reach his eyes or his heart, "In these times, duty calls to us all. Please, do not feel obligated to stay a moment longer."

Turning to my other dinner companion I continue with the necessary social pleasantries, "Prince Alexandros, it has been a pleasure, but I have much yet to accomplish this evening. If you will excuse me."

"Of course," he replies, jumping to help me with my chair, "Shall I escort you to your chambers?"

Oh God, no! "Thank you, but no. I believe I can find my own way. The walk will give me a chance to put my thoughts and my duties in order."

"Until tomorrow, milady," swifter than thought, Prince Alexandros captures my hand, ushering it to his mouth.

With the caress of his lips, my pulse races and my legs turn to jelly. I lock my knees in order to remain upright, giving a brief dip of my head as he releases my hand.

I slather my muscles with self-control to keep from either running from the room or straight into his arms. Stretching out my legs for long quick strides as I retrace the route Szames used when depositing me to my seat. I am relatively sure of the way back to my rooms as I cross the foyer outside the dining room.

"Hey, where's the fire?" The English idiom from behind cuts through the swirling fog of my scrambling thoughts. I slow down, giving Jamison a chance to catch up.

"That was some dinner, wasn't?" I babble trying to calm my frazzled nerves.

"You said it. I can't believe they sat you right next to the king, but then again, after what I heard from Rose, it kind of fits." My eyes bore into him, waiting for him to continue. "Let's wait until we meet at breakfast in your chambers to go into that." his clumsy implication for the necessary security is clear as he glances around, "I noticed you acquired a royal escort of your own?" his voice takes on a suggestive note.

"You mean Szames?" Jamison tries to leer, looking more curious than sensual. I chuckle, "I assure you, our association is strictly business, at least as far as I am concerned. We just happened to get done modifying the shield about dinner time."

Smiling, Jamison mutters, "Sure... right."

Holding out my left hand, I display the diamond straddled by two emeralds on my ring finger, "I'm married, remember? You even saw a wedding photo this morning."

"If you say so," He shrugs, a ghost of a smile still playing about his lips.

Like I don't have enough to worry about with the attention of one prince. I'm just glad Szames seems content with a friendship. Then again I don't have the kind of attraction for him that I do for Alexandros. Dark, smart, sophisticated, that's my weakness. I never went for those blonde hunky types.

I change the subject, "So are you packing it in for the night?"

"Yea, I'm bushed. I could use a full night's rest. How about you?" I sense a weary echo in him as we begin to climb the stairs, "Boy what I wouldn't give for an elevator."

"Already missing the modern world?" I continue as he shrugs. "Sleep would be nice, but I have way too much on my plate. I'll be lucky to make it to bed by dawn. Thank goodness my recuperative mage abilities are functioning. With just a few hours rest I woke invigorated this morning," The list of things needing my attention flashes through my mind, "At least I hope they are working."

"I'm beginning to wish I had developed my character a little better. So much is needed, even though they have so much already," he pauses as we reach the top of the staircase. Turning to look back the way we came, his gaze travels up to the entry doors, over the ceiling, and back along the floor.

His voice turns hoarse with emotion, "Isn't this place amazing. Marble floors, vaulted ceiling, and beautiful alabaster wood everywhere you look."

"You said it. I never expected people of this age to have so much refinement." I mumble wondering if they have artists. *Hey, that gives me an idea. Maybe I can use Prince Alexandros's attention to my advantage after all.*

We continue in a companionable silence, each lost in out own thoughts. Jamison retires to his room as we reach the turn toward my chambers.

Even without numbers or markings it is pretty easy to find my way. The solitary set of double doors in this hallway belongs to my suite of rooms. In the reception chamber a fire blazes. The page stands waiting for my instructions.

"William." I nod in acknowledgement, moving toward the bureau.

Seeing a stack of correspondences resting on top of the desk I change what I intended to say, "If you will have a seat, I will be with you in a moment."

Taking the stack with me to the center of the desk I begin skimming my way through letters containing invitations to do this or that with people I have yet to met.

I don't have time to answer all these, even if I work through the night. Well, I'd say it's time for a little magic. Let me see, if I use the ink, the paper, and the wax it should conserve energy. Something like this should due the trick:

"Time is precious and much would be wasted
To answer you politely 'no' signed and dated.
So for each letter here a reply will be made,
Sealed to be delivered by my waiting page."

I draw in a deep breath as the exhilaration of power oozing from my body washes through me. Thickening blue fog envelopes the stack of paper and other utensils on the desk until the items are hidden from view. As the mist dissipates a new stack of correspondences lays next to the pile of opened letters.

"William I am going to need more parchment. Can you fetch some?" I ask my wide-eyed page.

"Yes, Milady ArchMage. I can get some from the library," he is a little less composed than before.

As the boy leaves, the door to the bedroom opens and Crystal appears, carrying a miniature lamp with a candle for fuel instead of oil, "Milady, I have a question concerning the pot chamber."

"Oh, I completely forgot about that. The new device is a "toilet." It is used to… take care of bodily functions," I phrase its purpose delicately.

"That much I surmised, milady, but I could not figure out how to remove the 'toy-let' for cleaning," her temper sparks, "And if you still wish me to be open with you - well, milady, if you warn me of future engagements I might be of more assistance in preparing you for them, that is, after all, my duty."

Noting her fear, probably that a disheveled appearance on my part will reflect badly upon her, I lower my eyes in acknowledgement, "Point taken, Crystal. I apologize for the lapse. I will try to keep you informed in the future."

I continue, keeping my promise, "Tomorrow I will be addressing the commoners, I have a luncheon with the princess, a meeting with King Arturo and the military officers, and Prince Szames will be joining me here for dinner," Crystal bobs her head in approval as I relate tomorrow's itinerary, "As for the toilet, besides a wipe down on the outside surface, it won't need cleaning," *If she didn't know how to clean it, I wonder if she has figured out how to use it?*

"Any of the staff may use the toilet, you simply sit down, placing your bottom over the open hole. It is constructed to hold any amount of weight, so don't be afraid to relax. After you have finished, the small roll of white stuff is made to unwind, just pull on the end. Clean yourself with it. Place the soiled tissue in the water, either through your legs or behind you. When you stand, magic will take care of the contents."

"All that, just to replace a chamber pot? This world of yours must be rich in sorcerers to afford such things," she shakes her head but adds with a smile, "Not having a pot to deal with is an unheard of luxury! Milady, will you be bathing at first light again?"

"Yes, thank you." I answer, "I have much to do, but I will not require any further assistance. Feel free to call it a night."

"Thank you, milady. If you require anything, please knock on my door, it is next to the bathing room," I feel her gratitude and amazement as she takes me up on my offer. "Shall I leave this light for you, milady?"

"No thank you," I set my mind on the work ahead, dismissing her from my thoughts.

The pad of paper and pen I conjured yesterday is in one of the desk drawers. I bring out the modern materials to begin composing a speech. By the time William arrives with the parchment I have used all but a few pages of the yellow notepad: I flex aching fingers. *That's more writing than I've done since high school.* Massaging my right hand I sit back with a satisfied smile. *Next time I'll magic up a computer or a typewriter at least.*

Beaming at the stack of papers I chuckle. *One speech, more shield modifications, two new personal defense spells, an enchantment for the material and my first effort at a trans-dimensional portal. Not too bad for a night's work.*

"William, I have a short list of duties for you tomorrow. These letters need to be delivered and I will need a guide from here to Princess Szeanne Rose's chambers a mark before mid-afternoon bells," He nods looking very proper and attentive even though the midnight bells have just rung, "And seeing how you seem to be such an efficient and knowledgeable page, I thought you could handle some additional responsibilities." When William smirks, I stretch out my empathy to gauge his reaction.

"One of the survivors of last night's attack was a boy who will be assigned to me," *Shock, fear,* "Your workload is light, so I assume you will have plenty of time to get him through the basics before your other duties pick up," *Interest, curiosity, slight fear.* "This is a large responsibility. Even though you are young I believe you are ready for this assignment," *Pride, interest, curiosity, slight fear.*

"He is from town and has most likely never even been in the castle. Maybe never even met a noble. He is going to need your guidance and instruction if he is to be a good page," *Pride bordering on arrogance and still a slight fear. Let's see if he has any sympathy.*

"You must remember he has lost everything - even his parents, all in a single night," *Arrogance, slight sympathy and fear,* "I am putting my trust in you to show him compassion," *Confidence, arrogance, sympathy and slight fear. Where is that fear coming from? I can't seem to reassure him.*

"I expect you to keep in mind that although your apprentice my not be someone of equal lineage, he is a person, just as you or I. If you are not up to the task, please let me know and I will find another option," *Confidence, Pride, but still with a bit of fear lurking in the background.*

"Milady, it would be my pleasure to accept any apprentice you assign. I will do my best to see he feels this is his new home and to disregard his prior stature," William states with manly sophistication well beyond his age. I perceive honesty, pride and a small amount of fear. *That will have to do: I'm beat. I will have to try and puzzle out what it is he fears some other time.*

"Good, William I put my trust in you. It is late, you should turn in. I will be changing my sleeping pattern to prepare for the upcoming battle. I might need your services late into the night. Take any opportunity you have to get some extra sleep," William gives a nod in recognition of orders received and bows before departing.

Tony, I wish you were here: you are so much better with people than I am. Somehow, I think a transdimensional phone call will take more energy than I can spare.

Hmm, I'm going to try out that new spell tomorrow, I could send a short note. Taking out the inkwell and parchment, I compose my thoughts. Quill in hand I begin:

> Tony,
> By now you are probably worried about me. I want you to know that I'm fine, besides missing you terribly. I guess I should start from the beginning. As to where I am, well, it all started with that flash of light in the foyer of the hotel

Yawning, I pause. *At this rate, chronicling my time here will take forever.*

"A letter home is what I've started,
About my trip since I departed.
The hour is late, I'm tired too,
So I leave the telling up to you.
Make it personal, as I would have done,
If I had written more than just line one."

Light surrounds the ink and parchment. In a matter of seconds I have a stack of written work and an empty bottle. I take a closer look at the letter where I left off.

> Color seeps back into my vision, inky blotches fade from the world around me. Amid the cloudy haze in my mind a slow but startling realization of my surroundings penetrates my thoughts.

Yes, that sounds about right. Now I'd better sign it before I forget.

Turning to the last page I notice it illustrates my time here right up to our first battle. I add a few lines letting him know that I am okay then sign it with my normal "Love, Hugs, and Kisses," securing the folded pages with a ribbon and wax.

Another extended yawn overpowers me. Knowing I have another long day ahead I stumble toward the bedroom. I scan the dim interior noticing my staff next to the bed. *I still have quite a bit of energy left.* Another yawn pries my jaw apart, *magical energy that is.* Taking the dark, smooth pole in both hands I begin a basic enchantment.

"The day is over, finished and done,
I give you energy till need comes.
Any who wield you without consent,
Give them a jolt until they repent."

Aqua radiance surrounds my staff, sinking into the wood. The pins and needles in my hands as the power flees from my aura nearly takes my focus from the staff. Whispering, "sight," I see the rod now has blue luminescence.

Leaning the weapon on the wall beside the bed I slip on the awaiting nightgown. Following the same routine as the night before, I intone my nightly grace, which acts as restorative spell as I sink into the luxurious feather bed.

I drift into sleep, thinking of the warm body that is supposed to be located next to me. As unconsciousness overcomes me, I lay dreaming of my husband's embrace. His shape begins to shift. The features become refined, the complexion turns light, the hazel eyes change to a more brilliant green, and the shoulders broaden. The jet-black hair remains the same, but it lengthens bringing a hint of wave to the silky locks.

Chapter Fourteen

"ArchMage Reba... m'lady? It is a mark after morning bells," Crystal mumbles beside me.

Yawing, I rub the sleep from my eyes, "Is the bath ready?"

"Yes, milady," she holds a thick cotton robe open for me.

"Then let's make it quick. I've got a long day ahead," Oh yeah, she doesn't know yet. As we head into the bathroom I clue her in to the upcoming alterations in my sleeping pattern. Dashing into the pot chamber, I take care of my morning business. When I return, Crystal helps me disrobe. It takes considerable effort not to let the fact that she was willing to sleep with me totally creep me out.

"We will need to change the bath to noon bells tomorrow. I am a light sleeper so I would appreciate it if you can keep all of the staff out of my chamber until then," I ease down into the warm water, letting it cover me to my neck.

Crystal motions to the extra bucket and I nod 'yes' to a warmer bath. *Let's see... if I concentrate I should be able deactivate my temperature shield. Ah...much better.*

The hot water sooths my muscles, but my imagination keeps me paranoid about being naked and alone in a room with someone who might be bisexual. I extend my empathy trying to reassure myself. *Placid with a slight curiosity and underlying boredom. Nothing to worry about there.* Still I find relaxation just out of my reach as the blond chambermaid hands me a soapy sponge. *Maybe if I get to know her better...*

"So... you started here at the castle when you were fourteen, of your own accord. You have already worked your way up to the top of the staff. That is quite an accomplishment," She mumbles acquiescence to my recollection as she takes down my hair and begins combing out the tangles.

"What made you decide to seek work here? Was it due to some family mishap?" As I make the tactful inquiry I sense her trepidation.

"I don't mean this as an interrogation, I'm just curiosity. I'll tell you what, we will have the same arrangement Prince Szames and I share: an information exchange," Surprise overwhelms her, so I expound.

"I want to get to know this world better. I don't think we have servants who function the same way as the ones here, but before I can be sure I need to know more about what kind of system runs this kingdom. I realize you might be similarly curious about my world. An exchange will only be fair. I will answer one of your questions for one of mine," after the shock wears off I perceive her relaxing attitude.

"M' Lady, I thank you for your kind offer. Never have I dreamed I would be treated with the same consideration as royalty. You are truly from a different world," Crystal clears her throat as she pours water over my head. The remaining tension disappears as she washes my hair, massaging the scalp. I lean back, the tension sloughs off my shoulders.

"My parents own a small inn located on the western edge of the tanning district. It isn't impressive, but they keep it clean. Mom is known throughout the NorthEastern Quadrant for her fine meals. One night just before my fourteenth birthday I overheard my parents talking about a betrothal offer from an established merchant who was a regular guest at our place," Her story is interrupted she rinses out the shampoo. She hands me a towel then waits with a bathrobe.

"His name was Rhine, he was old, fat, bald, and even shorter than I am. He offered more gold than we saw in a year and valuable connections, which could lead to long list of regular customers. The price to riches was merely the hand of their daughter," She is calm, but I feel the hurt behind her statement.

"I realize now that they meant well, but I was appalled at the idea of being married to the man and terrified of the mysteries of the bed chamber." After I use the odd-shaped wooden toothbrush she directs me into the next room.

I sit at the vanity table and state the obvious, "So you ran away from an arranged marriage. But why did you choose this line of work? Besides, don't girls usually get an early introduction to romance? You know, 'a roll in the hay' so to speak?"

Crystal chuckles as she answers the direct questions, "Yes, most girls my age would have had many 'a roll in the hay,' as you say it. However, most girls do not have two older, very protective, brothers. My brothers kept boys at a distance and fed me horror stories of what takes place between men and women once love has dawned."

"Oh I see…" I mumble, "And you were prevented from your first roll in the hay, or love's dawning."

Crystal's brow furrow's and I sense trepidation which causes a hesitation, "Please be open with me, Crystal…"

"Milady, forgive me for the misunderstand-ing," She continues apologizing as if she has been the one to make a mistake, "Here, in Cuthburan, it is believed love is like the beginning of a new day. Often people refer the beginnings of a romantic tryst as 'love's dawning.' When lovers consum-mate a relationship, physically, it is 'love's day' and when a couple decides to part, it is 'love's sunset.'"

"Oh, I see." I smile encouragingly, "Thank you your enlightening explanation."

Crystal dips her head, in acknowledgement of the praise, then continues on her original topic, "I decided to face my fears before I was resigned to life with a man I found repulsive. Thaddeus was the son of the cobbler. He was quite handsome. Love dawning had begun when my brothers were preoccupied elsewhere. We even managed to be alone a couple of times: it was from him that I received my first kiss."

"I asked for him to meet one evening at midnight bells in the hayloft and I had my very first time with a man," Crystal smiles at the fond memories as she turns me around, "I guess a roll in the hay is an appropriate term for the adventure." She applies lip-gloss then pulls a few strands from the enchanted clip she has expertly placed.

"It wasn't at all like my brothers told it. Maybe it smarted a bit, but it was… fun: nothing at all to be afraid of. I spent several days thinking about my options. I heard stories about the castle chambermaids. One of them left the service of the king. She opened her own brothel with the money she saved by providing 'extra services' when they were needed. She hadn't even seen her twenty-fifth year and she had her own business! Service to the king could be no worse than fulfilling my wifely duties to a fat pig."

Stepping back for a better look she adds with a nonchalant shrug. "I knew a lot of men found me attractive. With sex being nothing to fear, well, at least I had something to trade on. I found my way to the castle's servants' quarters. Hestur interviewed me even though it is unusual for the castle to enlist outsiders: most are born into the service. As it happened, they had a visiting dignitary who was known to have a taste for young, inexperienced girls. Having no staff to fit that description, he chose to take me into service. I received instruction in the duties of a maid and was told to give him anything he wanted while reporting everything I heard."

Nodding with satisfaction she heads over to the

armoire. I trail behind her as she adds with a tone of pride, "I have been told that I have made pleasing both men and women a work of art. I pride myself on being able tell what a person wants or needs without being asked."

Unbelievable! She really seems to like what it is she's doing. She finds nothing unethical about it. "Thank you, Crystal, for sharing that with me. I have one more question, then it is your turn for some answers. Do all who provide services for the king do so of their own free will?"

"Of course, M'Lady. What good would it do to have someone gathering information if they are forced into it?" She replies as I dress in the clothes she picks out.

"Now I get to ask you something I am curious about?" She arches delicate blond eyebrows.

"I will do my best to fulfill any curiosity you have," I reassure her.

"Well, there is one thing I can't puzzle out. It is why you had me so confused at first. I know now you are married, it stands to reason that a woman of your stature would be. But you used that as a reason for me not to provide you with pleasure while you're here. You also refused to let me provide you with a male substitute, again stating your marriage as a reason. Why would marriage prevent you from enjoyment? After all you are a sorcerer: preventing pregnancy won't be a problem."

What is she confused about? Marriage is marriage, right? Let's see: 'marriage' in Cuthburish means: A union of two people for the providing of heirs. No mention of love, commitment, or monogamy in the definition.

"An interesting question, and a fair one. I'm afraid it is going to take some explaining, though. My world is different from yours in more ways than I can describe, but perhaps marriage will be a good place to start," I pause in my rambling, realizing that to explain why our marriages are what they are, I need to explain more than just the difference in the vows.

"We have many items that are as convenient as the

toilet but use science, not magic. This allows my people to have a great deal of time for recreation. Most people have to work for one third of each day and only five out of seven days. Because we have this luxury, our society has evolved. Women are treated as equal to men, mostly, which has allowed the relationships between the sexes to evolve as well."

"In my kingdom we no longer have arranged marriages. Most people marry for love. In the vows we take when we are joined together we promise to forsake all others and to be faithful to each other 'until death do we part.' So for us, pleasure in the arms of another is not an option," Walking over to the mirror to take a look at the new outfit I ask, "Marriage here doesn't include vows such as these?"

"Milady, I am afraid I still don't understand your reluctance. It is true most here are joined into marriage by either an arrangement made by their parents or for political reasons, however, a few have been known to marry for love. In their passion, they exchange vows as you stated. But the cycle of love is as unchangeable as the coming of each day. Eventually the passion of love's day wanes to evening. It they are lucky, both husband and wife come to this realization at the same time and with the aid of a simple spell they find other romantic partners to fulfill their desire while keeping their pledge to provide heirs," I stand, staring blank-eyed into the mirror seeing nothing in my astonishment at this world's Roman society. *So here, marriage doesn't even mean you must share the same bed, except to become pregnant!*

Crystal, seeing my loss of composure, hastens to explain, "If one of a pair finds their interest lies elsewhere before the other, well, a bitterness has been known to build, turning what started out so beautifully into a living nightmare. M' Lady, have you and your husband not yet reached love's sunset? Most of the time the woman reach the sunset first, for a man finds his satisfaction much quicker than a woman and most men don't have the patience to bring their women much pleasure after the first year, so I hear. How can any world prevent the cycle of love? Do you marry for passion, or is it something else?"

I take a look at my reflection to give myself a few minutes to form a reply. *Not bad. Blue and sliver, the colors of the Kingdom of Cuthburan, which my robe will accent nicely.* The silver belt is perfect. The strands of loose hair add a soft feminine aspect. *Never thought I could look this good without make-up or a curling iron. Now how to explain... what? Commitment? Maybe explaining sensuality is the place to start.*

Motioning to the chairs I invite her to sit with me. She obliges, looking disconcerted as she perches on the edge of the seat. "Let me start by reassuring you that my world does have passion. That passion is part of what enabled my husband to win my hand in marriage. You see, I believe when either party has the ability to dissolve a marriage it causes both parties strive to maintain the physical pleasure and emotional closeness, which makes a lifetime union possible. I have been married for over seven years now, and although the flames of desire do not scorch the sun as they once did, our desire for one another still remains intact. Sunset has not come upon our love."

"You mean," Crystal pauses to compose herself, "Milady, do you mean that he still brings you to a climax? That he continues to do so after seven years?"

"Oh yes, he gave me great pleasure before we married and continues to do so," I mumble, remembering our first time together, "Even now one of the things I miss most are his hands."

"They're not hands, large or powerful, but refined and perfectly formed. Yet they still possess the strength of a man. With nothing but these wonderful tools he has brought me pleasure the likes of which I never knew before experiencing his touch," sensing Crystal clinging to disbelief like a lifeline, I close my eyes loosing myself in the memory.

"He begins by caressing, not rushing but easing, teasing his way from one erotic spot to another. With unending tenderness he fondles each breast as if he had never held a thing of such beauty. Then with sensitivity and patients belying his own throbbing anticipation, these same hands trail across your skin, moving to another erotic zone. With unhurried deftness he coaxes and teases first one area, then the next."

"Your flesh heats, your pulse quickens and sweat forms, though you have hardly moved at all. And then he slips his finger inside, just a finger. With unerring ability that seems magical, he caresses 'the spot.' All your thoughts scatter as your world is reduced to the sensations he creates across your body as you pant his name." *Tony... oh Tony... yesss...* "As you near the peak and beg for more he relents, entering your wetness, setting every nerve aflame."

"Tingling waves of passion rip through you as he thrusts and thrusts and thrusts again. You climax, screaming his name; spikes of intense pleasure rip through you so strong, so overwhelming, it sends prickling sensations clear to your palms. You collapse, drenched in sweat."

"But he is not through. He continues, moving slower, his hands once again roaming across your flesh. As seconds pass, feeling returns and desire begins to swell once more. It builds faster this time and he increases the speed and power of his movements as his engorged manhood pounds within you, harder, faster..."

"You begin to pant, unable to form words. Pure animalistic grunts, fly from you lips, louder and louder, beyond your ability to control. With one last powerful thrust you let out a scream of pure elation. An orgasm so powerful erupts within you and the world goes dim around the edges. He collapses on top of you, the moisture on your flesh mixing with his, too tired to move, exhausted yet satisfied in mind, body, and soul, unwilling to move away from the one you love, the one who has made such wonderful love to you."

I sigh, opening my eyes. A rosy hue infuses Crystal's cheeks.

My maid makes a visible effort to close her open mouth, swallowing with an audible "gulp." Sighing like a lovesick teen her hands flutter as she straightens her blouse then her hair, whispering so quietly that it is almost beyond my range of hearing, "To have a man touch me like that, just once, much less twice in one night..." Her voice strengthens as she becomes resolved, "Milady, I think I can see why you have such a strong commitment to your marriage. To share such passion, to open oneself in such a fashion - intimacy beyond intimacy - you share with each other your fundamental selves. If both believe in the vows you took and both work to maintain the emotional closeness, yes, I see now Love's day wax long, perhaps forever."

A knock sounds at the reception chamber, interrupting my thoughts. *Breakfast already?* I move to follow Crystal as William ushers two children before him.

"Milady ArchMage Reba, these are your new servants, Keth and Phedra," William nudges them reminding them to bow. The newcomers stand with their hands clenched to one another, glancing wide-eyed around the room.

Keth is blond and blue-eyed. Skinny and gangly as any eleven year-old I have seen. His clothes are well kept, but plain. His sister has curly blonde haired with sparkling blue-eyes. *She is so small it is hard to believe she is eight. Not much smaller than my niece Misty was at her age.*

I address the youngsters as adults, hoping they are bright enough to understand. "Keth and Phedra, I take none into my service who do not come of their own free will. Before you accept assignment with me there are two things you must know: I am new to this world and my ways are strange. I expect questions to be asked, at the proper time, when my behavior confuses you. I will try to answer any concerns you have. The other thing is magic. I am a mage; it is like being a sorcerer. I use magic often and have many enchanted objects. For this reason, you must be comfortable with sorcery. Do you still wish to be a part of my personal staff?"

"M'lady," Keth begins with an awkward bow, "I's always liked magicians. Servin' be a pleasure." I nod in response as he bows again, grinning from ear to ear, revealing teeth that will benefit from braces.

On a hunch I whisper "Sight." Not a powerful aura, but he has a definite affinity for corporeal magic. *I will keep an eye on him, if he has brains and a strong will, I'll see if Merithin can take him as an apprentice.* Phedra, though, seems to have no ability at all.

"M'lady," Phedra shuffles her feet, "I'd like to serve you, too." *Not said with grace, but I feel it comes from the heart.*

"Service accepted," I affirm, "Keth you will go with William. He will provide instruction as to the duties of a page." I nod to William who leads the new employee from the room.

Turning to Phedra, I indicate Crystal standing beside me. Although my voice remains firm, it takes on a softer tone, "Phedra, this is Crystal. You will report to her. Do you have any skills or interest? Do you know how to read or write?"

"I got no teaching. Keth's suppose ta take over the shop," I strain to catch her murmur, "but he passed on some he learned to me."

I turn to address Crystal, "I might have need of a scribe, please see both she and her brother have the proper training in reading and writing," Discerning waves of dismay from Crystal I add, "This is a direct command from the ArchMage. If anyone has a problem following my orders have them report to my reception chambers at evening bells. I will reassure them this is an order I intend to have obeyed," The head chambermaid radiates amazement as she bobs her head in acceptance.

"Is there a place where Phedra can sleep close by

you?" I inquire as an afterthought.

"Milady, I could make a pallet on the floor in the corner of my room…" There is hesitation in her voice.

"Show me your sleeping quarters." *There must be a better way than a pallet on the floor; even my dog sleeps on her own couch.* I follow Crystal over toward the bathroom and the curtained doors leading to the balcony. Another doorway lies in the corner of the room. As she swings this inward I get my first look at the servant's quarters.

The walls of the tiny room are bare. It contains only two pieces of furniture, not that it would hold much else. The bed is even smaller than a twin-size, more like a cot. A rough-hewn chest sits at its foot. As I surmised yesterday, another door leads out at the opposite end of the room providing a backdoor into my chambers. *No wonder she was reluctant to share her room, this isn't much bigger than a closet! Maybe I can make this arrangement a little more bearable.*

Inspired by the child at my side I start a limerick:

"For my staff this will not do,
We need bunk beds made for two.
Chest of drawers too,
Of magic I create you;
With a 'Bibbity-Lanity-boo'."

A heavenly smile graces my lips as cerulean mist fills the room with the beginning of the rhyme. As the bells toll in the distance, I utter the last line. A bright flash goes off, like a spark set to a room filled with gas fumes.

"Oh, now there are two beds!" Phedra takes a step back.

Crystal has no such reservation. She walks into the room and, after taking a closer look at the solid oak beds, still narrow but complete with a ladder to the top bunk and drawers underneath, she examines the five-drawer dresser stationed at the foot. With her chin on her breast and eyes downcast she whispers, "Milady, these things... they are much too nice. I have no way to pay you for them."

"Nonsense. I didn't ask for payment. It was my choice to increase my staff and it took very little effort to upgrade the available quarters to accommodate for it. Besides you will be loosing your privacy. This is the least I can do in return," feeling the overwhelming sense of appreciation my explanation trails off as tears gather in the corner of her eyes. *And I thought that life might have pushed her beyond caring.*

A rap at the outer door interrupts the awkward silence, "I'll get that," I declare as Crystal makes a hasty effort to compose herself, "Why don't you get the newest member of our staff settled in?"

The smile Crystal gives as I turn to go is more than enough payment for the minor spell I have cast. *This is the first time I have actually felt the smile when she gave it.*

Chapter Fifteen

"Don't you guys look sharp," My thin lips nearly disappear as I smile when the gang files through the door.

"O-o-h, imagine that, Reba actually has to answer her *own* door," my spirits are so high Allinon's jab doesn't even faze me. But Charles seems to take offence, nailing him with a dirty look and elbowing him on his way past.

"I apologize. That was rude and ill mannered of me," Allinon bows in my direction. *Has an alien replaced my least favorite companion over night?*

"That's never stopped you before," seeing the abashed look from my aggressor I jest, "Besides, what do you think I'm gonna to do, get pissed off zap you?"

I perceive genuine fright from the elf as the five of us cross the threshold of the secured dinning room. The entire group radiates an uncomfortable feeling. "Ok spill it. What is going on here? You guys feel like you are walking a tightrope."

Allinon and Charles exchange glances. As we assume our places Charles lets out a sigh, "You'd better tell her. Like all women she's gonna hang onto this like a pit-bull. I'm bettin' she won't let go of this 'til one of us is dead."

I turn a questioning gaze to Allinon, "It's nothing really…" As I arch an eyebrow at him, he relinquishes, "Fine, if you must know, yesterday after the meeting I was complaining to Charles about Duke Rokroa: That jerk continued being a total pain-in-the-ass after you left the council. Charles pointed out his resemblance to me, to my attitude. When Jerik agreed, I figured the three of you, along with my wife, couldn't all be wrong. Charles has agreed to help me... how did you put it, 'improve my social dialog skills.'"

"Admirable goal, and as they say: knowing is half the battle. Now down to business. How comes the training?" with time in short supply today I am anxious to begin, "Anything you need from me?"

"Allinon and I..." Charles pauses as he yawns. It seems contagious as Allinon follows his lead, mouth gaping wide. "Excuse me. I was trying to say, we have been working with the twenty best swordsmen they have, one from each division. They are pretty quick learners and in another day or two they should have some of the needed techniques down. They'll then be in charge of training each of the--"

Again, both men are overcome with tiredness. Charles draws a hand across his face, shaking his head before concluding: "Each will pass on the training to their division."

"Problem sleeping last night, or too much recreation?" I try a little humor even though I am thoroughly pissed they have chosen entertainment over their duties.

"Pppsshh, I wish it was recreation. That was the other thing I thought you should hear from us," after an extended pause Charles mumbles, "We lost six archers last night."

The chair's legs scrapes the floor as I bound to my feet, frost cloaking my voice, "And why wasn't I woken?"

The swordsman holds out his hands as if to ward off a blow, "Hey, now... the duty officer didn't wake us till a couple of marks before sunrise to get our opinion on the matter," Holding my tongue, I give a tight nod inviting him to elaborate.

"There was no fault in your shield; it was a matter of human error. The demons are much craftier than we have given them credit for. A couple of marks before sunrise, groups of the monsters appeared on all sides of the castle." A seriousness I haven't seen before grips the clown of our group as he continues, "with the quietness of the night prior, the men must have been half-asleep. The guards rushed to the edge of the battlements to get a few shots off. In a matter of minutes winged demons swooped down from above.

"It was a massacre. But the fault didn't lie in your defense. Since the shield wasn't penetrated we didn't wake you. Instead Allinon and I did a round on the battlements to reassure the men and reinforce the need for maintaining a distance from the edge. Allinon even managed to get off a couple of shots with his long bow. He took out a couple of those flying bastards."

"I see... thank you for the update, I appreciate your consideration for my rest." Dismissing the topic with a sigh, I try not to let the fact that six men died in the night get me down. "Jamison how are the Healers progressing?"

"Training is going better than expected. They have a much better grasp of the human body than any medieval society I have read about. They're even aware of germs, on a hypothetical level. That makes training just a matter of showing them how to access and use their powers. I will be checking out the Physician's Consortium this afternoon," he reports.

After an extended pause I urge, "And exactly what did you hear about the Prophecy?"

A wide grin encompasses his handsome face, "Well let's just say they sat you next to Prince Alexandros for a good reason. It seems everyone expects you to marry Alex," As Jamison drops the bomb my mouth falls open. Nonplussed I stare, unwilling to believe what I have just heard.

Marrying Tall Dark and Handsome? hmmm... "But...But... I'm already married!" I stammer, shaking the betraying thought from my head.

I change the subject. "I don't have time to worry

about this crap!" having nearly shouted the denial, I add in a more reasonable tone, "besides I am having dinner with Szames tonight. He is supposed to relate the entire prophecy word for word. It's probably just obscure wording people have interpreted to mean marriage. After all, didn't they also expect me to be a man?" *Why are they still radiating such unease?*

I continue with the business at hand, "I am working on several spells to aid in the personal defense for the soldiers, but I still need to test it. I'd rather not say any more 'til I am sure it will work. Right now what I really need is a huge favor. Will you let me try out my speech?" I beg, wishing I had more than just an hour to practice.

Receiving shrugs and grunts from the guys I launch into the dissertation I composed the night before. By the time the table has been set for breakfast, I am finishing the monologue. While the guys sit quietly drooling over the bounty before us, I finally get the hint: I help myself to the new type of cheese that has been placed on the table. Finding it tastes like blue cheese, I grimace, placing the small chunk to the side of my plate.

Each man mumbles a non-committal patronization about the speech. Like when you ask: does this outfit make me look fat?

"Come on guys, I know I suck at public speaking. I wish one of you could give it, but they've put me up to bat." I plead, looking to each one of my comrades, "Don't hold back, give it to me straight, I am open to any suggestions,"

"The words are great. But you might try a slower delivery," Jerik takes the lead, his deep rumble unusually tentative, "And a pause in between the three major parts."

"Put some emphasis here," Jamison chips in, indicating one of the paragraphs, "And again… maybe there."

"Loosing the stuttering wouldn't hurt," Allinon smirks, which earns him a kick under the table from Charles, "Oh, I'm sorry, I guess that was a little harsh."

"A little…" *If I can't do this in front of people I know, how am I going to do this in front of a crowd!!* Shaking my head I take my emotions in hand before I breakdown into a teary mess, "Yes, it was a little harsh, but it is something I needed to hear."

Still sensing an undercurrent of unease I slam my silverware down on the table. I pin them all with a mock glare, "And there is more… I know there is. Out with it, all of you. I am empathic, remember? What is going on here? It's not just Allinon, it's like you all are skirting a minefield."

Allinon ducks his head and Charles finds something infinitely intriguing on his plate as Jerik massive shoulders raise in bafflement. I lock eyes with Jamison who gives a disconcerted smile.

"Reba, I'll ride this wave with you. These guys," Jamison dips his chin at Charles and Allinon, "All I hear from them is about that meeting yesterday, about how you walked into a room with a King, a Prince, and a bunch of nobles and put them in their place. All anyone is talking about is how in one day, you've broken more traditions than what has been done in generations. It has got me all weirded-out. It's like I don't know who you are…what to expect from you," As the others nod, agreeing with what only Jamison has had the nerve to say, I let out a sigh of relief.

"You must be kidding. I'm the same old housewife you were introduced to a few days ago."

Charles interrupts me before I can even begin. "No, you aren't. You are still you, but you're different. Yesterday, you stood right up to the King and said, 'Excuse me, but I don't think so; don't be a fool.' Maybe not in those words, but that was the gist of it. All I's able to do is stand there hoping my shorts would be clean for the execution," Charles finishes his exaggerated interpretation of yesterday's events.

"Since you put it that way, yes, you're right. I guess I have changed. I was just telling Jamison about it the other day," The healer gives me a blank look, "I have been granted a tremendous amount of power on this world. I mean, look, yesterday I flew, just like Superman," I see the light dawn in Jamison's eyes and feel him relax as I continue the antiquated allegory for the rest of the group.

"I might not be a queen, hell, I'm not even nobility, but I am beginning to see that I wield more power than any other person on this planet. This realization has given me a great amount of freedom: I don't have to worry about anyone threatening to execute me or even us, for that matter. I simply won't permit it," Jerik lets out a grunt of approval, but Charles and Allinon are still as the marble surrounding us.

"With all this power comes an even greater amount of responsibility. There are demons out there. An entire civilization is counting on us to save them. I am not going to let some old fashioned ideas prevent me from keeping as many of these people alive as possible. But I can't do this without you, all of you. I need your open honest input, nothing less. Everyone here is so scared of me, I am lucky they don't wet themselves when I speak to them, much less give constructive criticism," As the others begin to nod I tease, "I mean, I know I've got a temper and all, but I am still the same person; it's not like I'm gonna blast you or somethin'."

"That thought never crossed my mind." Jerik gives a hearty laugh, "No offence Reba, but you just aren't the killer type. Now if my wife had your abilities… watch out, we would've all been fried before the first sunset!"

"Reba, if we can just get you to give your speech sounding like what you just said to us, we would have it," Jamison's sincere advice gets us back on track.

By the time we are marching out the door for the public address everything has returned to normal. Charles and Allinon take the lead, with Jamison and I following. Jerik trails in the rear guard position.

"Don't stress it Reba, that last time sounded pretty good," Jamison encourages.

"Yea, I only stuttered once," *And in front of a live audience I'm going to be a hundred times worse. Where is my twin when I need her? Lani did great in drama: she never had stage fright! Oh, why didn't I work harder in speech class? Wait a minute...*

"This will be the last time I have a problem talking." I declare aloud as the perfect words blaze to life in my mind.

"Speeches have never been my forte,
However that now changes today.
Stuttering no more as speeches I make
My voice will carry strong, never break."

Giving a push, a tingling sensation cascades from my head to my shoulders.

"Awesome, dude!" Jamison grins. "That's the quickest I've ever seen someone get over a speech impediment."

"Yea, too bad we can't bottle it and take it home with us!" I quip, my spirits lifted.

"Why not?" the healer rejoins.

"Why not what?" I echo.

Jamison expounds, his breath forming a white cloud around his head as we step out into the brisk winter day, "Why not make a pill or something to cure a disease? If you make it here, there is a chance it might work once we get it home. It is worth a shot."

"Hey now, you're the healer. I don't think I could make a cure for much more than a headache," Mulling the idea over, I revise my position, "Maybe we could work together. I could make something that might extend life, like a general boost to the immune system to help the body rebuild itself, but as for fighting a complex disease that already has a hold on someone, it would have to be all you."

"Before we leave we will set aside a day to try it. I'll work on the cure-all and let you know when I figure something out," Jamison promises as we approach the guard's station. The royal family is cloistered together, close to, yet apart from the elegantly clad nobles milling about.

"Your Majesties," I greet the King and Queen as the guys step to either side, forming an escort, "Your Highnesses," I add nodding to their sons who flank them.

"ArchMage Reba and the Crusaders of the Light, I present to you, my wife, The Lady Szacquelyn, Queen of Cuthburan," Even though King Arturo has stated my companions and I first in the introduction, implying I outrank her. I bend low, wanting to show my respect. I am rewarded with a smile that feels genuine. *Her children have inherited her blue eyes, among other things.*

Queen Szacquelyn's hair is golden except for a few strands of gray at the temples. Her age would be impossible to determine if not for the fine webbing of lines around her sparkling sapphire eyes. She comes to King Arturo's chest, short as all the women I have met have been. Her figure is almost identical to Rose's, her curves more athletic than voluptuous in perfect petite proportions. Although I stand a good six inches taller than her, she somehow manages to meet my eyes without seeming to look up.

"Milady Reba, it is my pleasure to make your acquaintance. Perhaps you will have time for tea?" Queen Szacquelyn invites in a voice that is low pitched, yet still quite feminine.

"I would be delighted, Your Majesty," I return her smile as the mid-morning bells toll in the distance.

"I believe it is time to begin the address. Ladies, if you will follow me." King Arturo indicates the guard's station.

The nobles form an isle for their monarchs. I turn to Szames, who is standing off to one side, a smile lighting up my sparkling eyes, "Your Highness, if you have a moment after the ceremony another shield modification is in order?" *If I keep close to him maybe I can avoid his* brother. *I really don't need any more stress right now.*

"Milady Reba, I would be delighted," He bows, a somberness in his response at odds with the serene smile gracing his lips: as if I just asked for the keys to the kingdom and he is unable to refuse.

With everyone waiting on me, I fall in behind the monarchs, hoping Szames will volunteer as my escort. Prince Alexandros steps close, holding out his arm. With the slightest of bows he indicates his wish to fulfill the role. Placing my hand on his, I nod to show my consent. *God Bless!! Just what I don't need! Ok, just calm down, he is just a guy, nothing special. Please, please, Please, just don't speak to me.*

"Milady Reba, you look radiant this morning. Do you find your chambers satisfactory?" Prince Alexandros interrupts my skittering thoughts.

"Very, Your Highness," I keep my reply brief, hoping to end the conversation as we enter the guard station.

"If there is anyway I can aid your efforts to prepare for the upcoming battle with the demons, I would be honored to assist you," Alex states. *Why do I sense jealously?*

I whisper "Sight." His aura is much stronger, almost back to normal. He doesn't have enough energy to even consider mage training but there is enough that he could help a little… that's more to store tonight, right?

"Do you know if the irreparable armor has been gathered as requested?" I query.

"It has. It waits by the northern side of the training grounds." His voice holds a note of curiosity.

"Your Highness, if you have an opening in your schedule I will be handling those soon. I could use your assistance in the preparation." I regret the extended invitation as trepidation washes through him. *Perhaps he has his father's dislike for the arcane?*

"I would know no greater pleasure, milady," The lie slips effortlessly from him as Prince Alexandros gives a heart-melting smile.

Even though I perceive the dishonesty of his words,

my knees weaken as I gaze up into his eyes. I yank my thoughts back to where my feet are traveling to avoid stumbling over the bottom step. I move quickly to take the lead on the battlement stairway, aiming to put some distance between us.

At least his distraction is good for something... I am no longer anxious about giving this speech, only about holding to my marriage vows! How does this man do it?

As I turn another corner on the stairway, a lighted doorway appears. Stepping out onto the battlement, squinting until my eyes adjust, I hear the rustling throng below. Thanks to the parapet I can see only the farthest fringe of the waiting audience. Prince Alexandros immerges, once again taking a position beside me.

Prince Alexandros extends one perfectly manicured hand, gently brushing my cheek as he tucks in a stray lock of my hair caught by the breeze. Looking up to my escort the words on the tip of my tongue disappear, swallowed beyond recovery. My vision is narrowed to a gorgeous pair of emerald eyes and lips more sensual than any I can recall. My body heats and my pulse quickens as desire to fall into his arms consumes me. *I have...got... to...get... a grip! Who in the blazes is this guy to have me quivering like an oversexed groupie with no more than a brush of his hand?*

"ArchMage Reba, I present to you ArchBishop Prestur," Szames ushers a balding gray-haired elder toward us.

"Your Grace, it is an honor," I bow. *Thank God for small favors!*

The ArchBishop nods his head in recognition of the homage I have paid him. "The honor is mine. I have often prayed that your arrival would occur within my lifetime. Perhaps when you have a moment you will visit the Holy Sanctuary, Saint Alfred's Cathedral?" Even though his invitation is formed as a polite request, I am determined to comply as quickly as possible. *Intuition or malicious manipulation?*

I know God is still with me, even here. I refuse to fear a pagan imposter. "I would love to. Will this evening be convenient?"

"Just ask for me when you arrive," the Archbishop smiles warmly.

As Szames and Prestur move off to either side of King Arturo I notice the rest of the entourage has lined up along the far side of the battlement. Meeting the King's inquiring gaze, I give a firm nod indicating my readiness. While trumpets blare, he steps up on the wooden platform, turning toward the crowd to begin his speech.

"My loyal subjects, I come before you with wondrous news," King Arturo's voice booms out, "You may have heard rumors that the time of the Great Change has come. I, your King, declare this is true: for behold, my son Prince Alexandros, who lay mortally wounded only two nights ago, is returned to full health," With these words Alexandros steps forward. Shouts of elation arise. Arturo holds his palms up for silence.

"Two days ago, Chief Advisor Merithin, summoned from across the plains a group of warriors led by a mage, who is more powerful than any magic user in the history of Cuthburan," The masses, on the verge of become a mob, stir at this pronouncement.

"This ArchMage brings change that will allow us to triumph over the demons threatening our gates. You have already beheld the workings of this mage when you look up at night and see our enemies turned to ash as they come into contact with the shield overhead," The restlessness continues, but the King pays no heed.

With a half turn in my direction, he holds out his hand introducing Cuthburan's newest arrivals. *Clever... never referring to my sex. I wonder if it is for shock value or to prevent a revolt?*

"But judge for yourselves the validity of the rumors for here to address you is ArchMage Reba and the Crusaders of the Light," Making his final pronouncement, he and Alex step back making room for my companions and I between them.

A calm encompasses me so completely you would think I have been giving speeches as often as a presidential candidate. I step forward. In one fluid motion, I up on the platform before the parapet and remove my concealing hood.

Absolute silence enfolds the crowd, as if my cowl is a death shroud enveloping them. I open my senses, absorbing the emotions of the throng before me, sharing the crowd's astonishment at my appearance. As I fill my lungs, the rasping sounds of the inhalation echoes in my ears. I begin the prepared monologue.

"People of Cuthburan, we have come a vast distance, from beyond the stars above, to aid you in the upcoming battle. But the five of us alone are not enough to win this war:" I pause to let the meaning of my words sink in. As fear begins to rise I qualify, "it will take the combined efforts of every man, woman, and youth for us to be victorious in the conflict to come," As the populace stirs with unease I continue, "Yes, you heard me right, I said a combined efforts of every man, woman, and youth."

"This is no ordinary war we waging: The foes we face do not wish to be the new rulers of this nation. This is a fight for the very lives of every person in this city. Nay, not only in this city, or even in this kingdom, but a fight for every human life on this world. These demons do not wish to rule us, but to destroy us!" As gasps arise from truly frightened people, I pause.

"I have been brought here to keep you safe, but no one lone individual can break the tide of evil threatening our race. So with me, I bring the greatest tool at my disposal: change. Things I ask of you, each and every one of you, are going to sound odd, perhaps even unthinkable, but I, ArchMage Reba, guarantee; if you do as I request, no matter how it goes against tradition or propriety, I guarantee we will be victorious!. People of Cuthburan will you follow me to victory?!"

After the last word, voiced in a triumphant shout,

I pause. The multitudes before me begin to chant my name. The feelings of faith, hope, self-importance, determination, and awe fuel an overwhelming high more earth shattering than any drug on earth. Detaching my emotions from them, I begin my requests.

"Any man, woman, or youth who has any skill or knowledge of herbs or medicine please report to the Physician's Consortium when this gathering is concluded. I have brought with me a new kind of magic, a healing magic. Any who come will be tested and if you desire it, the magic inside you will be set free and instruction on its use will be given. I intend for this war to claim as few lives as possible. With your help that will be accomplished." I ease the emotional shield down, sensing agreement, hope, and awe from the crowd.

"Any woodsmen or farmer taking refuge from the demons, your help is also needed. I will not have us win this war to be defeated by famine. One of my men possesses a type of earth magic that will enable you to speed the growth of plant life and strengthen the land once the battle has been won. If you desire to help in the recovery of the fields and forest, please report to the guards."

"We still have the battle, the Great Battle, to win. For that reason I ask any man, woman, or youth who has any skill with a sword, a bow, or knives, and are willing to fight for your kingdom, report to the front gates." A whispering ensues. Stepping up onto the lower rung of the parapet I raise my voice.

"Yes, I said *women*! Any hand courageous enough, with any amount of skill, is necessary if we are going to turn aside the horde gathering outside our gates," Slight fear mixes with hope and awe along with a newly forged determination.

"If you do not fit into any of these categories, do not fear, you still have an important roll to play in the waging of this war, for much is needed," Their attention is focused on me once more, as if I were Elvis at the height of his career.

"We have a proverb in my kingdom: united we stand, divided we fall. It is united as one that we will overcome the darkness. For they, as individuals are much stronger than we, but together, joined as one, there is nothing we cannot overcome." A little more fear, and a lot more determination transfuses the populace.

"It is for this reason, even though you will be compensated for any materials donated to the war cause, I ask you freely give your time and your skills to the kingdom in this time of need," *Shock, awe, disbelief,* "Yes, you will be justly compensated for any materials you donate to the cause. You will be given a token and after we win this war, King Arturo will provide compensation for your aid," I pause, filling my lungs as the crowd filling the street cheers. Holding up my palms for silence I continue.

"We need the services of cloth merchants and seamstresses, we need two hundred poles, five inches in diameter and thirty feet long, and we need animals for slaughter and butchers to attend to them. We also need fruit, grain and other staples as well as bakers willing to use these items. We need volunteers to travel to the river and bring back wagonloads of sand." Terror seeps crowd like a wave coming ashore at high tide. I hasten to make an addition.

"Do not fear the demons. You will be safe as long as you are within these walls at dusk. For peace of mind, an armed guard will accompany the brave men who volunteer to gather what we need." The panic abates. A renewed sense of hope and determination settles over the people of Cuthburan, as they realize their safety has been considered.

"In parting I ask but one thing more. Put aside any differences or disputes you have with your neighbor: now is the time to unite. Volunteer to cook a meal or watch over their children if your neighbor's wife is at the Healers Consortium or volunteering in some fashion.

Share your surplus, not only with kinsman but the deeper relations - the relation of mankind."

I pause, whispering the name of the Man of Steel, "Superman." Stepping off the edge of the parapet, I drift downward, stopping when I am a several feet above the closest heads. In a kneeling position, stretching out my hands, I beseech the people before me. "Most of all, be kind to one another, for our compassion is what makes us human, and is it not humanity for which we are fighting."

With the gathered throng cheering wildly, I float back over wall, landing on the battlement beyond the crowd's sight. The outpouring of emotion is so strong it threatens to overwhelm me, destroying my self-control. I snap a mental barrier into place, blocking out the waves of adoration projected from the throng of people who have gathered for my first oration.

The silence of not perceiving any outside emotions for the first time since my arrival has a calming effect on my spirit. The emotional lull eases reality back into focus. I shake the rest of the fog from my brain realizing ardent highs like this might prove addicting.

"Well said, milady, well said," King Arturo nods, as he and the queen pass on their way to the staircase.

I bow my head in acceptance of his praise then turn to look for Prince Szames intent on escaping as quickly as possible. Jamison and the others give assorted pats on the back, nods and winks as they pass. Spotting Szames standing with his brother, I make a beeline in their direction.

"Your Highness, if you're ready I would like to leave for the shield modification." When he bobs his head I hold out my hand, turning to address his brother. "Your Highness, is now a convenient time to meet you at the training grounds?"

"I am at your service, Milady Reba," He smiles. *Is he still nervous about helping me?* I don't dare release my empathy shield until I get some distance from all that emotion ebbing from the dispersing crowd.

When I look to Szames, he nods firmly, so I lift us from the ground. We are a few hundred feet away from the multitudes who have descended on the front gates before I release the shield around my emotions. I feel a sense of awe - this time it's coming from Szames. Horrified at the change in the stoic warrior, I pause in mid flight.

"So what did you think of the speech?" *What else could have such an effect on him? After all, we have flown before.*

"Honestly?" He continues, as I dip my chin, "Alexandros, it is said, has the strongest gift of oration since King Sheldon, the first of the great monarchs of our line. Being his brother, a Prince of the Kingdom, and the Commander of the forces of Cuthburan, I have been to every speech he has given."

"I can unequivocally say, Reba, I have never seen the equal to the performance you have given. When you spoke to the audience, you seemed to become one with them, or maybe the driving force behind them. It was an amazing sight to behold," The honesty ringing from his compliment is unsettling.

Blushing before his praise, it is shame coloring my complexion, not pride. Unable to perpetuate the falsehood I ask, "Szames, as a friend, can I take you into my confidence?"

"If it is your wish, all that you reveal to me I will take to my grave," His vow is as solemn a pledge as the fealty I gave him.

I sigh, wondering if the course of action I have chosen is wise, "I cheated when I addressed your people. I don't deserve the praise you bestow on me. If we are to have an honest friendship, I cannot mislead you," I pause. *How much do I tell him?*

"Cheated? How? Did she weave a magic spell with her words to capture the hearts of all who listened?" my keen ears pick up Szames' mumbling in the silence of our isolation. I feel some of his awe dissipate as his mind puts reason to the sight he has witnessed. Then, in a blink, I feel nothing at all from him.

"Not exactly a spell.... but magic of a kind was involved," As we hover right below the center of the force-field, Szames gives me a quizzical look. *Of course you can't be satisfied with just that, can you? Oh well, in for a penny in for a pound.*

"I can't reveal the exact nature of this magic, not here. My dinning room is secure. I am afraid you will have to wait until tonight to find out more," I elude, hoping he will forget about it by then.

"A wise precaution. You give me one more reason to look forward to the coming of night, when just a few days ago it was night we dreaded." The spark in his eyes and the troubled look behind them tell of an internal battle at which I can only guess.

"Are you ready to begin?" When he nods, I concentrate on pooling the energy above our heads.

"Perfect in form and function you've been,
So now I enlarge the size of your skin."

The rush of pleasure coursing through me as the magic melts into the shield is only a fraction less exhilarating than the earlier emotional high. Swooping down, heading for the practice grounds, I hint at the modifications I have made.

"The demons will take no more lives from us tonight. If you will bring your twenty best archers to my dining chambers, and come half a mark earlier, I will clarify the purpose of the work we have completed?" *Will he let me get away with one more secret?*

"I will now count the marks in anticipation of hearing the bells sound so I may see you again." Szames's smile is meant to be debonair, but doesn't quite make it. He only succeeds in looking like a mischievous boy, and barley escapes looking goofy.

He relinquishes his grip on my hand as I bring us,

feather-like, to the ground ten feet from his brother, "Until then, Prince Szames," I state in parting, holding back laughter. He gives a slight bow as we part. I curtsey in return. *Surly someone such as this won't take too much offense when he finds out about empathetic magic...*

Chapter Sixteen

"Your Highness." I bow, "Have you been waiting long?" Winged insects plague my insides once more. *Why have I put myself in this position?*

"I arrived only moments ago," Alexandros dips his head in greeting, "besides being a marvel to behold, it seems flying is more expedient than walking."

"Your Highness, it would be a pleasure to take you aloft sometime. The city takes on a new aspect from the vantage point flying gives." *Uh-Oh...* I sense unease blossoming within my soon to be working partner.

"Perhaps when the world is more at peace I will take you up on your generous offer." The Prince's smile is kind and sincere. *He feels so upset by the idea he can't possibly intend to ever try it.*

"Your Highness, why don't we get started?" I ask, hoping to get away from him as quickly as possible. "I am sure you have more important matters, needing your attention,"

"Milady, nothing is more important to me than discovering more about the angel we have called from the heavens to guide us through this time of peril," his smile relaxes into one that melts my heart, "I consider being in your company my top priority. I have since first gazing into your eyes as I was whisked from oblivion's doorstep."

"Your Highness, there is some--" I begin to disclose

223

my marital status, only to have him silence me with a caress on my arm that makes my heart pound and my loins ache.

"Please, call me Alex, for I feel that we are destined to become great friends. After all did not fate bring us together?" His husky voice is almost a whisper.

Looking into his adoring gaze, I am overwhelmed with the irresistible urge to fall into his arms, while he smothers my mouth with his. *What the hell is going on?! This guy couldn't find the truth if it bit him in the ass... and I... will not... collapse... at his feet... Like some simpering court maid... who has left her sense of morality back on her home world!* Exerting my will power to the limit, I take a step away from Alex, toward the pile of rusted armor, trying to regain my self-control.

"Well… Alex, in friendship I ask that you not speak to me of such things, for I have always considered 'Destiny' the King Trickster and 'Fate' his Court Jester. Save such talk for court maidens whose virtue may be swayed buy such nonsense." I let Don Juan know his place. "I assure you that I am not one of those. I choose the path I take and I don't need fate or destiny to blame for my actions."

Coming up beside me, his demeanor is astonishingly playful, "Touché. At long last I have found a worthy opponent in the field of courting. I wonder if you spar as well with the staff it is said you carry as a weapon?"

What is it you want from me, other than the obvious quick romp? First you treat me like a simpleminded, week-willed woman - now this? Maybe if I best you on that field, too, you'll let me be.

"If time allows, perhaps we will find out… I warn you, though, there's an infamous tale in my kingdom. Our most famous swordsman, said to be the best in all the land, was so accomplished he lost just one fight--"

The prince interrupts the folktale with a bored harrumph, "Let me guess, by a man wielding a staff," he pauses so long I glance over to gauge if he is done. When our eyes meet the intensity of the glaze forces me to turn and face him. "And I would also bet he could not hold a flame to the beauty that is your fire…"

Blushing I ignore his last remark as a compliment, "It is a bet that you would win, on both accounts. The person to best our most fabled swordsman was an old peasant farmer who was protecting his home with nothing more than a staff, for he was not wealthy enough own a sword."

Man, I feel like a bitch in heat. Even his corny come-on lines turn me on! I was with Tony the night before I left… how am I going to resist when I've been here another week!

Inspecting the material as if it makes a difference, I bend down, giving myself a few minutes to order my thoughts. I quickly decide the best course is, as always, the direct one. Dusting off my hands I rise, prepared to do battle once more.

"Alex, am I correct in assuming this will be the first spell-casting in which you have taken part?" When he nods I notice tension building.

"In order for this to work we must link hands and you must be unequivocally relaxed. You will feel a tugging sensation within you, here," I tap my chest, to draw his attention away from what he fears.

"Resisting the urge to fight the pull takes willpower as well as trust in the caster. If you struggle against the draw, it will cost more energy to extract aid from you than what will be obtained by the joining. This is why it is not desirable to partner with someone who has any reservations about magic or the wielder. I appreciate your offer of assistance, however with these items to work with I will be able to cast the spell unassisted," I pause before continuing, "Perhaps I shouldn't have asked, we have only just met. I won't take offense if you wish to postpone the giving of your aid until we have become better acquainted. You may need more time to trust the magic I wield," Having given him what I consider a graceful way out of a hastily made obligation, I wait.

Relief, logic... in the background lurks envy and jealousy. Within seconds hope flares, which could only mean one thing: Alex has developed a scheme.

"If I am to be King in this time of change I must be willing to change also..." Taking me by the hand Alex maneuvers my position as if we are on a dance floor, bringing my face close to his, "Reba, if you will let me gaze into your eyes, as I did when you pulled me back from the edge of the abyss, any reservation I might harbor is sure to melt away like frost under a warm spring sun," the caress of his hand on mine and his imploring gaze convinces me to give in, though I know sibling rivalry is at the core of his request.

"How can I say 'no' to such an artful entreaty..." Inspired by my own wording I arch a brow, "I will do my best to ease your passage in to the world of magic. Perhaps in return you will listen to a suggestion I have."

"My Lady," he coos so that the words no longer resemble a title of respect, but take on a whole other meaning, "I will listen attentively to all that passes those diminutive blossoms, however much progress we make in the arena of sorcery."

"Ahem... yes... well... that is what friends do... is it not?" I stammer, feeling as if I need to catch my breath, "Listen to one another."

"Among other things," he breathes so softly I am unsure of what I have heard.

It is going to be a very, very long couple of weeks! "Let's get started... as I open my eyes I will form a connection between our energies, then chant the spell. You should feel an even, continuous pull throughout this process."

Alex moves with the poise of a prince, capturing my free hand like a fragile dove. Eyes closed, I calm my racing heart and gather my scattered wits. Calling to mind the spell I created last night helps me focus on the task at hand. Making a quick change to the last few lines to include my unanticipated partner, a long breath steadies my racing mind, as I block all other thoughts except the results of the spell. My stare is blank when I open my eyes, I see nothing but the objects I intend to create.

"You are old, damaged, and abused—
That doesn't mean you can't be used.
With these words your shape will change,
Matter and substance rearrange.

I place upon you a serious duty,
Now you will be worth a lot of booty.
If you are given with the intent to deceive,
In their hand you will heat without reprieve.

If you're used with an honest heart,
Peace they will find as you depart.
Stainless steel, you'll never tarnish or rust;
Double-sided, engraved with our busts."

My intense concentration shatters as the world comes back into focus and I find myself taken prisoner by Alexandros's piercing green eyes while orgasmic energy penetrates every fiber of my being. Time slows to a crawl when, as gracefully as an eagle, the prince swoops down on his paralyzed prey.

Am I a startled rodent to be pinned in place by this... The thought speeds through my mind breaking the hold he has on me. Swifter than a gazelle in flight I step back before his lips meet mine. Stooping I retrieve one of the magically forged coins.

"You did well, Alex." I flip the coin in his direction, "Would you like to see your handiwork?"

"I helped create this? It has my portrait on one side and yours on the other... how perfect," For once Alex's emotions agree with what he is saying, "Our craftsmen will demand to know how this work of art was created."

"It's more than meets the eye. Indulge me: think of misrepresenting something - like your horse, selling him for twice what he is worth." My smile twists sardonically.

"You want me to think of selling something for more than I know it is worth?" With an uncharacteristic lack of grace, he complies.

"Ouch!" Alex exclaims, throwing the coin from him, "The blasted thing stung me?" Picking up the same coin, I hand it back to him.

"Not satisfied with one scar... you intend to inflict matching ones?" He grumbles, gingerly taking the coin in his other hand.

I hold my laughter in check, not wanting to offend him more than I already have. "I'm sorry, I suppose that was rather malicious. I promise this time will be better. Just think of selling the same horse for what he is worth, without any deception."

"Hurmmph." He flips the coin back to me, "So we have created a coin that will keep merchants honest... I bet they disappear in an octal!" My mind puzzles out the unfamiliar word, coming to rest on the Cuthburan definition - a unit of measurement, eight consecutive days - while I note his caustic commentary, "There are not many 'honest' merchants."

"These aren't for trade. They are tokens. Call them Fire Tokens if you wish. Your father said I could promise the people fair compensation for goods used in the name of this war. These coins will make sure that when its time to pay, the price you give will be fair. Simply have them hold it in their hand while they recite to your treasurer the list of supplies given and their worth. *Voila*! Instant honesty!"

"Fire Tokens. The name is very appropriate." The Prince mutters, rubbing his singed hand. "Reba, you are much more manipulative than you appear. It is a quality I respect in a woman." Alex grin turns sly, "These Fire Token will be very useful."

"I'm glad you approve." Reaching down I gather two large handfuls of coin. Securing them deep in my pocket,

I stand to address the prince once more.

"Alex, if you will see these get to the front gate, I must be on my way. There are many things demanding my attention," *And staying as far away from you as possible is first on that list!*

"Of course, but I still owe you a favor. The spell-working turned out better than I would have believed possible. Perhaps you could share your ideas with me over dinner tonight?" I perceive lust and desire behind his smoothly delivered proposal.

Alone in a room with you? Not on your life... not if I can help it. "I'm afraid I already have a dinner engagement tonight, but if you have a few minutes, I could use an escort to the woods on the northern side of the castle grounds. We could discuss my idea along the way."

"It would be an honor," Alex bows gracefully, though I discern disappointment, mixed with curiosity and envy.

I notice the page standing a few feet away as Alex signals him to approach. After giving brief instructions for the disposition of the tokens, the prince extends his arm with a slight bow. Unlike his brother, this gesture suits him to a tee.

Alexandros's thick hair looks as if every strand has been frozen in its place. The raven locks are tied in a ponytail, which suits his chosen attire. The velvet Musketeer-type clothing wasn't worn on Earth until well after the Iron Age in the Sixteenth Century, but here it seems suitable, even with the massive saber strapped to his hip instead of the more delicate rapier. His entire appearance is well groomed, manicured, princely, and very handsome.

I place my hand on his, holding in a sigh as my blood heats again. *This guy is going to give me wet dreams if I'm not careful...*

"Alex, am I correct in presuming the majority of your subjects cannot read?" I attempt to stay focused on my earlier inspiration.

"About two-third of the nobles can read and write, the rest have scribes. This has something to do with the idea you mentioned earlier?" He shrugs, impatient to get on with the conversation.

"Yes, it does. Do any of your MasterArtist inhabit this city?" again I try to arouse his curiosity, instead of his male member. His feelings, however, are sill centered in his pants, or getting into mine, as he nods yes.

"Then my idea has a chance to succeed." *Maybe if I stimulate his vanity... Lord knows that shouldn't be too hard.*

"Alex, you are the prince who is going to fulfill a prophecy your people have been waiting for all these generations. Your name will go down in history. But how much does a name really tell people about you? Especially when only two out of three of the nobles, and almost none of the peasants, can read about your marvelous deeds?" I give him time to absorb the new line of thought.

"Now imagine a place dedicated to historic events, events in which we are now taking part. Imagine a grand hall, bearing your name, dedicated to the artwork you commission to be created. It will depict all the wonders taking place in your fathers and your reign. It will show the world what has occurred and the part you played in it!" *Pride, confidence, and, yes, conceit. Talk about vain!*

"A historic hall, dedicated to paintings showing history... Reba, your idea sounds revolutionary. If I were King, I would have the papers drawn up to set your proposal in motion," his enthusiasm is genuine. Unfortunately, so is his disappointment. "However, I am not King, and my father sees no use in social artistry. I doubt I can change his mind, at least not in the middle of the biggest war our country has ever seen," Alex sighs, "He holds onto his gold tight enough in times of peace."

He took the hook. Now let's see if I can reel him in. "If funding is the problem, I might have a solution, at least until your reign begins."

"Really? An artist who paints without being paid a

commission?" His smile is calculating as he continues to guide me behind the castle toward a grove of trees on the northeastern side, "More of your tokens?"

"No, not tokens, but magic all the same. An enchantment that will be passed down through generations. Still interested?" I must reel him in gently.

"More magic? Like with the healers?" Anxiety rises, but curiosity and ego are still warring for the top position among his emotions.

"No, it will be more of an enhanced memory spell that can be passed down from one individual to another," I give a shrug, "It would require a minimal amount of support from you right now, and a promise of a grand hall to display the art work when you reign as King."

"If you can persuade MasterArtist Yivgeni to use his talents without a commission paid for each piece, you have my word I will support you," The his voice drops, oozing sensuality, "now and when I am King,"

At the edge of the grove of trees he stops, taking both of my hands in his. The castle stands in the distance, a small cloud passes over the sun, and as I look up to Prince Alexandros, a breeze ruffles his ebony hair. My breath quickens as he gazes down at me. I feel my moral resolve weaken along with my knees. *No! I... will... not... give... in!*

I recover in time to curtsey instead of swooning. "Thank you, Alex. For the escort."

Taking a step back, so my arms are extended pushing me as far away from him as possible, my voice is brash, "If you are serious about accepting my plan, then I leave it to you to arrange for a room at the castle for MasterArtist Yivgeni so he and his apprentice may work and reside close to their subject. If you can also arrange for the necessary supplies to be purchased, that is all I require from you at this time. I will inform the artist of the plan to build a place where his works can be displayed to the public when you assume kingship. All of this, with your approval, of course."

"Yes, Milady Reba, you have my approval. I will see to it that the MasterArtist Yivgeni of Everand reports to your chambers first thing tomorrow," the smile in his voice and the smug feeling convinces me the attempt to hide my reaction to his close proximity hasn't been entirely successful, "Beautiful maiden, I am sure you will be able to charm him to our cause without even the of promises of magical gifts."

"I appreciate your confidence in my abilities, Alex." I refuse to react to his words on any level but the business at hand. "Tomorrow afternoon will be a better time for the meeting, though. I, too, am in the process of changing my sleep pattern."

Alex gestures around us. "May I ask what brings you to these isolated woods?"

"I wish to try a new spell. I am unsure of what the results will be." Perceiving his curiosity rise along with the usual tension, I expound with vigor, "I didn't want to expose anyone to the danger of an enchantment where the results may very well be hazardous."

"With magic, I defer to your knowledge," fear urges him to give up on the idea.

"Is there a way I can aid you on the morrow? When the situation permits, I look forward to becoming better acquainted with the arcane realm," His emphasis on 'acquainted' and the lust I sense from him makes his intentions clear.

"I could use some assistance with the sand," I solicit. *I can't spurn him completely if I expect to continue receiving his cooperation,* "What time will you be available?"

"Mid-afternoon will suffice," in one swift movement he steps close, bringing my hand to pursed lips. As before, a wave of heat washes over me, this time accompanied by wetness between my thighs, "Until then, My Lady," He whispers, low and seductive.

Still as the trees surrounding me, I watch Alex make his way back to the castle. It is all I can do to stand watching instead of calling him back, or worse, running after him. Alex angles toward the eastern side of the castle, entering through a camouflaged door. My enthrallment dissipates as he disappears from my sight. *He is way too good looking to be that charming, which makes him a very dangerous man...*

Shaking off my heightened arousal, I refocus my attention on the woods. Maneuvering my way deep into the forest, I spot a large boulder lying close to the center of a small clearing. Kneeling down next to the rock, placing my hands on the stone, I begin the limerick I composed the night before...

"The laws of magic, which rule this place
Say that, once, may I bridge time & space.
So now I weave into your substance,
Memories of my Earth in abundance.

When the word 'trans-dimensional' is said,
You will assume the burden in my stead.
Using the info that you now possess,
Finding my world so I don't transgress.

Open a gateway to the land of my birth,
Keep it stable until all is passed your girth.
You will deliver what rests upon your surface
To he who's present in the memory's preface."

As I intone the last word, my skin tingles into numbness as I push power into the stone, while recalling the most vivid memories of my life, starting with the first time I saw my husband. *Huddled under a blanket, Tony's ebony head peaks through the door. "Come on in..." I invite, wishing I hadn't taken off my make-up before bed.* The stroll down memory lane continues, until I have imbued the rock with a third of my energy reserves.

Lightheaded with exhilaration, opening my eyes I whisper "sight." The stone now glows a bright blue. Squinting, I discern a web-like pattern of blue laser-light spreading through the boulder. *Makes sense: a spell is like a chain linked together, interwoven. All parts of a single enchantment have to be connected for it to work.*

From a pocket hidden within my robe, I remove the large bundle of papers addressed to my husband. Placing the memoirs on the center of the stone, I close my eyes. With a silent prayer I say "trans-dimensional."

The boulder's light intensifies, the pattern of the web, blurring. The magic within me feels the memories come alive, spreading outward, or maybe inward: the search for a match has begun. My heart surges with joy as a connection is made. *It has located Tony. I've found my home!*

A corner of the power-web expands, encompassing the letter as magic forms a link between the two worlds. But as the returning energy reaches its place of origin, the glow of the rock goes up a notch and I sense something is amiss.

Leary I watch, wrenching my conscientiousness away from the death throws of the misdirected enchantment. A wave of dizziness consumes me as the letter twists, crumpling as if a giant pair of hands are wringing water from a dishtowel. A red glow mixes with the blue. The radiant hue turns purple as the rock heats. The pages of the letter darken. Within seconds, the entire manuscript bursts into flames.

I fall to my knees. Through a teary blur, I watch the destruction of the spell I hoped would bring my husband to join me.

I refocus on the world as the azure radiance bleeds from the stone. The rock shines an angry crimson. The surface of the boulder begins to roll and bend. The stone liquefies, spreading like butter too long in the sun. Flames flicker to life where the molten rock touches dry winter grass.

I jump to my feet as the ring of fire expands. I need a water spell! I look up into the clear blue sky for help. *No clouds, a rain spell will take too long to work.*

Unable to think of a quick rhyme, I charge the flames. Stomping like a Native American in a war dance, tears of frustration keep the smoke from my eyes as I smother the misbegotten fruits of my labor.

"Flames are not alive but flames may die,
Without oxygen you'll light no funeral pyre."

The desired results are firmly implanted in my mind for the quickest spell I have ever composed. Though the riddle makes little sense, the flames are extinguished in a blink.

With my jaw hanging, I stare at deflated slab puddled where the boulder once stood. *So much destruction from the dissolution of one spell!* My mouth snaps shut. The iron resolve that got me through a troubled childhood reasserts itself, as I grind my teeth.

"So much for my first attempt," I grumble, rubbing moisture from my face.

I hear bells chime in the distance as my eyes travel outward from the burned circle of grass. *Noon already!* Looking down, I notice the bottoms of my pants are singed halfway up my shins.

Turning on my heel, I leave the ruins of the trans-dimensional spell, power walking toward the castle. *Let's see, can I find the entrance Alex used?*

Chapter Seventeen

I re-enter the castle from a new direction, confidant I can either make my way to my chambers or ask for directions. Turning left as soon as my eyes adjust to the dim interior, I see a staircase leading upward. The distinct ringing of metal on metal reaches my ears. I freeze in place with my foot on the first step.

Combat instincts come alive, senses heightening with the anticipation of trouble. I gather magical energy around me, whispering a spell I created for the Renaissance Games. *I hope this medieval world can comprehended the 'Trecky' reference to the Klingon shields!*

"Life is precious and the danger apparent,
So saying 'cloak' will make me transparent.
To once again make myself seen,
Using 'uncloak?' will sound so keen."

Sweat springs to my brow. Even though the enchantment is a minor one, I feel the drain on my powers. The miss-enchantment has cost me in more ways than one. After a tingling sensation spreads through me, I whisper, "cloak." A devil's grin spreads across my face as I look at the floor where my feet should be.

Nimble as a cat, I edge my way past the stairs and around the corner. The wall to my left has narrow gaps stretching from floor to ceiling. Getting closer to the sounds of battle, I distinguish two tones in the grunts accompanying the noise. Breath whistles in between clenched teeth, as I peer into the adjoining vastness.

In the cavernous room, five high-set windows let in a good amount of sunlight. One figure towers over another figure by more than a foot. The odd pair, covered in white-padded outfits, square off in what is obviously practice.

A son of a noble receiving instruction in the sword? I am about to release the invisibility spell when an all too familiar voice rings out.

"Now I know you can do better than that. I thought you, at least, would not to treat me like an invalid!" Teases Prince Alexandros to his sparring partner.

"Your Highness," Begins a voice that I can't quite place, "a mere servant… would not dare…" It continues, pausing in between swings, "to judge the health….of the crown prince." Intrigued I remain hidden.

"'Your Highness' is it now?" The prince taunts back once more.

"Of course, Your Highness… a friend would not… keep a friend waiting…for over a mark… without even an apology." *Is he sparing with a woman?*

"Is that what this is all about? My punctuality has never troubled you before?" Alex parries his attacker's efforts, and un-winded he continues to addresses his opponent, even managing to shrug while doing it. "I am sorry, it could not be helped. A romantic tryst with the ArchMage was a necessity," he gibes.

Not a wise move if she is anything like the kind of "friend" you want me to be. You may be a prince, but you still make the stupid typical mistakes only a man can make!

The short swordsman reaches to her mask. In a flourish, she flings the covering to the floor. In the next second Andrayia swings her sword around in a hard slash at Alex's arm, followed by a flurry of attacks, proving she is a true swordsman. The prince manages to parry the enthusiastic charge, but his breathing is no longer quite so relaxed.

"It is about time! I thought we would...never get to...some real practicing," He reaches up to remove his helmet.

"Is that what I am to you now? Practice? And after just two days..." His mistress retorts, stepping back. Her dull practice sword clatters across the floor as she flings it from her. When she continues, I sense tears in her voice. "Well, you can just get the ArchMage to be your sparing partner, as well as your wife!"

As she turns to go another sword clangs, joining the other on the floor. Price Alex grabs her arm, swinging Andrayia to face him, "Is that what is behind your mood?"

I feel Andrayia's heart breaking as well as Alex's compassion and love for the diminutive woman, "I am a fool. It was insensitive of me to taunt you. That is all it was: a bad jest. The councilors kept me, that is all, nothing more," Gathering her in his arms he strokes her hair.

Holding her out from him he looks down into her eyes. I perceive more honesty from him than ever before as he continues in a voice I strain to hear, "I may have to bed and even marry that witch, but my heart will always belong to you, my love."

That pig! Here he is trying to seduce me, all the while stringing her along! My eavesdropping becomes uncomfortable as Andrayia falls into his arms. Turning from the window, I lean against the wall.

He does love her - that much is painfully clear. And she loves him more than is good for her. But still, how could he take such pleasure from chasing my skirt while feeling such love for her!

He's a complete jerk! A rutting PIG! But wouldn't all men be in a society that says it is ok to sleep with someone when you get the urge? What kind of world have I fallen into!

I start to leave when Alex speaks once more, "My love, I sincerely apologize for my tardiness, but I am afraid I must go. My father has asked to lunch with me."

"Then go. He won't be as forgiving as I if you arrive late," Andrayia eases away from him.

Standing stock-still, I hold my breath. Having given 'his love' a quick peck, Alex rushes past me then up the stairs. Holding my position a few more minutes, I give him time to get a head start. Before I can be on my way, a figure approaches from the opposite end of the hallway entering the room the prince has vacated.

"Your Majesty," Andrayia pauses in her gathering of the equipment to bow her head with a deep curtsy.

"Andrayia," King Arturo's tone is curt. The distaste in his voice is obvious as he continues, "I see you are still practicing the sword with my son."

Taking a cloth sack out of his robe, coins jingle as they hit the floor, "Compensation. Your presence here is no longer desirable. I expect your rooms to be vacated by tomorrow morning. Make no mistake: attempt to use Alexandros to sway me and the life of your son will be forfeit."

Having given his orders, King Arturo turns on his heal striding past me on his way to the stairs. Andrayia collapses to her knees, burying her face in her hands. *Hmph. Can't have the mistress distracting the prince while he's courting 'the witch.'*

Marching into the room I whisper, "uncloak." Clattering fills the air as Andrayia scrambles to her feet hastily wiping her eyes. Her feelings about me burn so strong you can almost smell them as she curtseys. *Great! She hates me. And I've done nothing! Nothing yet, anyway.*

"So which are you? The weeping, spurned maiden or the warrior I saw earlier," I use my hardest, most sarcastic voice, turning my vocal cords into a whip.

Her chin comes up. Defiance sparks in her blue eyes, but her tone is polite when she speaks, "What ever you wish, milady."

"There is some fire left in you then?" My voice softens a little, "One more question. It is obvious you love the prince and he you, but how strong is your love for him?"

"I would die for him," She proclaims, a little hatred creeping into her voice.

"You just might have to." I mumble. Fear rises swiftly in her, but she stands her ground, "Good, you are brave as well."

"No I'm not going to kill you. And rest assured, I have no desire nor any intention of marrying your prince," *Shock, disbelief, curiosity, along with a slight easing of fear,* "In fact, if you will do as I say, you have my word that I will do everything in my power to see you betrothed to him, not me."

"I will do anything you say, if there is the slightest chance it will lead to our union," she declares, though she still radiates the same emotions to a lesser degree.

The world turns white. I blink to clear the spots as the premonition takes over my world. My presence hovers over an octagonal room. The pews are lined with nobles in their finest. Walking stately down the isle making a be-line for the alter is Alex, next to him my likeness. The vulgar parody of a wedding dress looks like I am going to explode through the bulging middle. But the radiant glow of expectancy is missing. Gloom hovers around me like a disturbed nest of killer bees. A third of the way down the isle, the bride wavers. Now a regal blonde that can be none other than Andrayia is striding along with Alex.

White blinds me once more. A knowing forms.

"More than a chance, I'd say. But it will be dangerous. It may even cost you your life." *Can I handle having her death on my hands if things go wrong?*

She drops to her knees whispering, "What is it you wish of me," A slight hope rises within her, but she is still dominated by fear and hatred.

Words of rhyme blaze to life in my mind. I begin to chant….

"Warrior, these clothes will never do,
Speed and freedom are needed too.
Stronger than steal so death will be cheated,
Soft as silk when protection is needed.

To overcome the trials you face;
You lack in muscle but have grace.
The molecules will rearrange

Your sword I now also change.

Now titanium and razor sharp,
So with your life you won't part."

The outfit and the new sword are implanted in my mind as I set the enchantment. Andrayia lets out a gasp as her clothes transform from the bulky sparring garb to black-suede, loose fitting slacks, complete with a matching cloak and a scabbard for her sword.

"In case you missed it, I addressed the populace today. I asked any man, woman, or youth with the ability to wield a weapon report to the barracks. You now fit that description. Since the king approved my request, I see no reason you can't move your things into the vacant wing of the new barracks across from the infirmary. That is now the women's quarters," My voice is smug as she rises looking over her new duds. "No demons claw will penetrate those clothes. I'd be careful with that sword; it will be lighter now, and much stronger. In addition I will see to it you are given special training from my men,"

Stepping back I size her up. "If you survive the upcoming battle, I give it a three-to-one chance it will be you Alex takes as a bride, not me. Are you willing to stand at my side facing a horde of demons in the battle foretold by your prophecy?"

"Gladly will I face the most evil demon, milady. But there is the matter of my son. What of him? Will his life be forfeit? Will he be required to fight by your side as well?" Andrayia inquires with sarcasm and a little trepidation.

"Of course not." *What kink of monster does she think I am?* "Where is he now?"

"Currently he is being watched by a friend." She eyes me warily.

My eyes turn blank as I search for an answer. "Can this friend care for him while you train for battle?"

"I believe she would, if told of the importance,"

Andrayia nods.

"For my plan to work no one must know of our bargain. You can stress the importance of your staying close to the prince, but no more."

She holds out the bag of coins. When I make no move to take them she explains, "Payment for your assistance."

"That is not necessary. What I give, I give freely. Besides you take much more risk than I," Her hatred has abated a little, but mistrust rises with my statement.

"If we are to have a bargain, a payment must be made, milady," She waivers.

I take the bag from her, shrugging, "Your ways differ from mine. If you wish to seal this bargain with a payment, let it be done. With this payment and your aid in the war against the demons, I agree to do all in my power to aid you in your pursuit of marriage to Prince Alexandros," I add, "My time is short, lead the way to your friend, then I will take you to mine for training."

Placing her sword in the scabbard, she ushers me farther down the hall. Entering a door about halfway down, I follow her into a classroom where several well-dressed children sit quietly at six short tables. The teacher curtseys, lowering her head as I enter.

I dip my chin, acknowledging the teacher's show of respect. "Andrayia, why don't the two of you go into the hallway? I will watch the children while you make the needed arrangements."

When the two adults leave the room, ten pairs of eyes are fixated on me with awe and a little trepidation, except one beautiful emerald pair. As I lock eyes with Prince Alexandros's son, he smiles.

"Hello, Andertz. Tell me, what were you studying before the teacher left?" I squat to his level.

"History. About the olden times," His comprehension astounds me.

"Well, I don't know any of your history. Were you learning it in songs?" I ask.

"We do songs tomorrow. Today we are doing history," Interjects a cute brown-haired girl sitting beside him.

"Oh, I see," I stand so I can address the entire class, "Where I come from, before all the people learned to write, we passed on our history in songs. These tales we call folksongs."

A blonde-headed boy raises his hand. When I nod at him he implores timidly, "That sounds like a lot more fun than boring old history. Could you sing one for us?"

Grins break out around the room and I smile back. *If I can sing my nieces to sleep, surely I can sing for these kids.*

"Hmm, let me see if I can remember one," Then in my native tongue I whisper,

"Singing for these kids I will now do,
With better rhythm and tone-control too."

Now instead of being adequate, maybe I can give a good showing of one of those old tunes… which one… ah, yes - perfect!

"How about a really old story called a 'fairytale' about a prince and magic and frogs?" I bubble with childish enthusiasm as my troubles melt away in the presence of such beauty.

"Yeah!" is the fervent response from the awaiting audience. With no further ado, I begin one of my favorite songs.

"Do you remember in the fairy's-tale,
How the wicked witches spell
Changed the handsome prince to a toad?

By the power of her potion,
She handed him the notion,
That he's lower than the dirt in the road."

I stroll down the isle between the tables, sing a verse

to each table.

"Thou she left him green and warted,
Her evil plan was thwarted,
When there happened by a young miss.

Who in spite of his complexion,
Offered her affection,
And broke the wicked curse with a kiss."

Stopping at Andertz's table, I can't resist blowing a kiss in his direction.

"And that's the secrete to frog kissin'
You can do it too if you'll just listen,
Just slow down, turn a-round, bend down and kiss you a frog."

By the first chorus, I am acting out the motions just like I did for my nieces when they were this little.

Once upon-a-time ago,
I was down and feeling low,
Like a lonely frog in a pond.

Life was just a jokin',
I was very near a croakin',
I was zapped by life's wicked wand.

But in the depths of my depression,
There came a true expression,
Of love from a guy so-o sweet.

He gave me a warm fuzzy feelin'
A feeling that was healin'
Knocked me off my little-webbed feet."

The up-beat tempo has me tapping my feet. The

studious facade the children wear cracks as excitement takes hold. Some of them hum the next chorus.

"And that's the secret to frog kissin'
You can do it too, if you'll just listen.
Just slow down, turn a-round, bend down, and kiss you a frog."

    Several of the youngsters let out giggles as I come to a stop, spin around and squat down in pretense of kissing a "warted" companion.

"There's a happy ever after land,
Deep in the heart of man,
Where a prince or princess abides.

They got the full potential,
But they're lacking one essential,
To enable them to shine like a star.

But all we get are glimpses
Of these handsome prince or princesses,
Cause they're covered by a green 'n warty hide.

That's to have some guy or misses,
Smother them with kisses,
Love'm while they're still like they are.

Last chorus...

That's the secret to Frog Kissin'
You can do it too if you'll just listen,
There's a world of opportunity under each and every log.

So if you've never been a charm breaker,
If you've never been a handsome prince maker,
Just slow down, turn around, bend down, and kiss you a

frog!"[1]

At Andertz's desk once again, I place my head on my hands, uttering, "Ribbet, ribbet." It doesn't surprise me a bit when the child leans forward, placing a kiss on my cheek.

Amid peals laughter I ask, "So what do you think of folk songs?"

"That was great!" A small child of about eight pipes up, "Can you sing us another?"

An older girl, the sole child with black hair in the entire class, shoots her a look that says she should remember her manners. Primly, she raises her hand.

"Yes, what did you think of the song?" I speak as if addressing a grown-up.

"It was fun and it rhymed, which will probably make it easier to remember." She sounds entirely too grown-up for her small stature, "Do you know any about love and courting?" *Well, the women here tend to be on the short side, she could be approaching her teens.*

One of the boys raises his hand, waiving it about. "How 'bout one with monsters?" *What have I started... one with monsters and courting?*

On the table, next to the dark-haired girl, I notice a wooden cup and plate with a pair of leather gloves, "Would it be ok if I borrowed these for an enchantment?" Oohs and ahs breakout among the kids.

"Please do," is her meticulous rejoinder. Chairs scrape the floor as kids move to get a better look.

Figuring they will all benefit form a little exposure to The Arts, I take the items to the front of the class. Feeling inspired by the last song I use a new format.

"With words that rhyme I am doing fine,
Songs will improve with a guitar's chime,
With these materials here for my use.

---

[1] *Frog Kissin'* by Chet Atkins

Only one thing needs your backing,
Talent I will no longer be lacking,
Because I have magic as my muse."

   I smile at the playful limerick more than the ecstatic wave of tingling as the wooden dishes meld together and the gloves mold around them. The entire bundle expands, in a matter of moments I hold an old-fashioned guitar case.

   Gasps along with ooh's and augh's echo in the chamber. The children are smiling. I perceive no tension in the room. Removing the instrument from the case so they can observe, I proceed with some instructions.

   "All of you can help me. After I sing the first verse and you catch on to the tune, sing the second verse with me." With no further ado, grasping the newly made instrument in my hands, I begin another folk song, one that my dad played for me when I was a kid.

"Frog went a courtin' and he did ride, uh-huh.
Frog went a courtin' and he did ride, uh-huh, uh-huuh.
Frog went a coutnin and he did ride, sword and bo-ow by his side, Uh-huh, uh-hhuh, uh-huuuhh."

   I exchange the word 'Bow' for 'pistol' unfazed when I fail to find a word for a gun in versatile Cuthburish. A couple of the kids join in on the second verse.

"He rode right up to Molly Mouse's den, uh-huh.
He rode right up to Molly Mouse's den, uh-huh, uh-huuh.
He rode right up to Molly Mouse's den, said 'Molly Mouse are you within,' Uh-huh, uh-hhuh, uh-huuuhh."

   As I pitch my voice real deep to imitate Mr. Frog on the last line, the youngsters break out in giggles. I stroll around the room encouraging the rest of the kids to sing as well.

"He took Miss Mousy upon his knee, uh-huh.
He took Miss Mousy upon his knee, uh-huh, uh-huuh.
He took Miss Mousy upon his knee, said Molly Mouse won't you marry me,Uh-huh, uh-hhuh, uh-huuuhh."

"'I don't now what to say to that,' nah-uh.
'I don't now what to say to that,' nah-uh, na-uhh.
'I don't now what to say to that, until I speak to Uncle Rat.' Nah-uh, nah-uuh, nah-uuhh."

The children laugh at the first line. Most of them sing the second verse, imitating the high, squeaky tone.

Uncle Rat went to town, uh-huh
Uncle Rat went to town, uh-huh, uh-huuh.
Uncle Rat went to town, to buy his niece a weddin' gown, Uh-huh, uh-huuh, uh-huuuhh

Where will the weddin' supper be, uh-huh
Where will the weddin' supper be, uh-huh, uh-huuh.
Where will the wedding supper be? Way down yonder in the old oak tree, Uh-huh, uh-huuh, uh-huuuhh.

What will the weddin' supper be? uh-huh
What will the weddin' supper be? uh-huh, uh-huuh.
What will the weddin' supper be? Two green beans and a black-eyed pea. Uh-huh, uh-huuh, uh-huuuhh,

Well, they all went sailin' on the lake, uh-huh.
They all went sailin' on the lake, uh-huh, uh-huuh.
The all went sailin' on the lake, and they all got swallowed by a big black snake....
Uh-huh, uh-huuh, uh-huuuhh."[2]

As I pitch my voice in my deepest tone, gasps arise from the girls while the boys cheer.

2   *Frog Went A Courtin'* by Doc Watson

Looking toward the doorway, I am abashed to see Andrayia has returned with her friend. Turning to hide a flush, I put guitar in its case. On my way back to the door I set the encased instrument on the ground, leaning it on the table next to the dark-haired girl from whom I borrowed the items, "Would you like me to change it back?"

"You, mean I can keep this…" As she struggles for the proper words I supply her with the word "guitar" as I nod yes.

"I can really keep this beautiful, magical instrument?" She grins from ear to ear.

"It is yours to keep, but I am afraid there is nothing magical about it. I used magic to create it, but the instrument is merely a different type of lute. Perhaps your parents will let one of the court musicians teach you how to play it?" I elucidate.

The girl trails her fingers across the case, "Yes, I will ask if I can learn to perform."

I finish the journey to the door where the grownups are waiting. Both of the women look at me as if I have grown wings… A lot of the hatred eases in Andrayia as we leave the students in the capable hands of their teacher.

"You're good with children, do you have any of your own?" Andrayia remarks as we hang a right into another hallway.

"No, I have not been so blessed." Now that we are on a feminine topic, her whole attitude transforms. "How old is Andertz?"

"He will be six this summer. He's small for a male of the royal line, but it's not uncommon for boys to come into their height at a late age. Milady, is it true? Are you taking in the orphans from the attack two nights ago? You have seen to their education?"

"Yes, on both accounts." *Word sure gets around fast.*

"ArchMage Reba, as part of the bargain, may I request, in case of my untimely demise, that you see to it Andertz is likewise taken care of?" Andrayia petitions, even though I discern a hesitation within her.

"I hope I need never fulfill that stipulation, but yes, I will make suitable arrangements for him if the worst should come to pass. Actually, Andertz is already showing signs of the Healing Gift, his future might be predetermined," With her son's future taken care of, I feel the hesitation leave her.

The hallway ends in an opening beside the Grand Staircase. We continue on in silence. Reaching the practice grounds, locating Jerik and Charles is relatively easy: they tower over the rest of the men by almost a foot. After introducing Andrayia and requesting she receive additional training sessions, I charge back to my chambers knowing the mid-afternoon bells can't be far off.

Chapter Eighteen

"Squire William, Squire Keth, I'll be ready to leave for Princess Szeanne Rose's apartments momentarily," I rush past the teenagers and into my bedroom.

Not seeing Crystal, I go to the armoire. The portable closet is already full of clothes! *I've only been here what, three days? Not that I'm complaining.*

Spotting a black pair of the loose-bottomed pants, I snag them from the wooden hanger while wiggling out of the scalded slacks. *I have to remember to send a thank you note to the tailor - or even better, I will commission outfits to be made for any women who show up...* My train of thought is broken as the rear door to the bedroom opens.

"Milady, can I assist you?" Crystal sounds offended. "Are you looking for a different color perhaps?"

"I think I have found what I need. I'm afraid that I have already ruined one pair of pants Edward made. There was a slight magical mishap--" I pause in my explanation as tolling sounds in the distance, "--and I am supposed to be at Rose's by mid-afternoon bells. God, how I hate being late!"

"Milady, perhaps if it would be possible for you to let me know in advance of any… experimentation… we could prevent any further tardiness." She admonishes.

"Schedules were never my strong suit, but I'll try. I won't be back until after the evening bells for dinner,"

My lips twist sardonically at the imposition of having to constantly report an itinerary.

I snatch my staff from beside the bed then hustle into the next room where William and Keth lead the way down the hall. William has enough forethought to set a fast pace, and I soon discover Rose's rooms aren't too far from my own, just down the hall and around the corner.

Noticing the princess is wearing a pants outfit similar to my own makes me smile. Glancing past her, I see the table has already been set. Lunch is waiting.

"Rose, I apologize for my tardiness, it was unavoidable." I hesitate, unsure of what is proper in a case such as this.

"No apology is necessary. I am sure your schedule is becoming quite full. If you are ready, so is our lunch," Rose's honest, caring attitude is a soothing balm after the double exposure to Alex's duplicity.

My stomach rumbles as she ushers me to the table. The presence of a solitary servant is unobtrusive. As I help myself to some of everything, except the blue cheese, I begin to relax, a quiet sigh escaping my lips.

"A long day?" the princess queries.

"And then some. It seems I solve one problem only to discover five more demanding my personal attention. My biggest frustration, though, is a particular spell," I pause, unsure whether her inquiry is just polite small talk, "I am trying to revise a portal spell."

"What type of issues are you having?" Rose is genuinely interested, "Is there a way I can be of assistance?"

"I think the problem might be the focus I used," Seeing her blank look I explain, "I placed the main components of the enchantment in a boulder, which melted before the spell was completed. It could be the spell was too complex, causing it to overheat."

As my eyes travel across the table to my new friend, the sparkling emerald necklace hanging around her neck absorbs my attention, "Actually, you have just helped more than you know. A gem should allow for the intricacy the enchantment requires! I'm going to need a sizeable stone. Tell me, which are the more common jewels?"

"Emeralds are quite common. You know I might have something you can use," Placing her fork and knife aside she goes to her vanity, returning with an emerald the size of a chicken egg. The stone is set in a metal stand resembling a star. She hands the treasure to me. "Will this do for your spell?"

I nod yes in response to her query, reluctantly pushing the jewel back toward her. "In good conscious I cannot accept this. The incantation I'm working to perfect is not a battle spell or even a defense spell. It is a personal work. With the results of my last effort, I can't guarantee the gem will remain intact."

"I insist. This stone only serves to remind me of what I would rather forget. It is not precious to me. I will be glad to see it put to use," Having said her peace, she places the precious rock next to me.

My lips curve with gratitude. I change the subject, not wanting to reveal the rest of my frustration concerning her brother or my plans for Andrayia, "Any word from your father?"

"The war preparations have him thoroughly occupied. I am ashamed to admit it, but a part of me is sorry there are no more patients who need my help," *The bird no longer wants to reside in the gilded cage?*

"You know, in my oration today I called for the aid of anyone with skills or knowledge in healing. Your father approved of the idea. I know Jamison can use your help at the Physicians Consortium."

Sputtering, she chokes on the drink she was attempting to swallow. "You mean go out of the castle grounds without an escort?"

"I need to stop by on my way to the church. I'll be happy to escort you as far as the Consortium. Jamison can bring you back," With a second thought I ask, "Are there many dangers for a member of the royal family outside the castle grounds?"

"Our Family is well loved, but even in times of peace, caution is advised to all who are close to the king." Rose mulls over the idea.

"If the possibility of danger is all that is stopping you, I can spell your clothes so they will be stronger than armor. I can also show you a few tricks that will aid you in defending yourself," I tempt.

"I will take you up on your offer of a spell, but" With a mischievous glint in her eyes, she jumps up again, this time going to her armoire. Opening the bottom drawer, pushing aside the clothes, she brings out a slender, short-sword in a tooled scabbard, "but we can save the defense lessons for a more convenient time. I think this will do for now. I am out of practice, but if I look the part I think it may deter any possible threat."

I smile as we dig into our plates with renewed vigor. Even with my faster than normal pace of consumption, Rose is finished with her meal before me, "Could you send my squires to ready the horses?" I ask.

By the time I clear my plate a second time, Rose has belted the sword around her waist. Hastily she finishes buttoning on a robe. After I perform a revised version of the spell I used on Andrayia's clothes, we hurry out the door.

I set a quick pace but slow when I notice my short friend is nearly jogging to keep my pace. We arrive at the front steps of the castle as the horses are being led to the cobbled entryway. Unexpectedly, there is a third horse and rider accompanying ours.

"Milady, Your Highness. I happened by the stables when your boys arrived. Thought you might use an escort if you're venturin' out." Lieutenant Craig drawls.

I look to Rose, who shrugs, "An escort is welcome."

We mount our steeds unassisted, the princess being an able horsewoman. I turn to our escort, "If you'll lead the way, Lieutenant, we need to go to the Physician's Consortium."

With a nod Craig prods his horse. The princess and I don our hoods, hanging back a few feet for some privacy. After passing the castle gates, I turn to Rose, "So are you going to tell me about the emerald? Or perhaps why a princess seems to be an able swordswoman? You've got me more curious than a cat staring at a mouse hole."

"The two stories are related, in an odd way." Her eyes take on a far away look, "When I was six years old, Szames began his arms training. He and I were inseparable. He took me everywhere with him, including the fencing lessons. I was fascinated by the swordplay. The maneuvering it requires reminded me of a dance. "

"Szames was tutored with Alex for the first few years. Alex had a two-year lead on him, and two year's growth, as well. Szames usually got a sound trashing. Trying to compensate, he practiced for hours, using me as a sparring partner. We kept it very private, between the two of us only. Everything went fine for the first year or so."

Her story takes on a life of its own. As I listen I am overcome by sense of love and adoration for her brothers.

....

The royal duo, opposite as day and night, looks for the appropriate practice weapons. Raven locks disappear beneath the sparing mask of the lanky teen as he takes a first stance position, poking his brother with the wooden tip. "You feel lucky, Szamesy? It will take an act of Andskoti for you to score a point."

"Almost got you yesterday," a hallow clack echoes across the chamber as wood meets wood when the golden headed younger boy swivels to stare defiantly up at his brother.

"Is that a challenge, little brother?" The patronizing continues, "You know we are supposed to wait for ArmsMaster." A lazy parry fails to move the wooden barrier blocking his path.

With a disdainful "harrumph" at his short, blue-eyed opponent, Alex makes a slash at the head standing a few inches lower than his own. Green eyes pop open as the attack is not only deflected but countered by a stab at his middle.

Red-faced, Alex jumps back, "You asked for it!" He swings for Szames's shoulder, "And if you go crying to mother I will thrash you twice tomorrow!"

Szames holds his own at first, but within a half-mark Alex is using every trick in the book to remind his baby-brother who is eldest. Szames is pinned in a corner as Alex hovers over him, hitting first one side then the other.

Grabbing one of the smaller swords, Rose bellows, "No, not again... not again!" She leaps into the fray. Alex is forced to turn and face the attacker who is half his size.

Within minutes the blonde pair has Alex's back to the wall. Zach, the ArmsMaster's son, recovering from the shock of seeing the pigtailed princess wielding a weapon, rushes to the aid of his mentor, "Two against two is more fair."

The foursome, embroiled in battle, never see the hulking figure watching from the narrow window. "Hold!" the single word halts all movement, as if the king himself has spoken. Eyes wide in fear, knees trembling, they form the line he demands.

Rose stands with her chin held high as the ArmsMaster glares down at them. Like the sun appearing over the horizon, a grin begins to spread. Giving a chuckle the master of arms nods his head, "It seems I no longer have a need to find additional sparring partners. If I'm not mistaken, I have just uncovered the reason Szames has been coming along at a breakneck pace." One large hand cups Zach's, shoulder, "Son, you have some catching up to do, unless you want to be whooped by a girl!"

....

Rose shakes herself out of the memories as we turn off the broad, main avenue entering the narrow side streets. "That was the day sword lessons began, as did my friendship with Zach."

"Was it he who gave you the emerald?" I prompt, when she appears lost in the past.

"Zach? No. He gave me this necklace. One day he asked me to meet him for an extra practice session: We often sparred together when our schedules would permit. I was fourteen. He had gotten a growth spurt and shot up past me in both height and reach, but I was quick, so it took him a while to best me. When he did, he gave an elegant bow presenting a box in his open palm."

"'For you, m'lady. A token of feelings I dare not speak.' The seriousness of his voice made him sound years older. I remember... my hands trembled as I opened the box, it was the first gift I had received from a boy.

One look told me he saved for months. The stones may have been inexpensive, but the metalwork was intricate. 'It's absolutely beautiful' I said, meaning every word. As he reached to place the treasure around my neck, I looked into his eyes and saw the love of which he never spoke. I leaned forward to him to give him the one thing I could: my first kiss. Afterward, I rushed from the room so he would not see the tears in my eyes," Rose pauses, a catch in her throat.

"Was is love's first dawning?" I query, though I discern no trace of the emotion within her, only a terrible sadness as she speaks of him.

"I never even considered him when I thought of love, which is why I cried myself to sleep that night. He is common born. Even if I marry with an agreement, anything between us would be impossible. That I was the recipient of feelings so genuine, from someone I admired, yet never dreamed... it devastated me."

Again she pauses, fighting the old feelings. "It was then I had a most profound epiphany: I will never have what those flighty, annoying court girls, chatter about: a true day of love. Zach had seen me with my hair a mess, clumsy, and red-faced with frustration, yet he loved me. He knew me as no one but my brothers had. Not the picture of perfection, the Princess Szeanne Rose, but as me, Rose. Yet, because of our situation I had not even considered him as anything more than a friend."

"So love's day ended before it even begun?" Large buildings surrounded by a lush park, undoubtedly the Physician's Consortium, lay at the end of this street.

"A few weeks later, my father decided it was not appropriate for his daughter to be in the company of common soldiers: I have not seen Zach since. The egg came from Alex. When he found out about the necklace, he belittled the size of the gem. At the Winter Festival, the stone was his gift to me. He meant well, but to this day it just reminds me of the impossibility of love in the life of a princess," I perceive desire for love in her, and the despair of never having it. *Somehow I don't think this is a problem I can fix.*

I leave Rose alone with her thoughts as we approach the Physician's Consortium. We dismount at a broad, well-groomed path leading to a three-story stone structure, "Lieutenant, please take care of our mounts. I will be back shortly."

A crowd mills around the side of the building as Jamison, perched atop a gigantic boulder, gives instructions. Seeing our approach, he hustles over.

"I thought you might be able to use an extra pair of hands," I indicate the princess who drops her hood. A wide smile spreads across his face. I feel perceive emotion oozing in gooey waves from both sides. *Maybe love dawning in her life isn't as hopeless as she thinks.*

"You bet we can. We have almost 100 new additions to our healing staff. Some don't have a trace of healing in their aura, but they are willing to do anything that might save a life. Reba, I think I've come up with how we can use them...." Jamison's explanation trails off as a healer passes, dragging a couple of screaming kids by the back of their shirts.

"Malegur, wasn't it?" I approach the physician who is manhandling a group of five children, "What seems to be the problem?"

"No problem, milady," He ducks his head, "just handling a nuisance."

"But we's just want t' help. Weren't no problem!" shouts the largest of the ruffians, a brown haired boy whose toes barely reach the ground while Malegur hauls him by the shirt. "Flame-haired said kids could help too, and that's all we want, is t' help!"

Taking down my hood I address the outspoken child, "Actually I said men, women and youths. May I have the names of those who wish to help so sincerely?" Upon seeing my hair the smallest child, a dark-haired girl, hides behind the boy whose eyes have just about popped out of his head. "And for God's sake, let go of them Malegur."

The boy's face is white as a sheet under the grime as he mumbles, "I'm Todd, M'lady. We's meant no offense." I smile, encouraging him to continue, "M'lady, I'm not so young, just turned nine. My sister Maria, she's seven, so is Erik. Chazan's eight and Araine's five."

"Well Todd, you're right, you aren't so young." I close my eyes for a second as goose bumps make their way up my spine. Intuition spurs me to inspiration, " Hmmm, you know I have the perfect job for you. It is a very important one. Maria can you find me a small rock?" She nods her head enthusiastically and soon locates a pebble.

"This is a very good rock. Did you know that, with a touch of magic, even rock can be many things?" I hold the stone in the palm of my hand so they can all see it.

"A rock you are and a rock you may be,
But for you I have a different need.
You'll carry water, and never rust,
Sturdy, but light, a handle's a must."

A quick surge of power centers on my open palm. The children gasp as the rock expands, changing color. Within seconds I hold, resting on my hand, a one-gallon, stainless steel bucket, complete with a metal handle.

"Now, what I need is someone who can go down to

the river and find a whole bunch of rocks, just like that one," I raise an eyebrow, handing the bucket to Erik.

Todd, the obvious leader, bellows above all the exuberant shouts of 'me, me,' "We can all do it, it'll be faster!"

"But you have to be inside the gates by the time the sun touches the hills. The demons are still out there. Even though they can't get inside the castle, they will hurt you if they find you outside after sunset," As their eyes double in size, I pull a Fire Token out of my pocket, "Show this to the guards when you go out. When you get back, show it to guards at the castle gate. Leave the rocks there for me. I'll have an empty bucket waiting for you in the morning."

"This is a very important job; do you think you can do all that?" As they nod with the jubilance of the young I continue, "Now repeat the instructions back to me," They begin talking all at once, so I ask the eldest, Todd, to recite the orders.

"We go the river like the men get'n sand, 'sept we get rocks like the one Maria found an' bring them back to the castle gate, show'n the coin to all the guards," he proclaims.

"You forgot t' part 'bout being back b'for the sun touches!" Maria pipes up, eager to correct her brother's mistake.

"Very good. Maria, you make sure they don't forget the part about the sun, because I wouldn't want the demons using my number one gathers for monster snacks. Now you'd better hurry if you are going to get rocks today." They take off at a run with Araine trailing behind, but not by much.

"You have a way with the young. Do you have a use for a bucket of rock?" Rose inquires as I join them.

"Actually I do: an important part of defense in fact." I dismiss the topic, knowing I have to keep moving if I am going to make it to the ceremony with the king and the troops on time. "Jamison, how many awakenings do you need?"

"At least twenty, but I don't have them organized yet. I will have more accurate numbers at breakfast tomorrow," Jamison's eyes keep wondering in Rose's direction, although it is me he is talking to.

"How 'bout I set up an awakening spell in that boulder? You could have the applicants place both hands on the surface and repeat the Healers Oath after you." I give some quick instructions, glad there is now one less thing I need to do. "The enchantment will react to the words and perform the spell to release the gift."

"You can do that?" Now I have Jamison's complete attention, "What about the…. you know?"

His ever so sly hint at the empathetic read makes me smile, "I think I can incorporate everything into the spell that is normally part of the ceremony," I reassure him, "I would like to test it first, though, and make sure the rock will hold the necessary power." *I don't think the healers would appreciate having a molten pool in their courtyard.*

Five minutes later, the enchanted bolder is surrounded by a group of healers securing it against unauthorized use. I release Rose into Jamison's custody after making luncheon arrangements for tomorrow. Unsure of the location of the religious sanctuary, I ask Lieutenant Craig to escort me to my next destination.

Starting out at a trot toward Saint Alfred's Cathedral, groups of commoners in drab clothing pause to point at us as we pass. I quickly replace my hood to conceal my telling locks. It seems only minutes pass before we stop in front of one of the few three-story structures in the city. Made out of pure ivory marble, the building is hard to miss.

"Lieutenant, would you mind taking care of the horses again?" I hand my reigns to him without waiting for an answer.

The majestic towering doors are made of cherry wood, with two-foot bronze hinges. Grasping the bronze handle, an ominous chill spreads down my spine. I begin to wonder what has called me here.

My eyes adjust to the dim interior as I pass through the vestibule. Another six paces and the hall opens into a large foyer. Padded wooden benches line the walls: five-foot tall candelabra in the corners provide illumination. A young priest in a plain, white robe approaches as I try to get my bearings.

"May I be of some assistance?" queries the plain priest, as I hesitate in the entryway.

"I am here to see Archbishop Prestur," I declare.

"Do you have an appointment?" The timidity of question is at odds with the confidant set of his shoulders.

"Nothing specific." I respond by rote, focusing my attention on picking out the details of my surroundings. "He asked that I stop by to see him this evening,"

"Matthew, are you having problems with even so simple a task as reception duty?" demands a figure entering from the next room. The new arrival is older than the priest who greeted me. The short man's robe is golden with a maroon border. The pig-eyed priest also sports a large paunch, a balding head, and a haughty look.

In a voice dripping with self-importance, he sneers, "Archbishop Prestur is occupied with important matters. If you leave your name, you will be notified when he becomes available."

My hands reach for the hood of my robe as I address Chrome-Dome, "You may tell your superior ArchMage Reba is here, accepting his invitation." Recognizing at whom they are speaking, both men step back. I look to the young priest; "I await his reply, eagerly." The youth takes the hint, dashing off through the lighted doorway ahead.

"I am Brother Christopher," The older priests' tone is politer, but still self-righteous. "Perhaps you would care to wait in the inner sanctum, milady?"

"That will be fine." I acknowledge before probing

for information. "What is the history of Saint Alfred's canonization?"

"He was the bearer of the *Prophecy of the Flame*. Through his death, when the first Church of Eldrich burned, he gave us the words of the prophecy." Christopher ushers me through the doorway into a polygonal sanctuary I immediately recognize from my earlier premonition.

Drastically different from any church I have ever attended; it takes me a few seconds to adjust to my surroundings. The walls of the congregational center are set at distinct angles. I am standing in the octagonal room. Eight sets of candelabra, varying in height, are placed in each corner. Twenty pews, varying in length to accommodate the interesting shaped room, are arranged in two rows. The priest leads me down the nave and up eight steps to an apse where he kneels to pray at an eight-sided marble altar.

I ignore the pagan's babble as a marble statue to my left absorbs my attention, exquisite in its extraordinary detail. The sculpture depicts a man, his robes are royal blue marble and the face is alabaster stone polished so that it seems to glow. The features are engraved is such detail you sense the peace the priest is feeling as the flames, depicted in bronze, devour him from feet to waist. *Hmmm, was it from serenity that he prophesied or agony?*

"Ahem," Christopher clears his throat, "It is required that all who enter pay respects to Andskoti," he indicates the spot next to him.

"My beliefs do not allow me to kneel to any God but mine," I shrug off his request.

"B-but, it is required of all who enter, regardless of their beliefs," sure of his sacred duty, his voice rises, "You must kneel in respect. No homage is expected, just acknowledgement."

"I am not a child of your world." The tension in the room becomes almost palatable. "I worship God who does not allow me to bend a knee to any other god, not even in the giving of respect or acknowledgement." *Where's my staff?* My eyes narrow as I recall leaving it tied to the saddle.

Brother Christoper grabs my arm as three doors open simultaneously, one in the chancel behind the altar and two lying to either side of the main doorway.

A judo twist frees me from the man's grasp. I step into a corner beside stone table, keeping the platform between the priests and me. Having obtained a secure position, I note the new arrivals. *Eight to one, even without a weapon I'd say the odds are in my favor unless they've had combat training.*

"What is going on here?" demands the oldest priest, whom I recognize as Archbishop Prestur, "Christopher, I asked you a question. What is going on here?"

"Archbishop, I was…" his voice takes on a whine, "she…. she refused to kneel…"

The Archbishop looks to me for an answer. Our eyes meet. The room glows as if I am looking at the world through sunlit glasses. The luminescence is accompanied by warmth, like being huddled up in your favorite blanket on a rainy day. Although the sensation is pleasant to my senses, I tense, knowing there is no god but mine and wondering if I will have to fight to prove it.

A deep voice comes from everywhere at once, reverberating throughout the room. "You, Reba of the world you call Earth, are a child of the One God, Yahweh. His mark is upon your soul, therefore I declare it unnecessary for you to kneel before me."

"You know My Heavenly Father?" I question the bodiless being.

The voice brings a sense of veneration as it continues, this time inside my head, *"We all know of the One: the Alpha, the Omega. He is what we all struggle to become, omniscient, omnipotent, and loved by millions upon millions."*

Uncomfortable with the intimate contact of sharing thoughts with a being I do not know I demand. *"Who are* you?"

"*I am the one called Andskoti.*"

Sensing no malice, only honesty and caring, I attempt to get some much-needed answers, "*What do you wish of me? Why have you brought me here?*"

My face betrays nothing as the alien thoughts of Andskoti penetrate my mind once again, "*My time is limited. I will tell you what you need to know. I stand blocking a gateway linking this world to another. I will choose one who will accompany you in the campaign to find the gate's location. You must leave immediately after the battle, traveling in a circular route around Castle Eldrich: we do not have a luxury of time. All is lost if the gate is not destroyed.*"

Andskoti pauses briefly, continuing, answering even my unasked question, "*Your faith in Yahweh keeps you from many of the limitations of our world, but your powers are not infinite. Yes, the Priest may perform a Blessing, and I will work through them to aid the soldiers. No, your power cannot aid you in breaking the First Law of Magic concerning Portal transfers. Neither can I break it. I will guide you to select the one of my flock who is to accompany you...*" The voice in my mind trails off and the lighting returns to normal, seeming dim now to my eyes.

"As it was in the past, so it is now, eight are called to witness when Andskoti speaks. Let it be written: ArchMage Reba need not kneel," Prestur's voice is filled with both reverence and authority, "Tell us, ArchMage, what message did Andskoti give you for us?"

"You must gather all of your order immediately, here before me: one has been chosen to accompany us on the campaign after the Great Battle. Andskoti also wishes you to bestow a blessing upon the king's troops. His final words were of warning, time is short and we must not tarry," no sooner does the last word leave my mouth then seven of the priest spring into action, leaving me alone with Archbishop Prestur.

"There was more that Andskoti said?" Prestur states more than asks.

"Yes, Andskoti stands blocking the gateway to the Demon World. If the gate is opened your world will be flooded by monsters that will devour mankind. One of his priests must be present at the gate when we close it. Time is crucial, we ride with the troops on the day after the Great Battle," I relate more than the words I heard, I translate the feelings accompanying it.

Prestur comes to stand beside next to the altar, "You were right to withhold this information. If the word spreads that Andskoti is aiding us in this battle the masses will panic. It is said, anything the gods take a hand in is deadly to man."

Priests file in through six of the eight doorways. Their robes vary in color, some are plain white, some are gold, and some of each have a colorful trim around the bottom edge of the gown. Prestur, however, is the only one who has a maroon robe with golden trim. More than forty men file in, taking a place on hard wooden pews. How will I ever know which one I'm supposed to choose?

The door to my right opens and a young priest in a plain white robe enters, hastening to find a seat. A soft golden glow surrounds him like an aura, without Sight activated.

"Archbishop Prestur, the one who just took his seat," I whisper, "he is the one Andskoti has chosen."

"Fellow Guides on the Passage of Light, hearken to my words. Andskoti has spoken. Our god has chosen one of you to accompany the troops after the Great Battle. Brother Matthew, come forward," The clergymen begin to whisper as the priest who greeted me makes his way to the altar.

"How can it be that he is chosen above us all?" Christopher falls silent as the Archbishop raises his hand.

"It is not for us to judge. At your rank, Bishop, you should not have to be reminded of such things. Perhaps assuming Brother Matthew's duties while he is occupied with the upcoming journey will help reinforce the Neophyte lessons you seem to have forgotten," Prestur's tone softens as he turns to Matthew, "Place your hand upon the Altar of Andskoti, my son."

Matthew visibility trembles as he follows the orders of his superior. The feelings reverberating through him cause me to flinch. *He expects to die when he touches it.* The golden glow crowning him moves to the marble table. Every man in the room gasps as light radiates from the rock. I dip my head in acknowledgement. The task of choosing a priest to accompany our troops wasn't as hard as I expected.

"ArchMage Reba, I thank you for your assistance here today. I assure you, Brother Matthew will be ready when he is needed." His dismissal is unmistakable.

"It was an honor, your Grace," I take my leave with a bow.

Chapter Nineteen

Galloping toward Castle Eldrich, we turn onto Royal Boulevard with the darkening sky hovering above. The guard at the front gate is in a wrestling match with a figure half his size, while three smaller figures attack him from all sides.

I urge my horse into a full-out run. Within seconds I recognize the children I sent to gather rocks. The smallest figure, which must be the five-year-old Araine, stands between the brawl and the metal pail. Scattered around are bundles of bread and meat that were distributed to the volunteers as they returned from collecting sand.

"Hold!" I demand, bringing my horse skidding to a halt. The guard straightens up, releasing the child. "What seems to be the problem?"

"ArchMage," The guard bows, "These children are thieves. They try to claim payment for a bucket of stones with a Fire Token."

"Lieutenant Craig, report to the courtyard and inform King Arturo that I will be there directly." As Craig remounts, I turn to the guard who retains a tight grip on Todd's shirt. "Release him at once." Letting go of the child the guard comes to full attention.

"Soldier, what were you orders concerning the Fire Tokens?" My voice is as hard as the steel he wears.

"They were to be given to any who contributed supplies, in lieu of payment, Sir. All materials arriving with them are to be placed in the field next to the stables," he barks out his instructions.

"I suggest you follow those orders to the letter. Leave the judgment of value to others. You will now personally see that the bucket and its contents are delivered to my quarters." His fear is punishment enough. Does he expect me to vaporize him?

The guard gives a crisp salute, taking possession of the bucket. As he calls for assistance, I am mobbed by the kids who begin chattering like a group of chipmunks, "It's ok, it's ok…" I shush them, gathering the smallest ones into my arms.

Maria and Araine soon quiet down. Todd elbows Chazan, who also stops babbling. "I'm sorry, Ma'am, we tried to do what ya' say, but he wouldn't let us…" Todd pauses to glare over his shoulder as the evening bells toll in the distance.

"Well that won't happen again. And if you guys are still willing, I could use a second pail of rocks tomorrow."

"Yes, milady, we can do it!" Todd exclaims over the other shouts of agreement.

"Then come back to this gate tomorrow morning and I'll have an empty bucket waiting." They gather up their foodstuff, bounding home with youthful exuberance. The true treasure of a country, indeed, lies with its youth.

With haste I make my way to the courtyard, where the officers of Cuthburan are waiting. As expected there are close to thirty men lined up, standing at attention. To my surprise, Merithin and Alex are standing with King Arturo on the lower steps.

"Your Majesty, your Highness, Merithin." I bow, "If you arre ready?"

The Monarch nods his head solemnly, so I continue, "I plan to tie an enchantment to your sword, Your Majesty. Three key words, spoken in Cuthburish, will activate the spell: king, kingdom, mankind. I thought perhaps you could use them in performing something like a second knighting ceremony."

Figuring that they pulled Merithin out of his sick bed to keep an eye on the proceedings, I explain my intentions, "Whatever you touch with your blade as you say the last word will be the recipient of the spell: leather armor will become stronger than the strongest steel and all cloth stronger than chain mail."

"I will be the one controlling the spell?" King Arturo is incredulous.

"Yes, but I can imbue only so much energy into the sword. Tomorrow night it will need to be recharged at least once." Smiling at the elder sorcerer, I ask, "Merithin, if you are feeling up to it perhaps you could assist King Arturo with the recharge?"

"By tomorrow evening I'll have strength enough for all but a major working," Merithin still looks pale, in face as well as aura but his nod is firm.

As the king hands his sword to me I recall the lines of rhyme I composed for this incantation. Focusing my attention on the blade, I begin to chant.

"Those who gather to protect this land,
Are now in need of a helping hand,
All the leather they are wearing,
Titanium strength will be bearing,

Clothes that move and bend,
Chain mail strength times ten,
Key words you will find,
'Konung, riki, mannkyn.'"

Picturing the knighting procedure and the intended results, my hands holding the blade vibrate with power as I set the enchantment. "Sight," the radiant glow reassures me that the spell has taken.

"Your Majesty, if Merithin will accompany you, I see no need for my presence. He will be able to inform you if the spell fails to transfer," I hand the sword back to its owner.

"Of course, Milady ArchMage. Go with our gratitude," King Arturo dismisses me.

"Milady Reba, will you require an escort to your next engagement?" Alex proposes.

"Thank you for the offer, your highness, but I think I will take the direct route," I glance upward. Please let his fear of flying outweigh his curiosity.

The prince relinquishes his offer with a slight nod. I bow to the king turning to leave. Ten paces later I whisper "Superman," and lift myself from the ground. Flying around the corner I look toward my balcony. Catching a glimpse of the starlit sky, I manage to keep my attention focused on my landing, but not by much. My feet land on the secured perch. I swivel around, gaping at the heavens above.

Stars are sprinkled throughout the dark, grouped in odd clusters: not a trace of the Big or Little Dipper, or even Orion's Belt. But consuming my attention, are three moons. One is full and bright, one is three quarters illuminated, and a third is invisible to the naked eye, but my magesight reveals the florescent teal sphere.

We really are on a whole other world. Shaking off the chill lodging at my nape, I step into my chamber. Figuring I should check for messages I amble toward the desk.

More than a mark later, I look up from the new stack of correspondences. I flex my right hand, fingers cramping from more writing than I have done since high school, while my other hand rubs a neck throbbing from the unaccustomed stress of the life and death decisions I have put in place. A knock sounds on the reception chamber door. Crystal comes in from the bedroom with Rhachel in tow, ushering in Prince Szames and a group of archers.

I rise to greet them, "Your Highness, please follow me."

"ArchMage Reba. As you requested, I have my twenty best archers." Szames states as his men file into the dining room behind him. Why do I perceive such a clear feelings from everybody else, but nothing from him?

"I have an important task for you men," I begin, my voice loud enough to carry to every soldier in the room, "Today Prince Szames and I have enlarged the shield, it now reaches the outer side of the battlement walls. Each of you are to reinforce the guards as the bells toll midnight. After a few marks, start to wander toward the outer edge of the battlement. Lord willing, we will be rid of more demons by sunrise. You may even be able to pick off any of fliers that manage to avoid the wrath of the defensive shield. "

The men grin in anticipation as Szames dismisses them. Within minutes we are alone in the extravagant dining room. Without a word he pulls out the chair at the head of the table then takes a seat. The prince sits, looking expectant.

I sigh, "Szames, what I'm about to tell you must never be revealed. I trust you with this knowledge for two reasons. Most importantly, you seem pretty open-minded about magic. I also feel that if we are to have an honest friendship I shouldn't deceive you, or even mislead you." He waits for me to continue.

"I possess a small amount of 'Empathetic Magic.' Unless I shield myself, I can form a link with the emotions of others, discerning what they feel. That is how I was able to deliver the speech so well. In a way I did become 'one with the audience.' I was able to feel their reaction to what I said. I don't deserve praise for the performance… it was the first speech I have ever given," Should I mention that I can't feel anything from him?

"Empathetic Magic, hmmm. As it is said, you bring a whole new dimension to sorcery as we know it. How much can you sense of what others feel?" bristling with emotion I cannot fathom, his question is almost a demand.

I answer cautiously, "I can sense different levels of

emotion from different people or I can shield myself from sensing anything at all."

"Are there any here that have this Gift lying dormant, like the healing one?" Prince Szames persists.

"It is a relatively new magic on my world so we don't know much about how it works." I hate the minor deception, even though I know it is necessary. I cock my head, exploring the new line of thought, "You know, I haven't thought about looking for the empathetic trait in Cuthburan." I continue, pleading for understanding, "I'm unsure how your people will react to this type of sorcery. I prefer to keep my abilities private, for a while at least."

"I assure you, your secret is safe with me," Szames mumbles, more somber than I have seen him. Crystal enters followed by a whole troop of servants to set the table around us as he mumbles, "Perhaps my brother has a type of magic after all."

I make a mental note to follow up on that idea with my gang and proceed along what I assume is the same train of thought as my dinner companion. "Speaking of your brother, I would love to hear your view on him, if it wouldn't be betraying a confidence," without warning waves of emotion cascade through me, my face betrays nothing as impressions threaten to overwhelm me. The foreign feelings echo those I have felt countless times. Unbidden, a vivid memory springs to mind....

....

My hand trembles as I hold the note, re-reading it for the fourth time.

Becky,

I need to talk to you. Can I give you a ride home today?

Thanks,
Richey

Can it be? He wants to see me, not Lani? For once a guy has chosen me over my more outgoing, more confident, not to mention poised and flirtatious, twin sister?

I make a conscious effort not to stumble on the way to his car as he pulls up outside the school. Floating on cloud nine all afternoon, it is the best day of my life. Within minutes my fantasy world comes crashing down around me.

"I'm glad you could make it. I know are friends and all, so I thought you might be able to help." Richey hesitates before blurting out the reason for the unexpected invitation, "Can you tell me what Lani likes to do? I want to ask her out but I don't know what she's into."

Lani wins again. We are twins, yet wherever we go the guys choose her over me.

....

Szames's emotions mirror the ones I have felt for so many years: disappointment, diminishing self-esteem and rejection, all mixed together with resignation and a little frustration. The feelings disappear like the light of fireflies on a chill evening.

"Of course. What is it you wish to know?" His voice is as bleak as is the barren ground of my empathy.

I try to make amends without letting on that I had even a brief look at his innermost emotional state, "I know your brother is a playboy. But how any woman could be stupid enough fall for his obtuse advances is beyond me. What I need know is, is he as good with the nobles as he thinks he is with women? Will they follow behind him if he backs my ideas?" After he closes a sagging jaw, Szames's face lightens although I still feel nothing from him.

"Yes, as you have surmised, Alex is extremely good with the nobility. I believe he could charm the feathers off a bird if he set his mind to it. If he backs you, your voice will be heard," Szames relaxes, as I help myself to the fare placed before us.

"I'm no good at political games and court maneuverings. I hope all I have to do is get Alex on my side and let him take care of the rest." I probe further, "What kind of king is he going to be? Does he care about his people, the common man?"

"Like all the kings of the line before him, he seems to have a knack with the peasants as well. Although, with your stirring speech, you have probably replaced him as their favorite noble." His smile is sincere.

We eat in companionable silence, as I explore the new information. Alex will be a good king and has the backing of the nobles. How am I supposed to assume power? Why would I want to? It's time to hear that prophecy.

"So is it my turn for a question?" Szames queries as I pause to refill my plate, "The few items you have made, and those you describe, makes it appear that your world is much more scientifically advanced. Just how far advanced is it?"

"I would hazard a guess that our world is a several hundred years ahead of your own, which isn't all to the good. We have made many mistakes over the last couple hundred years. We are only now seeing the results." I keep my reply vague. "Because of this, much of the technology we have I will be unwilling to reveal, even to you, for fear of the harm it might cause in years to come."

"What technology could be so devastating?" Szames counters. "Could you tell me the results of the advancements at least?"

"We have weapons of war that poison the air and land for decades into the future. The making of these weapons, among other things, has poisoned our oceans. We destroy our forests to make room for overpopulation and hunt many animals into extinction for sport." I sigh. "But plagues no longer sweep the land, the average person only works five out of seven days, and the average life expectancy is ninety in my country."

"Longer life, more time for pleasure and good health. The price is merely the destruction of the land and seas. The price is too high. I admire your decision. I will honor it," Szames echoes my thoughts as I finish sating my appetite.

"Thank you, I'm relieved to find an ally on this subject. Now it's my turn?" When he dips his head I prompt, "I seem to recall a promised recital?"

"The Prophecy of the Flame? Let me give you some background first." As he begins, a shadow passes across countenance. Pushing his plate aside his tone is somber, "Rikard of Kempmore was in the process of laying the foundation of this city, when a group of Disciples of the Path of Light journeyed here claiming they had been instructed to build a temple. Ever respectful of Andskoti, Rikard finished the area they requested first, then left them to their own."

"A few years later, as a solitary wing of the castle was finally complete, King Sheldon visited. On the eighth night, the freshly consecrated temple caught fire. A novice priest was trapped inside, Alfred. He climbed to the bell tower. As flames engulfed him he shouted with a voice, said to be heard over the entire city. Thus 'The Prophecy of the Flame' was born." He pauses to sip the mulled wine provided with dinner.

"'Hearken to my words: our salvation is revealed by our beloved Andskoti. In the darkest hour, when the fate of mankind is threatened by darkness, our savoir will come with hair aflame, by that you will know him. Embrace that which is brought, for it will be your only salvation. Change will sweep the land like fire across a summer meadow. Magic will rise as the entire fabric of our kingdom is rewoven. Through the bond of marriage, magic will be brought onto the Throne of Cuthburan at last. So I have been shown. So let it be known.' As the last words were uttered Alfred was engulfed in flames." Szames gives a resigned sigh.

While servants place desert in front of us I raise my

glass, stalling for time. I'm already married! There is no way in Hell that I will marry that... that... pig, Prophecy or no! Ok, calm... I've gotta remain calm. Think rationally. It's a prophecy. It could have many meanings, surely.

"You know, all I have read about prophecy says they are a dangerous thing. Often the meaning lies hidden, what seems forthright and obvious can mean something entirely different," Szames is blank-faced so I continue as we start on desert, "Take the fact that it seems to describe a man: perhaps in translating the original, it was assumed any help would come from a man, not a woman. Also, the part about 'through marriage bonds' seems, likewise, a simple enough prediction: but there must be a deeper meaning. I am already married."

Szames chokes on what he is attempting to swallow, "Pardon me. Did you say you are a married woman?"

"For several years now," I smile at his astonishment.

Incredulous he asks, "Is it one of the men with whom you travel? Do you have children?"

"Unfortunately no to both. Merithin failed to bring Tony, my husband, when he transferred us. I am working on a way around the Portal Law so we can be rejoined. If I can't find a way around it, I will have to return with the others when we've completed our mission here."

Again Szames's wine seems determined to strangle him. Coughing, he clears his throat, "You are planning on returning to your world?"

I'd better watch when I drop those bombshells or I might have to practice CPR. "Most likely. If I can't find a way around this law about portals, I will have to return with those of my group wishing to go home. The way I see it, there is a good chance the marriage of the prophecy is not my own, but a marriage I set into motion or one of the new types of magic I'm introducing to this realm." I steer us back to the original topic, "Even the most simplistic of predictions can be misleading."

As we return our attention to our desert, I get a stray feeling from Szames, one of skepticism. It is so strong it is almost a denial. I need to get the word out that I will not be marrying Alex before they try to force me into it.

"Look, let me be candid with you. I would not marry your brother for all the gold in your treasury, even if I weren't already married. He may be an excellent diplomat and turn out to be a wonderful king, but I simply don't find him to be suitable marriage material," Szames's disbelief intensifies.

"I also have no interest in being queen. Politics are incredibly boring," Still unconvinced._ In desperation I mutter, "and your brother is a narcissistic womanizer."

"Tell me, did magic help you figure out my sibling so quickly?" Szames radiates pleasant astonishment before all emotion disappears again.

"Who could fail to recognize him for what he is with his gigantic ego pointing the way?" As a deep chuckle escapes my dinner companion, I continue, "Good, now that we have that settled, I was wondering if I could get your help with an experiment." When Crystal takes our dishes I ask for the bucket delivered earlier.

"A magical working with rocks?" Szames stares at the contents.

"It doesn't take much to hold an enchantment." I hint.

He raises his eyebrows, smiling to let me know he is still game. Taking one of the small river-stones in my hand I begin an incantation.

"If with my essence you are placed,
You will afford a 'saving grace.'
Make a barrier around the skin,
Titanium strong, you'll be thin.
Also behave as a Paladin Shield
Giving an edge on the battlefield."

My tingling palm opens as magic penetrates the stone, drawing deep inside. The blue light dissipates, the rock turns clear: all of the color withdraws to form a dark core in the center of the opaque stone.

"I need a little help with a test. The stone should form a shield around the bearer, slowing down incoming attacks as well as forming an almost indestructible shield lying next to the skin. The problem with testing this charm is that a weapon must be trying to injure the wearer of the stone for the effect to be seen."

"So you need someone to attack?" Szames shrugs, "With the new healing power you have brought, the danger should be minimal."

"It's not that simple. The intent must be to injure. I'm not sure I can do that, at least not if I am holding the weapon. If you will remove your mail, I will throw one of my knives at you. The blade will then be a weapon intent on harming you," Use you as a pincushion? "I wish there was another way to test it, but the danger must be real…"

I hand the pebble to the hunky blonde. With a smile he strips off his tabard then his mail. "Let you throw a knife at me? Without my mail? You ask a lot of a dinner guest." His lopsided smile is contagious.

"Only the ones I like." My eyes twinkle, "Are you ready?" Pulling a blade from my leg sheath I hold it by the tip. It feels so comfortable, like the blade is an extension of my hand. Let's just hope that I can hit what I aim at, too.

"Ready and waiting," When I hesitate to throw he asks, "Reba, would it be easier if I closed my eyes?"

"That's not necessary." Filling my lungs to capacity, I hurl knife, praying I won't see a crimson river flowing from his stomach.

The blade flies true. The knife becomes more visible about two feet from Szames's midriff as the stone slows the weapon's momentum. The Paladin Shield fails to stop the knife: It slices into his padded undershirt. With a thud the throwing knife hits the floor.

"Are you hurt?" I rush around the table.

Szames pokes his finger into the hole in the material,

moving it around. "It cut right through the undershirt but did not even scratch the skin."

"It worked!" Excitement bubbling over, I grab him by the hand, pulling him over to the bucket, "Szames, when I finish the duplication spell, toss the rock into the pale."

The replication goes off with out a hitch, "If you will distribute these among the men, we can make more tomorrow. In a few days we should have enough for all the troops, maybe even the support staff."

"Reba, you intend to make more than two thousand of these?" His eyes bulge.

I shake my head, "More than four, if we can get enough stones."

"You are handing my kingdom immeasurable power. I am beginning to wonder, what price do you set for your aid?" Although the question sounds suspicious, his tone is friendly enough.

"All I ask is that your family continues to rule justly with fair consideration to all in the land." If I could perceive something from him. I could reassure him better.

"That is why you were curious about my brothers ruling ability?" Szames inquires.

"Yes, among other things," I raise an eyebrow, "Szames, perhaps you would be willing to relate more of your kingdom's history to me, say, over dinner tomorrow? We could take care of the stones at the same time."

His blue eyes twinkle. "I would love to dine with you again. However, I insist we keep our evenings for relaxation. Our physicians tell us, in times of stress we need to set aside a mark or two to recuperate from our duties. Is there perhaps another time when we can take care of the magic stones?"

I shrug, "The rocks are to be delivered to the front gates at sunset. If you meet me, we could take care of them as they arrive."

"I have had a delightful evening, My Lady Reba. I will see you at sundown," he replies formally, "Will a mark after mid-night bells suffice for dinner on the morrow?"

With bucket in hand, he turns to leave.

I follow the prince into the reception chamber. I saunter on to my bedroom when he dips his head again in parting. After meditating on what's needed for a revised portal spell, I place an enchantment on the egg-sized jewel. Bells toll signaling night is now three-quarters done, as I crawl into bed after performing my nightly ritual.

Chapter Twenty

"Charles the Paladin, MasterHealer Jamison, Allinon the Druid Elf, and Jerik the Dwarven MasterSmith, I present to you MasterArtist Yivgeni. He will chronicle this crusade in paintings and sketches. He is sworn to reveal none of what he sees or hears, except in paintings," Yivgeni bows while Jerik's bushy eyebrows shoot up to his hairline. The others merely nod, ambling into the dining room.

"Reba, placing the awakening spell in the stone was brilliant. We have been able to thoroughly screen the volunteers before we take them through the process," Jamison announces as he crosses the threshold into the secured chamber.

"I wish my first attempt at a disassociated enchantment had gone that well." While the servants begin setting the table under Crystal's watchful eye, I reveal my failure.

"But why go through the trouble of using a focus to offset the portal spell? We just need to cast it once?" For once Allinon's question contains no trace of sarcasm.

"I was hoping I could send correspondence home or even bring out our significant others. At the church today I found out our job doesn't end with The Great Battle, as they are now calling it. It appears a gateway has been constructed between this world and the Demonic Realm. We've been instructed to travel on a circular route around our position until we find it."

"Hey now, I agreed to break the siege, not to be a crusading hero. I've got a kid I want to see grow up. " Charles is adamant, "I didn't sign up for a two-year tour! Reba, just who gave you these instructions?"

"Their god, Andskoti," Yivgeni chokes on his drink, reminding me of his presence. I pop a bite of sausage into my mouth while I wait for the shock to wear off.

"You are joking, right." Allinon puts a stranglehold on the irritation I sense bubbling up him. Seeing no way around it, I relay the details the entire encounter.

"That's heavy, man." Jamison lapses into English, but continues in Cuthburish. "You are a Christian and he recognized you as one of God's children? It looks like we are in for a little campaigning."

"There's no way! We were brought here against our will," seething with emotion, Charles slips into English, spiting each word out as if it is covered in bile, "I won't do it".

"Reba, you have got to find a way around that law or take us home after the battle. My wife will declare me dead if I'm missing for more than a couple of weeks." The honest sincerity in Allinon's voice rattles me almost as much as the shiver of premonition making chilly tracks up my spine.

I continue the trend, sticking to my native tongue, "I think a vote is in order. This is a decision affecting the entire group. There's no guarantee I can find a way around their First Law of Magic. But let me tell you, I don't think they will win the battle for the gateway without us. My vote is for staying until we finish the job. Jamison how 'bout you?" The icy fingers of fate refuse to release their hold on the back of my neck as Jamison agrees with me and Charles votes no.

"This is not our war, and we were not asked to join. We were taken from our world. As for bringing those we love out…" Allinon can't just give a yes or no, he delivers a speech, "Well, with their different perspective on morals, I would think twice about testing the strength of your wedding vows. I vote for going home after the battle."

"My vote will be the tie breaker." Jerik's quiet voice lacks its usual boom, "I say we compromise. No one should be forced to fight against their will, but we also can't leave these people with a war half won. Reba, let's do one circuit around the castle, take eight days to a couple of weeks. If we haven't found the gate, those of us that wish to leave should be sent then. I, for one, will not be one of those going home. I will stay here," the dwarf's closing revelation shocks us all.

"Jerik, you've got a wife. There is no guarantee I'll be able to cast the spell a second time." I plead with him to reconsider, "I told you what happened with my first attempt. I will try with the emerald, but if I don't find a solution before I leave, you will be stranded for who knows how long."

A long breath escapes the short man, "My wife and I are separated. I have nothing to go home to. For the first time, I feel as if I belong, even if I'm the only dwarf in this kingdom. When I am working in the forge, it fits like architecture never has. I have been here three days and yet I have no doubt: I belong here."

"I understand. Jerik, I'm sorry you won't be coming home with us," I turn to the rest of the band, "I can't agree to abandon these people right after the battle. I can't explain it, but I know there is something else I have to do. I see no other choice but to agree to the proposed compromise. If the rest of you will stay and fight until we have completed at least one round of the area surrounding the city, you have my word that I will take home any who want to go, at that time." As the men agree to the revised plan, Charles gives us an update on the battle training.

"Three other women reported in yesterday. One has a thief's skill with knives and the other two have some basic training with blades. Between Allinon and I, in a week's time, we might have them proficient enough that they won't hurt themselves," Charles' jovial demeanor is dampened as he contemplates the ladies in battle, "More than that I can't promise."

"That Andrayia, on the other hand, she's got some skill. With the titanium sword you made, she is quick. I'd say her ability is equal to or better than that of the men we trained," Allinon's optimistic view makes me wonder if perhaps he and Charles swapped bodies in the night.

"If you think they can handle it, I can copy your skills to the women as well as Andrayia's equipment..."

"You mean give them our knowledge? You could do that?" Charles's good nature reasserts itself, "Any chance at me getting a Don Juan ability while you're at it? Not that I need it."

As we laugh our reservations away, I steer us back to the business at hand, "Allinon, I should be ready for you and any druid students by mid-afternoon. Jamison, I will have some of those Paladin stones delivered to you, but not until tomorrow after sunset. Is there anything we missed?"

"How about that prophecy," Charles eyes twinkle devilishly, "Didn't you have a line on that?"

With a sigh, I recite the verses Szames revealed to me. The room is as quiet as snow on a frigid December morning as I finish the ominous sounding litany.

"Wheew, so you're here to save the world and become queen. Are you sure you want to leave?" Charles is only half-joking.

"Come on, don't tell me you took the bait." I beseech the most logical of our group. "Jamison, you at least, must be able to see through all the smoke and mirrors?"

"Well, since the prophecy is over two-hundred years old, and has obviously been translated at least once, it could have many possible meanings," Jamison removes the smile from my face with a qualifying remark, "But if enough people believe in one interpretation, they could have enough power between them to make what is expected to happen come to pass. That is the danger in a prophecy that is so popular."

"You guys have to help me spread the word. There is no way I'm going to marry that conceited, egotistical, male-chauvinist they call a crowned prince. He has all the morals of a rutting elk. He only intends to make me part of his herd," Quiet as deaths shroud I snarl, "On top of that he seems to have some sort of, as you put it Charles, 'Don Juan' ability that makes me want to forget I've got a husband."

"Are you sure it's not those broad shoulders and those baby-blues of his?" Tall, dark, and handsome gives his best leer.

"Of course I'm sure." at least I think I'm sure, I dismiss Charles' attempt at humor as bad taste. "Look, I can't stand lies. Empathy lets me spot his deceptions as clearly as a bad comb-over on a chromed-dome. Even when he is lying he turns me on. It must be a charisma based ability or something similar. Let's compare his aura with what we know of all of ours. Maybe we can come up with a theory or two." Again I try to rally the troops. "In the meantime we have got two hundred years of skewed perception to get back on target. I need to know how to combat this."

"I can tell the healers you're working to bring out your husband. They come into contact with mega people. If I can get them talking about it, word will spread in a day or two," Jamison volunteers.

Charles' grin is malicious as he contemplates this new duty, "I will work on getting the War Council ready for the campaign directly after the battle and let them know of our impending departure. With that and your turning out to be a woman it should be enough to shake some of their certainty concerning the impending nuptials."

"The more doubt we stir up the better." I heave a sigh of relief before interrogating the others about their magical and charismatic abilities, making a note of aura coloration.

Jamison is the first to rise from the table, "Well, if there's nothing else, I've got an appointment to keep. I'll be escorting Rose to the Physicians Consortium. You can reach me there."

"And I still have a stack of weapons to work on," Jerik adds, "Matter of fact, unless I'm needed, I would like to skip breakfast tomorrow."

"Sounds good. If you need anything, you know where you can find me." Apprehension nags me as our meeting dissolves. Something tells me this ride is far from over.

"I apologize for the necessity of excluding you from parts of our conversation, Yivgeni, but the times dictate strict security measures," I address the sole person left in the room.

"I understand, Milady ArchMage Reba. I appreciate your letting me stay. The intimate exposure to you and your men will allow me to capture you more accurately." He follows me into the Reception Chamber, "If you wouldn't mind, I would like to accompany you for the remainder of the day."

Yivgeni remains with me throughout the afternoon as I take care of the issues sent to me, via sealed correspondence early this morning. Being diligent to uphold his part of our bargain, the artist is still trailing behind when I meet Alex at the stables.

"Reba, I see you have managed to sway Yivgeni to our cause. I had the utmost confidence you would," Alex flashes a dazzling smile my way.

"Thank you," I mutter, trying to get a firm hold on my surging hormones.

While the prince leads me over to the large pile of sand delivered to the meadow next to the livery, I covertly observe his aura, "How's your shoulder?"

"Good as new," He flexes his arm, "Healing magic will be invaluable in the weeks to come. You must see very few losses in the wars of your world, with the Gift to aid you."

"Our wars are much different than the ones you wage. Facing an opponent on a field of honor is not something regularly practice on my world." my rejoinder is as bleak as my mood.

"Then your world must be as boring as ours was prior to demon invasion. Until a few months ago I thought I would never put to use the swordsmanship I have worked so hard to perfect. Now I have more than I could have ever dreamed: a fierce foe, battles that will be talked about for centuries to come," turning to face me as we reach our destination, he whispers, "and a beautiful maiden with whom to share my glory."

My knees tremble, my body aches for him to take me into his arms. "Glories of battle, Alex? Like the one that almost cost you your life?" I force my mind to evaluate his words in the harshest light, "Not to mention the lives of over fifty of your men."

"But with you here, the magic you bring, we are sure to be victorious in every conflict. When you are by my side, most beautiful of maidens," he captures my hands, drawing me within reach of the lips I long to kiss, "I know there is nothing we cannot overcome."

"I am afraid I must correct you once more, for I am not a maiden," fighting the carnal urges wreaking havoc in my body and soul, I free my hand from his startled grasp, "this ring symbolizes my union with another. It is a married woman to whom you speak." I hope I can manage to remember that!

"Married? But you can't be…" For the first time, Alex looses his composure, "the prophecy?"

"Yes, I have heard about your 'Prophecy,'" I exude nonchalance, pretending to examine the sand. "I am sure there are other possible meanings which have been lost in translation."

"I see. Perhaps the outcome of future events are not as predetermined as we assumed," with a heart-melting smile that feels forced, he rallies his offenses once more, "All the more reason we should take time to relish the company of one another. It is said 'what the gods bring should be pondered endlessly.'"

"Yes, perhaps in the days to come events will allow

us to spend more time together, but today I have too many duties to waste time on pondering frivolities. If you are ready I believe this sand will suit my purpose." The sooner I get Tony out here, the better.

"This time I'll need you to join me on the ground, next to the sand, if you think you are ready for the next step," Alex lowers himself gracefully, extending his hands. His arousal at the prospect of the closer proximity is almost palatable with my empathy. My face freezes and horror grips my mind as my stomach does a flip-flop: I am unsure weather the queasiness is due to disgust or nymphetic anticipation.

"Reba, with you I am ready for whatever may come," the seductive leer of his voice causes my cheeks to flush and my panties to dampen.

"Just relax and hold tight; the ride will soon begin," A sardonic smile creeps across my face as a puzzled feeling replaces the arousal of my partner when he fails to understand the English quip. I focus on my spell, beginning as our joined hands come into contact with the sand.

"Basketball sized and shaped you'll be,
Unbreakable crystal and hollow to see.
Drawing energy in, all the while
Giving off light in abundant style."

'Illuminate' causes you to glow.
'Transparent' will end the show.
If an opposing foe harms your being,
An exploding force will be freeing."

When the sand under our hands rises, swirling to construct a miniature cyclone, tension blooms in my partner. I struggle to ignore the distraction. Within seconds a clear globe lies beneath our hands.

Since the stress didn't escalate during the spell I ask, "Alex, if you're ready I would like to copy this one as we did with the coins."

After he gives a tight nod, I proceed with the duplication riddle. The dune ascends over our heads, spiraling like a dust devil. The whirlwind contorts. Contracting like a squashed balloon, it gives birth to a hundred mage-globes. They clatter to the ground, spreading out in a semi-circle around us.

Alex gallantly assists me in rising. He retains custody of my hand, "Thank you, Reba. These will be of great use, not only in the battle to come, but in the future of our kingdom." Taking my other hand, his voice drops an octave, "As always your abilities astound me."

Whispered as they are, the words send blood surging through my veins. With agonizing slowness Alex leans toward me. My mind is overcome by fervid yearning to feel his mouth on mine, to taste him, to be one with him. I lean into the embrace. Against reason, my lips part and my breath quickens.

"Your Highness. Reba, I'm glad I caught you," in the silence of the passion encompassing us, Allinon's loud soprano jars my brain into action.

My face flushes as I realize what I have nearly done. Dropping his hands like hot rocks. I take a step back from tall, dark, and hansom, pivoting so I can address my approaching savior.

"Allinon, is there someway I can aid you?" I pray for an excuse to escape.

"Not at the moment, except to remind you that Jamison is looking forward to your visit. I also wanted to confirm breakfast tomorrow. Will mid-afternoon bells be agreeable?" Perceiving a sense of urgency in his request, I assent.

Thanks to Allinon's timely arrival, I am able to extricate myself from Alex's company without any additional moral lapses, but not without promising to meet Heir Apparent at dusk tomorrow to transform another load of sand. I continue on my way with the MasterArtist in tow.

Love's Dawning

Chapter Twenty-One

"Szames, I am sorry I'm late. I hope you haven't been waiting long." I smile at the towheaded prince.

"I arrived moments ago." He smiles back, "I have only just now located the needed stones."

Less than a quarter-mark later, we have completed the needed enchantments, giving the new Paladin Stones to the waiting page. I wish dealing with his brother were this easy.

"Thank you," my curiosity about the differences in the two brothers gets the best of me. "You enjoy dealing with the arcane?"

"Typically, anyone unable to cast a minor spell has never been allowed to participate in anything of a magical nature." His deep voice is so unlike Jerik's: smooth where the dwarf's is gravelly, yet something in it strikes me as familiar.

"When I was a child they told me there was a strong possibility I would become an apprentice. For this reason I was allowed to study the history of magic with Merithin. It fascinated me more than the rest of my studies combined."

"Did you ever study the language of magic or spells?" I ask, wondering how much security we really have.

"Unfortunately, no. When I did not develop the Gift, my father called a halt to my studies. He insisted I concentrate on military research since I would be assuming the post of General of our Armed Forces," Szames shifts topics, "Speaking of duties, have you received a copy of the supply list I had sent to you.?"

"Is there something in particular for which I should be looking?" A frown causes my forehead to crease.

"Your idea of pooling resources was brilliant. But with the additions to the Healers' Academy and the Army, even the increased provisions will not last more than a day or two." He seems surprised at my lack of knowledge of such routine matters. "I was thinking: if you had the available energy, could you use a duplication spell on some of the staples?"

"A duplication spell for the food we will need? Szames, that's a great idea. I can't believe it never occurred to me. If you have got a list of the shops supplying us, I will make a run by them tomorrow night." Am I wrong about him? Sure he's big and brawny like a jock, but he's resourceful, intelligent and almost studious.

"Milady Reba, I will take my leave now, unless you have other errands?" Yivgeni interjects, "May I accompany you on the morrow?"

"Thank you Yivgeni, that sounds like a good idea. Meet me at the stables at evening bells," I turn to Szames, "I have really got to be going, there is an experiment I must conduct before I loose daylight."

"Another spell? If you would like some assistance, I am free for the moment," Szames volunteers with a grin.

"To tell you the truth I could use the help. I must warn you, though, my last attempt didn't go so well," I frown with the memory of the failure, "I'm not sure what the outcome will be."

"A work in progress, it sounds incredibly intriguing," Szames is undaunted.

"Perhaps, but if the spell fails, it could prove to be dangerous," I urge caution.

"All the more reason I should be there. If there is an issue of safety, you may need my aid," His valiant protectiveness is touching, if unnecessary.

Grasping his hand, I lift us into the air, drawing most of the needed energy from him. The sun colors the horizon with brilliant shades of pink as we set down in the meadow with the melted rock. I place the emerald and the folded bundle of correspondences on the flattened stone while there is still light in the sky. Szames takes my hand once more and my palms turn orgasmically numb, as energy surges from our souls.

"Trans-dimensional," I pronounce into the coming night.

Energy is sponged into the emerald. The crystal glows as teal light shoots out in all directions, disappearing into the approaching dusk. Another beam forms an octagonal doorway around the parchment. The laser-light pattern within the gemstone becomes brighter and brighter until, without warning, a sapphire ray returns from out of nowhere, seeming to come from everywhere at once. Tony's letter disappears. Having formed a mental link to the missive, I feel it race through time and space streaking toward its destination.

My face turns slack and my mouth falls open when then pattern inside the crystal begins to shimmer. I release Szames, cutting him from the link. I reach out a desperate hand as the emerald begins to vibrate in its stand.

My connection to the manuscript inexplicably disappears, as magical reserves wrench and twist inside me. A wave of dizziness causes me to sway like a tree in a tornado. Szames knocks me to the ground covering my smaller frame with his as a thunderous explosion leaves my ears ringing.

Rolling to the side, Szames gently helps me sit up, "Reba, are you ok? Your arm, it's bleeding." In a daze I watch him tear off a piece of his shredded tunic, using it as a makeshift bandage, "Are there any other injuries?"

"No... I...I am... ok," unable to focus on my surroundings, I look at the world around me feeling as though I am surrounded by soupy fog.

The rock has a large crack running across it. Its pitted

surface is a testimony to magic gone awry. Looking to my partner, I see other evidence of destruction.

"How about you?" a more complete sentence is beyond my fuzzy mind.

"Nothing but a few bruises, thanks to the chain mail. Do you think you can stand?"

"If you will assist me in rising," I am weak, but resolved, "With a little food I am sure I will be fine."

Szames practically picks me up, setting me on my feet, all the while maintaining a hold on my arm. Struggling to lift my foot, my legs give out from under me. Before my knees hit the ground Szames swoops me into his arms. Carrying me like a child he hustles for the castle with long, quick strides. Thick blackness of unwanted sleep steals over me as the rhythm of his steps rocks me like a babe in her father's arms. I wake as the smell of food tantalizes my senses through the light doze.

The haze surrounding my brain clears after a few sips of mulled wine, but is immediately replaced by a skull-splitting headache. The anxious look from Szames makes me feel even worse.

"I should have taken greater precautions... I'm sorry..." my apology trails off as the ache in my skull multiplies with each word. I choke down some of the bread and cheese for lack of anything better to do.

"You did warn me of the dangers. Are you sure you are okay?" His worry is touching.

"I'll live." What I wouldn't give for some Tylenol.

Looking down, I pull back the sleeve of my robe. The shirt underneath is torn and bloody. Now I've ruined a blouse; Crystal is going to kill me!

Missing the sound of the door opening over the throbbing of my head, I jump as Merithin appears at the end of the table.

"Quite the headache?" When I nod yes, the sorcerer turns to the prince, "Your Highness, I will see the lady to her chambers where she may recover. I am sure you have other matters to attend."

Szames takes the hint, rising to leave, "Milady, will you be feeling up to dinner this evening?"

"I must eat, whether or not I can think through this headache," I wince at the sound of my own voice.

As Szames leaves, Merithin moves to help me rise. Shamefully, I am forced to lean on someone more than twice my age as we make our way to my rooms.

"What exactly were you doing, if I may ask?" Merithin queries as we enter a deserted hallway, "I know it was an extensive work having to do with portals… I also have no doubt the backlash was felt for a few thousands paces."

"I was using an emerald as a focus to hold the majority of a portal spell so I could send a message to my home world," I mumble, trying not to antagonize the pain that is subsiding to a dull throb. Cautiously, I apply a touch of healing magic.

"You were trying to get around the First Law? You have broken the Fourth Law against flying, and you may be the One Who Brings Change, but this is one law you won't be breaking," Merithin's tone is surprisingly bitter.

"Merithin, I've got to find a way around it. I have a husband, we need to be together." Pleading with the elder, I feel like a scolded child. The situation with Alex worsening by the day, I am desperate. I gesture for him to take a seat in the reception chamber. "Surely it can be bent, if not broken?"

"Milady, you have my greatest sympathy. I understand your desire to be with the one you care for, but I am afraid I can offer you no good news," his voice turns softer, kinder as he explains. "With your experience on another world, it is expected some of that which is unattainable to us might be possible for you. As you well know, the usual enchantment relies solely on the spoken word and information in the mind of the caster. But the portal spell uses the essence of the individual performing the spell. A piece of the aura is necessary to complete the transfer. That is the reason it can only be preformed one time. Only the aura of a MasterSorcerer holds the needed essence, and once cast, the aura is depleted of the vital substance making the spell possible. Any attempt without the needed ingredient destroys that which is to be transported and, depending on the strength of the spell, the caster as well."

Muted through the haze of pain I perceive an inexplicable sadness in the graying gentleman, "I can see by your aura you were still in contact with the process when it failed to find the portal essence. Most Master Level sorcerers would be unconscious right now. With your abilities I suspect you will merely have a headache that will make you wish you were dead. It will take a day or so for your aura to sort itself out and regain its vitality. I suggest, if you have any more ideas concerning modifying a portal spell, talk it through with me first." The grandfatherly manner with which he delivers his advice makes it impossible for me to resent him for the restriction.

"Merithin, I promise I'll talk to you before I perform any more portal experiments." With the pain abating, I can think straight. I blush at the folly of my actions. "But right now I need to hurry over to the infirmary."

"That, milady, is out of the question. You are going nowhere but to bed. Without a nap, at the very least, you are going to find working even a minor spell incredibly difficult," he informs me.

"I don't have time for this! Merithin there are things I need to do. I have to at least enchant those sashes." When I shake my head for emphasis a sharp knife slices through my skull causing me to wince involuntary.

"If you don't rest now, give your aura time to settle, it may take you weeks to recover. Do you have a spell ready for the defensive sashes?" After I give a cautious nod he continues, "Let us go over the enchantment and the desired attributes."

Since the majority of the magic is a duplication spell from my silver cloak, Merithin manages to assume the responsibility with very little effort. Minutes later, after handing over the enchanted garment, I stumble into my bedroom. Not bothering to undress, I collapse into a heap on the inviting featherbed.

The sensation of tumbling in a black void engulfs my subconscious. Once sleep overcomes me I am unable to wake. After what seems like hours to the confusion of my muddled senses, a soothing balm penetrates my comatose state: I discern the presence of another. My eyes pop open.

"Sleeping Beauty awakes with my touch. Does this mean I'm a prince?" Recognizing Jamison's accent, I sigh with relief.

"Who me? Sleeping Beauty? I'm more like a sleeping giant around here. But Jamison, you are a prince among men. You took away the headache." As Jamison examines the wound on my arm, Crystal and Rhachel enter.

"Another experiment, milady?" Crystal gives the blouse a disapproving look. "You will need to change."

"Removing the shirt will make my job easier, if you don't mind." Jamison colors as he makes the request.

As I unbutton the shirt I notice blood on the slacks. Seeing no reason for modesty - after all, the undergarments I am wearing are more concealing then a bikini - I take those off as well.

"Crystal, I guess I'll need a whole new out fit while we're at it."

As I turn back toward him, Jamison lets out a whistle, "Not a beauty my ass," the healer puns shamelessly, staring at my butt. "That tail is a black man's dream."

"Jamison! What happened to doctor's medical detachment?" mockingly, I take him to task, "I suppose I'm built decently if you like the tall athletic type."

"Now you must be joking. You've got the perfect slim figure and a great butt, if I may say so," he trails off as he begins working on my arm.

"Well, I'm proud to say that's an original piece of

equipment - my dad's bubble-butt," Noticing Rhachel's open mouth I explain, "Good friends come in both male and female on my world; openness is not uncommon."

Still bewildered at the platonic exchange she bobs her head, "As you say, milady."

"Jamison, I hope they didn't drag you all the way from the Hall for this little scratch." I remark as he comes out of the trance.

"What? No... I escorted Rose back. I heard what happened I stopped by to see how you were doing," looking up from his work he gives his final diagnosis, "Your arm should be as good as new, but I'm afraid it was only a temporary fix on the headache. When the boost I gave you wears off use your healing ability to keep the pain to a minimum until you aura sorts itself out."

"Thanks a million. Crystal, I am famished. Can you send for a snack?" Crystal whispers to Rhachel who darts off as I begin dressing.

"I don't think I'm gonna make breakfast tomorrow, but if you have a few minutes, can I join you for your snack?" With his request I sense something troubling him. I don't have to wait long to find out what's bothering my friend: as soon as his feet cross the threshold he begins pacing.

"I've been thinking about what Jerik said this morning, about not going home. Reba I have got no one back there that will miss me much. I see my foster parents a couple times a year, I don't have anything close to a love interest."

"Jamison, hold on a minute. If you're thinking about Rose...."

The healer takes a defensive stance, "What do you mean, 'thinking about Rose?' What if I am?"

"I'm empathetic, remember. Being between you two is like being submerged in chocolate: all warm and gooey," the joke fails to lighten the mood.

"You mean she digs me, really digs me?" The huge grin spreading across his face tears at my heart because I know I am going to have to break his.

"Did she happen to mention that King Arturo has arranged a marriage for her?"

"Married?" The strangled tone makes me wince, "That," he stutters, "that doesn't matter. The real reason I'm staying is Healing. It's just like Jerik said: when I use my Gift I feel complete. I feel like I belong somewhere for the first time in my life. My decision still stands. I'm not going with you."

"If that's what you want. You can always change your mind. You're gonna have at least another couple weeks to explore this place before we go."

When Crystal and Rhachel enter with a plate of food I change the subject, not wanting news of our splintering group to get out before I am ready for the questions it will arouse. Jamison, congenial as always, follows the change in topic, promising to try and make breakfast day after tomorrow for an update.

Chapter Twenty-Two

"Reba, I am delighted you have recovered enough to join me. How are you feeling?" The honest caring the princess exudes is a soothing balm to my wounded pride. She's related to Alex?

"Thanks to Jamison, I feel almost back to normal." At the mention of his name I get a rush of intense passion laced with a warm fuzziness.

As we sit down to lunch, I broach the topic with my new friend, "Rose, it's obvious, at least to me, how you and Jamison feel toward each other. Part of me is happy, but I'm also worried about the eventual pain any type of relationship is bound to bring."

"He feels the same?" her surprise isn't as great as Jamison's, but the overwhelming happiness it brings is a mirror image of the physician's response, "I expected as much. I am touched by your concern, however, I hope you will not be offended when I do not heed it." Stunned by her frankness it takes me a few minutes to reply.

"I understand your position. We have a saying," raising my glass for a toast I plagiarize shamelessly, "'It is better to have loved and lost then to have never loved at all.' I wish you both the best, until duty separates you."

As Rose sets her glass on the table she gives a slight nod of her head, as if acknowledging something, "I love both my brothers, however I feel I should give you counsel in return for your thoughtfulness."

My mind races through possible revelations while I wait for her to continue as she chews a bite of meat, "Jamison has told me some about the ways of love and marriage on your world. Ours ways differ greatly. It is expected that you will marry Alex. If it should come to pass, no matter what promises he gives, I do not believe Alex has the capacity for monogamy. Do not trust him with your heart, no matter what he pledges."

"Thank you, Rose, I will keep your words firmly in mind." I respond to her support even if the information is unneeded, "Hopefully the issue will never arise."

The rest of our lunch passes too swiftly. When I leave for my chambers she goes to the Healers Academy. Being unable to cast even a minor spell leaves me with little to do but organize supplies and created the enchantments I will need. Surprisingly, these activities take the rest of the evening.

"Yes, Milady ArchMage Reba." William bows as I finish listing tomorrow's duties. Why do I still sense trepidation?

"Yes, milady ArchMage Reba" On his second day, Keth's mimicking Williams behavior perfectly. A quick study. I'll have to talk to Merithin about his training. I don't even know at what age the Gift is supposed to appear.

A knock sounds on the outer door and my newest squire moves to answer it, beating William to the punch. When Szames enters, both boys bow before taking their leave.

"I wondered what was keeping Alex's other squire so busy. How are you finding his services?" Szames ushers me toward the dining room table.

"Alex's squire?" I am blindsided by the revelation.

"You mean he failed to disclose where he received his training? Who assigned him to you?" Szames's bewildered tone changes to disgust as he enlightens me. "Like father like son, I suppose. William is Duke Rokroa's son. The Duke is one of Father's most loyal subjects. What is said in his presence might as well be whispered in Father's ear."

"Szames, you have just solved a riddle that has plagued me since William's arrival. A sense of fear shadows the child. I think he's been terrified I will discover he is reporting to your brother," chuckling at the thought of someone fearing me, Szames and I exchange knowing smiles.

We both dig into dinner, concentrating on food instead of conversation. As our hunger diminishes Szames breaks the silence.

"So, Reba, what can you tell me about the world from which you come?" He lets me make the decision of what to contribute for the information exchange.

"Hmmm, let's see. Our worlds are so different. Why don't I start with something close to home? It has been pointed out, by several people now, that my marriage differs from the ones here in one very fundamental way." Needing to make my lack of sexual freedom clear, I begin a lecture I know I will be giving quite often.

Explaining relationships to him like I did with Crystal, minus the dramatic recreation of our lovemaking, I find his openly displayed astonishment extremely amusing. "You are welcome to ask questions. We can discuss any topic. But I want you to know that whatever my behavior may imply on his world, my gestures are completely platonic."

"So if I understand correctly, you and your husband still find your... relationship... satisfying?" The emphasis he places on "relationship" leads me to ask the obvious.

"You are talking sexually?" I chuckle as Szames turns a bright red. "It's not as earth-shattering as it once was, but it's still extremely enjoyable. Making love has lost some of the urgency you find when the relationship is new, but we have overcome many obstacles, which has caused our love grow. Now we share a greater intimacy in our coupling." I finish quickly before I bore the playboy to death with monogamous details. "Both of us know that when we get old and fat there will be someone who will still want to cuddle and express the love we have nurtured throughout the years; that each wrinkle will be loved."

"I have often dreamed, but never believed such could be true." Szames' sigh would sound facetious if it isn't so solemn.

"Come on, now. You don't expect me to believe a guy like you would be interested in monogamy. You're tall, built, and totally gorgeous, not to mention your princely status. You must have women throwing themselves at you right and left. Being "you" is a man's dream," noticing crimson infusing my dinner partner's face, I halt my rebuttal.

As his color returns to normal he asks, "You do say exactly what you mean?"

"I am afraid so." I work to keep my disappointment from showing. "If you'd like I can try to be a little more circumspect, but I make no guarantees,"

"I am not offended, just surprised. I will try to be as direct with you as well." Clearing his throat he begins, "I had a lot of fun, as you implied, when I was younger. Being a prince does have many advantages. There were, still are, many women of all varieties willing to take a stroll in the garden late at night. But after a few years it grew tiresome. I began to want more, someone who would be there for more than just a few nights. One would think it would not be so difficult to find," Szames takes a long sip of wine before he continues, "It took years, two and a half to be exact. My relationship with Kealla lasted almost as long as it took to find her,"

The sadness in his voice is unmistakable, even without empathetic aid, "I discussed my desires for an exclusive relationship. She agreed. Like a fool I thought, even though we had a few problems, that once we worked through them everything was fine. Then came the day she could no longer look into my eyes, all the while telling me how foolish it was that we tried to make our relationship into something which could never be."

"Szames, I am so sorry. I had no idea." With out thinking, I place my hand over his, offering what comfort I can. With the contact I perceive a small ache that's outshadowed by astonishment before all emotion disappears like superman from a kryptonite hailstorm.

"She cheated on you?" I speak hastily to cover my shock at sensing anything.

"It was not even necessary to ask who enticed her. I had seen her in the company of my brother for the last couple of weeks. It was the same as every other relationship, it just took longer this time," Szames shrugs off Alex's betrayal as a fact of life.

"Believe it or not, I know exactly how you feel." When he gives me an incredulous look, I retrieve the pictures I conjured for reality facts.

"This is me on my world, in the transfer my appearance was altered. And this is my twin sister, Lani. Here's one of us together."

"You are a twin? I have never met someone from a dual birth." his amusement is so exuberant, even without empathy I know it is genuine, "Is she gifted as well? And these, what did you call them? Pictures? Like miniature paintings..."

I overlook his ignorance and continue on with the topic original, "Lani is a warrior. Like you she loves the challenge of combat. Unfortunately, that also includes the conquering of men. It never mattered if I had fallen for the guy or not. Most men weren't as interested in what I had to offer: unconditional love, understanding, and a relationship, as what she offered. It caused me a lot of heartache when we were growing up. But like me, I'm sure you will find someone unaffected by your sibling rivalry."

"I appreciate the thought, but I am afraid I have already stopped looking." His wistful tone leaves me doubting his word.

I shift subjects, "Szames, I forgot to thank you for coming to my rescue. If you hadn't been there I would have come away with much more than a scratch and a headache."

The comical, wanna-be debonair, totally contagious smile eclipses his face as he sloughs off the compliment, "Rescuing damsels is a prince's first duty."

"Then I had better keep you close by, something tells me I am going to need a lot of rescuing." We chuckle. The merriment causes me to follow my heart and ask about something I have been curious for a while. "You mentioned King Sheldon a few times. I would like to hear more about him and your ruling lineage."

"King Sheldon is one of my favorite topics. Let me see, where to begin?" Snapping his fingers he gives a boyish grin, "I have the perfect thing, if you are recovered enough for an adventure?"

Unable to resist, my smile is just as childlike, "Always!" Hard to believe I'm having a good time in the middle of all this war. I am glad I decided to trust him.

Szames leads me through a maze of cobwebbed corridors. In a matter of minutes, I am completely lost. Arriving at our destination, we sit on a dusty attic floor. He takes me into the past weaving a story with paintings as references for the characters.

Two men standing side by side look out over the rail of a sailing ship. One is tall and lanky the other short and stout. Although physical opposites, something about them speaks of a true friendship.

"But, Sheldon, the Council will rebel if you bring this… this savage… home as a bride. She is beautiful, and her body is the stuff of legends, but there are many such civilized women. I beg you, think this through. They still have not adjusted to the idea of you telling them who they can and cannot marry!" implores Markus, King Sheldon's most trusted counselor.

"I advise you to watch the manner in which you refer to your new Queen. Her name is her Majesty Milady Monique," because of the sharp edge to the normally jovial voice, Marcus bows relinquishing his position.

"Marc, Let me worry about the Council. By the time we get back, they will have had time to review the research I have compiled. They will come to see the wisdom of the 'Cousin Edict.' My Rosa would still be here if that law had been passed generations ago."

Marcus can find no words to comfort his king: Sheldon's continual remorse at the loss of his wife still puzzles him. Yes, she was his best friend growing up, as well as his first cousin. And yes, her passing came unexpectedly at a time when they were still young: the love they found was still strong. But there is a time to let go. In Marc's opinion, that time had come and gone long ago.

What Markus could not understand was the sole reason Monique, Princess of the Isles, had fallen in love with the still grieving monarch. Beneath Sheldon's comical appearance, was a heart as enormous as it was fragile. The king has a pair of boats for feet. His six and a half foot stature would be a boon if not for the scarecrow body that wore it. What is more, ears and a nose far too big for his ill-proportioned head serve as to disguise the most precious man she ever met.

When she gazed into his eyes for the first time, she perceived his pain. The kindness with which he treated everyone, her people and all of his subjects; the tenderness he showed when she took him to her bed; these were the reasons she agreed to marry this King of some great land far away -- not as an act of rebellion. It pained her that her father could not, or would not see it any other way.

Even if she had to clothe her body in strange coverings, even if she had to cross the great waters, she would give this misunderstood giant of a man what he needed most: love. Perhaps one day the sadness in his eyes would be gone, perhaps not. But she would love him regardless. And she knew he loved her, and that was all that was important.

In the end, the nobles grew accustomed to the strange

ways of their new Queen. Did they not have an even stranger King? When Sheldon ordered the Consortium Of Knowledge be built, they agreed. Their kingdom was the richest in all the known lands thanks to the Cuthburan line of rulers. The people were content to follow the whims of their beloved, if eccentric, rulers.

Curiosity cocks my head to one side, "What a beautiful story. Tell me, did Sheldon ever stop grieving for his lost bride?"

"He developed a lung sickness, and was bed-ridden for the last two years of his life. In his delirium it is said he called repeatedly for Roseanne, his first love," somberly, Szames helps me rise.

"So it was a tragic love story. Is that why he is your mentor?" I frown.

"Hmm, I never thought of it in that light before. I guess I have always idolized his dedication to learning and knowledge. His most famous saying is: 'Those who cannot think, fight.' It was he who began most of the treaties we still honor today."

His grin turns sarcastic as we head to the door, "A poor attitude for a leader of an army. I have always thought Alex and I should have been switched at birth, he has the warrior mentality, not me."

I shake my head, "To the contrary. I would be worried about the magic I'm initiating if the army were lead by someone with Alex's attitude. Thinking of battle as glorious is a dangerous attribute in a commander. The best military leaders are those use their brains first and the sword as a last resort."

Noticing my yawn on the way back to my chambers Szames makes a polite departure after setting a dinner date for tomorrow.

Chapter Twenty-Three

"Wow, what's up with the do? Don't tell me the king's putting on another dinner," Charles asks as I open the door.

"Not precisely, I'm having tea with Queen Szacquelyn after breakfast," I sigh, tugging on one of the curls, "Crystal thought a change in hair style was necessary."

The elf, Charles, and I enter the security of my dining room. "Allinon, please tell me the urgent matter is good news, I could sure use some," I plead.

"How would you like an explanation for your near-fatal moral lapse?" The elf's smug tone flies right over my head: hope floods through me, eclipsing everything else.

I address him in English, for additional security. "Don't keep me in suspense. The color in his aura isn't even close to Charles' charisma."

Sipping on his tea, Allinon takes his time, milking the moment for all its worth, "When I saw your intimate proximity to Alex, I switched to mage-sight. What I saw made me think about his aura coloring. Tendrils of his aura extended and mixed with yours. The closer you came to him the more entwined the colors became. Add to that the intensification of the burgundy and gold glowing in your aura and the answer is obvious."

"Not to me…" Bewildered, Charles shakes his head.

"The dominant color for Alex is mauve. If we took

paints and mixed fuchsia for charisma with gold for telepathy I bet we would get a shade close to his color. The real give away was Reba's empathy and telepathy glowing like a receiving beacon. He has a kind of telepathic charisma."

"So it is magic… of a kind. He exerts his charisma on a telepathic level. If my empathy is drawing in emotion, I get a double dose. Allinon you're a lifesaver," The tow-headed elf glows with self-righteousness. "Today I will go in with my empathy shielded and see if it makes a difference."

As we dig into breakfast the conversation ceases. After clearing my plate for a second time I broach the topic of the portal. Starting with my recent failure with the emerald and ending with Jamison's revelation that he won't be going home, I have the perfect lead-in.

"Guys I gotta tell ya, I really know what they are talking about. This world is so vivid. It's like all my senses have come alive. Colors are brighter, odors stronger. For the first time in my life I enjoy eating - everything has a distinct flavor. And when I use magic, I feel a sense of rightness, wholeness."

"Are you staying too?" Charles interrupts.

"I would love to, but I have a husband. I am going to talk to Merithin about performing a portal exchange. Since I can't perform more than one portal spell, I want to try to bring Tony out when I send you guys back. Unless you will give this place a second chance. With magic I can give you practically anything your heart desires. Consider letting me zap your families out here?" My twinkling smile crumbles as their faces cloud over.

"We had a deal, remember? You lead because you are sending us home," a note of sarcasm creeps into Allinon's voice. He immediately works to restrain, "It wouldn't be fair to bring people here with out their permission, especially when it's a one way trip."

"I'm with him. Reba, I might look the part, and the motions come natural, but I feel like a fish out of water.

The fact that I am the solitary African American in this entire kingdom doesn't bother me, it's even kind of nice. The ladies are all curious...." Charles takes the time to leer before resuming, "Talk about getting a major refund on the black tax I've paid all my life."

When our Caucasian eyes stare blankly he explains, "Back home I hade to do everything twice as good as yo whities, usually for less chedda," He flashes his pearly whites. "no offence." His jocular voice takes on an unaccustomed strain, "but the thought of spending the rest of my life hacking at people with a sword makes me want to crawl out of my skin. I'm sorry, but the sooner you send us back the better," That explains Charles constant mood swing. His new persona is at odds with his true character.

"I gave my word. I will stick by it, come Hell or high water. Unless the vote is unanimous, we go home after the crusade, even if I have to go too," I reaffirm my pledge. With little more to discuss, minutes later I leave for my next engagement.

Although I find Queen Szacquelyn's presence as enjoyable as her daughter's, it is difficult to talk about simple pleasantries when so many other things are on my mind. I excuse myself from tea as soon as it seems polite, racing over to the front gate to work on more Paladin Stones with Szames.

With my tight schedule, I appreciate his magical proficiency even more. Less than a half-mark later, I proceed to the practice grounds to meat Allinon and Charles. Word has gotten out: Fighting abilities will be given to the untrained. Four new female recruits have enlisted. Now I must fulfill my part of the bargain.

Weaving the magic transfer spells, endowing the women with martial art skills and sword mastery, I sigh. I hope I get to stay._ I stride toward the meadow to meet Alex.

Spotting Lieutenant Craig, I ask him to accompany me so I can use his energy to put the final touches on the thirty-foot poles. As the Lieutenant and I approach the stables, I erect an empathy shield, bracing myself for the coming ordeal.

"Reba, you look positively picturesque this afternoon," Alex greets, flirtatious as ever.

"Thank you, Alex. I hope you weren't taxed from yesterdays spell?" Perhaps I can talk my way out of working with him yet.

"I did find myself able to sleep quite soundly. It seems contrary to how it looks, magic takes a lot of energy." My heart still flutters as he flashes his most charming smile but uncontrollable desire doesn't threaten to drive me into his arms.

My tolerance for pleasantries evaporates, "I am pleased you, too, have arrived early. I have many duties vying for my attention."

With a tight smile, I motion for him to progress before me. Since Allinon was kind enough to leave one of the mage-globes, I simply use the duplication spell on the pile of sand. Unable to discern anything, I assume my partner still finds the process tolerable.

"I think your magic lessons are coming along wonderfully. If you would like a little more experience you can help me put the final touches on the globe holders," I gesture to the waiting soldier. "Lieutenant Craig has enough resources to aid in the final duplication."

"It will be my pleasure to experience whatever you will allow," Alex replies in a sexy bedroom voice.

"Then please, follow me," I effortlessly ignore the seduction. The corny come-on line still excites me more than is warranted, and looking up into his eyes makes melting into his arms seem a matter of urgency, but the feelings aren't as overpowering as they were yesterday. A prickling slides along the back of my neck: a warning that magic is afoot. Would have noticed that days ago if my hormones weren't on the rampage every time I am within ten feet of the man.

Turning on my heel, I saunter over to the poles

Allinon completed yesterday. Using his druid abilities the Elf encouraged one end of a wooden stave to grow new limbs, intertwining themselves around the mage-globes. Each rod has developed according to an inner chaotic pattern, securing a globe at one end. Holding the opposite end of the shaft in one hand and Alex's hand in the other, I begin setting the spell to activate with spoken English words for added security.

"Pointed and sharp this end will be
With the magic I now give to thee.
'Penetrate;' in a meter you will sink.
'Release' will bring you to the brink."

The stave lengthens forming a spear at the base, but other than that there is no discernable change to the naked eye. Mage-sight reveals a cerulean glow.

"These should be adequate for the function we discussed in the Council Meeting."

"Reba, as always, it is a pleasure working with you," turning me to face him his voice lowers, "Has anyone ever told you how enchanting your eyes are in this light? The sunset makes the amber dance. They echo the color in your enchanting mane."

"Yes, actually, they have," I retort dismissively. Even though my pulse has quickened and the pull of attraction nags me, I release his hands, motioning for Craig to assist me. Denying Alex knowledge of the stimulation gives me a vindictive pleasure.

"Lieutenant, if you're ready it will be just as we discussed on the way here." With an empathy shield in place, I can't tell if Craig's bothered by the contact with the arcane.

"There. That's all there is to it." I ignore Alex, hoping he will go away. "What did you think?"

"Milady, it's about to the most interrest'n experience I've had," he drawls, "I'd be glad to lend a hand whenever ya need."

"I appreciate your willingness, Lieutenant. As a matter of fact, if you are available perhaps you could guide me around town. There are several stops where I'll be required to cast the enchantment we just performed. Your aid will be welcomed," Craig agrees, leaving to ready the horses.

With a prolonged blink, I take a deep, steadying breath before trying to extricate myself from princely company, "Alex, I am sure you have many pressing matters to attend, so I won't monopolize any more of your time. As enjoyable as I find your company, I am afraid duty calls us both."

"I, too, have enjoyed the moments we share," pausing, giving a half smile, he looks hesitant, "I can make an opening in my schedule with a little effort. I will join you. I long to spend the afternoon indulging in the splendor of company so fair."

"If you are sure it won't be an inconvenience." Ah Hell, you had to get all cocky and open your big mouth.

"For you, milady, I have all the time in the world." With an elegant bow the raven-haired prince strides to his waiting squire.

I fell like I'm on a first date with the high school quarterback. As we begin our ride, I address Lieutenant Craig, hoping to rid myself of the unwanted feelings. The prince, however, still manages to dominate the conversation.

I try, once again, to bring Craig into our discussion, "So Lieutenant, you have an interesting accent. What part of the kingdom do you call home?" Anything is better than listening to more of Alex's monologue about sword expertise and awards he took in last year's Festival.

By midnight bells I have had about all I can stand. I hold in a sigh as the guard at the front gate pulls Alex aside to deliver a personal message. The "thank you," I give, as the crown prince politely excuses himself is more gratefulness for his departure than gratitude for his accompaniment. The Lieutenant, respectfully silent, continues to escort me to the barn. When the StableMaster fails to greet us, I turn to my escort.

"Craig, if you will point me toward the proper brushes I'll gladly see to the care of my mount." I could use the relaxation before dinner. _I begin to unwind with the familiarity of the chore as I tie the animal to the hitching post and unbuckle the saddle.

"Right this way, milady," the Lieutenant ushers me into the barn.

Craig opens a cupboard. As I squeeze past him to take a look at the supplies, I feel a hand brush my waist. Turning toward the officer, the touch turns into an embrace as he draws me to him. Defensive instincts kick in: I step backward to put some distance between us but his grip is firm. My effort takes me nowhere.

"Lieutenant!?" the growl in my voice doesn't register as he leans in to cover my mouth with his.

With adrenaline pumping, options run through my head at light-speed: with my arms pinned I can't get a back-swing to land a solid punch. I can't use a judo throw with his hands locked behind my back. Only one choice.

"Hiiigggh yyyaaa!" I jab my knee into his groin. The stringy, longhaired soldier gives a grunt of pain as he topples to the ground. With all the new skills I still use the oldest trick in the book: hit him where it hurts.

"What'd ya' go an' do that for?" His voice is a few octaves higher as he grunts out his complaint between gasps for breath, "Ya' been comin' on to me all night…"

Releasing my shielded empathy I know his words are honest. Damn that man! If I hadn't needed these stupid barriers to fend off Alex's advances I would have sensed this building!

"My apologies, Lieutenant, if I have misled you. I suggest in the future you make absolutely sure of the other persons inclinations before you make a move like that: especially when it is a Mage you are pursuing," sympathy for the hound-dog evaporates, my apology turns into a growl, "You're lucky I didn't turn you into a toad."

Having lost any desire to groom the borrowed mount, I stalk out of the barn. Spotting Merithin in the predawn light, I flag him down to present my latest portal idea as we stroll into the castle. The elder is quick to inform me that a transfer only goes one way. During an exchange items may become mixed, the results of which are unpredictable. Our discussion ends as the bells toll. Realizing I am late, again, I race to my chambers.

"Szames, I'm sorry. This is the second time I have kept you waiting," I sigh for more than just my tardiness, "You must think my manners are deplorable."

"To the contrary, I am grateful you can fit me into your schedule." The blonde knight comes to his feet, "I must say... you look beautiful tonight."

"Thank you," my tone is curt. God, please, no more compliments!

Szames pulls out a chair for me, and as usual takes a seat across the table. With the long day weighing me down, conversation is sparse. I give another terse response to Szames' inquiry as the servants set the table for desert. I find myself apologizing once more, "I'm afraid I am not very good company tonight. I am taking out my frustration on you and you are the last person who deserves it."

"You know, I have two very capable ears if you would like to talk about it." The kindness in his voice is touching, but I hesitate to take advantage of it.

"Are you sure you want to hear it? It involves your brother..." Should I reveal what I've learned?

"Now you must tell me. I am used to mending the broken hearts of the women Alex has left behind. This will be a first: someone upset before he has bedded her?" Szames jest falls flat as I glare acidly across the table.

"Are you implying that I will allow him to bed me?" My voice takes on a steely edge. Seeing his abashed look, I make a hasty apology. "I'm sorry... again. It's just... I'm as mad as an old wet hen. My feelings toward Alex are not very kind right now." I take a long sip of wine before giving in to the urging of my conscience.

"You know, now that I think about it, you might be very interested in this, but it is a somewhat sensitive topic," turning to Crystal I continue, "The cleaning can wait till morning. You're welcome to turn in as well. Thank you for your service tonight."

While the servants clear the room, my dinner companion waits expectantly, "You may not believe it, but your brother has magic, of a fashion. Kind of like empathy, charisma, and telepathy combined," Szames looks baffled so I expound, "Alex's aura reaches out to those near him to persuade them in whatever manner he wishes. Allinon pointed it out when he saw us together yesterday. Today I tested the theory."

Szames still looks doubtful, so I offer the only proof I can, "If you would like I can give you the ability of mage-sight. All thing of magical will then be revealed."

"You mean you could let me see the magic we have been doing?" Szames interrupts me, so astounded he looses a little of his properness.

"It's something I should have done days ago. But you will have to take my word on it until tomorrow. Your brother has a Gift of his own. And unfortunately my empathy makes me twice as vulnerable to him," I admit the last with a shake of my head.

"So Alex is courting you." Szames exudes nonchalance, but his gaze threatens to penetrate my very soul.

"I suppose some may call his advancements courting, but I call it a pain in the ass," I sigh, reigning in my temper, "Thanks to Allinon's observation, all I have to do is keep my empathy shielded but, let me tell you, it was a close call for a while there."

"You are serious?" Dumfounded, Szames's scrubs his face with a hand. "My brother uses magic in his courting?"

"You have no idea how infuriating it is to feel yourself react to a man you find abominable. Your mind clouds over and your body betrays you." Recalling my first few days here, my blood heats in a different way, "Alex is the kind of guy I have always despised: he thinks he's God's gift to women. He is so full of himself he sure every woman will fall at his feet."

"He uses magic to sway women." Szames's face mirrors the disgust on mine.

"Yes, and I was almost a victim. By shielding the empathetic ability within me, I have a fighting chance." I take a deep swallow of the spiced wine, "Tonight I spent the entire evening in his company. With my shields up it was like walking a tight rope with one eye closed. And I still had to fend off his continual advances!"

I slam my fist down on the table in frustration. "If he wasn't a prince, I would have slapped him for half the things he said! Or maybe it was the way he said it. And to top it all off, I tried to distract Alex by including Lieutenant Craig in our discussions: The man took everything I said the wrong way. I had to physically discourage the Lieutenant's advances!"

Fury blazes in Szames's eyes, "Craig did what? Did he hurt you?" As I shake my head in denial, he growls. "I will have a talk with the Lieutenant." The way the growls it leaves no doubt there would be very little conversing to it.

"Thank you for your concern, but I have already handled the matter. I think it will be a long time before he tries anything like that again." I sooth his anger before mine reasserts itself, "And now I'm so frustrated with that idiot brother of yours, I could just spit!"

"You know," Szames's anger melts as he chuckles, "I bet you are not half as frustrated as Alex. You are dead right when you said he expects every woman to fall at his feet. And here is the most exotic beauty of all, the one everyone tells him he is supposed to marry, and she repeatedly rejects him!"

Some of the day's tension drains away as we both get a good laugh imagining Alex pacing like a caged lion.

When I regain control of my senses I feel a creeping headache.

"Thank you, Szames, I needed that," I sigh, with relief this time, "That is one of the things I miss most about my husband. He is great a looking at the bright side of things. He always makes me laugh."

"Do you miss him terribly?" Szames whispers.

Having drunk more wine than usual, I find myself opening up, "The time I miss him most is snuggling in bed. The rest of the time this world of yours has me so captivated he doesn't enter my thoughts. But in the quiet moments, or when I need someone to talk to...." My voice turns husky as it trails off.

"Reba, I hope you know that whenever you need someone to talk to, I will be happy to listen," the resonant bass in his words has a familiar quality to it.

"I appreciate it, Szames. The feeling is mutual. Whenever you need an ear…" My smile is genuine. I can't believe I have found a friend here.

Szames flushes as he shrugs, "Do not worry, you will get a turn. I will probably bore you to death with details of supply demands."

"Does that mean that we are on for tomorrow night?" My Dinner Date nods so I continue, "That reminds me. I should let you know of our impending departure. Unfortunately, I was unable to find a way around the Portal Law. I would love to stay - your world feels more like home than my own, but I'm out of options. It looks like you will be loosing three of us after one crusade around the castle."

"Only three of you are leaving?" His somberness is a deeper echo of mine.

I shake my head, "Yeah. If Allinon and Charles would just change their minds, then I could stay too, but I don't think there is much chance of that."

Szames tilts his head, "If you want to stay, why do you not? I am sure Arturo will offer you a position as counselor."

"And what kind of advisor would that make me. I am married, that means that I have taken a vow before my country, my family, and God. What kind of person would just throw away a sworn oath because they found someplace they would rather be?" I sigh, "No, I can't. I'll probably regret it for the rest of my life, but I can't break that vow."

"Reba, I admire your integrity," I look away, blushing at the adoration in his eyes. Deftly he changes topics, "In the meantime, is there anything else I can do to make your time here more enjoyable?"

"Got any aspirin?" I crack a joke to lighten the mood.

"Au-sp-rin? I will try to find some for you, if you will be kind enough to tell me what kind of thing they are." The handsome prince takes my request to heart.

"It's medicine to relieve a headache, and boy is this one coming on fast." I mumble, "I almost regret using up my healing power…. almost."

"Was someone hurt?" Szames inquires. "Do you want me to fetch a healer for your head?"

"No… I mean yes. Let me start over. One of the new female recruits received a going away present from her husband in the form of a few bruises, so I healed her. And no I don't want someone to come all this way for a headache." I grate my teeth against the stabbing pain. I begin searching through my hair for the pins holding the flaming mass of curls on top of my head, "If these damn pins weren't digging into my skull it might be bearable."

My attention is focused on searching through mop of tresses for the few dozen pins gouging into my skull. Suddenly, I feel a large hand covering mine.

"Here let me…" Deftly, Szames begins removing the bobby pins. As the giant warrior slowly and ever so gently combs his fingers through my locks searching for any missing pins, a quiet moan slips through my relaxed lips.

"I am afraid you've found my weakness. If you're not

careful you will put me to sleep," I whisper, not wanting to antagonize the pain that is beginning to ebb.

"Sounds like just what you need. I will even deliver you to the safety of your bed, if you will let me," Szames murmurs.

In disbelief I ask, "You'd do that for me?"

"What else are friends for?" He breathes quieter than my whisper.

Without another word he continues stroking my hair. Bit by bit, working their way from forehead to neck, massive hands massage my scalp. By the time Szames gets to my shoulders I am sound asleep.

The gentleness with which he picks me up doesn't penetrate my consciousness nor does the tenderness he shows laying me down.

As he looks with longing at my sleeping form a muffled groan escapes the giant man, just loud enough to draw attention from the shadowed corner. Silently the prince slips from my chambers.

Chapter Twenty-Four

"Crystal, in the last couple of days something about Prince Szames has struck me as familiar. Maybe a little more information will help me place it. What do you know about him?" In the short time since my arrival, relaxing in the tub has become one of my favorite activities. The fact that two other people are in the room hardly registers.

Crystal demonstrates her duties to Rhachel as she replies, "My first year, the prince was the talk of the castle. He came into the baritone with which he speaks at a mere twelve winters. Still small for a prince of the royal line, he already he spoke with the voice of a man. It was considered a good omen."

"A voice that deep must have been quite comical in a twelve-year-old boy." I snap my fingers, "That's it! Now I know why it strikes me as so familiar! I can't believe it didn't occur to me sooner. After all, their names are so similar."

"You knew a boy with a deep voice, milady?" Crystal sits down to start on my hair.

"Did I know him? Hmmm…" I sit back enjoying her administrations, "In a way, I guess. We went to school together. I had a thing for him, starting when I was about your age, Rhachel."

"What's a 'sk-oo-l?' What kind of 'thing' did he give you? Was he a prince, too?" Rhachel nails me with several questions then adds a quick "milady" when Crystal shoots her a look. Chuckling at the child's exuberance I try to answer the questions without creating new ones.

"All kids receive learning in my country, kind of like the tutors for the nobles." The amazement on her face reminds me just how far from home I am. "James wasn't a prince, just a regular boy who was so-o-o cute. He had these incredible blue eyes. And 'a thing' that is what my people call it when you are really, really, attracted to someone."

I can't help but smile at the memory, "And boy did I have it bad. I would drop my books whenever he walked by. Heck, if I just saw him across the room I couldn't control myself: I would speak either way too loud or just plain forget what I was saying," As Rhachel giggles, Crystal shoots her another look.

"It was pretty funny. My sister Lani didn't even have to see him. Just by my reaction she would say 'Okoy, Sis, where is he? Why don't you just go talk to him?' But before I could get a grip on myself he was always gone. Then one day, when I was fifteen, we moved away," I pause, the innocence of those years captivating my heart.

"So you never got to talk to him…Milady?" This time Rhachel manages to remember the title without Crystal's help.

"Not for a couple of years. I spent many afternoons lost in daydreams about him. Oh how I wished I had gotten up the nerve to talk to him. Then, when I was seventeen, we moved back. Not into the city, but close enough that I was allowed to spend a weekend with my best friend. Visiting new places, exposure to new cultures, gave me the time to figure out who I was. It built up my self-esteem. I decided long ago that if I ever had the chance to talk with him I would take it," I revisit the past as the story unfolds for my staff....

"You can't be serious!" Jennifer was incredulous, "He's the star quarterback! You can't just go to his house and introduce yourself."

Rebecca's twin sister jumped in on Jennifer's side, "Yah, what are you going to do just say, 'duh, my name is Becky and I had a crush on you.' He will think you're a complete idiot."

"Get off it, will ya!! You of all people know I have to do this," Lani's granite expression softened a little with the hurt embedded in her twin's words until Becky added, "Come with me, then you can see for yourself."

"No way! There is no way you are dragging me into this mess," as if Medusa stood before them, Lani turned back to stone.

Jennifer, likewise, remained unmoved, "I've gotta to go to school with the guy, you're on your own."

They didn't even wait outside on the street. "We will meet you at the park when you're finished humiliating yourself," was Lani's parting remark after they shoved out of the car around the corner from his house.

Rebecca's knees quaked as she approached the door. Stomach churning, she waited for someone to answer the bell. "Hello-o..." Leered the six-foot four gorgeous hunk that didn't in any way resemble the boy she dreamed about for more than two years.

"Hi.... I'm looking for James.... James Cutter," Rebecca forced the words past hesitant lips.

"He's out, won't be back until late," the giant, who must be a brother of the shortish, blond-haired boy she remembered, smiled, "Do you want to leave a number or something?"

"No... I'm just in town for the weekend," Rebecca struggled to keep the tears in her heart out of her voice, as well as her eyes, "I'm staying with a friend."

"Well, you could come by tomorrow. He should be in all day," the interest this total stud of a man showed was so unexpected it made her smile.

"Sure.... I can do that. I'll be by tomorrow morning." Rebecca dipped her head decisively as she headed back down the walk.

Twenty-four hours later, having once again donned the formfitting, string-tie khaki one-piece that showed off her long legs and slim figure, Rebecca stood before that same door. Knots wound her stomach so tight it is all she could do not to squirm as the hunky older brother bellowed behind the door he just closed, "James! She's here!"

Minutes crawled by so slow it seemed a year passed before a tousled blond head eased the door open. "Yes..." said the voice that haunted her dreams for almost three years. The face had changed. The man--for the boy had grown into a full fledge hunk--who stood before her was more than she ever dreamed possible. Well over six feet, thick blonde hair, shoulders to die for and the face of a GQ model: here before her is every woman's dream. But the pair of deep pools of blue were the same, and so was that resonate bass voice.

When Rebecca's knees threatened to give way so she locked them in place. Nervousness forced words out in a rush, "Hi, you probably don't remember me but I used to go to school with you, I'm one of the twins."

When the flushed girl paused for breath James supplies, "Becky and.... uhhh--"

"Berta, she goes by Lani now," the silence stretched out into an uncomfortable pause. Figuring she might as well go the whole way Rebecca rushed on, headlong, "Yeah, well, back when we were kids I used to have the biggest crush on you. But I never had the nerve to say anything. I'm in town for the weekend, I though I would stop by, see what you've been up to, how your life has turned out."

After James recovered from her blatant honesty, he was most congenial, "Would you like to come in? My mom has a scrapbook."

Following him into the kitchen she noticed his backside was just as perfect as the front, "Would you like some tea?" James's mom offered, as her son dug out a photo album.

James had been in the news many times: he was, after all, the starring quarterback for one of the biggest schools in Phoenix. After twenty minutes of listening to him drone on about his greatest moments on the field, boredom set in. Becky changed the topic, "So what's your GPA? Have you applied to any colleges?"

"Grades? I'm one of the hottest players. Tons of colleges will be begging me to come," James shrugged.

"What kind of major are you looking for?" She continued.

"Who knows. Maybe I'll go professional ball before I have to decide." the jock dismissed the trivial topic of future plans, "Did I tell you I am dating the Prima Ballerina at the Phoenix School of Art?"

"Really," Rebecca was baffled by the new direction of the conversation.

"I was dating the head cheerleader for a while. Then 'the team' got volunteered to help a local dance studio. They needed us to help the girls get used to being lifted over someone's head, since we were so strong and all. Well, I was the Captain, so I got paired up with the Prima Ballerina. After a couple of weeks we started dating and then she got the lead part in a ballet so I figured I'd better break up with the cheerleader before attending the opening show."

"Yes, well, I appreciate you taking the time for me today, but I've got friends waiting. I had better be going." Disgusted with his two-timing attitude, she excused herself.

"If you're free tonight, maybe we could get a burger? Or I could call you sometime?" The thickheaded jock had the gall to ask her out when he was dating another girl!

"I'm sorry, but have a boyfriend. I am kind of a one-man woman." She wasn't even tempted by his proposition. "If I am ever single and in town again I'll give you a ring."

I shake my head, coming out of the memory, "That

was the last time I saw him. I knew he wasn't what I was looking for. He was what I have come to refer to as a 'Dumb Jock' -- all brawn, no brains and totally controlled by what's located in his pants. I couldn't believe I wasted years dreaming about him. I vowed never to do that again. From that day forward I lost my shyness. If I was interested in someone, I went up and said 'hello.'"

"Wow...." Rhachel is awed.

"Milady, it's very hard to picture you as a shy, awkward girl," Crystal helps me back into a robe.

"Well believe it. When you were buxom and beautiful, I was awkward and gangly," I chuckle, "I still have my clumsy moments."

A knock sounds on the outer door as I am getting into my clothes. When Rhachel comes back from answering it, she seems troubled. The new apprentice goes over to Crystal. Fierce whispering ensues.

A soldier at the door is insisting to talk with you," Crystal hesitantly asks, "Milady, would you like me to send him away?"

"No, it's okay, I will see him." I shrug, "My day is packed, and I would like to take care of it now, rather than later."

The uniformed youth comes to a smart attention when I enter. The fear and awe I sense are pretty typical, but at this close range it is a little disturbing.

"Milady ArchMage Reba, Sir," he salutes then bows.

"You requested to see me?" I smile, trying to ease his trepidation.

"I was instructed to leave this package in no hands but yours." The soldier hands over a cloth bundle that has a note tied to the top of it. No sooner have I assumed possession of the package than the deliverer stoops before practically dashing for the door.

"Sight," When the package fails to give a tell-tail glow I untie the strings, freeing the attached note.

"Ah, crap!" my hand slams down on the desk.

Crystal comes running from the next room, "Milady, is something the matter." She anxiously searches for the source of the trouble.

"I apologize, I didn't mean to startle you. As long as you are here, maybe you can help me with this." I hand over the letter.

"Last night this gentleman - and I use the term loosely - assumed I wanted a roll in the hay with him. I thought I set him straight. Obviously the implied threat to turn him into a frog was not enough to discourage him." Rhachel's eyes turn globular, as she enters the room with my last remark. "Not that I would actually do it, turn him into a toad, that is, but I figured at least it would scare him off," I amend hastily, before I continue, "Crystal, can I send this back? Tell me, what's the proper etiquette in this situation?"

"To send a gift back would be the greatest of insults. It is considered very poor manners, milady. I take it you have no wish to encourage any further courting?" As I nod she explains, "Then simply don't wear the necklace."

"But how can I take a gift from someone I find detestable? Wouldn't that be a sign of acceptance?" I am dumbfounded.

"In a way, milady. Keeping the gift shows you acknowledge his feelings for you. If you wear it, it will mean you wish him to continue courting. If you send a gift of your choice back to him it will signify your willingness to speed up the relationship," she finishes as Rhachel ushers Jamison into the room.

"Well, I suppose you must see this finds a place… somewhere." I hand her the necklace with three sapphires the size of my thumb set into it.

"Reba, you realize that with a little flirting you could leave here a very rich woman," Jamison is all smiles as he takes a seat across from me.

Without the others of our group, breakfast passes all too rapidly. After Jamison yawns for a third time, I relent and ask the obvious.

"You mean your empathy didn't tell you?" He ribs me for the third time this morning.

Concentrating, I strain my senses. The love feeling is twice as strong as yesterday and he has a sort of 'the cat that ate the canary' satisfaction.

"You bedded the princess?" I take a wild guess.

"Well, we never actually made it to the bed..." the perma-grin he sports is now accounted for.

A Princess! "But what about her impending marriage?" I am stunned at his audacity.

"We had a very long talk. We decided to live each day to its fullest." He shrugs.

"What if she gets pregnant?" I arch my brows.

"Okay, Mother dear," The smile stays in place, reassuring me he means it in the best possible way, "I have healing magic, remember. With a slight touch, there is no chance of any 'oopses.'"

"It seems you've thought it through. Jamison, I'm happy for both of you," I spoon out a dollop of honey onto the empty saucer in front of me, "While you are here, why don't we work on those pills you suggested?"

I bring to mind a spell I have been working on.

"Across space, thru a portal you will go,
Keeping safe this enchantment with a glow.
Gel-cap you will be easy to swallow.
Magical benefits soon to follow."

My fingertips tingle as the honey rolls into itself. Seconds later the expected pill is ready for the next step. Repeating the much used duplication spell, I drop the squishy oval into the honey pot. Retrieving one of the capsules I hand it to Jamison for the next step.

The hair on the back of my neck rises as he works his healing magic. In a flash it occurs to me. I could probably imbue one of the tablets with the same spell I used my first night here. Who wouldn't kill for a magic pill that keeps you in the best shape you have ever been in?

By the time Jamison has completed his lifesaving enchantment, I have a caplet sitting in front of me. I stare, unable to look away. The pills have a soft blue or green glow without active Magesight!

"Well, if this makes it through the transfer it should cure every thing from cancer to AIDS, in addition to speeding up the body's natural healing process for cuts and breaks. It might even regenerate missing limbs." Jamison wipes sweat from his brow, "I missed most of your limerick, what does your pill do?"

"Puts your body in perfect physical shape and uses magic essence around you to keep you that way. If it works, it will double the average lifespan, maybe even triple it." My smile turns to a smirk, "seems like we will even be able to tell if they work before we use them. If they loose the glow the spells didn't make it through the transfer."

"Awesome man, with these," Jamison's smile broadens, "who needs jewels? You can make enough off these pills to be set for life."

"Yah, but besides family, who would believe they'd work?" Handing over the rest of the blank pills, I put the blue one in my desk drawer to duplicate later, "I suppose seeing the Grim Reaper approach will make a believer out of anyone, but somehow I wouldn't feel right charging a fortune for these."

We journey to the gate, joking the whole way. Seeing the large blonde figure waiting for me I realize Jamison's not the only friend I will miss when I leave.

"Now I know I'm not late this time; it's not even dark yet," I remark when I am within earshot.

"I was just retrieving today's report from the guard station," Szames indicates a bundle of parchment.

"Can I talk you into taking another flight with me? And maybe get your help on the staves as well? I don't think your brother has the necessary energy and I would rather not have to use the Lieutenant again." I extend my hand when he acquiesces.

As our feet leave the ground I recall the promise I made last night at dinner, "Would you like to see the magic we are doing?"

"You can do that here?" Szames glances at the ground a few hundred feet below.

"Sure, just hold tight." With a thought, I withdraw most of the needed power from him, only taking from my reservoir what is needed to manipulate his energy.

"Great help and a wonderful friend
To me you have continually been.

Therefore I give to you
The ability to see what I do.

'Sight' and magic you can see.
Once more and your vision is free."

I graze his forehead with the last line, feeling lightness in my arms and euphoria with in. A satisfactory glow envelops his head melting into his eyes.

"All you have to do is say 'sight'" I pronounce the English word slowly, "while thinking about seeing magic. Saying it again will return you back to normal."

"So all I have to do is say 'si-te?'" His brow crinkles as he stares at me, "So the pattern of colored light surrounding you, that is your aura? They were right – it is brilliant… gems, sparkling like the sun. It is the most beautiful thing I have ever seen," as my cheeks brighten to pink he stops gaping at me, looking instead, to the force field.

"If you're ready, it will take a moment for me to make today's alterations," I set my mind back on the work ahead.

Repeating the same spell we used last time we were aloft, I enlarge the shield by another ten feet. Seeing Alex waiting for me in the meadow I take us there. I sense Alex's shock at our landing. When he spots our linked hands I perceive jealously as well. I snap my empathy shield into place, releasing Szames.

"Reba, timely as ever." When we near, Alex takes my hand, delivering a courtly kiss. "I had no idea flying makes you look so radiant, perhaps I will have to take you up on your offer and accompany you one days soon."

Butterflies have come back to haunt my stomach by the time he is through. As he retains possession of my hand, it is all I can do to break eye contact with him. Reluctantly, Prince Alexandros releases me.

"When you want your first flight, just let me know. For now we have these poles to take care of. I didn't want to exhaust you, so I brought Szames for additional support," I indicate his unacknowledged sibling.

I stand holding the hands of both princes in either of mine as I recite the duplication spell. When I utter the final words, the fair-haired prince touches the enchanted shaft to waiting poles.

"While you are both here let me demonstrate these for you. It will be necessary for you to train several of your men so they can distribute them before the battle." I bend to pickup one of the light-posts. Both princes jump to assist me. Being in the way, now that there are three of us trying to stand one shaft upright, I take a step back, instructing them to hold it perpendicularly to the ground while pressing downward.

"Pen-e-trate," I make an effort in the pronunciation.

When the lamppost sinks five feet into the ground Alex takes a backward step. Szames wiggles the pole testing its durability.

"Il-lum-i-nate," instantly the mage-globe brightens. I ask the brothers to hold the shaft once more then intone, "Re-lease" followed by "Trans-parent."

Szames and Alex practice the unfamiliar words. Alex has more trouble than Szames, however, after a few tries both are able to accomplish setting the lamppost.

Stating my need to speak with my rock bearers, I am able to extricate myself from Alex. Easily we match long quick strides, as Szames accompanies me to the front gate.

Noticing my silent companion still has sight activated, I ask "So I take it you believe what I said about Alex?"

"I am sorry I ever doubted you." He gives a tired shake of his head, "Tell me, is it like that every time you are near him?"

"More or less. This was his strongest effort since I started shielding myself. Most of the time it isn't as intense but the barrage is more incessant."

A look of disgust slides across Szames's face as we close in on the gate. His countenance speaks volumes about his disapproval concerning his brother's actions.

"Szames, don't get me wrong, he is still something that a woman can resist. You just have to want to bad enough," I clarify my position.

A nod to the guards at the gate is all it takes to get us onto the street. In the dusky light of the coming night it is easy to spot the group of children. I smile seeing that, once again, they all have a bundle of the food intended for distribution to the workers as they re-enter the gates at dusk.

Upon recognizing my silver robe, the youngsters dash toward us, all except the tallest, who is carrying the pail of rocks. Recognizing my large companion they skid to a stop about a foot away, sketching awkward bows, keeping their eyes on the ground before them.

"Prince Szames, I'd like you to meet five of the most helpful children in your city: Maria, Araine, Erik, Chazan, and Todd is the one carrying the bucket."

"Milady, these are your stone collectors? They are young to be dedicated to such a noble cause." When he bows back to the children, Maria blushes a bright red while Araine hides her face in her brother's shirt, "The kingdom is most grateful for the service you have rendered."

Taking the stones from Todd I address the kids again, "You guys have been doing such a wonderful job; I don't know what I would do without you. If you think you're up to it, I've got another task for you."

"Yes, m'lady." Todd's back is board straight.

Squatting down to their level, I use a stone to form another pail and explain that we need two full buckets for the next two days.

"Momma's so happy I'm help'n, I know she'll let us go earlier," Chazan volunteers.

"I knew I could count on you. Now this next part is real important," I lower my voice as the circle of their cherub faces closes in around me.

"Each day I also need you to find eight rocks the size of two of your hands. I am going to give you a very special stone, one that will protect you from being hurt." A tingle of warning creeps down my spine so I add, "When you go out again, I need you to stay real close to the grown-ups, there might be demons out there. Okay?" As all five nod solemnly, I tell them to repeat the instructions. During their impeccable recital I notice Erik's stuffy nose.

"I'm okay, m'lady. Please don't tell my mom, she will keep me home for sure," his voice sounds like someone has applied sandpaper to his voice box.

"How 'bout if I fix it for you?" As I gather him in my arms I try for healer's vision. "Can you tell me how it feels?"

The brave lad describes the symptoms of the common cold. I place my fingers where the infection has taken hold. When my sight indicates a full recovery, I hand the cloth wrapping from the unwanted necklace to him.

"Now blow." In a matter of seconds he is unable to loosen anything more from his nose.

"My head don't hurt…and my nose stopped it's runnin'," giving me a hug he adds, "Thank you, m'lady."

"You are very welcome. Prince Szames, are you ready?" I stand, anxious to get back to work.

"I have the Paladin Stone, milady," there is a reverence in his voice that causes me to blush.

After transforming the contents of the bucket, I hand

a stone to my volunteers. "Now, I want each one of you to spit on the stone, then put it in a pouch with a lock of your hair, and tie that around your neck. Can you do that for me?" As all five immediately complete the first step I smile.

"You'd better get home now, your parents are probably looking for you," I shoo them on their way.

"You have a way with kids." Szames remarks as we turn back to the castle.

"And so do you. I don't think any of them will ever forget: the Prince paid them a compliment." A smile of disbelief plays about my lips, "You know, for a noble you aren't all bad."

When I notice Szames's squire, Herald, waiting for us at the gate, I ask to borrow his services. I don't get the sense of fear or awe from him that I do from most others. I suppose when you are serving a prince, dealing with an ArchMage is no big deal.

"Herald, there is a staff next to my bed, could you fetch it for me please? We will see you at the practice grounds."

Herald's darting glance to Szames for conformation is barely perceptible before he replies, "Yes, milady," exiting with a bow.

"If you have time for an extra stop, I could use your help getting a few of those new lamps over to the practice fields," I invite my favorite magic partner to join me.

Chapter Twenty-Five

"Charles, how's the training?" I shout as we approach the small group of new recruits.

The Paladin gives some final instruction to his trainees before joining us. "Damn good, considering only two of them had touched a sword before."

"The requested lampposts are here," I indicate the four poles with mage globes attached to one end. As we set them up around the perimeter of his designated area he fills us in on the details.

"After they got over the shock of 'knowing' what to do, they increased in proficiency tenfold. Now they are better than the majority of the troops: what they lack in strength, they more than make up for in speed and skill. Even with my additional power and reach I'm hard pressed to best them," then with a leer he adds, "But there's not another soldier I'd rather be hard pressed with."

Chuckling, not so much at the dark man's pun but his return to good humor, I shake my head. A moment later, when Herald returns with the requested staff, I unbutton my robe, "If you think they're up to it, it is time I got in a little practice myself. Besides, it will let me see first hand how they adapt to a different opponent with a new weapon."

"This should be interesting," Szames takes my silver cover while Charles nods in agreement.

"Tell you what, let's make it really interesting. With

my mage talents, I have lightning speed and agility, heightened intuition, not to mention six inches of reach. They all have a Paladin stone?" When Charles indicates yes I give a firm nod, "I will take on three of them."

"I assume you have a stone or something?" Charles arches an eyebrow.

"Actually, no. So if I've guessed wrong we might need Jamison's services by the end of this." I shrug.

The three of us enter their sparing area. The women form a line, coming to attention.

"At ease, ladies. I'm just here to get in a little practice. Mikaela, Auricle, and... Rucela, wasn't it? You three against me, and don't pull any punches. I won't either," the recruits jump to obey my no-nonsense tone.

The indicated women circle my position in a triangular pattern while I stand with my feet shoulder-width apart, braced for their attack. Mikaela gives a minute nod of her head and all three close in. I rush at Auricle, since she is in front of me, to buy a few seconds before I have to deal with all three.

When the woman's eyes dart to her partners', I land a bone crunching strike across her wrist. With the shield active, the blow is reduced to a bruising force that causes her to drop her sword. "Hei-Ya!!" a quick karate-kick to the stomach and Auricle is out for the count. I pivot to face the others.

Sparing with the remaining two is like nothing I have ever done. Taking a deep breath I let go, allowing my body to react, without my mind's supervision. Swifter than thought, I parry the duel attack. I feel the sweat of exertion bead up on my brow, as I fail to find an opening to disable either one. Minutes drag by: I sense a crowd of onlookers gathering. I force my mind to stay focused on my opponents. Patiently, I wait for the opening I know will bring the mice within reach of my claws.

Men begin cheering, some for me, some for the Cuthburan women. Rucela darts a quick glance in their direction. My staff swipes her feet out from under her.

The next strike knocks the wind out of her. Mikaela's attack takes on a desperate fury, as we square off one on one. When I see Rucela moving to rise, leaving herself wide open, a quick swing that would have split her head, leaves her unconscious.

Mikaela is good: a master swordsman by any standards. But with my enhanced abilities she is outmatched. Another five minutes and she is disarmed, but still unwilling to yield. When I aim a strike at her head she blocks with her wrist, and although it hurts like hell, her face is set in stone.

With her attention focused on the staff she misses the leg sweep coming right on the heels of the charge. My redheaded opponent lands flat on her back, unable to breathe. My stave halts, mere inches from her nose. The match is over.

"Not bad, against three miniature swordsmen, but how would you fair against full-sized attackers?" The biting sarcasm in Alex's voice surprises me more than hearing from the prince at all, "Brother, I bet you and I alone could best her."

Although he has addressed his sibling, his remarks are loud enough to be heard by all the hundred or so men watching the sparing match.

"Is that so, Your Highness? I would rather see the two of you matched up against these ladies, if you are so contemptuous of their skill," I shoot Charles warning glance when he begins to chuckle at my proposed challenge.

"Since you are secure in their abilities, why not take one as a partner if it is the odds that concern you," Alex issues the challenge and I am overcome with desire to acquiesce.

Snapping my empathy shield in place my reply drips like honey, "If I am to have a partner, I insist that you take at least a third man on your team."

"Agreed. Stezen, up to a little sparing?" The Crown Prince's ethics, or lack there of, do not keep him from trying to recruit the ArmsMaster standing beside him.

"With all due respect, Your Highness, you got yourself into this and you can get yourself out of it." Stezen recognizes the true skill of the newest additions to the army.

"Szames, are you going to desert me, too, brother?" Alex's smile is crooked.

"I stood beside you when we faced a hoard of demons, these odds do not look much worse," the crowd chuckles as he gives a slight lift of his chin, "Count me in."

Alex's last choice for a teammate makes me shake my head at his gall. "Charles, now is a good time to find out how well we will work together."

"At your service, Your Highness," Prince Charming roles his eyes as he bows.

"And your choice, milady?" Alex's smile is smug.

I saunter over to where the women have huddled into a group, noting every word of the exchange, "How's the arm feel? Mikaela, you up to another round?"

"Milady I received worse than this from Scott on a weekly basis. I'd be proud to help you teach these men a lesson," by the sneer in her voice when she refers to the opposite sex, I suspect her husband will be better off if he never sees his magically endowed wife again.

"No use in starting off already bruised, it's going to be a close match," I take a moment to heal her arm and whisper, "Don't let your anger get away from you. Alex still favors his right shoulder." Mikaela gives a terse nod.

The number of onlookers has doubled in size by the time we take our place in the center of the field. Standing side by side as we watch the men approach I begin an enchantment I hadn't gotten around to implementing.

"A woman I am, and a warrior I must be,
Bones stronger than steel will keep harm from me.
'Schwarzenegger' will give ten times his strength to thee."

A moment later I whisper Mr. Universe's name as Charles begins to pan right and Szames edges left to divide our attention. Turning back to back, we wait for the men to make the first move.

Being experienced fighters, the first few strikes are mild, as they try to determine our weaknesses. Seeing Mikaela has no problem holding her own, I concentrate on finding an opening in Charles's master level swordsmanship. Because his Paladin shield slows down my increased speed, we are evenly matched… almost.

Alex's continual taunts at my companion begin to get on my nerves: my next parry has more force behind it than I intend. Charles dexterously moves the sword to his left hand while he waits to regain the feeling in the right one.

"A little stronger than I remember," Charles chides playfully.

"Just call it my new 'Conan' spell. Figured I'd need it against you," I tease.

The compliment has the anticipated effect; Charles's strikes become cocky. Ducking his next swing instead of parrying it, I bring my staff down solidly on his foot. He manages a clumsy back-swing, but it leaves his head open for a second, which is half a second more than I need. I remember to pull my blow just in time to keep from crushing his skull.

Turning to stand beside my partner I notice she too has her sword in her left hand. Mikaela is momentarily distracted by my appearing beside her, which allows Alex to land a solid blow on her thigh taking her down. Even injured, she manages to roll out of the way so she won't interfere.

"It looks like we have the desired match after all, milady," Alex's charming smile makes me want to zap him with a stun spell and be done with it.

Taking a step back, I bow as if we are starting the duel over again, "As you wish, so it is done."

I move a few more paces back then sprint toward the royal pair. Planting my pole just out of arms reach I vault over the princely brothers. Twisting in mid-air, both feet hit the ground making a solid landing between them. With my increased speed, I land a kidney punch on Szames before he has time to turn and engage me.

With a back swing, I take Alex off his feet and come up to parry his brother's first blow. Concentrating on my intuition, I manage to avert the attacks from both sides as well as land another blow to knock the wind out of Szames.

"Hei-Ya!" Swiveling around like a ninja, I block Alex with my staff, aiming a foot at his head. The raven-haired prince manages to block both attacks by the skin of his teeth. I am forced to cartwheel while holding my staff in order to recover.

"It seems she has as much fire on the field as she does off the field," Alex's blatant insinuation is accompanied by a suggestive leer.

As the crowd erupts in hoots, Szames struggles to his feet, "I must agree, her beauty is unsurpassed when she is angered. But, brother, I do not think antagonizing her is the best course of action."

With laughter flowing like a river around me, I devise a plan, "And how would you like to find out just how fiery I can be, Your Highness?" I coo, leaving my implied wager clear, "If either of you best me, he will be the one to find out."

The pair circles me, making half-hearted attempts at scoring a strike, "And, milady, if you best us both?" Alex asks as we come into eye contact again.

"You will knight these ladies so they may become the Royal Guard," I flick my staff in their direction.

As Alex utters the word "deal" he levels a strike at my right side. Parrying his flurry of blows isn't difficult, but with Szames behind me it is tricky business. As I hoped, Alex shuffles right, trying to put his brother in the line of fire. When I have both on either side I cease holding back. I attack at full speed. Alex goes down first with a blow to the stomach. His brother soon follows when my staff makes contact with his sword arm followed by one a jab to the right side of his ribcage.

As the crowd cheers wildly I remark loud enough to be heard by those around me. "When you insist on playing with fire, Your Highness, sometimes you get burned."

Chuckling Szames adds, "Alex, it looks like she has bested you on both fields."

The Crown Prince eases to his feet, dusting himself off. With a gentlemanly bow his voice rings out, clear for all to hear, "I stand humbled in the face of your prowess, ladies. Those of you who prove themselves in the coming battles shall be knighted and receive with it, a title."

The sincerity oozing off Alex must be effecting the crowd for they cheer wildly, thumping anything in arms reach. When the noise begins to die down he turns to me. Silence hovers over the playing field as men strain to catch every word.

"Milady, perhaps I can get those private lessons we spoke of, on either field of your choosing," Alex bows as if making a courtly gesture.

This time the hooting is accompanied by several men chanting his name. Alex's blatant innuendoes and the fact I still find myself attracted to him, lights an inferno of anger.

"Yes, your highness, I can see you are, indeed in need of lessons, of many kinds," Half the bystanders laugh, the other half back Alex's position with an ominous "Oooohs."

"Alex, by my count, she is ahead two to nothing," Szames smiles as he puns his brother's defeat, "I do believe this is the first time you have failed to score."

"But the game is far from over, Brother, far from over," Alex's murmur is missed by most of the soldiers.

Disgusted, I shake my head. Is that what this is? Just some kind of game with me as the prize?

When Alex leaves he takes the majority of the crowd

with him. A mark later, I have seen all the women fight. It is obvious they have one common fault, "Charles, once they learn to keep focused on the battle at hand and ignore any outside distractions these women will be able to best any of the regular soldiers."

"I hope I can drive that point home, otherwise there may be none left to be knighted. There is a lot more going on in an actual conflict than there is here. If attention lags for even a moment it will be a slaughter," he is uncharacteristically solemn.

I notice quite a few men are still hanging about the edges of the practice field, interested in our workout. Approaching the largest group I invite them to spar.

"Perhaps when they are bested by men with half their ability the point will sink in," a mischievous glint enters my eyes.

"If nothing else it will give them an opportunity to fight against people of varying skills," Charles optimism still fails to exert itself but as I hear the midnight bells toll I realize I am out of time.

"I leave you in the capable hands of you instructor," I nod my head in dismissal.

Hurriedly, Mikaela steps forward. With a curtsy that looks odd in her pants suit, she bows her head, "Milady, we women have been discuss'n it. We have decided there's much we owe you, for what you have given us," the defiant redhead rises to look me in the eye as she finishes, "all that we ask is that you either set a price on your aid or let us set one for you. Andrayia has told us that you give what you do, expectin' noth'n. But we believe, if you give noth'n in return, then what's been given has no mean'n--"

Her speech comes to a stumbling halt as I raise my hand. "Do all of you feel the same?" As the rest of the troop voices their agreement an idea springs to mind.

"Then a payment I will set. All eight of you have the skills to become the greatest warriors this kingdom has ever seen. Because of this, I ask that until the day you have been appointed as the Royal Guard, you act as my personal defenders, standing beside me when we take the field. Since I am a mage, the enemy will be throwing all they have my way, so the payment I ask is high. The price may very well be your life."

Several of the women pale, but all of them proclaim, "Yes, milady."

"We accept the price you ask, milady," Mikaela curtsies formally.

Feeling the need for privacy, I head to the woods before going to my chambers. Wandering through the peaceful forest gives my mind a chance to unwind. Focusing on the world around me, I find myself in the meadow with the miss-enchanted rock.

"Ah Tony, I wish you where here. You must be going crazy, worrying about me." I sigh, kneeling on the stone. "You would've found a better solution for the women."

I am plagued by doubt about the decision I have made. Is having them close where I can try to protect them worth the added danger of being close to a high priority target? Relenting, knowing the choice has already been made and fretting about it is getting me no where, I make my way to my rooms and the stack of papers waiting for me.

"Is that all for tomorrow's schedule, milady?" Crystal valiantly fights another yawn.

"With the Great Battle, night after tomorrow I refuse to waste time on social engagements, so no, there won't be anything else for the next two days."

"Milady, if I may presume to ask, what of the day after the battle? I have heard rumors that you are to go on campaign?" Crystal's eyes bat sleepily.

"Have you now?" Word spreads fast, "Yes, those rumors are true. I suppose your duties will be light for the following ten days or so."

Puzzled she tilts her head, "How so, milady? Will I not be accompanying you?"

A startled laugh escapes me until I see she is sincere, "Go with me? You're not a warrior, why would you go on a campaign?"

"You are still a lady. As such, you will need at least one female servant to care for your needs," the chambermaid explains, "Since I am your Personal Maid, it is my privilege to accompany you wherever you go. It would be very improper otherwise."

"Crystal, can you even ride a horse?" All I need is another life in my hands.

As she shakes her head 'no' I continue, "Then the matter is closed, you cannot ride, therefore you cannot accompany me."

Feeling guilty for my harshness, I expound, "Crystal, I appreciate you thinking of my reputation, but it really doesn't matter to me how inappropriate it is. I will be leaving when I return from the trip. I don't wish to endanger your life needlessly."

I feel a stunned gratitude emanate from her and make a hastily addition, "And about this yawning: it is obvious you need some rest. If you will instruct the servants that they can leave after dessert, I would like you to take the rest of the night off. Get some sleep."

The new topic doesn't help her emotional state. Tears are threatening to overflow as she curtsies to leave. What am I supposed to do, ignore her needs? By her reaction you'd think I just gave her a million dollars. "Hmmph." more likely it's the only kindness that she's seen in several years. A knock on the outer door brings me out of my internal musings. I jump to answer it. Don't want her to think I have reconsidered.

I smile in familiar greeting to my favorite dinner partner. Following Szames into the dining room I notice he is walking rather stiffly, "A little sore from practice?" A hint of a smile in enters my voice.

"Practice? You mean that massacre? I had forgotten how painful it can be to lose," his smile widens, "but it was worth it to witness Alex's frustration first hand."

"You really think it bothered him?"

"Believe me, there is no end to the frustration your

encounters are bringing him." Szames smirks.

My brow crinkles in puzzlement. "But he thrives on the 'game?'"

"Do not mistake me: your evasiveness in no way keeps him from enjoying it immensely." I miss the wince as Szames takes his seat.

I harrumph dejectedly. "I just wish he'd give up already," casually, we serve ourselves dinner as we continue the conversation.

"I would wager he has not seen a challenge this like this since he courted Andrayia." He shrugs. "It took him a full two years to win her to his bed."

"Two years! He's insane!" recognizing the panicked quality to my voluminous riposte, I clear my throat, "That man has all kinds of women surrounding him, what would make him continue to pursue someone who rejects his advances?"

"I think it has to do with the greener grass syndrome. If someone tells him that he cannot have something, that is exactly where he sets his mind," our conversation lags while we dig into dinner.

As desert is served Szames asks, "Did you know half the men have placed bets on the two of you?"

"Bet's on us?" My question is a thrust of steel, when the nature of the contest hits me, "what are the odds?"

"If you will excuse the crudeness, they are two to one that he will bed you before the battle and even odds that it will be after." The glint of laughter in his eyes sparks a fire under my temper.

"What are odds that I won't be bedded at all?" I demand icily, "I suggest you place your money there."

"I am pretty sure no one has even considered that possibility," Szames chuckles.

Relaxing in the company of someone, whom I now consider to be a good friend, the tension of the day drains away. The impending battle seems a distant future. I sip mulled wine while Szames struggles to get the last piece of cobbler on his fork, a fork he is wielding with his left hand.

"Is your wrist still sore? I must have hit you harder than I thought." I make my way to his side of the table. "Here, let me take a look at it."

"It is fine, really," he protests, "I will have one of the physicians look at it tomorrow if it is not whole by then."

Standing with my arms folded across my chest I give him my best mothering glare. "I've got plenty of healing power left. Off with the chain mail already."

Heaving a sigh he removes his tabard and mail. The sleeves of the padded shirt underneath are just tight enough that he can't get it up far enough for me to examine the wound, so he removes that as well.

I wince at the sight of his bared flesh. "Oh Szames, I am so, so sorry."

An ugly purple bruise covers the center of his chest, another one covers his right side, and a particularly nasty one is only inches from his spine.

"Just part of fencing," he shrugs, then, noticing the guilty look he adds, "Now surely you must have more sense than Rose? You know that this is not your fault."

Willing the tears not to fall, straining to keep emotion out of my voice, I reach for his arm, "But I landed every one of those blows; the least you can do is let me heal them,"

I put all my effort into attaining a new level of healers-sight. Confident I have achieved my goal I work on his wrist then move on to the rest. Half a mark later I heave a sigh.

"I've got the majority of the damage repaired," I muse, "but I don't have enough energy to fix those knotted muscles in your back."

Szames interrupts my thoughts. "Ahhh, that was amazing. The pain has disappeared. The rest of those knots truly have nothing to do with you," Muscles ripple as he struggles into his shirt. "It is only stress that has plagued me since we first got word of the demons."

Placing my hand on his arm I halt his dressing, "You took care of my head last night, I insist you let me take care of your back tonight. It just so happens I give excellent backrubs, even if I am a little out of practice."

"On… your bed?" The strangled words finally make it.

I put a strangle hold on the sudden case of the giggles threatening to burst forth. I smirk, "It sure as hell will be a lot more comfortable than the floor."

"But your husband…" he stutters.

"Szames, unless you are more like your brother than you seem, I think you can be trusted to behave like a gentleman, even on my bed," my lips pucker with mock seriousness, "Do I have your word you won't take advantage of the situation?"

"Reba, I would never…" Seeing my lips cure he hastens on. "If you are sure you wish to."

"Look, I used to give them to all my male friends growing up. There is nothing immoral about it," holding my breath I manage to contain a sigh. Am I pulling teeth or trying to make him feel better? "The practice of massage is something I find quite relaxing. Boy, could I use some relaxation right now."

With the hesitant blonde in tow I head into the next chamber. Szames drops his things on the couch. When he looks to me, I gesture toward the waiting plateau. He shucks off his boots and crawls onto the mattress. Without the distractions of the bruises, I notice the body I have been working on.

Wide, heavily muscled shoulders, a chest with defined pecks, and a washboard stomach make a very broad 'v' shape leading to a shapely butt. Szames's hulking form makes the gigantic mattress look like a normal king-size. My hormones kick into overdrive. God it's been a long time, maybe this wasn't such a good idea. But after that speech there is no way I am backing down!

"Flat on your back, now," Just pretend this is one of your sisters: this is just a simple massage. The litany does little to calm my awakened libido. I hurry to remove my shoes, blushing as I crawl onto the pillowed surface with Mr. Universe.

I feel his muscles tense underneath my hands as I place them on his shoulders. "Szames, for this to do you any good you are going to have to relax," I chide.

When he takes a deep breath I feel the tension ease, somewhat. Kneading his muscles with my fingers, I make my way across his back. Thank goodness for the added strength or my hands would never hold up to these massive tendons. Trancing, I use my power to augment the massage, easing the stressed areas. Scanning with sight I notice a knot of pressure still exists in his lower back even after all my effort.

I refocus my attention there. When additional rubbing fails to release the tightness I reexamine the problem. After several minutes, I my face begins to burn. For the entire duration of this massage, Szames has been stiff as a board!

Applying the last dregs of my healing energy I calm his surging hormones and decrease the blood-flow to the aroused area. I smile in satisfaction as the last indications of stress leave his body. Disabling my sight, I continue the rubdown the old-fashion way, magically unaided. As anticipated, the process is comforting, if slightly arousing.

When my hands become too tired to continue, I look up. The sun is peaking in through the curtains. Having had time to fully unwind I find myself exhausted.

Szames is sound asleep. I finally got him to relax, the last thing I want to do is wake him. I glance at the austere looking couch, recalling the trials of my youth: how difficult it can be not to follow your instincts when you first wake with your senses muddled, I am still unwilling to be that uncomfortable. I decide, nonetheless, to play it safe. I complete my bedtime rituals then mumble a couple of lines to release the bindings of my brassier, tossing it off the side of the bed. Lying down I intone:

"Sleeping here is a must,
Morality can't be a bust,
So snoozing I will remain,
Until hormones are restrained."

Peacefulness overcomes me. Slipping into slumber my lips curve. Having another warm body in the bed makes me feel a little less lonely in this world so far from my home.

Szames freezes, not daring to blink. Feeling a soft, feminine, body sleeping next to him he struggles to throw off the haze of sleep. As his eyes adjust to the darkness he realizes most of the illumination is coming from the curtained balcony to his right, not the dying embers of last night's fire.

His muscles tense. The slight state of stimulation multiplies tenfold as he groggily recalls the last place he remembers being and who the long slender shape molded to his left side must be.

Feeling the body next to her stiffen, Reba's subconscious acknowledges it. Trailing her hand across Szames's abdomen, she places a kiss on the chest where her head resides before rolling over so her sleeping partner can get comfortable. It was a nightly ritual with her husband so the motions come naturally, even in the haze of sleep.

A groan of desire escapes Szames. It goes unnoticed by both parties on the pillowed plateau, but is studiously noted by a third.

The prince fills his lungs as he fights to control the passion sweeping through him. Using a will stronger than the iron sword he wields, a will he has worked a lifetime to hone, he denies the surmounting carnal urges. Methodically, he slices all thought of seducing her sleep-shrouded body out of his brain. Still, it is several minutes before he trusts himself to move.

Szames eases himself off the side of the bed. In the dim firelight, the outline of his fully engorged manhood can be seen as he gazes down at the sleeping form. Without thought, his hand gently brushes a strand of hair from her face.

"Am I a coward or a fool? No man would pass up this opportunity. My love, as much as I desire to take you in my arms I dare not. I have given my word. Our friendship is too dear, even if it is destined to lasts no more than a few weeks."

Neither the husky whisper nor the sounds of his leaving disturbs the spell-shrouded Reba. The shadowy figure a few feet away, however, observes everything, noting even the smallest, and especially the enlarged details.

Carrying his belongings before him so anyone he meets will not see the telling snugness in his britches, the prince stumbles back to his own rooms.

Lying on his bed, his chest throbs where her warm lips caressed his flesh. Searing warmth tingles his ribcage where her supple breast pressed against him. A pain begins to form when he remembers the silkiness of her touch across his midriff. As thoughts of her run through his mind he struggles for the illusive tranquility of sleep.

Chapter Twenty-Six

"Boy, did I have the strangest dream last night." I remark to Crystal while easing into the warm water.

My handmaiden raises her eyebrows waiting for me to continue, "Szames and Tony were battling. Szames with his sword and my husband was wielding a saber made of fire," I make a half-hearted attempt to explain a Star Wars light-saber in gothic terms, "as the two came together sparks flew."

"The strangest part of the dream was my behavior. I just stood by, helpless, not doing anything. Crystal, I don't think I have ever been truly helpless in my entire life," my last remark gets a disgruntled "humfp..." from the maid. This time I pin her with questioning stare.

"Milady, the dream's provocation is obvious, considering last night's activities," her condescending tone leaves me speechless. Her bitterness spikes as she continues, "So much for the idealistic relationships of your world. It took less than an octal for my world to defeat what you supposedly cherish."

Even though I know it is neither required nor expected, I begin to explain, "I know what you think you saw, but you have jumped to the wrong conclusion. What transpired last night was nothing that transgressed my wedding vows. I only gave a massage to a friend who fell a sleep."

Crystal opinion remains unchanged, "Perhaps last

night was innocent enough, but the next time probably won't be."

Guilt fuels my temper, "Look, I had everything under control: I spelled myself not to wake until he left. I'd bet my life Szames isn't the type to rape someone while they sleep."

Crystal looks at the floor, but hurt anger seethes in her eyes, "Please, talk freely."

The words barley pass my lips when she barges on, "He is only a man, how long is he expected to resist a woman with whom love has obviously dawned. Last night was a close matter: I observed the testing of his self-control as he stated his feelings for you. Unless he finds something to relieve the state he is in, he's likely to wind up with man-cramps so bad he won't be able to stand to fight in the Great Battle."

She harrumphs with a wry twist to her mouth, "Take it from someone who knows. Any man can be broken. Maybe not on the first attempt, and maybe not even on the second, but eventually passion will overcome even the strongest of men."

Her determination makes me re-examine my behavior as I lean back into the vanity chair, "You're right, Crystal. It was inconsiderate of me to put him in such a position. I thank you for pointing out the oversight," having conceded victory to her on one point, I rebuke her other observation, "but about one thing you are gravely mistaken. There is no way Szames is in love with me. He doesn't even know me. Men often substitute 'love' for 'lust' when desire overcomes them."

"As you say, milady," Crystal doesn't buy into the idea. "If I may ask, how would that husband of yours feel about what happened between you and the prince?"

"Ok, ok already, it was a really bad judgment call. Tony would be pissed as hell, but he would forgive me." A rare case of pessimism asserts itself as I mutter, "he'd better after all I have put up with from him."

"So your relationship isn't as picturesque as you have

led me to believe? Has he been unfaithful?" the grief in Crystal's hushed tone prompts me to reveal parts of my marriage I would rather forget.

"I never said it was a perfect relationship. I only said we are committed to staying together, that we are both working to achieve that goal. As for being faithful, I guess that depends on your definition of the word."

I pause trying to figure out how to explain our problems in terms that will make sense to her. I am relieved when she dismisses Rhachel to her studies. Having finished with my hair, I gesture for her to take a seat with me in the living area.

I begin hesitantly, "Even in the advanced society of my world where you marry for love, mismatches are made more often than naught. Many people choose to dissolve the relationship rather than work to sustain it. Less than half of the marriages make it until 'death do you part.'"

"Tony and I have always agreed separation isn't an option, even when we discovered we have a major difference in opinion on a sensitive issue that is, in essence, the main vow we took: faithfulness," I have her attention now.

"Remember those miniature paintings I created? Those are called pictures. They are commonplace on my world. They come in many sizes and shapes. People can even call up these pictures at will, they can look at anything they wish," Crystal absorbs my description of this amazing feat.

"My husband is addicted to some of those pictures… ones that are harder to come by, but still quite prevalent. Photos depicting other couples engaged in sexual acts."

My revelation gets a blank look so I explain, "He uses intimate pictures of other couples for the fulfillment of his fantasies: needs I cannot meet. I have always considered this a transgression on the vow to remain faithful. When Tony courted me he pledged to give the practice up before we married. But it wasn't as easy as he thought it would be. We have worked for years to come to an understanding, but the problem still plagues us," I close my eyes against the agonizing stab, an ache I had hoped my heart would be numb to by now.

"Milady, I can see how disturbing this is to you, but I am confused as to why this should be. It seems to me your husband found the perfect aid to keep the vow you both cherish. After all, he has lain with no other woman, he merely uses their likeness to satisfy the normal human urge for sexual conquest," Crystal's honest puzzlement forces me put aside my own dislike for the topic.

"Perhaps your view is valid. Perhaps many more of our unions would last if we embraced other methods to explore our fantasies. But I cannot," vividly I recall the chest-seizing anguish when I first learned what Tony believed was a simple Playboy habit was and is an all-consuming addiction.

"As a child I saw my parent's marriage become more and more destructive until it dissolved. Pictures, like the ones my husband uses, were blamed for much of that. And my religion also speaks against it, saying we should resist the basic animalistic temptations and concentrate on the love and emotion in the intimate act to keep it sacred between the beloved pair. But what hurts most are the lies he tells: the deception."

"Two years into our marriage I discovered Tony had been lying to hide his continual exploration of sex-pictures. After a year of discussion with a professional, I decided to give his way a try, regardless of my beliefs," A tear slides down my face as I finish revealing the state of our holy union. "No matter my effort, I couldn't hide the pain accompanying each of our attempts at integrating his fantasy world into our bedroom."

"Being the thoughtful husband he is, Tony couldn't continue doing something he knew hurt me. At first, he lost almost all interest in sex. It kills me to know that every time my attempt to sway him into a romantic entanglement fails, it is because I am not enough to stimulate him: He desires something I can't provide. He still slips when we are apart for extended periods." Shaking off the negativity, I concentrate on the good side.

I attempt a smile, "It only occurs occasionally now, a week here or there. So we have overcome the trial and now our union is stronger for it."

"He's given up something and you are still hurting. Sounds like a wonderful arrangement. Perhaps the two of you are a mismatch," Crystal makes her harsh statement matter-of-factly with no sense of ill will accompanying it.

"Crystal, are any two people ever perfect for one another? The whole point of a marriage is compromise. Growing close together through the trials of life," she looks thoughtful, but shrugs it off as she goes to answer a knock at the door.

Settling down to a familiar breakfast with the whole gang helps me shake off the remnants of last night's dream, but not Crystal's warning. As we wind up the meeting I decide the line I have been walking with Szames is a dangerous one: a little distance will be for the best. Gloom plagues me as I head out for the day.

"Reba, sorry to keep you waiting," Szames approaches at a fast walk.

Seeing him striding my way makes me smile. It gives my spirit an upward lift. Very dangerous ground when one's husband is nowhere around. "Not a problem, it gave me a rest-break to complete the spell for those large stones. If you are ready, I have got about a million things to do today."

After completing the needed enchantments on the rocks, I take us soaring to enlarge the shield again. Following the same pattern as yesterday I set us down in the meadow where I promised to meet with Alex. As gallant as ever, Szames agrees to take time out of his schedule to accompany me while I have to deal with his brother.

"Prince Alex, Yivgeni, I am pleased both of you could

make it," I set us down only feet from their position.

"Milady, you are my favorite tutor to date, I would not miss one of your lessons for the crown itself," Alex coos.

"I'm delighted to hear it," I proceed with business, brushing off the flattery, "Your brother came up with a novel idea yesterday. I have given him the ability to see magic, much the way you activate these lamps by saying just a single word. I think it might be worthwhile if I did the same for you."

The color drains from Alex's face, "Reba, I appreciate the offer, but I like my world the way it is. Seeing forces I cannot control would not serve a great purpose for me. Szames is the General and my right hand, his sight will serve for both of us."

With his tone of finality, I let the subject drop.

Over a mark later Szames has mastered all the activation words, but Alex still fails one time out of every eight. Glancing at the position of the sun, I end the tutoring session.

"Now for the Demon summoning. I will need both of you to hold my hands and the light pole."

"All who are evil and malevolent, then come at my call. Drawn by magic, you cannot resist this glowing ball."

Following the litany, the sphere at the top now shines with a bright blue light to Magesight. I nod in satisfaction.

We prepare to go our separate ways as Alex turns to me. "Anything else I need to mention in the council meeting?" Don Juan steps closer.

"I have nothing more for the council, but if you wouldn't mind, I would like to request a private meeting with your father before the day's end. There are a few matters I wish to discuss with him," I allow his physical advance, putting all my effort into resisting his 'come hither' gaze, figuring a slap across his face him might hurt my chances of getting his assistance in this matter.

"A private meeting with my father? Tell me, milady, what must I do to get you to agree to a private meeting with me?" With his use of the title of respect the hair raises on the back of my neck.

"Your Highness, I beg you to remember that you speak to a married woman, one who has taken vows of faithfulness to her spouse. I am afraid unless it pertains to duty I must decline, even if I wish it otherwise," unfortunately, I mean every word.

"Then I will wait patiently for the day when you are released from those vows," with courtly poise he takes my hand, delivering a kiss that leaves me quivering with desire before he and his brother march off for the castle together.

Please God… let that day never come.

It occurs to me, as I hustle with Yivgeni to my next rendezvous, this was the first day since my arrival that Szames and I failed to make dinner plans.

Self-reproach keeps me preoccupied as I complete the day's business. Social failure is something I am accustomed to, but the familiarity does my self-esteem no good. It seems in the transfer diplomacy skills were not included in the list of improvements.

Checking back in at my chambers about mid-evening bells, I find a royal squire waiting for me.

"Milady, His Majesty, King Arturo asks that you join him for a stroll through the gardens at midnight bells," states the teenager with a bow. His likeness to William marks him as an older brother.

"It would be my pleasure," with my brief words he bows, taking his leave.

Several marks later I arriving at what turns out to be a lush rose garden. I purposefully neglect to dismiss William and Keth as they amble behind me.

"Your Majesty, I am please you have found room in your schedule to meet with me," I bow politely in greeting.

"I might be old enough to be your father, Milady Reba, but on a night such as this even I cannot resist the company of an enchanting woman," his eyes sparkle in amusement. I discern no lust in his words so I take them as a harmless.

"I am flattered, Your Majesty, that you find me so, for standing beside the beautiful flowers which you name wife and daughter, I feel unworthy of your notice," I retort.

"Milady, I applaud you. Never have I seen a more gracious return on an opening exchange. It seems my son was right, you do have a talent for word play," pausing, he indicates I should take a seat on the cement bench.

"As much as I would love to explore this enchanting side of the Prophesied One, I am afraid time limits us," he assumes a seat on the bench next to me, but not close enough to invade my personal space. "Alex informs me there are additional matters?"

"Your Majesty, let me start with my most trivial concern. Perhaps you've already heard, I was not born of noble blood, nor am I free to marry. I am already wed, as this ring symbolizes." Holding out my hand, I displaying my wedding ring.

"What a delicate masterpiece," King Arturo seems undisturbed by my announcement, "tell me, do you have children, milady?"

"No, we have not been so blessed. But I cannot, in good conscience, leave behind the duties or the vows I have taken. As much as I have grown to love your world, I intend to return to mine with some of my men following the first campaign." The monarch's lack of surprise leads me to believe he has already been informed of such.

"Milady, your presence will be a loss felt throughout the kingdom if that day comes to pass. I respect you all the more for holding to vows you have taken in the face of a more desirable option," King Arturo acknowledges my statement, but fails to take it as the certainty I have stated it to be.

"The rest of my concerns can be rolled into one: the state of morale in the armed forces. On my world it is not uncommon to knight and title an individual with a land-gift when one performs a great deed. Is there such a custom here?"

"Hmmm, an interesting concept. Currently the only way to obtain a title is through nomination, in the rare case of an estate failing to produce an heir," I perceive an internal chuckle before he continues. "I see no reason we can not start a new tradition. The foes we face are intimidating, to say the least. The added incentive will increase the men's hope. Milady, you are as intelligent as you are beautiful."

You don't know the half of it._"Thank you, Your Majesty. I must admit, you took to the idea much quicker than I believed possible. It seems my list of benefits is unneeded."

"Unneeded to convince me, but I am sure Alex and I will have a long night composing a list of our own for the council," knowing a polite hint when I hear one, I bid King Arturo goodnight before strolling back to my chambers for dinner.

I eat alone in my bedroom after creating another pad of paper. By the end of the meal I have completed the final force-field adjustment along with five battle spells for myself, the later of which I perform immediately so that a keyword will be all I need in the coming conflict.

Having had a very productive, if lonely meal, I dismiss a tired looking Crystal. The five of us have fortified the city, re-armed the military, bolstered their medical staff, while I snubbed the crown prince and destroyed a friendship with his brother. Crawling into bed, I send up a silent prayer to God who seems so far away, "Please let me get a full night's sleep before my first battle."

Chapter Twenty-Seven

"Reba, I ask one thing from this meeting: another reality check. We are heading into out first battlefield: I think a reminder that this is now real life - and real death - will be invaluable," Allinon opens the breakfast with a dismal, but courteous request.

"Why don't you start," I give him a brief smile of approval.

"Let me begin by saying that, Reba, I am amazed at the job you've done. I didn't think you had it in you. Now I am proud to be part of this group," seeing gratitude shining in my eyes, he moves on to the business at hand, "As I said before, I'm separated from my wife. After what I've learned, here, about attitude: I have hope for my marriage for the first time in years. So much makes sense now. For this reason I will be doing my damnedest to get through this war with my skin intact," Allinon's humble acknowledgement leaves us all speechless.

Clearing my throat, I try to lighten the mood, "Well, it looks like you've out done me this time. I don't have another 'DoubleMint' surprise to top that." Surrounded by masculine chuckling I struggle to think of something to contribute, "Well, I learned a valuable lesson last night: never activate a 'Conan' spell the night before you need it. It was said that Arnold Schwarzenegger used to push Maria Schriver out of bed without knowing it, back in his bodybuilding days. With ten times his strength I ripped my sheets to shreds." When I get a quartet of disbelieving looks I add, "Just ask Crystal if you don't believe me."

"Laks?" Charles asks my maid in this land's native tongue.

The look of exasperation she gives says more than my story did. As the rest of the group laughs, Allinon looks at me. I discern fear stirring in him.

"I don't think that really counts, after all, this is a reality check," a fraction of sarcasm enters the Druids voice. Poor guy, he is truly upset by this world.

"The only thing I can think of to contribute is something you men probably would never dream of even thinking about. I said before, I have no kids. It is not for lack of trying. My tubes were deteriorated by endometriosis: I will never be able to have the children I have wanted all my life. Also, another reason this prophecy is a bunch of bullshit: me marrying the next king wouldn't be very helpful if I can't produce an heir."

"Definitely not something that would ever cross my mind," Charles's joke falls flat, "Let's see… facts… when I get back I am going to propose to my girl. Women of this world have been fun, everything I have ever wished an then some, but I find myself missing the little things." The ebony engineer shakes his head. "I can't believe I miss her even more than my computer!"

"Now that's a shock," Jerik's voice grumbles into the silence, "I thought you were enjoying this bachelor's dream of moral decadents. Me, well my marriage has been screwed from day one. She got pregnant, we got married, and she had a miscarriage. In my opinion we both have been too chicken to admit we made a mistake. By staying here I am helping us both out," straight to the point, Jerik is as direct as the hammer he wields in the smithy.

"I guess that leaves me. Don't suppose that you'd let me pass on this one," Jamison murmurs.

"No way, it's your turn to spill your guts," Allinon's urging carries a trace of his old attitude, but its bearable.

"We all have."

"I had a totally boring life, there is nothing to say. A rich couple adopted me, but I don't know why. I might as well been an orphan because I was raised by nannies. Yeah, I know they care. I just don't feel all that attached, never have. That is why staying here is such an easy choice." Turning to Allinon he adds, "That enough gut's for ya'?"

"So the 'Annie' story isn't all it's cracked up to be? Yeah, I'd say that is a wake-up call," The druid nods his head.

As I hear the mid-afternoon bells toll I reaffirm why we are here, "Time's getting short. Guys you know where you're going to be?"

Allinon gives a firm nod, "I'll use my Druid abilities to hold the Northgate where I can pull strength from the forest."

Jerik motions to Charles, "We will team up at the Eastgate."

I dip my head in agreement, "Merithin will be at the Westgate with four of the soon to be Royal Guard. I will take Southgate where the strongest attack will likely come."

"I know I'm needed for the wounded. The teams of roving healers with stretchers will be useless if I'm not there to triage the critical patients," creases appear in Jamison's forehead as he frowns, "But I would feel better if I were out there with them. Your paladin stones will help, and they have the force field to duck behind, but only a handful of them have any battle experience. I feel like I am sending lambs to the slaughter."

"Hey, every pack of sheep has their very own guardian wolf! You made sure your healing teams were assigned a street thug who is quite handy with a knife." My analogy gets a half-smile from my chestnut-headed companion, "They are used to dangerous situations and staying safe."

"I still don't like it. We are split up around the wall.

Reba, as a mage you are vulnerable to physical attacks. At least one of us should be beside you," Charles's concern is touching, but the argument is getting old.

I smirk with irritation, "I am no more vulnerable than you, I bested you in practice. We have been over this! You approved the strategy."

"That was before I knew the expert swordsmen surrounding you would be the women, not me and Jerik," Prince Charming pouts, looking even cuter.

"I made a promise to The Guard. They will stand beside me. I barely got them to agree to protect Merithin as well." With a sigh, I go over the reasoning one last time, "Szames will be with there, with him I will have the emergency resources of the Royal Cavalry on standby, and a sword by my side as well."

"And that must irritate the heck out of Alex. His brother at your side while he watches over the Castle's battlement, not even allowed in the fight," Jamison's deft change of the topic is masterfully done.

Charles humor quickly reasserts itself, "Did you see the look he gave his father when Arturo tried to justify the position as a necessity by giving him a Cavalry unit. How did he put it? 'You will lead any critical charge in the event of a dire emergency.' If looks could kill it would've been patricide!"

"That is one meeting I'm sorry I missed…" my sentence trails off as a knock sounds at the outer door.

Hearing a familiar voice I rise to greet my Royal guest. Now I know why Alex had a change of heart about flying. I guess escorting me to the assembly outweighs his fear of heights and magic.

I lead the way into the reception chamber with the guys forming a half circle behind me. Using the same cues we created on our arrival, we bow in unison to the Crown Prince, magnifying the importance of the moment.

"Your Highness," I remain stooped, waiting for his acknowledgement.

"ArchMage Reba, gentlemen," the slight smile

playing about his lips lets me know the gesture hit a home run.

And what a set of lips they are. My mind wonders as I take in his total ensemble. Although he has exerted none of his charm, I can't help being aroused by the tall, dark, and handsome man in front of me.

The metal breastplate and cape highlight his broad shoulders and perfectly proportioned stature. The royal blue color provides the ideal accent to his eyes. When his fine-boned, manicured hand reaches for mine, placing it on his arm, I am alarmed at the similarity to Tony's. He escorts me past the bed on the way to the balcony. Why have I resisted him so fiercely when my life could very well be forfeited in the coming battle.

Principles, remember? Aand morals…and…

"Reba, I place my life in your hands. Perhaps something I should have done long ago, for who could resist an enchantress of your beauty," Alex's voice is husky, but I perceive no magic.

…and his conceited, manipulating flattery is an insult to the integrity of all women…

"I thank you for the trust you place in me, for both our lives will depend upon my concentration," I exaggerate the needed attention hoping he won't try to ambush me once we are airborne.

"If you are ready? There is just one additional thing you need to keep in mind, don't let go of my hand. It is all keeps you aloft," I get a surge of sadistic pleasure as his face turns ashen.

Grasping his hand in one of mine, holding my staff in the other, I take us off the ground in a smooth upward arch, soaring straight for the center of the shield. As we approach our destination, I address my partner in this magical endeavor, "If heights bother you, don't look down."

The comment has the expected result as Alex shoots a glance ground-ward. I hold in a chuckle as his grip on my hand tightens. Paybacks are a bitch.

"I am going to work the spell to add the new layer to the shield," closing my eyes I try to bring our joined hands up to the force-field.

Serves me right. Not only am I unable to move our hands, but when I try to draw energy from him the resistance is so great I am forced to take the needed energy from my staff instead. I begin the enchantment.

"You are strong, impenetrable so
Outward another layer will grow.
Like a stun setting on a ray gun,
Touching you they'll no longer run."

A teal-colored veil eases away from the original barrier. It continues moving until there is a thirty-foot gap between the two shining blue domes.

"The moat is now complete. Hopefully, waiting until today to activate final shield will prevent them from finding a way around our best defense," Alex gives a terse nod. Even though I didn't use him in the process, there is sweat on his brow.

Fighting off the guilt assaulting me, I take the scenic route, flying over the assembled troops lined up ten abreast, winding around Castle Eldrich. The men cheer wildly reaching up their hands as if to touch us.

"It seems your people adore you, Alex," I murmur.

"My people have always adored me. I do not believe that is the reason for this outpouring. Seeing us together invigorates their faith in the prophecy. It gives them hope that we will survive this onslaught," for once his response contains no flattery.

"Had I known that boosting the morale of the men could be accomplished so effortlessly, I would have put more energy into convincing you to soar by my side," I return his smile, finding myself relaxing in his presence for the second time this morning. Gracefully as an eagle landing on a mountain peak, our toes touch the ground.

"My beautiful Lady," he uses the possessive form

of address that is supposed to be reserved for intimate couples, "I always soar on hawk's wings when I am next to you, whether or not my feet leave the ground."

Not out of the air five seconds and already he starts with this nonsense! Ignoring his last remark I turn to bow to his father, "Your Majesty, I have no fear for the outcome of today's battle with you watching over us."

"With the Flame-Haired One defending our gates, I am certain of Our victory in the Great Battle. ArchMage Reba, We send with you our son, Prince Szames of Cuthburan, General of the Armed Forces and Second Heir to the Throne. May your return be swift and victory complete," dressed in my black leather combat uniform covered by the shining sliver robe I feel every inch a warrior, worthy of King Arturo's declaration.

As if on cue, Squire William and Squire Herald complete the last ten feet to our position, dutifully holding the horses while Prince Szames and I mount. Within minutes Merithin and the rest of the Crusaders of the Light are mounted beside us, forming a row of eight defenders. An equal number of priests line up to performing a blessing from their god, whose chosen number of strength is eight. Horns blare out into the quiet dusk of evening. The ritual continues, while we lead the army through CastleGate flanked by The Wizard's Guard of Eight.

The air is crisp and the skies are clear. Throngs of people line the streets. There is fear in the solemn eyes, but they hold their heads high as we pass, resolutely pounding wooden blocks together in a double-rhythmic beat. Their odd salute thrums in my ears, like the pulse of this strange world, as we march toward our waiting destiny.

Jerik and Charles are the first to depart the procession, turning down a street heading east. Allinon soon follows, traveling north. Two columns of soldiers follow both groups.

When Szames, four of the Eight Guards, and I turn

southward, three of the remaining six columns trail behind us. My thoughts turn inward. I use the remainder of the journey to make my peace with God, incase the unimaginable should come to pass.

We dismount, leaving our steeds with guards at the gate. With Szames as escort, I take my first step outside the city that has summoned me from my home. Twenty feet from the entrance we turn and face the troops. Andrayia and Mikaela stand beside me, and Sheridan and Keeton take up position next to Szames, my appointed Royal Defender.

Enwrapped in the silence of our own thoughts, we watch as the columns split to divide their number. They spread out along the marble wall encasing the Jewel of Cuthburan in a bristling fortification of steel and flesh.

Healers, designated by a green sash and shimmering canteens of healing potion at their waist, follow the guards. In groups of four they skitter down the wall carrying stretchers made out of wooden poles and cloth.

The screeching of metal echoes into the dimming night as massive bars are lowered, locking the gates behind us. The solitary entrance into the city is now a small door located beside the guard's station through which the roving teams of healers will deliver the wounded.

Shining helms along the top of the wall gleam in the starlit night as archers take their place. Lampposts are positioned twenty feet from the wall. They represent the safety line of the force-field. Darkness is upon us. The posts provide a ring of illumination around the city, so even those without magesight can see outwards of seventy-five feet. Hair along the back of my neck rises, telling me our enemy is gathering.

A breeze wafts past, carrying with it a putrid stench. The odor brings a feeling of death and waste. A chill creeps down my spine. Straining my senses, I peer out beyond the supernatural illumination. More than a hundred yards out, congregating beyond the light, odd-shaped patches of darkness form an approaching tide of evil.

How deep these waves of darkness extend I can't determine, but for the first time in my life I know true fear. A dread so overwhelming grips me that my bowls turn to water. Minutes pass before I remember to breathe.

I shake off the unwanted emotion like a coyote ridding itself of the morning dew. Reaching out to touch the arm of my Royal Guardian my voice remains rock steady, "Ready or not, here they come."

Chapter Twenty-Eight

"Present arms," Szames's voice booms out. The command echoes down the walls as field commanders bellow the command. The night air sings when hundreds of blades are drawn.

"Hupp," Szames turns toward the force field, bringing us even with the safety line.

Having strapped the staff to my back, my hands are free. I place them before me making a triangle with my thumb and forefinger. I whisper, "MageFire."

A writhing ball of blue flames appears in the space between my hands. The magical sphere of death races toward our foes, pulling in energy, growing larger the farther it travels. A trio of ogres is illuminated seconds before the orb disintegrates three demons and several others in the front line.

As if my opening volley is a cue, the monsters surrounding the Capitol City cry into the dark night. The demonic chittering makes my flesh crawl. A hellish scene worse than any nightmare vision springs to life. The oily darkness of the inhuman ranks surges toward us.

"MageFire, magefire, magefire...." I continue chanting, casting fireballs far down the line to either side. Over and over again, I release the balls of bubbling energy at the charging mass. Before the ashes have settled on the ground, more monsters flow into the places left by the vaporized beasts.

Arrows rain down from above and more dark shapes fall to be trampled by their own comrades. They come faster than I can destroy them, even with the help of the archers. The monsters reach the stun-shield, entering the moat.

A roar erupts from thousands of human throats when the demons tumble to the ground as they hit the shield. The monstrosities lay motionless, their nervous systems stunned into paralysis. Armored men rush forward. The true battle begins.

The earth is stained black with demons' blood and still they come, climbing over the bodies of their own kind. Having drawn my staff and switched to "laser" for the closer engagement the night wears on, passing in a blur.

A soldier climbs onto the pile of dark bodies, eager to dispatch a creature that rolls down the mountain of flesh, lying just out of the moat. Swooping down silently from above, a wyvern snatches the soldier in its talons before I can get off a shot. Another man slices into the neck of a four-legged monstrosity taking a life only to forfeit his own as the acid blood of the beast saturates his face, eventually penetrating the protection of the magic stone.

Out of the corner of my eye, I see a massive club begin to rise from the pile of dispatched demons. As the ogre swings the weapon in an arch toward Andrayia's back, I extend my hand.

"Laser." The spiked club explodes as the blonde warrior swings around. A chunk of timber the size of a two-by-four splinters off. A sliver of wood penetrates the shield protecting her, catching Andrayia in the left arm. Red blood is added to the dark substance coating her. Whispering "laser" again takes the life of the ogre who lay unconscious, hidden beneath his companions, for the last several hours.

The woman who, before this night, considered me her foremost adversary gives a nod, the thanks in her eyes saying more than word could.

As the battle lags, Szames calls out, "Stand down!" Listening to the confirmation echoing down the lines, I step forward as the rest of the men retreat back to safety.

"A burial pyre is undeserved by thee;
However, dissolved by fire demons shall be."

Hands, grown numb to any stimulation created by the power I wield, reach out to the pile of bodies. Blue flames engulf the monsters spreading faster than thought to anything in contact with them. Within seconds an azure ring blazes to life surrounding the castle in magical brilliance. The enchantment disappears. The field before us can be seen once again. A cheer arises from the throats of the soldiers.

Minutes pass, giving all a much-needed rest. Still no enemy appears. I walk back to where Szames is waiting with the Guards, "That can't be their entire strategy, throwing hoards of demons at us?"

"Before your arrival it would have been enough to breach our walls. But you are right, they have shown far more intelligence than that," Szames confirms my suspicions, "this is not over yet."

I look to our left in time to see an orange fireball streak out from the Westgate position. It travels across the sky, smashing into an immense red wall hovering in the heavens.

A brilliant white blinds my vision. I squeeze my eyes shut against the brilliance. As the world comes back into focus again, I see a ruby shield coming into contact with the force-field. As the area of contact spreads, lightning sizzles along our major defense. With an earsplitting "pop", the blue and red shields burst like a gigantic bubble. I watch helplessly as the Cuthburan Army is annihilated by the massive demon hiding behind that ruby cloak.

A brief flash of light and I see the Crowning Jewel of Cuthburan set to torch while thousands of voices shriek into the inky night. Eyes wide in horror, I am blinded by the next flash.

As the spots fade, I can make out a cerulean haze surrounding the castle. The scarlet cloud is still a fair distance off toward the horizon. There is still time.

"I am going help Merithin. Szames, use Magesight to keep an eye on this end. If something approaches, holler," my guardian nods tersely before whispering "sight."

Turning to the four women looking to me for directions, I make a quick decision. "Mikaela and Andrayia, you are with me. Mikaela, you've got a little mage energy, I'll barrow it so we can make better time."

I provide a short version of the standard explanation then take one of their hands in one of mine. Lifting our feet inches from the ground, we swoop down the moat corridor twice as fast as we could have traveled on horseback.

Touching down next to Merithin, the sorcerer gives a nod. "Impeccable timing, milady. What that shield hides I cannot tell, but it is magical in nature. I dared not drain my resources to reveal our enemy before your arrival: it will take most of my remaining power to break it."

I recognize a familiar face in the crowd around us. "With any luck, that won't be necessary." Grimacing, I hale the soldier, "Lieutenant Craig, your positioning is fortuitous."

As the lanky brown-haired man gives me a broad smile I expound, "The supply of magical energy is going to be a deciding point in this battle. We have a situation here that requires a substantial amount of it."

"My lady Reba, it would be my pleasure to assist you," he replies with a bow.

An annoyed huff escapes me, "I appreciate your willingness. However, I ask this as ArchMage Reba, the Flame-Haired One. This is no small undertaking. I intend to draw most of the needed energy from you. Depending on the strength of the approaching attacker the process could leave you unconscious or even dead."

Coming to attention the smile leaves his face,

"ArchMage Reba, sir. It would be an honor to die providing such a service."

Satisfied he understands the risk involved, I extend one hand to him and the other to Merithin, "I will supply the power, but you have probably had more experience disabling shields."

"I will assume the lead," the MasterSorcerer responds.

At a faster pace than is comfortable, I withdraw energy from Craig, adding to it a small stream from my own diminishing supply. I feel the slight tug that tells me Merithin has joined our powers.

"Magic called by another, I command you: Disperse."

Royal blue energy entwining with two lighter azure hues shoots from the hand of the sorcerer next to me. Hundreds of yards away, the heavens lighten like the Aurora Borealis as our power comes into contact with the enemy shield. Laser-like beams of blue and purple put on a show that would be marvelous to behold if we weren't surrounded by beings intent on eradicating the human race.

Long minutes pass while I draw energy from the lieutenant, passing it on to Merithin. The men who crowded the moat back up to the safety line as the approaching attacker grows closer and the size of our newest foe becomes clear.

Four hundred yards from us the demon's shield buckles under Merithin's constant barrage as Lieutenant Craig collapses to the ground. The men on the field tremble with fear. Heading straight for us is a creature straight out of myth and legend: The huge winged lizard is blood-red, has a broad fanged mouth, long sinuous neck and two sets of taloned appendages. The beast is a dragon from the fairy tales of yore. Larger than a 747 with a fifty-foot wingspan, the magic wielding demon descends.

Merithin releases a fireball at the monster. The blue magefire roles harmlessly off the beast's skin. "Laser,

laser," the beams have no effect on the vulnerable underside of the wings. I note it in the back of my mind when a healer tending to Craig pronounces that he will live, he has only lost consciousness.

"Merithin, the shields will never hold against a dragon. It is larger than anything I anticipated, and magical too." Frustrated, I lapse into English, "It's like trying to stop a charging grizzly bear with nothing but arrows."

"If your grizzly is anything like the giants of the north, I see your point," Merithin replies to the redundant statement I made in my native tongue. "I know an enlargement spell, perhaps between the two of us we could make a formidable arrow."

"That's it!" With the flying menace less than two hundred yards away, I leap to the lamppost. Whispering "release", I withdraw the thirty-foot spear from the ground. My Conan fingers grind into the wooden pole as I chant, pacing like a javelin thrower:

"To the neck you'll now fly,
To 'penetrate' as time goes by."

I chuck spear with all my Conan might. True to the words of the rhyme, it soars to the dragon. A tremendous bellow escapes the monster as the magically enhanced weapon drills into its neck. The winged beast pulls upward, hovering in mid-air less than a hundred feet away.

The intelligent creature swings its snout around, sneering at the object piercing its hide. The iron-hard shaft flexes like a bow as one huge claw reaches trying to snap off the impaling object.

Sprinting, I dart to another lamp.

"It doesn't shake like a bowl full of jelly,
But you will penetrate the tender underbelly."

As the second rod lodges in its stomach, the living

nightmare does mid-air summersaults trying to grasp both of the light-posts.

A rear-claw and a fore-claw slide down the twin shafts. Trying to remove the spears, the beast grasps the glowing balls at the end of the poles. Evil appendages wraps around the mage-globes. Crushing pressure is applied. A blinding light shatters the darkness as the luminescent balls explode mere feet from the dragon. The beast plummets earthward.

Having felt the creature's death, I nod at Merithin speeding back toward my designated position. The ground trembles under our feet as the goliath collides with mother earth. A cheer arises from the men as we continue our jog back to the Southgate.

"If that was a distraction, I hate to think what the assault will be," with Andrayia's shorter legs she is at a slow run just to maintain her position beside me.

The ground vibrates, like a convoy of MAC trucks skirting our position. As the ground quakes again I extend my hands to my companions. Taking our feet from the ground, I hurl us toward the danger I discern.

Chapter Twenty-Nine

"Nice touch, using those light-posts as spears," Szames compliments, as if a hundred-and-twenty pound woman throwing a thirty-foot javelin is an everyday occurrence.

"I got the idea from Merithin: bigger arrows," I smile.

In silence we wait, staring at the horizon, as the trembling grows stronger. Even with my night vision I cannot see the coming danger until it is two hundred yards away.

The next attacker is shaped like an arthropod. Each section of its multi-segmented body is as large as a minivan. Its jointed legs hit the ground with such force, the earth quivers with each step it takes. Like a giant centipede, it winds its way over rolling hills.

"MageFire," the first segment of its body disintegrates into ash, but the rest of the creature seems unaffected, "MageFire, magefire, magefire…" a popular arcade game comes to life as the beast's progress is unaffected by the repeated blasts of flame: several sections are disintegrated, but the monster continues on, like a preprogrammed robot. At fifty yards the demon still has more than ten bulbous portions.

"Pphhss..." the legs fold up as the monster hits the stun shield but the creature's momentum causes it to roll. "Laser" slices open the belly of the segment in front. Demons tumble out of the fifteen-foot sphere. Having played right into their hands, too late the purpose of beast is made crystal clear.

The remaining three sections hit the main-shield, dissolving with a fiery blaze as demon flesh comes into contact with the safety line, but only the outer husk is dissolved. Beasts are disgorged. Dozens of invaders spring to life in the midst of our sanctuary. The enemy waits for us in the moat, five times that number occupy the safety zone._We are surrounded!!

Soldiers charge from all directions, encircling the enemy on all sides. Even though the attackers are outnumbered eight-to-one, it does us little good.

Demonstrating cunning at odds with their grotesque forms, ogres hurl one soldier at a time through the shield. The waiting demons pounce on each man, their constant barrage breaking through the protective barrier created by the shield-stone.

"Laser, laser, laser," in the seconds it takes to clear the moat and destroy a half-dozen monsters, twice as many men lay dead in the moat.

Scanning the immediate area, I look for opportunities to take out a demon without endangering human life. Like a cat at a mouse-hole, I watch for an opening as Szames and two of the guards work steadily, keeping a ten-foot ogre occupied. The giants has several wounds, but they have yet to disabled him.

"'Ware, behind you!" Sheridan's warning comes from my left.

Pivoting in that direction, I bring up my hand ready for danger, but Sheridan's sprint to the approaching creature puts her between the beast and me. Twenty feet away, she levels a sword at the gremlin, separating its head from the shoulders. Time slows as the horror unfolds. "No-o-o!" I roar.

Sheridan looks over her shoulder at me, but continues to bend down: intent on retrieving the glowing red sphere the creature carried like a football. As her hand comes into contact with the maroon ball of demon energy her mouth contorts in pain. Black tendrils intertwine with what is left of the blue in her aura. The oozing strands brighten glowing fiercely.

An explosion knocks every man within ten feet of her to the ground. When the dust settles there is no trace of Sheridan. A ten-foot hole lies on the spot where she stood.

"Stand down to the moat!" I bellow at the top of my lungs.

As soldiers break off their engagements, retreating to safety, it gives me the needed openings. The remaining demons are history in a matter of seconds.

Men assume their stations again. The line is sparse now. More than ten feet separates the soldiers as Szames comes to stand beside me. Once again we peer toward the hills, wondering what they will throw at us next. With the moons setting, we don't have long to wait. The enemy knows the night will soon come to an end.

A buzzing fills the air, like a swarm of bees we can't see. From the northwest, three flying demonic shapes approach. Longer and slimmer than the wyverns, these demons are humanoid in shape. Landing a hundred yards out, they hold helpless humans before them, blocking my laser-fire. Two are soldiers and one has a green sash at his waist, labeling him as a healer.

"Take our lives swiftly, Flame-Hair!" cries one of the two men who remain conscious.

His captor sticks a long claw into his thigh, giving it a savage twist. The warrior's screams cease when the demon retracts its claw.

The creatures are six-feet in height and have clear, locust-type wings, but their appearance is more like a tarantula-wasp. Six arms are sprouted down their elongated chests. Black-skin bristles with stiff hair covering their muscled legs and arms. But it is the heads that cause me to clamp my jaws shut against a shriek determined to break free. A jutting jaw slopes back into a large cranium holding five eyes, providing a grotesque backdrop for a pair of human lips.

"A truce. We ask to confer under a pledge of truce," rings out a stilted, guttural, yet understandable voice.

"You attacked without provocation. What possible interest can you have in a talk of peace?" Szames's deep voice booms.

"It is not you to whom we wish to speak," the words slither out of their lips. "Sorceress, are not the lives of three of your men worth a mark of your time? Join us here on this field so that we may end this bloodshed."

I shout, "I have your word. You will release them to my custody, no matter the outcome of our talks?"

"Yes, you have our word that they will be released if you join us to discuss terms for a truce," The giant bug's reply grates irritatingly, even shouted from a distance.

"ArchMage, don't tell me you are considering taking them up on their offer. These monsters have no code of honor. It is clearly a trap," Szames's fierce whisper comes on the heels of the demon's reply.

"General, I agree with your assertion. However, that doesn't change the fact that I will take them up on their offer. I have got a few tricks left up these sleeves of mine. All I need to do is get within fifty-feet of them." I pause, unwilling to disclose my plan.

"I will stand beside you as your second," Szames proclaims in a voice that tells me I will need more time than I have to change his mind.

"There are three of the beasts. There should be three of us. I have sworn to stand by you throughout this battle, I will not be dissuaded from accompanying you," Andrayia states matter-of-factly.

Knowing when I am beat I turn, and in a tone that books no arguments, decree: "Agreed. Mikaela, you and Keeton wait here. Szames, Andrayia, watch for my signal, if my hand comes down to my side you must be touching some part of me, as well as the prisoners."

As all involved nod their assent I march double-time, leaving the safety zone I have constructed, flanked by a General and one of kingdom's most skilled swordswomen.

High atop the inner battlement, Merithin's apprentice, Nemir, shoves his way past the guards surrounding the Royal Family. "Your Majesty, Your Highness," he bows, not waiting for the acknowledgement before trying to speak.

"The Demons… coming… enhanced vision…" Having run the entire way from the castle roof, the young sorcerer is forced to report while gasping for breath.

"Slow down, breathe. We must hear your report in order to understand it." King Arturo reassures the shaken youth, "Now what is it you saw?"

Pausing long enough to gulp two deep breaths Nemir restarts: "Several leagues south: a mass of Demons approaches, fast. They will arrive at the ArchMage's position in less than a quarter mark."

"Father, Reba is heading out of the defenses to meet with those new flyers. She must be warned," Alex makes the statement, leaving the question unasked.

Arturo gives a curt nod of approval, "Take ten Cavalry with you to retrieve the ArchMage. Bring her back to safety, my son."

"I am here, as you requested, now release the hostages," I halt sixty feet from them.

"After the parley," closer now, the demons voice take on a clicking, chittering, echo.

"If their lives don't depend on the outcome, I see no reason for them to remain in your custody," I retort.

"What guarantee do we have that our lives will not be forfeited as soon as we stand unprotected?" Extending my empathy, I still perceive nothing from the monsters before us.

Sliding his sword home in the scabbard Szames growls, "Because we have a code of honor. If this truce is violated it will be by you. Trust must begin somewhere if the truce is to have a positive outcome."

A fly-like buzzing ensues as we wait for their decision. With no consideration for his wounds, the leader pushes his prisoner forward. The two other demons follow him.

As the healer and soldier lift the unconscious man between them, struggling toward us, hoof-beats ring into the silence of the night. Once again the ground beneath our feet begins to tremble.

Cursing I whisper, "To the wounded!" We dash to the prisoners. At the top of the knoll, I give the signal for my companions to bring all the defenders into contact with me.

I whisper "FireRin…" halting just short of releasing a fifty-foot circle of magefire as I feel the location and identity of the new arrivals.

"Alex!" Andrayia hails our galloping savior.

Alex charges into the spot we vacated seconds earlier as several jarovegi emerge from beneath the earth. Horses dance on hind legs, throwing their riders. Engraved in my memory is the picture of the Crown Prince falling from his horse, his head striking a rock.

Swiveling on my heal I hiss, "Laser, laser, laser," taking down the three truce negotiators. Turning back, I find Andrayia is no longer at my side, but fighting beside the new arrivals.

Swearing in frustration, I begin picking off the burrowing demons. When the ground around us begins to shake, I turn to Szames. "It's time to get back to the safety net. You feel up to carrying that one?"

Without a word he reaches down. Slinging the soldier over his shoulder he leads the way. Helping the freed prisoner with the leg wound, I follow Szames. The ground continues to vibrate under our feet as we reach our would-be rescuers.

Andrayia's feet are planted, anger blazing crimson on the fair complexion as she wields the deadly blade. Behind her is a crumpled heap, the one she loves. Before I can fire a shot, a second jarovegi falls before her shining steel. The healer, having stabilized both men, tends to the prince. Alex struggles to rise, the healer has stopped the bleeding, but dizziness still plagues him. Pointing southward he delivers the message that brought him onto the field. "ArchMage, a mass of demons, traveling at an unheard of speed."

"Then I would have you and Andrayia see the wounded back to safety. Szames will supply me with energy. We can fly back ten times faster than a horse."

"I will stay. I have assumed the field therefore I now lead this army, Szames, see the others back to the moat," the Crown Prince commands.

"Your Highness, you don't have the supply of power I need," I rejoin.

"I concur. Alex, on the battle field our combined votes override you, General and Magic Councilor," Szames announces as a cavalry soldier approaches leading two horses.

"I concede to your decision," Alex gives a slight bow of his head before swinging into the saddle.

To my amazement, Prince Alexandros gestures toward the unconscious man. By the time Szames has him draped over his brother's horse, Andrayia is mounted behind the soldier whose leg wound has been stabilized. With a salute to Szames, Alex charges back to the castle with the rest of the cavalry in tow.

I look to Szames. A dip of his head and we rush to higher ground. At first we see nothing, but within minutes the new threat crests a distant hill.

"By Andskoti's holy name..." Szames questions the sanity of what his sight relays.

An enormous round sphere is plunging straight toward the castle, as if a giant hand has released a bowling ball with earthshaking strength, hurling the oncoming object in our direction. Blacker than the night surrounding it, larger than most of the town's buildings, it bears down on our position.

"Magefire," I whisper as it crests the next incline.

The fireball hits squarely, taking out the top layer, but the monstrosity continues on, unaffected.

"Szames, a little height," I extend my hand. As if we have worked together for years instead of days, Szames responds. Pulling energy from him I take us aloft, conserving my dwindling reserves. We hover a few feet off the ground.

"Magefire, Magefire, Magefire," I chant over and over and until my voice becomes hoarse. Still the mass continues toward us. "Magefire, Magefire, Magefire…" I can now make out what the demons have thrown against us. Horror boggles my brain. I loose concentration and we drift back down to earth.

Threads of magic link the demons at the waist. What looks like a solid black ball is really a seething, boiling mass of the most grotesque, demonic shapes a mind can conjure. Using their arms, the beasts add momentum to the sphere of what started out as hundreds of monsters.

My continual battery has reduced the globe by half its diameter, but I know I don't have enough energy to finish the job, even if I milk Szames dry.

"Laserbeam," a bolt of blue light streams out from my hands.

I break off the beam of incandescent light, my attempt to cut the sphere in half, incomplete, "Sh*t… damn it… fu**ing shit!" Why didn't I try this sooner!

Regaining control of my anger I turn to my partner, "Szames, I am almost out of energy, if I take any more from either of us we will be in no shape to defend ourselves."

At his barely perceptible nod I hurl us toward the castle, sending a piece of my mind streaking across the night sky. Faint pictures overlay my sight, like a ghost shadow on a T.V. screen. When I spot a familiar stocky figure, I send a piece of my consciousness toward it, "Jerik, we're in trouble. We need back-up."

I watch with the rest of Cuthburan army, helpless to stop the incoming invasion force. The Demon-sphere whirls into contact with the outer force-field. The globe slows, but its momentum pushes the mass through the primary field where the stunned layer of demons is dispatched in a fiery glare.

"Blazing-staff," I pronounce. With sight I note the cobalt light gathering around the ends of my stave.

Dozens upon dozens of human size demons fan out inside the protective barrier. Two giants, larger than ogres, unfold themselves from the fetal position they held in the yoke. The soldiers use the force-field as intended, the two barriers creating a safety zone they can run to when out-numbered or when they need to regroup. Tag-teams of men harry the giants, keeping them from the gates. Even with the magical defense as a support, soldiers drop like flies.

"Hiii-yaaa," lacking magical energy, I wield my six-foot pole with deadly proficiency. Blue magefire pooled around the ends dissolves everything it touches.

"ArchMage!" a soldier bellows beside me. Swiveling around I aim the staff's end at the fiend I sense, taking him out. From the corner of my eye, I see another beast behead the man who just saved my life.

Again I try to get close enough to engage one of the giants: unlike the ogres these are monstrosities no human fairy-tale ever contemplated. Tall and wiry, covered in black scales shimmering as if with oozing slime, they have three segments to their arms, the last of which is double jointed and a spiked tail is responsible for more than one death. A quick evaluation of their fighting abilities reveals their most lethal asset: although their heads seem to be put on backward - the top cranial portion hanging as a shield over the three-eyes and wide fanged mouth - they display intelligence equal to the best soldier.

Followed by the Guard, I flank the two princes as we charge the closest monster. Side by side, the brothers fight, but it is all they can do to keep the right sword occupied while we apply ourselves to the left. Faster than lightning the beast parries the blows.

"I've got an idea, keep it busy!" I yell, dropping out

of the assault.

The other creatures have been dispatched leaving just two reptilian giants. I circle behind the beast as Jerik and Charles arrive with more than a hundred men to replace the ones lying in a deep circle around the other monster.

Keeping my eye on the five-foot sinuous tail, I take a deep breath, and then sprint toward the creature's backside. Planting my staff like a pole-vaulter, I spring upward. With my added strength, I soar into the night sky: over fifteen feet straight up. Coming down over the creature I use my staff to soften my landing, planting the stave in the serpent's skull.

Slicing through its head like a branding iron on a snow bank, the move does little to break my fall. However, the demon's limp body provides cushion enough. Having witnessed his companion's demise, the last monster raises to his full height, letting loose a bone trembling shriek.

"I don't think that trick is going to work a second time," wiping sweat off his brow, Alex looks toward the sky growing lighter in the east.

"But now we know they are vulnerable to magefire," pausing I take a moment to weigh the options, "Prince Alexandros, if I drain my reserves and those of the General's, I should have sufficient energy to release a bolt large enough to dispatch the last Demon. However, it will render both of us in a weekend condition, possibly unconscious."

"If you can dispatch this creature with one blow I will personally see you to safety," Alex declares.

"Andrayia and the others will aid you," unable to utter another word to the man to whom I must entrust my life, I extend my left hand to his brother.

"Laserbolt," I command the mammoth laser I installed in my arsenal last night. Black spots crowd the edge of my vision, but I hang onto consciousness: the shot flies straight and true, taking the monster in the head. Just before the blackness overwhelms my senses, I feel a pair of strong arms encircle me.

Chapter Thirty

True consciousness evades me as the remaining demons flee from the coming dawn. The siege of Castle Eldrich, the Pearl of Cuthburan, is broken. The city rejoices but I am unable to break through the corridor of darkness surrounding my mind.

"I saw Szames fall, is it a mortal wound," Arturo's words are winded, as if he has run a great distance. Seared with emotion, they echo into the dark that binds.

I struggle to open my eyes.

"He received no wound, Father. He fell while joined with Reba to destroy the last of the Lizard Kings."

"Has the Mage's life been forfeited along with my youngest son?"

The worry in the monarch's tone causes me to redouble my effort. I must be free of the darkness that is smothering my thoughts.

A hand brushes my forehead as the stretcher jostles to a halt. I feel a mind brush against my own.

"Her soul remains with her body... Reba did not deplete her reservoir completely." Allinon's sigh of relief is more for his ride home than the fate of his red-headed leader.

I feel a swinging sensation as the men caring the litter set off once more. Consciousness slips from me until I am place upon a feathered surface.

Arturo's fears have not been assuaged, "The enemy

is routed, but the gate has yet to be located. Will she recover in time for the Demon Campaign?"

"Your Majesty, in a day, two at most, I believe Reba will make a full recovery," Jamison pronounces over my still form before turning to Crystal. "Offer her water when she wakes and food should be brought within the hour."

With the kingdom's fate more certain, Arturo asks the question stabbing through his heart, "And my son? Will Szames wake as well?"

"Yes, Your Majesty."

Relief washes across the king's countenance. The monarch gives a grateful nod then strides into the next room. Jamison and Allinon follow at a respectful distance.

The rustle of clothing and clinking of armor dies as those privileged enough to be allowed entrance wait expectantly.

"Today's victory is the beginning, just as the prophecy stated: delivered by magic, unto magic. ArchMage Reba will lead the campaign two days hence. The Flame shall overcome the darkness!"

The shouted words reach my heightened ears as if whispered from a great distance. But I am comforted when I feel the emotional storm of worry depart for a new location. I know Arturo has left for his son's bedside and still true rest is elusive. Though my body is unable to rouse, my mind worries over what is to come.

The demon's strength is so much greater than we expected, their tactics so cunning: We have won the battle, but will we win the war?

My mind dismisses the topic, determined not to borrow trouble. Still, I am unable to find the peacefulness of true sleep.

Like a hound after a sent, I search for the root of the problem. Home? If I manage to save the glorious Kingdom of Cuthburan, nay, the entire world: Will I be able to return to the life of a wife, a mere housewife?

If I had an ounce of strength my teeth would be grinding. Hell yes I'm going home! I'm not staying on this decadent world where fidelity is considered folly.

As the thought crystallizes in my conscious-ness, an icy chill spreads down my back. A flash of white light startles me in the night that surrounds my senses. My body has been taxed beyond human endurance, but still muscles tense with expectation. One strand of magic still remains strong: precognition.

My destabilized mind is to week for the powerful vision. Instead of witnessing the event, I am drawn into it, experiencing it with all my senses.

....

A towering cliff rises across a rocky stream. The sky is bright but darkness overwhelms my soul. Tears trace twin paths down my cheeks.

I raise a hand and whisper a word. A bolt of light shoots out from my hand hitting something which glows red on the other side of the riverbank.

Hesitant word's I can't make out cause me to jump to my feet. I'm no longer alone. The sight of his compassion causes me to turn my back and hastily wipe the moister from my face.

Next to the shimmering water, Szames halts in his progress toward me…

Blackness crowds the vision from my mind. The premonition's drain on my body is too much. I slip silently into true unconsciousness.

Glossary

Armoire: A large ornate cabinet or wardrobe.

Tuvarnava: Kingdom to the northwest of Cuthburan.

Aura: The field of energy that surrounds every human being. Magesight allows the aura to be seen in color patterns representing different affinities: blue for magic, green for healing, fuchsia for charisma, gold for empathy, burgundy for telepathy etc.

AV: Aura Virus

Consortium of Knowledge: University of Cuthburan

Corinth: A soft metal prevalent in Cuthburan. When mixed with other metals it becomes malleable and prevents rust and tarnish.

Eldrich Castle: Home and ruling center for the Royalty of Cuthburan, located in the city now known as Eldrich.

Faux Pas: Social blunder

Jarovegi: A long limbed demon able to tunnel under ground at remarkable speed. The bight of this creature infects the aura of the wounded, eventually killing the victim.

Kypros: Country bordering Cuthburan to the southwest.

Lamppost: "Illuminate" activates the light, "transparent" causes it to dim.

Octal: A Cuthburan unit of measurement, eight consccutive days.

Perinthess: Cuthburan metal alloy composed of pewter and corinth.

Rapier: A long, slender, two-edged sword with a cup-like hilt, used with thrusting maneuvers.

Scry: A trance enabling out of body searching of large areas as well as other dimensions for a specific item or person or answer to a specific question.

wineskins: canteens made of animal intestines and covered over with the hide of the animal.

Wyverns: Commonly known as miniature dragons. A large flying demon with wings like a bat and claws like a dragon. It has two arms that support the tops of its wings.

Character Glossary

Names beginning with Sz denote the European J sounding like a cross between a "ssh" and a "j."

Alexandros: First born of King Arturo; Crown Prince to the Kingdom of Cuthburan.
Andertz: Son of Andrayia and Prince Alexandros.
Andrayia: Instructor in the arts of history, science, language and mathematics to the nobility of Cuthburan; also the mistress of Prince Alexandros.
Andskoti: Common name of the Deity of Cuthburan
Anzin, Count: Ruler of Gandrus
Araine: Stone collector for the ArchMage, age
ArchBishop: see Prestur
Arturo, King: Ruling monarch of Cuthburan.
Asdis, Marchionesses: Wife to Vinfastur of Rhymon
Eldhress, Baron: Ruler of Brightport.
Baulyard, Count: Ruler of Mountview
Bryson: MasterChief at Castle Eldrich
Chazan: Stone Collector for the ArchMage Reba.
Cheryl: Older sister to Reba.
Crystal: Head Chambermaid: assigned to ArchMage Reba upon her arrival.
Cuthburan: The kingdom over which King Arturo Rules.
Edward: MasterTaylor
Erik: Stone collector for the ArchMage, age seven.
Gabion, Duke: Ruler of Everand
Goran: Father of Gaakobah.
Herald, Squire: Second son of Marquis Vinfastur, Ruler of Rhymon
Hestur: MasterSteward of Cuthburan
Keth: Brother to Rhachel. Requested by ArchMage Reba to be added to her staff when demons killed the rest of their family.
Laeknaen: Oldest living Healer.

Lani: Twin sister to Reba. (RaLain)
Yivgeni: MasterArtist of Cuthburan
Malegur: A healer whose Gift is not activated at the first Awakening.
Maria: Stone collector for the ArchMage.
Mik: StableMaster of Castle Eldrich
Nemir: Apprentice to Merithin.
Prestur, ArchBishop: Leader of the Church of Cuthburan.
Rhachel: Brother to Keth. Made part of Reba's staff when Rhachel family and home were destroyed by the demons.
Rokroa, Duke: Ruler of Kempmore
Rikard of Kempmore: Stonemason who created Castle Eldrich and surrounding city; know also a Master Stonemason Rick.
Sheldon: First of the Cuthburan line of rulers. Joined with Roseanne his first cousin then after her untimely demise, Monique, Princess of the Isles.
Szeanne Rose, Princess: Princess of Cuthburan, third child of King Arturo, second born of Queen Szacquelyn.
Szacquelyn, Queen: Queen of Cuthburan, second wife of King Arturo.
Szames (Sha-mes), Prince: General of the Cuthburan Army, second born of King Arturo,.
Todd: Stone collector for the ArchMage.
Tupper: MasterHealer
Varpalava: Prince of Tuvarnava, betrothed of Princess Szeanne Rose of Cuthburan.
Vinfastur, Marquis: Ruler of Rhymon
William: Page to Crown Prince Alexandros; assigned to ArchMage Reba upon her arrival.
Youngmen: Captain the Cuthburan army and Childhood friend of Prince Szames.

Lynn Hardy

I was born in Phoenix, Arizona in 1971 where I attended school through the eighth grade. Although I attended seven different high schools throughout the Midwest and Texas, my heart remained in Arizona where I returned for college at Northern Arizona University.

In Flagstaff, Arizona, during my sophomore year, I met my Husband, Anthony. His continued love and encouragement gave me the confidence to begin the journey of publication. The unfailing love as well as the editorial support of my mother, Gloria Freeman, has enabled me to fulfill the lifelong ambition of sharing the worlds I inhabit each night in my dreams through my writing.

Yivgeni Matoussov

I was in 1986 in Russia. Since an early age, I have been interested in sketching and painting. At the age of 13 I attended the studio of Sergey Levin, a master artist with decades of experience. In his studio I studied the secrets of painting in oils and have been exposed to many lessons in art history. Since the age of fourteen, I have been selling my artwork privately as well as fulfilling commissions for portraits. Creating visual renderings of the human body is my passion.

In the year 2003 I emigrated from Israel to Canada. In 2004 I enrolled in Ontario College of Art and Design. I will soon enter the fourth and final year of my BFA.

My art evolves as I myself journey through life. I express my conclusions and discoveries about life through my paintings and drawings. My online gallery is located at www.yivgeni-art.com, you are welcome to visit it anytime.